'Isn't it abou[...] [...]r powers for go[...]

Knowing that she co[...] [...]r, she took a deep breath and slowly turned around. He was leaning against the stone pillar directly behind her, those dark eyes cool. His lower jaw was covered in golden stubble and his mouth was knifeblade-thin.

That hadn't changed.

A lot else had. She squinted... Tall, blond, built. Broad shoulders, slim hips and long, long legs. He was a big slab of muscled male flesh. When his mouth pulled up ever so slightly at the corners she felt a slow, seductive throb deep in her womb... Oh, dear. Was that *lust*?

Seb stopped in front of her and jammed his hands into the pockets of very nicely fitting jeans.

'Brat.'

His voice rumbled over her, prickling her skin.

Yep, there was the snotty devil she remembered, under that luscious masculine body that looked, and—oh, my—smelled so good. It was in those deep eyes, in the vibration of his voice. The shallow dimple in his right cheek. The grown-up version of the studious, serious boy who had either tolerated, tormented or loathed her at different stages of her life. Always irritating.

'I have a name, Seb.'

He had the audacity to grin at her. 'Yeah, but you know I prefer mine.'

Dear Reader

I write romances about finding love in the twenty-first century, and I love creating quirky heroines—women a little left of centre. Rowan, I think, is one of my quirkiest to date, and she came about when I was watching a travel programme and the female presenter captured my attention. Rowan ran into some minor trouble as a teenager, and as soon as she could left home to travel the world. She's spent years of bouncing from country to country, and I needed to work out what, and who, would make Rowan settle down—especially in her home town, which holds so many bad memories for her.

Seb is Rowan's best friend's brother, her childhood nemesis, and the person whose attention she has always wanted to capture and hang onto. When she finds herself broke and deported, dreading the idea of returning to Cape Town as the family screw-up, it's Seb she reluctantly turns to to help her out of trouble.

As they start discovering the adult versions of the children they used to be they both have to learn to trust, to believe in themselves, in each other and in love itself.

Writing romance is the best job in the world, and I hope you enjoy Seb and Rowan's journey to their happy-ever-after.

With my very best wishes

Joss

xxx

PS Come and say hi via Facebook: Joss Wood, Twitter: @josswoodbooks and Josswoodbooks.wordpress.com

THE LAST GUY SHE SHOULD CALL

BY
JOSS WOOD

MILLS
BOON

Published in Great Britain 2014
by Mills & Boon, an imprint of Harlequin (UK) Limited,
Eton House, 18-24 Paradise Road, Richmond, Surrey, TW9 1SR

© 2014 Joss Wood

ISBN: 978 0 263 91082 7

Harlequin (UK) Limited's policy is to use papers that are natural,
renewable and recyclable products and made from wood grown in
sustainable forests. The logging and manufacturing processes conform
to the legal environmental regulations of the country of origin.

Printed and bound in Spain
by Blackprint CPI, Barcelona

Joss Wood wrote her first book at the age of eight and has never really stopped. Her passion for putting letters on a blank screen is matched only by her love of books and travelling—especially to the wild places of Southern Africa—and possibly by her hatred of ironing and making school lunches.

Fuelled by coffee, when she's not writing or being a hands-on mum Joss, with her background in business and marketing, works for a non-profit organisation to promote the local economic development and collective business interests of the area where she resides. Happily and chaotically surrounded by books, family and friends, she lives in Kwa-Zulu Natal, South Africa, with her husband, children and their many pets.

Other Modern Tempted™ titles by Joss Wood:

TOO MUCH OF A GOOD THING
IF YOU CAN'T STAND THE HEAT...

I love the idea of my characters living happily ever after, but it happens in real life too. My parents and in-laws have been married for 110 years between them. It's a huge achievement and a shining example of the commitment marriage and relationships (in whatever form they might take) require. So this book is dedicated to Frank and Rose and Mel and Elsie for showing us, and our children, how it's done.

CHAPTER ONE

ROWAN DUNN SAT in the hard chair on one side of the white table in an interrogation room at Sydney International Airport and reminded herself to be polite. There was no point in tangling with this little troll of an Immigration Officer; she looked as if she wanted a fight.

'Why have you come to Australia, Miss Dunn?'

As if she hadn't explained her reasons to the Immigration Officer before her—and the one before him. *Patience, Rowan.* 'I bought these netsukes in Bali…'

'These what?'

'A netsuke is a type of miniature carving that originated in the seventeenth century.' She tapped one of the fifteen ivory, wood and bone mini-sculptures that had been stripped of their protective layers of bubble wrap and now stood on the desk between them. Lord, they were beautiful: animals, figures, mythical creatures. All tiny, all perfectly carved and full of movement and character. 'These are uncommon and the owner knew they had value.'

'You bought these little carvings and yet you have no money and no means of income while you are in Australia?'

'That's because I drained my bank account and maxed out my credit cards to buy them. Some of them, I think, are rare. Seventeenth, eighteenth-century. I suspect one may be by Tamakada, circa 1775. I need to get into Sydney to get Grayson Darling, an expert on netsuke, to authenticate them and hopefully buy them from me. Then I'll have plenty of money to stay in your precious, I mean, lovely country.'

'What are they worth?'

Rowan tipped her head. 'Fifteen at an average of two thousand pounds each. So, between twenty and thirty thousand, maybe more.'

The troll's jaw dropped open. 'You've got to be…joking!' She leaned across the table and her face radiated doubt. 'I think you're spinning me a story; you look like every other free-spirited backpacker I've seen.'

Rowan, not for the first time, cursed her long, curly, wild hair and her pretty face, her battered jeans, cropped shirt and well-used backpack. 'I'm a traveller but I am also a trader. It's how I—mostly—make my living. I can show you the deed of sale for the netsuke…'

Officer troll flipped through her passport. 'What else do you sell, Miss Dunn?'

'You've gone through my rucksack with a fine-tooth comb and I've had a body search. You know that I'm clean,' Rowan said wearily. She'd been here for more than six hours—could they move on, please? *Pretty please?*

'What else do you sell, Miss Dunn?'

God! Just answer the question, Rowan, and get this over with. 'Anything I can make a profit on that's *legal*. Art, furniture, antiques. I've flipped statues in Buenos Aires, art in Belize, jewellery in Vancouver. I've worked in construction when times have been lean. Worked as a bar tender when times were leaner. But mostly I buy low and sell high.'

'Then why don't you have a slush fund? A back-up plan? Where is the profit on those deals?'

Fair question.

'A large amount is tied up in a rickety house I've just co-bought with a friend in London. We're in the process of having it renovated so that we can sell it,' Rowan admitted.

And the rest was sitting in those little statues. She knew

that at least one, maybe two, were very valuable. Her gut was screaming that the laughing Buddha statue was a quality item, that it was by a famed Japanese artist. She hadn't planned to wipe out her accounts but the shopkeeper had had a figure fixed in his head and wouldn't be budged. Since she knew that she could flip the netsukes for two or three times the amount she'd paid for them, it had seemed like a short, acceptable risk. Especially since she knew Grayson—knew that he wouldn't quibble over the price. He was the best type of collector: one with deep and heavy pockets. Pockets she couldn't help lighten unless she got into the blinking country!

'The reality is that you do not have enough money on your person to last you two days in Australia.'

'I explained that I have friends...'

The troll held up her hand. 'Your not having enough funds has made us dig a little deeper and we've found out that you overstayed the visa—by six months—on your South African passport.'

Crrr-aa-aa-p!

Rowan felt her stomach sink like concrete shoes. That had happened over eight years ago, which was why she always used her UK passport to get into Oz. She'd been into the country four times since then, but they had finally picked up on her youthful transgression.

Bye-bye to any chance of getting into Oz any time in the next three years. Hello to a very sick bank account for the foreseeable future, to doing the deal with Grayson over the phone—a situation neither of them liked—or to finding another netsuke-mad collector who would pay her well for her gems. There weren't, as she knew, many of them around.

'You are not allowed to visit Australia for the next three years and you will be on the first flight we can find back to South Africa. In a nutshell, you are being deported.'

Rowan looked up at the ceiling and blew a long stream

of air towards the ceiling. It was the only place in the world where she, actively, passionately, didn't want to go. 'Crap.'

The troll almost smiled. 'Indeed.'

Sixteen hours later Rowan cleared Immigration at OR Tambo International in Johannesburg and, after picking up her rucksack, headed for the nearest row of hard benches. Dropping her pack to the floor, she slumped down and stared at her feet.

What now?

Unlike many other cities in the world, she didn't know Johannesburg, didn't have any friends in the city. She had one hundred pounds in cash in her wallet and thirty US dollars. Practically nothing in both her savings and current accounts and her credit cards were maxed out. All thanks to that little out-of-the-way antique shop in Denpasar...

Stupid, stupid, stupid, she berated herself. What had she been thinking? She'd been thinking that she'd triple her money when she flipped them.

'Hey.'

Rowan looked up and saw a young girl, barely in her twenties, take the seat next to her.

'Do you mind if I sit here for a bit? I'm being hassled by a jerk in that group over there.'

Rowan cut a glance to a group of young men who were just drunk enough to be obnoxious. One of the pitfalls of travelling alone, she thought. How many times had she sat down next to a family or another single traveller to avoid the groping hands, the come ons and pick-up lines. 'Sure. Take a seat. Coming or going?'

'Just arrived from Sydney. I saw you on the plane; you were a couple of rows ahead of me.'

'Ah.'

'I'm catching the next flight to Durban. You?'

'Haven't the foggiest.' Rowan tried to sound cheerful

but knew that she didn't quite hit the mark. 'I was deported from Oz and I'm broke.'

Bright blue eyes sharpened in interest. 'Seriously? How broke?'

'Seriously broke.' Rowan lifted her heels up onto the seat of the bench and rested her elbows on her knees. '*C'est la vie*.' She looked at her new friend, all fresh-faced and enthusiastic. 'How long have you been travelling for?' she asked.

'Six months. I'm home for a family wedding, then I'm heading off again. You?'

'Nine years. Can I give you some advice…? What's your name?'

'Cat.'

'Cat. No matter what, always have enough money stashed away so that you have options. Always have enough cash to pay for an air ticket out of Dodge, for a couple of nights in a hostel or hotel. Trust me, being broke sucks.'

She'd always lived by that rule, but she'd been seduced by the idea of a quick return. She'd imagined that she'd be broke for a maximum of three days in Sydney and then her bank balance would be nicely inflated.

It sure hadn't worked out that way… Deported, for crying out loud! Deported and penniless! Rowan closed her eyes and wondered if she could possibly be a bigger moron.

'Can I give you a hundred pounds?' Cat asked timidly.

Rowan eyes snapped open. Her wide smile split her face and put a small sparkle back into her onyx-black eyes. 'That's really sweet of you, but no thanks, honey. I do have people I can call. I would just prefer not to.'

Look at her, Rowan thought, *all fresh and idealistic. Naïve.* If she didn't get street-wise quickly the big bad world out there would gobble her up and spit her out. Travelling in Australia was easy: same language, same culture, good transport systems and First World. Most of the world wasn't like that.

'Your folks happy with you backpacking?'

Cat raised a shoulder. 'Yeah, mostly. They have a mild moan when I call home and ask for cash, but they always come through.'

Rowan lifted dark winged eyebrows. Lucky girl. Could her circumstances be any more different from hers, when she'd left home to go on the road? Those six months between being caught in a drug raid at a club with a tiny bag of coke and catching a plane to Thailand had been sheer hell.

Two months after being tossed into jail—and she still hoped the fleas of a thousand camels were making their home in Joe's underpants for slipping the coke into the back pocket of her jeans, the rat-bastard jerk!—she'd been sentenced to four months' community service but, thanks to the fact that at the time she hadn't yet turned eighteen, her juvenile criminal record was still sealed.

Sealed from the general public, but not from her family, who hadn't reacted well. There had been shouting and desperate anger from her father, cold distance from her mother, and her elder brother had been tight-lipped with disapproval. For the rest of that year there had been weekly lectures to keep her on the straight and narrow. From proper jail she'd been placed under house arrest by her parents, and their over-the-top protectiveness had gone into hyperdrive. Her movements had been constantly monitored, and the more they'd lectured and smothered, the stronger her urge to rebel and her resolve to run had become.

She'd tried to explain the circumstances, but only her BFF Callie had realised how much it had hurt to have her story about being framed dismissed as a lie, how much it had stung to see the constant disappointment on everyone's faces. So she'd decided that she might as well be the ultimate party girl rebel—sneaking out, parties, cigarettes, crazy acting out. Anything to live up to the low expectations of her parents—especially her mother—and constantly, constantly planning her escape.

It had come the day after she'd written her final exam to finish her school career. Using cash she'd received from selling the unit trusts her grandmother had bought her every birthday since the day she was born, she'd bought a ticket to Thailand.

Everyone except Callie had been furious, and they'd all expected her to hit the other side, turn tail and run back home. That first year had been tough, lonely, and sometimes downright scary, but she'd survived and then she'd flourished.

And she really didn't want to go home with her tail tucked between her legs now, broke and recently deported.

She didn't want to lose her freedom, to step back into her family's lives, back into her parents' house, returning as the family screw-up. It didn't matter that she was asset-rich and cash-poor. She would still, in their eyes, be irresponsible and silly: no better than the confused, mixed-up child who'd left nine years before.

'So, who are you going to call?' Cat asked, breaking in on her thoughts.

'Well, I've only got two choices. My mobile's battery is dead and all my contact numbers are in my phone. I have two numbers in my head: my parents' home number and my best friend Callie's home number.'

'I vote for the best friend.'

'So would I—except that she doesn't live there any more. Her older brother does, and he doesn't like me very much.'

Cat leaned forward, curious. 'Why not?'

'Ah, well. Seb and I have always rubbed each other up the wrong way. He's conservative and studious; I'm wild and rebellious. He's mega-rich and I'm currently financially challenged—'

'What does he do?' Cat asked.

Rowan fiddled with her gold hoop earrings. 'His family have a shed-load of property in Cape Town and he oversees that. He also does something complicated with computers. He has a company that does…um…internet security? He's a nice hat… No, that doesn't sound right.'

Cat sat up suddenly. 'Do you mean a white hat? A hacker?'

Rowan cocked her finger at her. 'That's it. Apparently he's one of the best in the world.'

'Holy mackerel…that is so cool! I'm a bit of a comp geek myself.'

'So is he. He's a complete nerd and we've always clashed. He's book-smart and I'm street-smart. His and Callie's house is within spitting distance of my parents' house and I spent more time there than I did at home. I gave him such a hard time.'

Cat looked intrigued. 'Why?'

'Probably because I could never get a reaction out of him. He'd just look at me, shake his head, tell me I was a brat and flip me off. The more I misbehaved, the more he ignored me.' Rowan wound a black curl around her index finger.

'Sounds to me like you were craving his attention.'

'Honey, I craved *everyone's* attention,' Rowan replied.

This was one of the things she loved most about travelling, she thought. Random conversations with strangers who didn't know her from Adam.

'Anyway, I could bore you to death, recounting all the arguments I had with Seb.' Rowan smiled. 'So let this be a lesson to you, Cat. Remember, always have a stash of cash. Do as I say and not as I do.'

'Good luck,' Cat called as she walked towards the bank of public phones against the far wall.

Rowan lifted her hand in acknowledgement. She sure as hell was going to need it.

* * *

Seb Hollis shot up in bed and punched the comforter and the sheets away, unable to bare the constricting fabric against his heated skin. He was conscious of the remnants of a bad dream floating around the periphery of his memory, and as much as he tried to pretend otherwise it wasn't the cool air colliding with the sweat on his chest and spine that made him shiver. The blame for that could be laid squarely at the door of this now familiar nocturnal visitor. He'd been dreaming the same dream for six days… He was being choked, restrained, hog-tied…yanked up to the altar and forced into marriage.

Balls, was his first thought, closely followed by, *Thank God it was only a dream.*

Draping one forearm across his bended knees, Seb ran a hand behind his neck. He was sweating like a geyser and his mouth was as dry as the Kalahari Desert. Cursing, he fumbled for the glass of water on the bedside table, grimacing at the handprint his sweat made on the deep black comforter.

Habit had him turning his head, expecting to see his lover's head on the other pillow. Relief pumped through him when he remembered that Jenna had left for a year-long contract in Dubai and that he was officially single again. He didn't have to explain the nightmare, see her hurt face when he wouldn't talk about the soaked sheets or his pumping breath. Like most women, and despite her corporate career, Jenna had a need to nurture.

He'd never been nurtured and he had no need to be fussed over. It wasn't who he was, what he needed.

Besides, discussing his dreams—emotions, thoughts, desires—would be amusing in the same way an electric shock to his gonads would be nice. Not going to happen. *Ever.*

Intimacy hadn't been part of the deal with Jenna.

Intimacy would never be part of the deal with anyone.

Seb swung his legs off the side of the large bed, reached for the pair of running shorts on the chair next to the bed and yanked them on. He walked over to the French doors that opened onto the balcony. Pushing them open, he sucked in the briny air of the late summer, early autumn air. Tinges of the new morning peeked through the trees that bordered the side and back edges of his property: Awelfor.

He could live anywhere in the world, but he loved living a stone's throw from Cape Town, loved living at the tip of the continent in a place nestled between the mountains and the sea. In the distance, behind those great rolling waves that characterised this part of the west coast, the massive green-grey icy Atlantic lay: sulky, turbulent, volatile. Or maybe he was just projecting his crappy mood on the still sleepy sea.

Jenna. Was *she* what his crazy dreams were about? Was he dreaming about commitment because he'd been so relieved to wave her goodbye? To get out of a relationship that he'd known was going nowhere but she had hoped was? He'd told her, as often and as nicely as he could, that he wouldn't commit, but he knew that she'd hoped he'd change his mind, really hoped that he'd ask her to stay in the country.

It hadn't seemed to matter that they'd agreed to a no-strings affair, that she'd said she understood when he'd explained that he didn't do love and commitment.

Women. *Sheez*. Sometimes they just heard what they wanted to hear.

Seb cocked his head when the early-morning silence was shattered by the distinctive deep-throated roar of a Jag turning into the driveway to Awelfor. *Here we go again,* he thought. The engine was cut, a car door slammed and within minutes he saw his father walking the path to the cottage that stood to the left of the main house.

It was small consolation that he wasn't the only Hollis

man with woman troubles. At least his were only in his head. *Single again,* he reminded himself. Bonus.

'Another one bites the dust?' he called, and his father snapped his head up.

Patch Hollis dropped his leather bag to the path and slapped his hands on his hips.

'When am I going to learn?'

'Beats me.' Seb rested his forearms on the balcony rail. 'What's the problem with this one?'

'She wants a baby,' Patch said, miserable. 'I'm sixty years old; why would I want a child now?'

'She's twenty-eight, dude. Of course she's going to want a kid. Have you told her you've had a vasectomy?'

Patch gestured to the bag. 'Hence the reason I'm back in the cottage. She went bat-crap ballistic.'

'Uh…why do you always leave? It's your house and you're not married.' Seb narrowed his eyes as a horrible thought occurred to him. 'You didn't slink off and marry her, did you?'

Patch didn't meet his eyes. 'No, but it was close.'

Seb rubbed his hand over his hair, which he kept short to keep the curls under control, and muttered an expletive.

'Don't swear at me. You had your own little gold-digger you nearly married,' Patch shot back, and Seb acknowledged the hit.

He'd been blindsided when he'd raised the issue of marriage contracts and his fiancée Bronwyn wouldn't consider signing a pre-nup. Like most things he did, he'd approached the problem of the marriage contracts intellectually, rationally. *He* had the company and the house and the cash, and pretty much everything of monetary value, so *he'd* be the one to hand over half of everything if they divorced.

Bronwyn had not seen his point of view. If he *loved* her, she'd screamed, he'd share everything with her. He *had* loved Bronwyn—sorta…kinda—but not enough to risk sharing his company with her or paying her out for half the value of the house that had been in his family for four generations in the event of a divorce.

They'd both dug their heels in and the break-up had been bruising.

It had taken him a couple of years, many hours with a whisky bottle and a shattered heart until he'd—mostly—worked it all out. He believed in thinking through problems—including personal failures—in order to come to a better understanding of the cause and effect.

It was highly probable that he'd fallen for Bronwyn because she was, on the surface, similar in behaviour and personality to his mother. A hippy child who flitted from job to job, town to town. A supposed free spirit whom he'd wanted—no, *needed* to tame. Since his mother had left some time around his twelfth birthday to go backpacking round the world, and had yet to come home, he'd given up hope that he'd ever get her love or approval, that she'd return and stay put. He'd thought that if he could get Bronwyn to settle down, to commit to him, then maybe it would fill the hole his mother had left.

Yeah, right.

But he'd learnt a couple of lessons from his FUBAR engagement. Unlike his jobs—internet security expert and overseeing the Hollis Property Group—he couldn't analyse, measure or categorise relationships and emotions, and he sure didn't understand women. As a result he now preferred to conduct his relationships at an emotional distance. An at-a-distance relationship—sex and little conversation—held no risk of confusion and pain and didn't demand much from him. He'd forged his emotional armour when his mum had left so very long ago and strengthened it after his experience with Bronwyn. He liked it that way. There was no chance of his heart being tossed into a liquidiser.

His father, Peter Pan that he was, just kept it simple:

blonde, long-legged and big boobs. Mattress skills were a prerequisite; intelligence wasn't.

'So, can I move back in until she moves out?' Patch asked.

'Dad, Awelfor is a Hollis house; legally it's still yours. But I should warn you that Yasmeen is on holiday; she's been gone for nearly a week and I've already eaten the good stuff she left.'

Patch looked wounded. 'So no blueberry muffins for breakfast?'

'Best you're going to get is coffee. No laundry or bed-making service either,' Seb replied.

Patch looked bereft and Seb knew that it had nothing to do with his level of comfort and everything to do with the absence of their elderly family confidant, their moral compass and their staunchest supporter. Yasmeen was more than their housekeeper, she *was* Awelfor.

'Yas being gone sucks.' Patch yawned. 'I'm going back to bed, Miranda has a voice like a foghorn and I was up all night being blasted by it.'

Seb turned his head at the sound of his ringing landline. 'Crazy morning. Father rocking up at the crack of dawn, phone ringing before six…and all I want is a cup of coffee.'

Patch grinned up at him. 'I just want my house back.'

Seb returned his smile. 'Then kick her whiny ass out of yours.'

Patch shuddered. 'I'll just move in here until she calms down.'

His father, Seb thought as he turned away to walk back into the house, was totally allergic to confrontation.

'Seb, it's Rowan…Rowan Dunn.'

He'd recognised her voice the moment he'd heard her speak his name, but because his synapses had stopped firing he'd lost the ability to formulate any words. *Rowan? What the...?*

'Seb? Sorry, did I wake you?'

'Rowan, this is a surprise.' And by surprise I mean… *wow.*

'I'm in Johannesburg—at the airport.'

Since this was Rowan, he passed curious and went straight to resigned. 'What's happened?'

He would have had to be intellectually challenged to miss the bite in the words that followed.

'Why do you automatically assume the worst?'

'Because something major must have happened to bring you back to the country you hate, where the family you've hardly interacted with in years lives and for you to call *me*, who you once described as a boil on the ass of humanity.'

He waited through the tense silence.

'I'm temporarily broke and homeless. And I've just been deported from Oz,' she finally—very reluctantly—admitted.

And there it was.

'Are you in trouble?' He kept his voice neutral and hoped that she was now adult enough to realise that it was a fair question. For a long time before she'd left trouble had been Rowan's middle name. Heck, her first name.

'No, I'm good. They just picked up that I overstayed on my visa years and years ago and they kicked me out.'

Compared to some of the things she'd done, this was a minor infringement. Seb walked to his walk-in closet, took a pair of jeans from a hanger and yanked them on. He placed his fist on his forehead and stared down at the old wood flooring.

'Seb, are you there?'

'Yep.'

'Do you know where my parents are? I did try them but they aren't answering their phone.'

'They went to London and rented out the house while they were gone to some visiting researchers from Beijing. They are due back in...' Seb tried to remember. 'Two—three—weeks' time.'

'You've got to be kidding me! My parents went overseas and the world didn't stop turning? How is that possible?'

'That surprised me, too,' Seb admitted.

'And is Callie still on that buying trip?'

'Yep.'

Another long silence. 'In that case...tag—you're it. I need a favour.'

From him? He looked at his watch and was surprised to find that it was still ticking. Why hadn't time stood still? He'd presumed it would—along with nuns being found ice skating in hell—since Rowan was asking for *his* help.

'I thought you'd rather drip hot wax in your eye than ever ask me for anything again.'

'Can you blame me? You could've just bailed me out of jail, jerk-face.'

And...hello, there it was: the tone of voice that had irritated him throughout his youth and into his twenties. Cool, mocking...nails-on-a-chalkboard irritating.

'Your parents didn't want me to—they were trying to teach you a lesson. And might I point out that calling me names is not a good way to induce me to do anything for you, Rowan?'

Seb heard her mutter a swear word and he grinned. Oh, he did like having her at his mercy.

'What do you want, Brat?'

Brat—his childhood name for her. Callie, so blonde, had called her Black Beauty, or BB for short, on account of her jet-black hair and eyes teamed with creamy white skin. She'd been a knockout, looks-wise, since the day she'd been born. Pity she had the personality of a rabid honey badger.

Brat suited her a lot better, and had the added bonus of annoying the hell out of her.

'When is Callie due back?'

He knew why she was asking: she'd rather eat nails than accept help from *him*. Since his sister travelled extensively as a buyer for a fashion store, her being in the country was not always guaranteed. 'End of the month.'

Another curse.

'And Peter—your brother—is still in Bahrain,' Seb added, his tone super pointed as he reached for a shirt and pulled it off its hanger.

'I know that. I'm not completely estranged from my family!' Rowan rose to take the bait. 'But I didn't know that my folks were planning a trip. They never go anywhere.'

'They made the decision to go quite quickly.' Seb walked back into his bedroom and stared at the black and white sketches of desert scenes above his rumpled bed. 'So, now that you definitely know that I'm all you've got, do you want to tell me what the problem is?'

She sucked in a deep breath. 'I need to get back to London and I was wondering whether you'd loan...'

When pigs flew!

'No. I'm not lending you money.'

'Then buy me a ticket...'

'Ah, let me think about that for a sec? Mmm...no, I won't buy you a ticket to London either.'

'You are such a sadistic jerk.'

'But I *will* pay for a ticket for you to get your bony butt back home to Cape Town.'

Frustration cracked over the line as he listened to the background noise of the airport. 'Seb, I can't.'

Hello? Rowan sounding contrite and beaten...? He'd thought he'd never live to see the day. He didn't attempt to snap the top button of his jeans; it required too much processing power. Rowan was home and calling him. And sounding reasonable. Good God.

He knew it wouldn't last—knew that within ten minutes of being in each other's company they'd want to kill each other. They were oil and water, sun and snow, fire and ice.

Seb instinctively looked towards the window and saw his calm, ordered, structured life mischievously flipping him off before waving goodbye and belting out of the window.

Free spirits...why was he plagued with them?

'Make a decision, B.'

She ignored his shortening of the name he'd called her growing up. A sure sign that she was running out of energy to argue.

'My mobile is dead, I have about a hundred pounds to my name and I don't know anyone in Johannesburg. Guess I'm going to get my butt on a plane ho...to Cape Town.'

'Good. Hang on a sec.' Seb walked over to the laptop that stood on a desk in the corner of his room and tapped the keyboard, pulling up flights. He scanned the screen.

'First flight I can get you on comes in at six tonight. Your ticket will be at the SAA counter. I'll meet you in the airport bar,' Seb told her.

'Seb?'

'Yeah?'

'That last fight we had about Bronwyn...'

It took him a moment to work out what she was talking about, to remember her stupid, childish gesture from nearly a decade ago.

'The one where you presumed to tell me how and what to do with my life?'

'Well, I *was* going to apologise—'

'That would be a first.'

'But you can shove it! And you, as you well know, have told *me* what to do my entire life! I might have voiced some comments about your girlfriend, but I didn't leave a mate to rot in jail,' Rowan countered, her voice heating again.

'We were never mates, and it was a weekend—not a lifetime! And you bloody well deserved it.'

'It was still mean and…'

Seb rolled his eyes and made a noise that he hoped sounded like a bad connection. 'Sorry, you're breaking up…'

'We're on a landline, you dipstick!' Rowan shouted above the noise he was making.

Smart girl, he thought as he slammed the handset back into its cradle. She'd always been smart, he remembered. And feisty.

It seemed that calling her Brat was still appropriate. Some things simply never changed.

CHAPTER TWO

SIX HOURS LATER and it was another airport, another set of officials, another city and she was beyond exhausted. Sweaty, grumpy and... Damn it. Rowan pushed her fist into her sternum. She was nervous.

Scared spitless.

It could be worse, she told herself as she slid onto a stool in the busy bar, her luggage at her feet. She could be standing at Arrivals flicking over faces and looking for her parents. She could easily admit that Seb was the lesser of two evils—that she'd been relieved when her parents hadn't answered her call, that she wasn't remotely sure of their reaction to her coming home.

Apart from the occasional grumble about her lack of education they'd never expressed any wish for her to return to the family fold. They might—and she stressed *might*—be vaguely excited to see her again, but within a day they'd look at her with exasperation, deeply puzzled by the choices she'd made and the lifestyle she'd chosen.

'So different from her sibling,' her mother would mutter. *'Always flying too close to the sun. Our changeling child, our rebel, always trying to break out and away.'*

Maybe if they hadn't wrapped her in cotton wool and smothered her in a blanket of protectiveness she'd be more...normal, Rowan thought. A little more open to putting down roots, to having relationships that lasted longer than a season, furniture that she owned rather than temporarily used.

She'd caused them a lot of grief, she admitted. She'd been a colicky baby, a hell-on-wheels toddler, and then she'd contracted meningitis at four and been in ICU for two weeks, fighting for her life. After the meningitis her family had been so scared for her, so terrified that something bad would happen to her—again—that they hadn't let her experience life at all. All three of them—parents and her much older brother—had hovered over her: her own phalanx of attack helicopters, constantly scanning the environment for trouble.

The weird thing was that while she'd always felt protected she hadn't always felt cherished. Would her life have taken a different turn if she had felt treasured, loved, not on the outside looking in?

It hadn't helped that she'd been a fiery personality born into a family of quiet, brilliant, introverts. Two professors—one in music, the other in theoretical science—and her brother had a PhD in electrical engineering. She'd skipped university in order to go travelling—an unforgivable sin in the Dunn household.

The over-protectiveness had been tedious at ten, irritating at fourteen, frustrating at sixteen. At seventeen it had become intolerable, and by the time she was nearly eighteen she'd been kicking and screaming against the silken threads of parental paranoia that had kept her prisoner.

After spending that weekend in jail she'd realised that to save herself and her relationship with her family she had to run far away as fast as she could. She couldn't be the tame, studious, quiet daughter they needed her to be, and they couldn't accept her strong-willed adventurous spirit.

Running away had, strangely enough, saved her relationship with her parents. Through e-mail, social media and rare, quick phone calls they'd managed to find a balance that worked for them. They could pretend that she wasn't gallivanting around the world, and she could pretend that they supported her quest to do more, see more, experience more.

They all lied to themselves, but it was easier that way.

Now she was back, and they couldn't lie and she couldn't pretend. They had to see each other as they now were—not the way they wished they could be. It was going to suck like rotten lemons.

Rowan hauled in a deep breath... She had two, maybe three weeks to wrap her head around seeing her parents, to gird herself against their inevitable disappointment. Two weeks to find a place to stay and a job that would keep her in cereal and coffee and earn her enough money to tide her over until she sold her netsukes.

She just had to get past Seb—whom she'd never been able to talk her way around, through or over. He'd never responded to her charm, had seen through her lies, and had never trusted her for a second.

He'd always been far too smart for his own good.

The image of Seb as she'd last seen him popped into her head. Navy eyes the colour of deep denim, really tall, curly blond hair that he grew long and pulled back into a bushy tail with a leather thong, and that ultra-stupid soul patch.

Yet he'd still turned female heads. Something about him had always caught their attention. It was not only his good looks—and, while she wished otherwise, she had to admit that even at his most geeky he *was* a good-looking SOB—he had that I-prefer-my-own company vibe that had woman salivating.

Live next door to him and see how you like him then, Rowan had always wanted to yell. *He's bossy and rude, patronising and supercilious, and frequently makes me want to poke him with a stick.*

Rowan draped her leg over her knee and turned her head

at deep-throated male laughter. Behind her a group of guys stood in a rough circle and she caught the eye of the best-looking of the bunch, who radiated confidence.

Mmm. Cute.

'Hey,' Good-looking said, in full flirt mode. 'New in town?'

I'm tired, sweaty, grumpy and I suspect that I may be way too old for you.

'Sort of.'

Good-looking looked from her to the waiter standing next to him. 'Can I buy you a drink? What would you like?'

A hundred pounds would be useful, Rowan thought. *Two hundred would be better...*

'Thanks. A glass of white wine? Anything dry,' she responded. Why not? If he wanted to buy her a drink, she could live with it. Besides, she badly needed the restorative powers of fermented grape juice.

He turned, placed the order with the waiter, and when Rowan looked again she saw that he wasn't quite so young, not quite so cocky. Tall, dark and handsome. And, since she was bored waiting for Seb, she might as well have a quick flirt. Nothing picked a girl up and out of the doldrums quicker than a little conversation with a man with appreciation in his eyes.

She thought flirting was a fine way to pass the time...

Rowan pushed a hand through her hair and looked at the luggage at their feet. 'Sports tour? Hmm, let me guess... rugby?' Rowan pointed to the bags on the floor with their identical logos. 'Under twenty-one rugby sevens tournament?'

'Ah... They are under twenty-one...I'm not.'

Rowan smiled slowly. 'Me neither. I'm Rowan.'

She was about to put her hand out for him to shake when a voice spoke from behind her.

'Isn't it about time you used your powers for good instead of evil?'

Rowan closed her eyes as the words, words not fit to speak aloud, jumped into her head. Knowing that she couldn't keep her eyes shut for ever, she took a deep breath and slowly turned around.

He was leaning against the stone pillar directly behind her, those dark blue eyes cool. His lower jaw was covered in golden stubble and his mouth was knife-blade-thin.

That hadn't changed.

A lot else had. She squinted… Tall, blond, built. Broad shoulders, slim hips and long, long legs. He was a big slab of muscled male flesh. When his mouth pulled up ever so slightly at the corners she felt a slow, seductive throb deep in her womb… Oh, dear. Was that lust? It couldn't be lust. That was crazy. It had just been a long trip, and she hadn't eaten much, and she was feeling a little light-headed… It was life catching up with her.

Mr Good-looking was quickly forgotten as she looked at Seb. She'd known a lot of good-looking men, and some devastatingly handsome men, but pure lust had never affected her before… Was that why her blood was chasing her heart around her body? Where had the saliva in her mouth disappeared to? And—oh, dear—why was her heart now between her legs and pulsing madly?

Rowan pushed a long curl out of her eyes and, unable to meet his eyes just yet, stared at his broad chest. Her gaze travelled down his faded jeans to his expensive trainers. Pathetic creature to get hot and flustered over someone she'd never even liked.

Hoo, boy. Was that a hint of ink she saw on the bicep of his right arm under his T-shirt? No way! Conservative Seb? Geeky Seb?

Except that geeky Seb had been replaced by hunky Seb, who made her think of cool sheets and hot male skin under her hands… This Seb made her think of passion-filled nights and naughty afternoon sex. Of lust, heat and attraction.

Thoughts at the speed of light dashed through her head as she looked for an explanation for her extreme reaction. She was obviously orgasm-deprived, she decided. She hadn't had sex for….oh, way too long. Right! If that was the problem—and she was sure it was—there was, she remembered, a very discreet little shop close to home that could take care of it.

Except that she was broke… Rowan scowled at her shoes. Broke and horny…what a miserable combination. Yet it was the only explanation that made a smidgeon of sense.

Seb stopped in front of her and jammed his hands into the pockets of very nicely fitting jeans.

'Brat.'

His voice rumbled over her, prickling her skin.

Yep, there was the snotty devil she remembered. Under that luscious masculine body that looked and—oh, my—smelled so good. It was in those deep eyes, in the vibration of his voice. The shallow dimple in his right cheek. The grown-up version of the studious, serious boy who had either tolerated, tormented or loathed her at different stages of her life. Always irritating.

'I have a name, Seb.'

He had the audacity to grin at her. 'Yeah, but you know I prefer mine.' He looked over at Mr Good-looking and his smile was shark-sharp. 'Lucky escape for you, bro'. She's trouble written in six-foot neon.'

As rugby-boy turned away with a disappointed sigh, inside his head Seb placed his hands on his thighs and pulled in deep, cleansing, calming breaths of pure oxygen. He felt as if his heart wanted to bungee-jump from his chest without a cord. His stomach and spleen were going along for the ride.

Well, wasn't *this* a kick in the head?

This was *Rowan*? What had happened to the skinny kid with a silver ring through her brow and a stud in her nose? The clothes that she had called 'boho chic' but which had looked as if she'd been shopping in Tramp's Alley? Skirts that had been little more than strips of cloth around her hips, knee-high combat boots, Goth make-up...

Now leather boots peeked out from under the hem of nicely fitting blue jeans. She wore a plain white button-down shirt with the bottom buttons open to show a broad leather belt, and a funky leather and blue bead necklace lay between the wilted collar of the shirt. Her hair was still the blue-black of a starling's wing, tumbling in natural curls down her back, and her eyes, black as the deepest African night, were faintly shadowed in blue. Her face was free of make-up and those incredible eyes—framed by dark lashes and brows—brimmed with an emotion he couldn't immediately identify.

Resignation? Trepidation and fear? Then she tossed her head and he saw pride flash in her eyes.

And there was the Rowan he remembered. He dismissed the feeling that his life was about to be impacted by this tiny dark-haired sprite with amazing eyes and a wide, mobile mouth that begged to be kissed.

He'd said goodbye to a kid, but this Rowan was all woman. A woman, if she were anyone but Rowan, he would be thinking about getting into bed. Immediately. As in grabbing her hand, finding the closest room and throwing her onto the bed, chair, floor...whatever was closer.

His inner cave man was thumping his chest. *Look here, honey! I'm a sex god!* He felt embarrassed on his own behalf. *Get a grip, dude!*

He hoped his face was devoid of all expression, but in his mind Seb tipped his head back and directed a stream of silent curses at the universe. *When I asked what else could go wrong, I meant it as a figure of speech—not as a challenge to hit me with your best shot.*

Rowan broke the uncomfortable silence. 'So…it's been a long time. You look…good.'

'You too.'

Good? Try sensational!

'Where did you fly in from?' he asked. Politeness? Good grief, they'd never been civil and he wondered how long it would last.

'Sydney. Nightmare flight, I had a screaming baby behind me and an ADD toddler in front of me. And the man in the seat next to me sniffed the entire time.'

'Two words. Business class.'

Rowan grimaced. 'One word. Broke.'

She shoved a hand into her hair, lifted and pushed a couple of loose curls off her face.

'Would you consider changing your mind about loaning me the money to get back to London?'

Rowan threw her demand into the silence between them.

Thirty seconds from polite to miffed. It had to be a record.

'Well? Will you?'

Sure—after I've sorted out climate change and negotiated world peace. 'Not a chance.'

Rowan tapped an irritated finger on the table and tried to stare him down. Seb folded his arms and kept his face blank.

Eventually her shoulders dropped in defeat. 'My mobile battery is dead, I have less than two hundred pounds to my name, my best friend is out of the country, my parents are away and their house is occupied. I'm in your hands.'

In his hands? He wished… Their eyes met and sexual attraction arced between them. Hot, hard… *Man!* Where was this coming from?

Pink stained Rowan's cheekbones. 'I mean, I'm at your mercy…'

That sounded even better.

'What is the matter with me?'

Or at least that was what he thought he heard her say, but since she was muttering to the floor he couldn't be sure.

What was cranking their sexual buzzers to a howl? *Dial it down, dude; time to start acting as an adult.* He dashed the rest of what was left in the tiny bottle of wine into her glass and tossed it back.

Think with your big head. It didn't matter that she looked hot, or that he wanted to taste that very sexy mouth, this was Rowan. AKA trouble.

Seb put his hands into the back pockets of his jeans. 'You ready to go?'

'Where to? Where am I sleeping tonight?'

'Awelfor.'

Awelfor… It meant sea breeze in Welsh, and was one of the few small holdings situated between the seaside villages of Scarborough and Misty Cliffs, practically on the doorstep of Table Mountain National Park. Her second home, Rowan thought.

The house had originally been an old school building, added to over the generations. The oldest part was made from timber and redbrick, and she could still feel the cool warmth of the Oregon pine floors beneath her bare feet. Nearly every room had a fireplace and a view of the Atlantic, with its huge rolling waves and its white beaches peppered by black-backed gulls.

She'd been raised next door, in the house that had been built by a Hollis forefather for—rumour had it—a favourite mistress. It had been sold off in the forties to her grandfather and separated from the Hollis house by a huge oak and a high, thick Eugenia hedge.

She knew Awelfor as well as she knew her own home:

which floorboard creaked if you stood on it the middle of the night, that the drainpipe that ran past Callie's window was strong enough to hold their combined weight, that Yasmeen the housekeeper hid her cigarettes in the flour canister at the back of the pantry. For most of her life she'd had two homes and then she'd had none; now she bounced from bed to bed in different accommodation establishments, depending on her cash flow. Once or twice she'd slept on beaches and on benches in railway stations, she remembered, even standing up.

Dots appeared behind her eyes.

Tired...so tired.

Rowan blinked furiously as the dots grew bigger and brighter and her vision started to blur. She reached out in Seb's direction and cool and firm fingers clasped her clammy hand.

'What's the matter?' Seb demanded as she abruptly sat down again. .

'Dizzy,' Rowan muttered as she shoved her head between her knees. 'Stood up too fast.'

Rowan opened her eyes and the floor rose and fell, so she closed them again.

'Easy, Ro.'

Seb bent down in front of her and held up three fingers. 'How many?'

'Six thousand and fifty-two.'

Seb narrowed his eyes and Rowan gnawed the inside of her lip, ignored the squirming sensation down below and tried to act like a mature adult.

'Sorry, I'm fine. Tired. I haven't really eaten properly. Shouldn't have had that wine.' Rowan rubbed her eyes. 'It's just been a horrible couple of days.'

Seb let go of the hand he'd been holding and stood up, looking away from those slim thighs in old jeans, that mad hair and those deep, deep eyes. She had always been gorgeous—hadn't all his friends told him that?—but for the first time in his life he saw her as something other than his sister's friend.

That felt uncomfortable and…weird.

His eyes dropped lower. Full breasts under that white cotton shirt, long fingers that were made to stroke a man's skin, long legs that could wrap around a man's hips…

This was *Rowan*, he reminded himself harshly. She was not somebody he should find attractive. He'd known her for far too long and far too well. Seb frowned, irritated that he couldn't break their eye contact. Her eyes had the impact of a fist slamming into his stomach. Those eyes— the marvellous deep dark of midnight—had amused, irritated and enthralled him. When he'd first met her he'd been a young, typical boy, and babies were deeply uncool but her eyes had captivated him. He remembered thinking they were the only redeeming feature of a demanding, squawking sprat.

Her face was thinner, her bottom rounder and her hair longer—halfway down her back. He imagined winding those curls around his fingers as he slipped inside her… Seb shook his head. They shared far too many memories, he reminded himself, a whole handful of which were bad, and they didn't like each other much.

Have you totally lost your mind?

'Let's get you home and we can argue later, when you're back to full strength.' Seb bent down and easily lifted her rucksack with one hand, picking up her large leather tote with the other. 'You okay to walk?'

Rowan stood up and pulled her bag over her shoulder. 'Sure.'

Seb briefly closed his eyes. It was a struggle not to drop her bags and bring her mouth to his.

'What's the problem now?' Rowan demanded, her tone pure acid.

He stared at the ceiling before dropping rueful eyes back to her face. 'I keep thinking that it would've been easier if you'd just stayed away.'

'Loan me the cash and I'm out of here,' she pleaded.

'I could…'

Rowan held her breath, but then Seb's eyes turned determined and the muscle in his jaw tightened. 'No. Not this time, Ro. You don't get to run.'

CHAPTER THREE

ROWAN SAT IN the passenger seat of Seb's Audi Quattro SUV as he sped down the motorway towards Cape Town. Although it was a little before eight in the evening, the sun was only just starting to drop in the sky and the motorway was buzzing with taxi drivers weaving between cars with inches to spare and shooting out the other side with toothy grins and mobiles slapped against ears.

Cape Town traffic was murder, no matter what the time of day. It came from having a freaking big mountain in the middle of the city, Seb thought. He glanced at his watch; they'd been travelling for fifteen minutes and neither of them had initiated conversation. They had another half-hour until they reached Awelfor and the silence was oppressive.

Seb braked and cursed as the traffic slowed and then came to a dead stop. Just what he needed. A traffic jam and more time in the car *not* speaking to each other. At the best of times he wasn't good at small talk, and it seemed stupid, and superfluous to try to discuss the weather or books, movies and music with Rowan.

And on that point, since it was the first time that Rowan had been in the same time zone as her parents for nearly a decade, he felt he owed it to them to keep her in the country until they got a chance to see her, hold her. Like him, they didn't wear their hearts on their sleeves, but he knew that they had to miss her, had to want her to come back. He could sympathise. He knew what it felt like, waiting for a loved one to come home.

He had never been able to understand why she didn't value her family more, why she rebelled so much. She had parents who took their jobs seriously; he and Callie had a runaway fickle mother and...Patch. As charming and entertaining as Patch was, he was more friend than father.

Rowan's parents, Heidi and Stan, had always been a solid adult presence right next door. Conservative, sure, but reliable. Intelligent, serious, responsible. On a totally different wavelength from their crazy daughter. Then again, it sounded as if Rowan operated on a completely different wavelength to most people, and he had enough curiosity to wonder what made her tick.

Since this traffic was going nowhere they had time to kill and nothing else to talk about, so he would take the opportunity to satisfy his nosiness.

He and Ro had never danced around each other, so he jumped straight in.

'I want to know why you're broke. I know that you consider yourself a free spirit, too cool to gather material possessions, but surely a woman your age should have more to her name than a hundred pounds?'

She'd known this was coming—had been bracing herself for the lecture. Because Cape Town was synonymous, in her mind, with being preached to.

Rowan pursed her lips as she looked straight ahead. Seb hadn't lost his ability to cut straight through the waffle to what he thought was important. Lord, she was too tired to tangle with that overly smart brain of his. Too weirded out by the fact that he made her ovaries want to dance the tango. What to say without sounding like a complete idiot?

Keep it simple, stupid.

'I was doing a deal and I was supposed to get paid for delivering the...the order when I got into Oz.'

'What were you peddling, Rowan?'

Seb's eyes turned to dark ice and his face hardened when she didn't answer. Of course he couldn't take that statement at face value. He needed more and naturally he assumed the worst. She knew what he was thinking...

Here we go again, Rowan thought, *back where I started.* As the memories rolled back her palms started to sweat and she felt her breath hitch. Even after so many years Seb still instinctively assumed the worst-case scenario. As her parents would... And they wondered why she hadn't wanted to come home.

'It wasn't anything illegal, Seb!'

'I never said it was.'

'I'm not an idiot or a criminal! And, while I might be unconventional, I'm not stupid. I do not traffic, carry or use drugs.' Rowan raised her voice in an effort to get him to understand.

'Calm down, Ro. For the record, back then I never believed you should have been arrested,' Seb stated, and his words finally sank in.

Rowan frowned at him as his words tumbled around her brain. 'You didn't? Why not?'

'Because while you were spoilt and vain and shallow— and you made some very bad decisions—you were never stupid.'

She couldn't argue with that—and why did it feel so good that Seb believed she was better than the way she was portrayed? Just another thing that didn't make any sense today.

But she knew that Seb's opinion was one that her parents wouldn't share.

'But, Rowan, this lifestyle of yours is crazy. You're an adult. You should not be getting kicked out of countries. You should have more than a backpack to your name. Most women your age have established a career, are considering marriage and babies…'

Shoot me now, Rowan thought. *Or shove a hot stick in my eye.* This was why she hadn't wanted to come home, why she didn't want to face the judgment of her family, friends and whatever Seb was. They'd always seen what they wanted to see and, like Seb, wouldn't question the assumption that she was terminally broke and irreversibly irresponsible.

Rowan's eyes sparked like lightning through a midnight sky. 'What a stupid thing to say! You don't know anything about me!'

'And whose fault is that? You were the one who ran out of here like your head was on fire!'

'I didn't run!' Okay, that lie sounded hollow even to her.

'Within days of writing your finals you were on a plane out of the country. You didn't discuss your plans with anybody. That's running—fast and hard.' Seb's finger tapped the steering wheel as the car rolled forward. 'What really happened that night?'

Rowan lifted her chin. 'I don't know what you mean.' He couldn't know, could he? Callie might have told him… No, she'd sworn that she wouldn't, and Callie would never, ever break her word. Seb had to be talking about her life in general and not that night she'd got arrested in particular.

That stupid, crazy, change-her-life evening, when she'd fallen from heaven to hell in a few short hours.

'Sure you do.' Seb scanned the road ahead, saw that the traffic wasn't moving and sighed. 'Something in you changed that night you were arrested… You were rebellious before, but you were never spiteful or malicious or super-sarcastic.'

Her attitude had been that of a rabid dog. In the space of one night she'd gone from being wildly in love and indescribably happy to being heartbroken, disparaged and disbelieved. That night *had* changed her life. After all, not everybody could say that they'd lost their virginity, got dumped and framed by their lover, then arrested all in the same night. And her weekend in jail had been a nightmare of epic proportions.

Was it any wonder that she equated love with the bars of a jail?

'You were never that hard before, Rowan.' Seb quietly interrupted her thoughts. 'Those last six months you fought constantly with your parents, with me, with the world.'

Rowan clenched her jaw together. Every night she'd cried herself to sleep, sick, heartsore, humiliated, and every day she'd got up to fight—literally—another day.

'Maybe I was crying because my parents, my sibling and everyone close to me left me to spend the weekend in jail when they could've bailed me out any time during the day on Friday. The party was on a Thursday night.'

'Your parents wanted to teach you a lesson,' Seb replied, his voice steady.

Rowan stared at the electronic boards above his head. 'Yeah, well, I learnt it. I learnt that I can only rely on myself, trust myself.'

When she dared to look at him again she saw that his eyes were now glinting with suppressed sympathy. Then amusement crept across his face. 'Yet here you are relying on me.'

'Well, all good things have to come to an end,' Rowan snapped back.

She was so done with being interrogated, and it had been a long time since she'd taken this amount of crap from anyone.

'So...' She smiled sweetly. 'Hooked up with any gold-diggers lately?'

Annoyance replaced sympathy in the blink of an eye. 'Sending me those sunglasses when you heard that we'd split was a very unnecessary gesture,' he said through gritted teeth.

'I know, but I thought you might need them since you finally saw the light. It took you long enough.'

'Very droll.' Seb's hands tightened on the steering wheel.

'Still annoyed that flighty, fey Rowan pegged your ex's true characteristics and you didn't?' Rowan mocked, happy to shift the focus of their conversation to him.

'Remind me again as to why I didn't leave you to beg in Jo'burg?'

'You wanted to torture me. So, are we done biting each other?'

'For now.'

As the traffic began to move Rowan watched Seb weave his way through the slower-moving vehicles to speed down the fast lane.

'Has the traffic got worse?' she asked when Seb slammed on his brakes and ducked around a truck. Her hand shot out and slammed against the dashboard. The last vestiges of colour drained from her face. 'Sebastian! Dammit, you lunatic!'

Seb flipped her a glance and then returned his attention to the road, his right hand loosely draped over the steering wheel. 'What's the problem?'

'The problem is that you missed the bumper of that car by inches!' Rowan retorted, dropping her hand. 'The traffic hasn't got worse—your driving has!'

Seb grinned. 'Don't you think it's a bit early in our relationship to start nagging?'

'Bite me.'

Seb flipped the indicator up and made a production of checking his side and rearview mirrors. He gestured to a sedan in front of him. 'Okay, brace yourself. I'm going to overtake now. Here we go.'

Rowan sighed and rolled her eyes. 'You are such a moron.'

Seb ducked around another sedan, and flew across two lanes of traffic to take the exit. Rowan leaned back in her seat, closed her eyes and thought it was ironic that she'd crossed seven lanes of motorbikes in Beijing, a solid stream of tuk-tuks in Bangalore and horrific traffic in Mexico to die in a luxury car in her home country at the hands of a crazy person.

Rowan sat up and looked around as they drove into a more upscale neighbourhood and she recognised where she was. 'Nearly ho... there.'

'Yep, nearly *home*. And, despite your inability to say the word, this *is* still your home, Ro.'

'It hasn't been my home for a third of my life,' Rowan corrected, thinking that she had a twitchy heart, a spirit that was restless, a need to keep moving. Coming back to Cape Town broke made her feel panicky, scared, not in charge of her own destiny. She felt panic well up in her throat and her vocal cords tighten.

Seb's broad hand squeezing her knee had her sucking in air. When she felt she had enough to breathe she looked at his hand and raised her eyebrows. Then she pulled her eyebrows closer together when she clocked the gleam in his eyes, the obvious glint of masculine appreciation.

'You've grown up well, Brat.'

Bemused by the sexual heat simmering between them, she tried to take refuge in being prosaic. 'I haven't grown at all. I'm the same size I was at eighteen—and don't call me Brat. And take your hand off my knee.'

The corners of his eyes crinkled. 'It worked to take your mind off whatever you were panicking about. You always did prefer being angry to being scared.'

Seb snorted a laugh when she picked up his hand and dropped it back onto the gearstick.

'Have you developed any other serious delusions while I've been away?'

'At eighteen...' Seb carried on talking in that lazy voice that lifted the hair on her arms '...you wore ugly make-up, awful clothes and you were off the scale off-limits.'

Rowan, because she didn't even want to attempt to work out what he meant by that comment, bared her teeth at him. 'I'm still off-limits.'

Seb ignored that comment. 'Is that why you are still single at twenty-eight...nine... What? How old *are* you?'

'Old enough to say that my relationship status has nothing to do with you.'

'Relationship status? What are you? A promo person for Facebook?' Seb grimaced. 'You're either married, involved, gay or single. Pick one.'

Rowan snorted her indignation. 'Gay? For your information, I like what men have. I just frequently don't like what it is attached to!'

'So—single, then?'

'I'd forgotten what an enormous pain in the ass you could be, but it's all coming back.' Rowan turned and tucked herself into the corner between the door and seat. At least sparring with Seb was keeping her awake. 'And you? Any more close calls with Satan's Skanks?'

She hoped the subject of his ex-fiancée would be enough of a mood-killer to get him off the subject of her non-existent love-life.

'You really didn't like her.' Seb twisted his lips. 'Was it a general dislike or something more specific?'

There wouldn't be any harm in telling him now, Rowan thought. 'She was seriously mean to Callie. I mean, off the scale malicious.'

Seb's eyes narrowed. 'I thought they got along well.'

'That's what she wanted you to think. She was a nasty

piece of work,' Rowan said, staring at the bank of dials on the dashboard. 'I really didn't like her.'

'I would never have guessed,' Seb said dryly.

'My "money-grabbing" comment didn't clue you in?'

'It was a bit restrained.' Seb's tone was equally sarcastic. 'Your efforts to sabotage our engagement party were a bit subtle too.'

'What did I do?' she demanded, thinking that attack was the best form of defence. 'And why would I do it since I was looking forward to you being miserable for the rest of your life?'

Seb slid her an ironic glance. 'Apart from spiking the punch with rum? And turning the pool that violent green that totally clashed with the puke-orange colour scheme? And placing a condom on every side plate? Anything I've missed?'

Rowan dropped her head back on the headrest. 'You knew about that?'

'I had a good idea it was you.' Seb's lips twitched. 'Okay, hit me. What else did you do?'

'Nothing,' Rowan replied, far too quickly.

'Come on, 'fess up.'

Well, he couldn't kill her now. She didn't think…

'I put itching powder in your bed.'

Rowan felt as if she wanted to dance to the sound of Seb's laughter. Despite her now overwhelming fatigue, she noticed the scar bisecting his eyebrow, the length of his blond eyelashes. Man, she wanted to link her arms around him, curl up against him and drift off.

'Ro, I knew about that too.'

He spoke softly and Rowan felt both warm and chilled, her nerve-endings on fire.

'Luckily we had a fight after the party and I chose to sleep in the spare room…she itched for days.'

'Good.' Rowan grinned and fought an enormous yawn. 'You had really bad taste in women, Seb.'

'She wasn't so bad. And if I didn't know any better I'd say you sound like a jealous shrew.'

'You really should give up whatever you're smoking.'

Rowan lifted her nose. As if she'd be jealous of that waste of a womb. Seb might be a thorn in her side but he was *her* thorn in the side—and Callie's, obviously. Nobody else was allowed to treat him badly. Especially not some lazy, stupid... Oh, dear God, the old oak tree was still on the corner of their road.

And there, through the trees, she could see the redbrick corner of Awelfor.

'No, don't panic. Just breathe. It's only a house, Ro.'

His house. And next door was her old home. And a life she didn't want to go back to—a life she'd outgrown a long time ago.

Seb turned into his driveway and parked in front of a new rectangular automated gate. While he waited for the gate to slide open he looked at Rowan, his blue eyes serious. 'Stay the three weeks, spend some time with your parents, and then I'll loan you the money to fly anywhere in the world.'

'Why?'

'Because I think it's long overdue.'

Rowan shook her head, suspicious. 'How much time, exactly, must I spend with them?'

Seb looked frustrated. 'I don't know! Make an effort to see them—have dinner with them—talk to them and we'll have a deal.'

It was too good an offer to pass up. It wasn't ideal but it was a solid plan of action. If she got some money together before that she'd go sooner... No, she couldn't do that. She was here. She had to see them. To leave without saying hello would be cruel, and she wasn't by nature cruel. Three weeks. What was twenty-one days in the scheme of things?

Twenty days too long in this city, her sarcastic twin said from her shoulder.

'I'll pay you back.'

Seb grinned. 'Yeah, you will. Yasmeen is on holiday and we're short of a housekeeper. You can start tomorrow: shopping, cleaning, laundry, cooking. You know what Yas does.'

'Are you mad? I'm not going to housekeep for you!' Rowan protested.

It wasn't that she couldn't—she'd worked as a maid before—but she wasn't going to pick up after Seb and his 'we'.

'We're? You said *we're* short of a housekeeper? Who else lives here?' Rowan demanded. If he had a live in lover/partner/girlfriend then she'd just go and sleep on the beach.

Seb steered the car up to his elegant house. 'Patch has hit a hiccup with his current girlfriend and has moved back into the second floor of the cottage.'

Oh, thank goodness. She didn't know if she could cope with Seb and any 'significant other'.

'So, housekeeping in exchange for your bed and food?'

'S'pose,' Rowan reluctantly agreed, thinking that she was jumping from the frying pan into... Well, the third level of the hot place.

After lugging Rowan's luggage up to Callie's old bedroom Seb finally made it to his office—the bottom floor of the two-bedroomed cottage Patch had moved into—temporarily he hoped! His workaholic staff worked flexible hours, so he was accustomed to seeing them at work at odd times, and Carl, his assistant/admin manager, like his hackers, was still around.

Seb listened to Carl's update and accompanied him into what they called the 'War Room'. The huge room was windowless, and a massive plasma TV attached to the far wall was tuned to MTV at a volume level that made his ears bleed. He picked up the TV remote that stood in its cradle on the wall and muted the volume. Two male heads and one female head shot up and looked in his direction.

His hackers needed junk food, tons of coffee and music. Deprive them of one of the three and he had their immediate attention. Seb walked into the centre of the room and rapidly scanned the long row of screens where computer code rolled in an unending stream. He read it as easily as he did English, and nodded when he didn't immediately pick up any problems.

'Anything I should know about?' he asked, folding his arms.

He listened while they updated him on their individual projects—testing the security of a government agency, a bank and a massive online bookseller—adding his input when he felt he needed to but mostly just listening while they ran their ideas past him. There was a reason why he'd hired all three and paid them a king's ransom: they were ethical, super-smart and the best in the field.

Nearly, but not quite, as good as him.

Seb wrapped up the meeting, left the room and headed for his office, which was diametrically opposite to the War Room. There were computers—five of them—with a processing power that could run most Developing World countries—but his office had lots of natural light, a TV tuned to ESPN, an *en-suite* bathroom and a door directly linked to the gym. Although he nagged and threatened, his staff members rarely used the up-to-date equipment.

Seb tossed his car keys and mobile onto his desk, hooked his chair with his foot and pulled it over to his favourite computer. Having Rowan return with her battered backpack and her world-weary attitude made him think of his mother and had him wondering where she was laying her head these days. He checked on her once or twice a year—

with his skills he could find out exactly where she was, how much money she had and pretty much what she was up to. He'd first tracked her down when he was sixteen and he'd found her passport and identity number on a supposedly coded list—ha-ha!—on his father's computer.

His fingers flew across the screen as he pulled up the program he'd written specifically to let him track her. Within minutes he found out that she'd drifted from Peru to Brazil and then moved around a bit within that country. She was currently in Salvador and running seriously low on funds.

He experienced the usual wave of resentment and anger, wondered if he was a hundred types of a fool—after all, what had she ever done for him?—and then transferred a thousand untraceable dollars into her account. It was less than petty cash to him, and if he didn't do it he'd lie awake at night, wondering what she'd have to do to dig herself out of that hole. She was, after all, his mother.

Rowan was in pretty much the same position, he thought, and he wondered how she'd come to the same point. He looked at his screen speculatively and thought that with a couple of clicks he could find out exactly what had happened to bring her home. He had everything he needed: her passport number, her bank details. He could, by inputting a line of code into that program, see her travel movements and everything she'd ever purchased with a credit or debit card.

It was that easy.

He'd done it before—not for five years at least, but once or twice a year before that, when her parents hadn't heard from her for a while and her father had asked him to take a peek. He'd skim over the information, not particularly interested, and report back that she was in London or Perth and reassure them that she seemed to have enough money to cover her costs. There were big deposits and big withdrawals, but there was always a savings account with excess funds. He wondered why she hadn't had one this time…

Seb dropped his hands to his lap and fought temptation. He could, but he didn't—as curious as he was, he didn't have the right to invade her privacy. She wasn't the child they had all worried about anymore, she'd grown up.

She was now the knockout she'd promised to be. Eyes the colour of night, wild hair, creamy, creamy skin and a body that was all woman. He felt his zipper straining and leaned back in his chair, spun around and stared out of the window to the pool area beyond his floor-to-ceiling windows. He wanted her. And, equally and as intensely, he didn't want to want her. She was everything he avoided in the opposite sex: complicated, gregarious, communicative…free-spirited and forthright.

Why hadn't he just loaned her the money and sent her on her way? Then he wouldn't be sitting here—being totally unproductive—with an urge to see if she slept naked.

He was such a moron.

'Gray, I'm really sorry…'

Seb propped his shoulder against the doorframe to his newly refurbished kitchen, with its sleek cupboards, black granite and black and white checked floor. Yasmeen had designed the kitchen and, since this was where she ruled from, he'd been happy to write out the rather hefty cheque. It was filled with light, modern appliances and Yasmeen's precious ferns and African Violets. If he let those die his life would be over.

He grinned. It was just another job he could add to Rowan's growing list of housekeeping duties.

'Grayson…take a breath. There's a monkey, a tiger with cubs, a squid, a seal and a horse. Those are the highlights. And a Hotei.'

What on earth was she up to? Seb wondered as he stepped into the kitchen and headed for the coffee machine.

'I'm pretty sure the Hotei is rare. It has that…class, a mastery that just can't be ignored.'

Rowan nodded when he lifted a cup towards her, asking whether she wanted coffee.

'Now that my mobile is charged again I'm about to e-mail you some photographs. Take a look and see what you think… Yes, I know that you won't buy anything without looking at it…'

Rowan murmured a couple of soothing phrases into the mobile before disconnecting the call. She quickly e-mailed Grayson the photographs she'd promised and placed her mobile onto the kitchen table.

'I *know* that you can't buy them without seeing them. I've only been dealing with you for ten years. Jerk.'

Seb handed her a cup of coffee which Rowan reached for with the enthusiasm of a true coffee addict.

'Thanks. You need a master's degree to operate your machine.'

Seb leaned against his counter and thought that Rowan looked a great deal better than she had when he'd picked her up. That was what a solid night's sleep did for you, Seb thought. She still had faint blue shadows under her eyes, but there was at least some colour in her cheeks. He'd checked on her a couple of times and discovered that she didn't— unfortunately—sleep naked, that she had a slight piggy snore and that she slept on her stomach.

'Are you trying to sell a zoo?' Seb said, his eyes on her long legs. She wore a simple pair of denim shorts and another button-down cotton shirt and had pulled her clean hair into a fat plait. She wore no make-up except for a slick of gloss on her lips.

She took his breath right away.

'Of sorts. I picked up some stuff in Bali which I hoped to flog when I got to Oz.'

And he'd thought that *he* was tight-lipped and uncommunicative. It made him want to shake her...or kiss her. 'You know I *could* just avoid pulling your teeth for information and find out for myself.'

'How?'

He wiggled his hands. 'Magic computer fingers.'

'Corny. And, like most men, I think you exaggerate your computer skills.' Her expression was a mixture of pity and disbelief, as if he was a child telling tall stories.

'Sweetheart, I hacked into the FBI's website and left them an Easter egg when I was sixteen—'

'A what?'

'An Easter egg. It's a surprise in a program that a hacker leaves...a signature or a message or a picture. It's non-malicious. Anyway, if I wanted to I could tell you what you had for breakfast six years ago, so finding out what you bought in Bali would be child's play.'

Rowan's look threatened to cut him off at the knees. 'If I find out that you've done that—ever—I will make it my personal mission to make your life on earth resemble the hottest part of hell.'

Seb knew that that she'd certainly try. And he'd watch her try for a while and then he'd get bored and haul her off to bed... Actually, that didn't sound like a bad plan at all. Entertainment in and out of the bedroom. Win-win.

'*Have* you ever done that?'

'Cyber checked up on you?' Seb slid his innocent expression into place—the one he'd been practising since he was fourteen and had discovered code and that he could speak it. And have some fun with it. 'Why would you think that?'

'Because I don't trust you further than I can throw you. Have you?'

Of course he had. She'd been nineteen, on her own in

countries where she couldn't speak or read the language. Her parents had been beside themselves with worry—actually, her father had. Her brother Peter had been concerned. Callie a little less so. Himself? Not so much… He'd always known that Rowan was stronger, smarter than they gave her credit for. He'd known that she'd be fine but he'd used his skills to check up on her so that the family and friends she'd left behind could sleep at night.

'Have you?'

He was saved from answering that question by her chirping mobile, which rattled and vibrated on the dining room table as if it was possessed. Rowan narrowed her eyes at him—a non-verbal threat that he wasn't off the hook—and frowned when she looked down at the tiny screen.

'Grayson…again?'

Rowan yanked the mobile up to her ear as her heart bounded up her throat. There was no reason for Grayson to be returning her call so soon unless she'd found the netsuke of the century or there was a huge problem.

It turned out to be both. Rowan listened to his garbled words and tried to make sense of what he was saying. 'Are you saying that my netsukes might have been stolen? From a West End art gallery a year ago?'

Rowan rested her forehead on her hand and tried to force the panic far away enough so that she could listen to Grayson.

'A seal, a stag antler, a tiger with cubs and a squid were stolen from the King and Cross Gallery. There's been a lot of interest in netsuke lately, and consequently a lot of theft. They are also easy to transport, being not much bigger than the size of a golfball.'

'If they were stolen, how did they end up in a hole-in-the-wall shop in Bali? They were covered in dust, forgotten. Nobody had looked at them for years.'

'I can't take a chance that these might be stolen. Didn't you get any provenance?'

'Gray, the guy said they were pawned. The owner never came back to pick them up and that was six years ago.' Rowan rubbed her neck. 'They are *not* stolen.'

Grayson was silent for a minute. 'Well, if these are genuine eighteenth-century netsuke and aren't the same objects that were stolen then I think you've got a heck of a find on your hands.'

'So, it's either really good or really bad news?'

'Essentially. Can you prove how you paid for them?' Grayson demanded.

Rowan's eyes flicked to Seb's face. He was listening to her side of the conversation with avid interest.

'Yeah. Every cent. I drained my bank accounts to pay for them.'

'That's good. Of course you might take a financial hit if they *are* stolen, but if you can prove you paid for them then it shows you didn't have criminal intent.'

'Yay me. And they *aren't* stolen.' Rowan closed her eyes at the thought of waving goodbye to twelve thousand pounds. She rested her forehead on the dining room table and tried not to hyperventilate.

'Of course if they are not stolen, then I think you've hit a massive pay-day,' Grayson added.

Rowan heard Seb move from his chair and thought that he was finally giving her some privacy. Instead she felt his hand warm and big on her neck, gently stroking the tense cords.

She wished she could just lean back and soak up his strength, ask him to help her sort this out. But she couldn't. She never asked for help...mostly because there had never been anyone around she could ask.

Besides, he'd just think that she was stupid and

irresponsible… And because she liked his hands on her skin a little too much she swatted them away.

'Do you have any documentation or photographs of what was stolen from that gallery so that I can compare them myself?' Rowan asked Grayson.

'No, that's not my problem—it's yours. I just know that it was those four subjects.'

And Japanese artists never did the same subjects. Damn Grayson! He was getting all paranoid and crazy without even knowing if the netsukes looked the same. Stupid man. Grayson was rich, but he wasn't bright.

'You need to do some research. Try to identify the pieces. Then we'll talk again,' Grayson said as Seb dropped his hand and walked away to refill his coffee cup.

'You know you want them.'

'And I'll buy them—after you tell me that they are definitely not stolen.'

'They are definitely not stolen.'

'Smarty pants,' Grayson said, before disconnecting.

Aarrrrgh. It wasn't as if she was a total amateur, Rowan thought on an internal eye-roll. She stared out of the window and tried to push her way through her panic to think the problem through.

'I can smell your brains burning,' Seb said, taking his seat again and pushing another cup of coffee in her direction. 'Sip and spill.'

Rowan instinctively shook her head. 'Don't worry about it. I'll figure something out.' She pushed against the table to haul herself to her feet. This wasn't Seb's problem, she thought. It was hers, solely.

Rowan looked down in surprise when Seb's hand snagged her wrist and tugged her back to her seat. 'Sit down, drink your coffee and tell me what's happened.'

'Seb…I can deal with it. It's fine.'

Seb shoved a frustrated hand through his hair. 'That's

the problem, Rowan. You don't need to deal with it on your own. Why won't you let me help you?'

'I don't need your help! This is minor, Seb. I *needed* your help nine years ago. I needed lots of help then! Since then I've learnt to rely on myself.'

Seb flicked his thumbnail against his bottom lip. 'Something happened that night—something more than any of us realised.'

Rowan shook her head. 'What is your obsession with that damned party? It was at a club, I got caught with a baggie, I did community service for it... End of story.'

'Really? I suspect you took the rap for that slick character you were so in love with. Jason... Jack...' Seb clicked his fingers in frustration.

'Joe Clark.'

He frowned. 'The same Joe Clark who runs that sports betting company? The one that's just been listed on the Stock Exchange?'

'I presume so. His father owned a couple of betting shops, so it must be the same family.'

'You haven't kept in touch with him?'

Revulsion passed across Rowan's face, accompanied by a visible shudder. Oh, yeah, there was a story here.

Rowan cocked her head. 'What's with the twenty questions? I feel like I'm back in the interrogation room at Sydney.'

'You're tough. You can handle it.' Seb looked over the rim of his coffee cup. Her remote, distant façade was back in place and it annoyed him. She wasn't cool and remote. She never had been. Loud, vivacious, spontaneous... He'd used to be able to read every emotion on her face.

'Are you in trouble—again?' If she was there was no way that he'd just sit back and watch her go through hell a second time. 'Tell me.'

Rowan recognised that determined look on his face and

realised that he wasn't going to be shrugged off. And she felt…relieved. Glad to have an excuse to tell him, to tell somebody.

Another part of her wanted to show him—tell him that she *wasn't* the ditsy, silly, crazy child who bounced from job to job, wafting her way through the world. Well, she did waft, but she worked as well. Being an art 'picker' took determination, time and a good eye. And hours and hours of studying jewellery, art, sculpture.

Maybe he could respect that—respect her?

Was it so wrong to want a little affirmation, a little admiration from a super-smart man? From anybody?

'Criminal trouble? No. Financial trouble? Oh, yeah. And to make you understand I have to show you something,' Rowan said, and walked out of the room to fetch her baby sculptures.

CHAPTER FOUR

'I LOVE THIS one,' Seb said, holding the chubby, joyful figurine of a Buddha in the palm of his hand. 'Simply stunning.'

'It's a Hotei, also called a Laughing Buddha, symbolising contentment and abundance and luck.' Rowan's finger drifted over the Buddha's cheek. 'I love him too. I think he's the prize of the collection.'

After Seb had spent at least fifteen minutes looking at the tiny ivory netsukes, pointing out details that she hadn't noticed, Rowan rewrapped the carvings and put them back into their box. Closing the lid, she wrapped her hands around her coffee cup. She wondered where to start. At the beginning, she supposed...

'After six months in Thailand I left and headed for Hong Kong, I had a job teaching English and was barely scraping by. One day, after I'd just been paid, I was on my way to buy groceries, and there was a little shop I passed every day, full of...curiosities, I suppose. Mostly junk, to be honest. I had some time and I went in. I was browsing through a box of costume jewellery and I found a brooch. I knew right away that it was special. The craftsmanship was superb. The owners thought it was paste but I knew it wasn't. Don't ask me how. I just did.'

Seb leaned his arms on the table, listening intently.

'I went straight to the Causeway District and found an antique shop.'

Seb's mouth kicked up in a smile. 'Don't tell me… It was solid gold and studded with diamonds.'

'Better. It was Fabergé and worth a freaking fortune. I was lucky. The owner paid me a fair price. He could've ripped me off. I didn't know what it was. The profit on that funded my travels for the next eighteen months, but I was hooked on the chase. I started studying antiques, jewellery, art. I realised I had an eye for spotting quality and, while I never found another Fabergé brooch, I *did* find Lalique glassware, Meissen pottery, minor works of art. I made some money.'

Well, that explained the deposits and withdrawals. Smart girl, Seb thought. Smart *and* gorgeous. A very dangerous combination.

'Most of my capital is tied up in a house I co-bought in London which I am planning on…'

'Flipping?'

Rowan tipped her mouth up. 'It's what I do.'

'So, coming back to these…'

Rowan told him what Grayson had said and waited through his resultant thoughtful silence. 'So, basically, you need to know whether these are previously undiscovered, undocumented netsuke or whether they've been stolen?'

'They aren't stolen. I'm pretty sure of that. But no one is going to buy them at the price I want without further information.' Rowan rested her chin on her fist. 'And obviously it also means that I'm going to be broke for a lot longer than I anticipated.'

Seb waved her money troubles away. Easy for him to do, Rowan thought.

'So, what's the next step?' he asked.

'Research. Lots of it. I don't know nearly enough about netsuke.'

'But you know that they are quality pieces? Do you need my computer skills?'

'I don't think so… I just need to trawl through databases of documented netsuke and see if I can find any of them.'

'Well, if you need to get into places that you can't get into…'

'Is that what you do? Poke around in places?'

Seb shrugged. 'At a very basic level.'

'What exactly are you paid so much money to do?'

Seb tapped his finger against his coffee cup. 'I guess you can call me a consultant. Companies hire me to evaluate their computer systems for vulnerabilities. So I go in there, try to hack their system—and pretty much always do. Then I point out where they have problems. Sometimes I fix the problems for them; sometimes they get their people to do it. Either way I get paid.'

'Huh. So you use your powers for good and not evil?' Rowan threw his words back at him.

'Yeah.'

'And you'd be willing to…poke around for me? Isn't that illegal?'

'Slightly unethical, maybe.' Seb's eyes were determined when they met hers. 'Look, I'm not going to use the information for personal gain, and if it helps you out of a jam then so much the better.'

Rowan nodded her understanding, thought for a minute, then said, 'Let me do some research. If I need your help, I'll ask.'

'Promise?' Seb shrugged at her gimlet stare. 'It's just that you don't have a great track record when it comes to asking for help, Brat.'

'Promise. Can I borrow a computer?'

'Sure. There's a couple you can use in my office, or there's a few you can use in my bedroom.' Seb deliberately wiggled his eyebrows suggestively and Rowan, as expected, rolled her eyes. Yep, time to bust her chops, he thought, and to banish the tension he saw in her eyes.

'I am not going anywhere near your bedroom, Hollis.'

Seb leaned back in his chair. 'Why? Scared you won't be able to keep your hands off me?'

'What? Are you mad? You're like my...my...er...'

'Don't say brother,' Seb ground out. 'That would be too creepy for words.'

'No...geez! *Eeuuuw!*' Rowan shuddered as she banged her cup onto the table. 'No talk of bedrooms!'

Seb liked the colour in her face and the snap in her eyes so he thought he'd wind her up some more. 'Okay, can we talk about what happens in bedrooms, then?'

'We could *never* have sex!'

'Uh, yes...actually we could. You see, my Part A would slot into your Plot B—'

Rowan's look was meant to freeze. 'Stop being facetious! It's a crazy idea! Yes, I think you've got some heat happening, but it would be a really stupid thing to do. We don't even like each other.'

Seb stood up and ran a hand over her head. Then he placed one hand on the back of her chair and bent down so that his face was next to hers. She just folded her arms and lifted a perfectly arched, perfectly arrogant eyebrow. *Man,* that look made him hot.

'Are you trying to intimidate me? It didn't work when I was ten—what makes you think it'll work now?'

'I was just wondering whether you taste as good as you smell.'

'You'll never find out.' Rowan pushed him away, stood up and put some distance between them. She placed her fists on her hips and tipped her head. 'Back to business. So, if I ask you for help what is it going to cost me?'

'What?'

'Your computer skills? I'm already paying for my food and bed by being the housekeeper...'

Seb looked at the stack of dishes in the sink. 'Not that you've done any housekeeping yet.'

'Give me a break. I'll get to it! So, what's the price?'

'We'll work something out,' Seb said, deliberately vague.

'And that statement scares the hell out of me,' Rowan retorted. 'As per usual you've managed to drive me crazy, so I need to leave. I'm going to do some shopping, since there isn't anything to eat in this house!'

'Want me to come with you?'

'I've been shopping on my own for a long time now. I think I can manage.'

Rowan made her tone even and unemotional, but Seb smiled at the twin strips of colour on her cheekbones. Her chest was flushed and her nipples were puckered against her shirt. Her mind and mouth might be protesting at the thought of them sleeping together but her body wouldn't object. He could reach for her right now and he knew that she wouldn't take much persuading...

Except that he wanted her to want this—him—with both her body and mind. He didn't want her to have regrets, to think that she was coerced. That would be giving that smart mouth of hers too much ammunition to chew his ass off.

Rowan wasn't known for playing fair.

'Money.' Rowan held out her hand and bent her fingers backwards and forwards. When he just looked at her, she sighed. 'I can't go shopping without money, Einstein, and I don't have any.'

Right. Try to keep up, Hollis! Seb reached into his back pocket, pulled out his wallet and handed over a wad of bills. He had no idea how much was in there and it didn't matter. Money was easy. She could blow every cent he had and he would just put his shoulder to the wheel and make some more.

People—it was people who baffled him, he thought as Rowan tucked the cash into the pocket of her jeans.

'Keys?' she asked.

'To what?'

'Your car. Or were you expecting me carry the groceries back in the basket on the front of a bicycle?'

'There is no way I'm letting you drive my precious car.' Seb walked over to a row of hooks by the door and lifted off a set of keys. 'Here's a remote to the gate and garage and the keys to Yas's runaround. Use that.'

'I can't use Yasmeen's car!'

'It's my car, and Yas uses it to do errands so that she doesn't risk getting her own dinged.' Seb tossed her the set of keys and Rowan snatched them out of the air.

Their glances clashed and electricity buzzed between them again. Except that this time—dammit—it wasn't all sexual, wasn't only a caveman impulse to score with a pretty girl. Rowan wasn't just a pretty face and a spectacular bod; she'd be easier to resist if she were.

She had a brain behind those amazing eyes, a sharp sense of business and a talent to spot art. Being physically attracted to her was enough of a hassle. To be mentally drawn to her as well was asking for trouble.

Yet he was having to fight to keep from taking those couple of steps to her, pulling her against him and making her his.

Seb placed his fists on his hips and blew out a long, frustrated breath. He needed to think this through, to rationalise this attraction he felt to her. Needed to try to find out where these crazy impulses to get her naked were coming from. He believed in being rational, in analysing that which he didn't understand.

And he didn't understand what was happening with him where Rowan was concerned. He needed to get a handle on these unpredictable and swamping impulses he had whenever she was in the same room.

Like the impulse to strip her naked and bend her over the back of that chair...

Oh, man. He was in a world of trouble here...

'Okay, well, I'll be back later.' Rowan flashed him an uncertain look and belted out through the kitchen door.

Seb gripped the back of a chair with both hands and dropped his head. What was wrong with him? He never went nuts over a woman—never, ever felt out of control. Sex was important and, like all men, he liked it—no, he loved it—but he had always been able to walk away. Always.

Until now. Until Rowan.

And she hadn't even been back in his life for twenty-four hours. She had already tipped his world upside down and Seb shuddered when he thought of the chaos she could create in the immediate future.

He was still so annoying, Rowan thought as she went into the empty, cavernous hall of the supermarket and walked over to the fresh fruit section.

'My Part A would slot into your Plot B—'

Seb's words rattled around her brain. A stupid phrase that had lust whirling in her downstairs regions, that made her feel light-headed—oh, dear, that made her sound like a heroine from a historical romance, but it was the perfect word—and created an impulse to reach up and yank that sardonic mouth to hers.

She'd never felt the impulse to yank—*yank?*—any man's mouth to hers, and that it was Seb's that she now had the urge to taste went against all the laws of the universe.

She could not believe that she—cool, competent and street-smart—was acting like a horny teenager, about to collapse in a panting, wet, drippy, drooling heap at his feet.

It was humiliating. Really!

Rowan pushed a tendril of hair out of her eyes and blew

air into her cheeks as her mobile chirped. Pulling it from
the front pocket of her shorts, she did an excited wiggle
when she saw the name in the display window.

'Ro? Honey?' The gravelly voice of her best friend
boomed across the miles.

'Why aren't you in Cape Town, where I need you?'
Rowan demanded. 'The one time I get back and you're
not here, Callie!'

'Sorry, darling. I got delayed... He's six-two and has
soulful green eyes. And I need to see a designer in LA
who can only see me next week. Or maybe the week after.'

'Naff excuse,' Rowan muttered.

'So, how and why are you back home?'

'It's a long story.'

Rowan gave her a brief synopsis of her last couple of
days. After thinking about and then refusing Callie's offer
of a loan, she sighed into the mobile.

'Something else is wrong,' Callie stated. 'Come on—
spit it out.'

'I don't know what you're talking about.'

'In the last fifteen minutes I think you said Seb's name
once. Normally you would've insulted him at least ten times
by now. What's going on?'

And that was the problem with knowing someone for
all your life. You couldn't sneak stuff past them. 'I don't
know if you want to know.'

'I always want to know. Spill.'

'I think I suddenly have the screaming hots for my best
friend's brother.'

When Callie stopped roaring with laughter Rowan put
the mobile back to her ear.

'Holy fishcakes,' Callie said. 'Sweetheart, when you
muck it up, you do it properly.'

Rowan frowned at Callie's uncharacteristically mild ex-
pletives. 'Holy *fishcakes*? *Muck* it up?'

'My temporary fling nearly had heart failure when I dropped the F-bomb yesterday; he's a bit conservative. I'm cleaning up my potty mouth.'

Rowan laughed and winced at the same time. That would last as long as the fling did: until Callie got on the plane to come home.

'Anyway, tell me about wanting to do my brother.'

Rowan grimaced. *Do* her brother? *Eeew.* Knowing that Callie wasn't going to drop the subject without getting something out of her, she thought about what to say. 'I've never had this reaction to anyone—ever! I just want to take a bite out of him.'

While she wasn't a nun, she'd had some sex over the years. Sporadic, erratic, infrequent, but it had been sex. Two one-night stands, a few season-long relationships, and once a relationship that had lasted a year.

'It's about time you ran into someone who set you on fire. The fact that it's Seb just makes we want to wet my pants with laughter.'

'Glad you find it amusing. I don't. I don't know how to deal with it,' Rowan muttered, leaning her hip against a display stand of orange sweet potatoes. Instead of discussing Seb further, she chose to shove her head in the sand. 'So, tell me about your fling.'

'Hot, conservative, sweet. And you're changing the subject because you don't want to deal with your sexy side!'

'Bye, Cal, love you.'

'Avoiding the issue isn't going to change it—'

'Miss you. Hurry home, okay? I need you!' Rowan interrupted, before disconnecting.

Rowan rolled her shoulders in frustration, thinking about her 'sexy side'. Sex had always just been nice and pleasant. Uncomplicated. It gave her a little buzz. But she could probably live without it if she had to. Just as she could live without having a permanent man in her life, being in a

permanent place. She had never given her heart away—
couldn't, because she still hadn't learnt not to look at a man
and wonder if he she could trust him. She didn't need sex
and she definitely didn't need love.

She'd managed without it all these years and probably
wouldn't know what to do with it if she found it. And if
she occasionally yearned for it then it meant that she was
human, didn't it?

She wouldn't mind some respect, though.

She'd loved Joe. Had been passionately, deeply, mind-
blazingly in love with him. The type of love you could only
experience when you were eighteen and everything was
black and white. Somewhere in the part of her that was
all woman—mysterious and wise—she'd known that Joe
would be the guy who would change her destiny, would
alter her mindset, would change her in ways that she'd never
believed possible.

She'd never considered that her love for him would spin
her life in such a different direction…

Rowan was pulled back from her memories by a store
announcement and found herself staring at piles of fruit,
multi-coloured vegetables, the perfection of the display.

Apples as red as the poisonous fruit in *Snow White*,
atomic orange carrots, purple eggplant. Six different types
of lettuce, herbs, sweet potatoes…and no people. At nine in
the morning the supermarket was all but deserted.

She looked down and saw the aisles, shelves packed full
of consumer goods. Where were the shouts of the vendors
in Tamil? The smell of lemongrass and hot oil? So much
abundance, so much choice, no people. So much artificial
colour, piped music that hurt her ears…no people. Where
was everybody? How could there be so much choice and
no one to choose?

She wanted to be back in the markets in Hanoi, standing in a queue to touch a statue of Buddha in Phuket, on a crowded train on her way to Goa.

She didn't want to be back here, in the city that held so many bad memories for her. She didn't want to deal with Seb, who set her blood on fire, made her feel things that were hot and uncomfortable. She didn't want to deal with her parents, revisit her past.

She wanted to be back on crowded streets, on the Inca trails in Peru, in an Outback logging town in the Yukon. She wanted to be on her own, having transient relationships with people who expected little or nothing from her.

She wanted her freedom, she thought as she left the supermarket empty-handed. Her independence, solitude.

Money in the bank.

Money… *Dammit,* Rowan thought as she turned around and walked back into the shop. She'd made a deal with the devil and part of that deal required her to shop for food.

Ugh.

After she'd spent a healthy amount of Seb's money Rowan drove towards the coast and onto the main road that led to the beach in the area. Behind her sunglasses her eyes widened with surprise as she took in the changes that had occurred since she'd left. Her favourite beach was still there—of course it was—but the buildings on the other side of the road had been converted into upscale boutiques and gift shops, restaurants and a coffee shop-slash-restaurant-slash-neighbourhood bar.

Rowan headed straight for the restaurant/bar and slid into a tiny table by the window. She ordered an espresso and a slice of cheesecake and silently told herself that she'd add it to the mental tab she owed Seb.

It was such a stunning day. She could see Table Mountain, blue, green and purple, a natural symbol of this incredibly beautiful city. The sea was flat, aqua and green, and the sun glinted off the white sand.

Rowan looked up at the waitress and pointed to the 'Help Wanted' sign on the door. 'I see you need another waitress?'

'A bartender, actually.'

Even better, Rowan thought. She loathed waitressing. 'Tips good?'

'Very. You interested? If you are, I can call the manager over.'

Rowan nodded and within fifteen minutes had agreed to tend bar on Friday night as a trial. If that worked out she could have three night shifts a week. Rowan agreed with alacrity… She'd do anything to add cash to her depleted coffers so she could leave this city as soon as possible.

A stream of feminine cursing distracted Rowan from her appreciation of the scenery and she turned to see a fifty-something fashion plate slip into a chair at the table next to her. She was fantastically turned out, with styled curly hair, large breasts and long legs in skinny jeans. She wore Audrey Hepburn glasses and a very sulky expression.

Rowan felt like a garden gnome next to her.

Rowan took a bite of cheesecake and sighed as the flavours burst onto her tongue. The lady gestured a waiter forward and pushed her sunglasses up into her hair. Fine lines surrounded her light green eyes and Rowan revised the estimate of her age upwards. Maybe closer to sixty, but looking good. She pointed to Rowan's cup and cheesecake.

'I think she wants the same,' Rowan told the confused waitress, and smiled when the blonde lifted her thumb.

'What do you mean you've made a mistake?' she shouted into her cell, in a French-accented voice. '*L'imbécile!* I booked the Farmyard on the fourth, and I don't care if you double-booked with the President himself. Unbook it!'

Rowan rested her chin in the palm of her hand and didn't

pretend that she wasn't listening. She was fascinated. What was the Farmyard? A brothel? A nightclub? A restaurant?

'How am I going to explain to my seven-year-old grandson that he can't have his party there? Are *you* going to explain?'

Or a children's party venue.

After swearing very comprehensively, in both English and French, at the Farmyard's representative, she snapped her mobile closed and rested her head on her folded arms.

Rowan felt her sympathy stirring and leaned over and touched her on the arm. 'Hey.'

She might not be able to make emotional connections to places or things but she'd never had a problem talking to anyone, making casual connections that could last a minute, an hour, a day...

The blonde head lifted, the sunglasses slid down the pert nose and Rowan noticed tears in the dark eyes. 'What's the matter? Can I help?'

The woman shoved her glasses up her nose and sniffed. 'Only if you can provide a venue for twenty-five kids in ten days' time, complete with horses and a mini-quadbike track and paintball shooting. And an army tank cake.'

'Pardon?'

'I booked this exclusive children's party venue for next Saturday and they double-booked it. I'm going to have to cancel the party and I am going to break my grand-baby's heart. I'm Annie, by the way.'

'Rowan,' Rowan replied as her mind started to whirl. She knew of a place that had horses, a paddock suitable to make a mini-quadbike track, and haybales to make up a mock battle field for paintball-shooting. 'What's your budget?'

The Jane Fonda look-alike frowned at her and named a figure.

Rowan swallowed and wasn't sure if she'd heard her

properly. Who paid that sort of money for a kid's party?
Were these people nuts? He was seven and not the Sultan
of Brunei's kid!

Rowan stood up, picked up her plate and moved to the
blonde's table. 'My name is Rowan, but my friends call
me Ro…let's chat.'

When Seb was twenty-two, Patch had told him that he was
handing over the family's property portfolio to Seb to manage and that he was going to open up a company in Simon's
Town, doing sea-kayaking tours.

Seb hadn't believed him, but within six months he'd had
the added responsibility of managing various warehouses,
office blocks and houses around Cape Town, Patch had
moved out of Awelfor and into a house in Simon's Town and
had started leading tourist tours showing off Signal Hill,
Lions Head and Table Mountain from a sea perspective.

The company had taken off, and he'd opened a branch in
Hermanus, but most days he still went out on the water and
led a tour. For Seb, Patch's Kayak Tours was just across the
peninsula, and he often found himself driving to Simon's
Town, running along the promenade and joining his dad
for an early-evening paddle.

Today it had been easy, paddling in the shelter of the
harbour, and he'd soon pulled ahead of the group in the
open sea, wanting to feel the strain in his arms and his
shoulders. Skirting a navy striker ship waiting to dock, he
headed south towards the world-famous Boulders Beach as
he kept an eye out for whales. He flew past the huge rocks
at Boulders, laughing at the penguin colony that stood on
the beach contemplating hunting for food, and after a half-
hour turned back and caught up with the sluggish tour.

Seb laughed again as two endangered Black Oyster
Catchers pecked at Patch's hat and with a pithy insult drew
abreast with him. He cursed when his mobile jangled in its

waterproof jacket. He put it to his ear and ignored Patch's hiss of displeasure.

'No mobiles on the water, Sebastian!' Patch said loudly.

Recognising the number at Awelfor, Seb ignored Patch and quickly answered it. 'Rowan, what's wrong?'

'Nothing. Well—um—I need to ask you a favour.'

Rowan's voice sounded hesitant and his face cleared. Oh, this should be good. Another favour? She was racking them up!

'What is it?'

'May I hold a function here on Saturday?'

'I thought you were broke! Do you have money to entertain?'

'It's not entertaining…exactly. I need a place to host a birthday party for some kids and I kind of suggested Awelfor.'

Seb thought that she had to be joking. 'You kind of *what*?'

'This lady will pay me a grotesque amount of money to organise a kid's birthday party and I need a place to make a track for mini-quads and to set up a paintball course.'

Seb dropped his hand, looked at his phone and shook his head. 'Are you nuts? I don't want kids all over my property!'

'You won't even be here! I saw that notice on the fridge for a trail run you're doing on Saturday!' Rowan protested.

'Rowan, you've been in the country two days and you've already managed to meet someone who can give you a job. How is that possible? And how do you know she's not a con?'

'Oh, maybe because she'll pay me sixty per cent of the fee up front,' Rowan whipped back. 'Yes or no, Seb? If it's no I need to go to Plan B.'

'Do you have a Plan B?' Seb asked, curious. Patch leaned over to yank his mobile out of his hand and he jerked away.

'No, but I will have to find one if you say no. Please don't say no.'

'Why do I suspect that you've already told her that you can host the party at Awelfor?'

'Because I have,' Rowan said in a small voice. 'Sorry. But I'll make another plan if you *really* mean no.'

He wasn't even surprised or, come to think of it, that upset. If anyone else took such liberties with his house and his property he'd have a fit of incredible proportions, but Rowan had been such a part of Awelfor for so long that it wasn't that much of an intrusion or an imposition. Weird, but true.

'Okay, knock yourself out. However, when you agree to house a shedload of monkeys, or a circus comprising of Eastern European acrobats, run it by me first, okay? Got to go.' Seb disconnected and shoved his mobile away before Patch could yank it away. He'd lost two mobiles to Patch's strict rule about 'disturbing the peace'.

'I'm going to ban you from joining my tours,' Patch complained.

'Sorry,' Seb replied, and picked up his paddle again and pulled it through the water.

They rowed for a while in companionable silence until Patch spoke again.

'So, what's Ro done this time?' Patch asked.

Seb explained and Patch laughed.

'Life certainly has been less…colourful without her presence.'

'But a great deal more sensible.'

'Sensible…*pshaw*! I had coffee with her this afternoon. It's lovely to have her home,' Patch said. 'I've always loved that girl.'

Seb sent him a measuring look. 'I know you did when she was a kid, but…'

Patch pointed out a seal to his group, exchanged some banter with them and turned back to Seb. 'But?'

'Doesn't she remind you of...Mum?'

Patch was silent for a minute and then shook his head. 'The only commonality between the two is that they both like to travel. No, Seb. Ro is nothing like Laura. Ro would never leave her kids—leave the people she loved and never make contact again.'

'She did for a couple of months,' Seb pointed out.

Why was he pushing this? What did he hope his father would say? *Yes, she's exactly like Laura and that he should run as if his tail was on his fire*? Would that make his big brain override his little one and cancel out all the X-rated visions he was having about her?

Patch's slow, measured words pulled him back into the conversation.

'Everyone seems to have forgotten that Ro sent Callie regular e-mails, asking her to tell Stan and Heidi and us that she was fine. She was a little lost and she was trying to find herself. When she had enough distance from her parents she made contact again. Ro didn't have it easy at home, Sebastian.'

'They loved her, Dad,' Seb protested.

'As much as they could. But she needed so much more. She wouldn't have run if she'd felt loved. They didn't understand her, and sometimes I think that's worse. Don't get me wrong—I like Stan and Heidi—but I think Peter fulfilled all their requirements for a child. Studious, quiet, introverted, brilliant and unemotional. Having to deal with an emotional hurricane like Rowan rocked their world.'

'Maybe. And she *is* an emotional hurricane.' And, because he could really talk to his dad, he cursed and muttered. 'And she's freakin' *hot*.'

Patch pursed his lips but his eyes danced with mischief. 'I might date younger women, but I'd never look at my second daughter and think she's hot. But I can see why my healthy son would think so. He might notice that she's grown up very well and has a killer bod.'

Seb twisted his lips. 'And I have a killer hard-on for her.'

Patch let out a low, rumbling laugh. 'Oh, geez, this is not going to end well. Especially since your modus is to bag her, tag her, and send her on her way when you're done with her. Isn't that the way you roll?'

Crude, but true.

'And if you hurt her I'll kick your ass,' Patch added.

Seb rolled his head around in an effort to relieve the knots he'd discovered in his shoulders and neck since Rowan had moved into his life. 'We have a history. My sister is her best friend. Her parents are important to me. I don't particularly like her; she's everything I'd run from in any other woman. Unconventional, free-spirited, slightly eccentric. And I forget all that every time I look at her. All I want to do is—'

'Don't say it.' Patch held up his hand and grimaced. 'Like Callie, I prefer to think of her as untouched and un-sullied.'

'Hypocrite.' Seb laughed and then turned contemplative. 'I've never had such a strong reaction to any woman—ever. So why her and why now?'

'It's fate bitch-slapping you. It likes to do that.'

'Sucker-punching, more like it.' Seb picked up his oar and dipped it into the sea. He glanced over to Patch as they easily covered the gap between them and the group. 'No pithy words of advice?'

'From me? The king of bad decisions pertaining to women? Nah! I'm just going to sit back and enjoy watching you making a fool of yourself over this girl.'

'That's not going to happen. My brain is still firmly in charge of my junk,' Seb lied through his teeth.

Patrick's deep laugh rippled across the sea. 'Yeah, you keep telling yourself that, my boy!'

'Thanks for your help,' Seb said dryly. 'I'm going to head back. Which bed are you sleeping in tonight?'

'The cottage, since crazy Miranda changed the locks on my house.' Patch shrugged. 'I'm really going to have to do something about her soon.'

'You think?' Seb did a quick turn, slapped Patch's hand and started to paddle away. His dad's soft words had him looking back.

'Is she okay? Your mum? I know that you…check up on her now and again.'

Seb blew out his breath. 'As far as I can tell, Dad.'

'Where?'

'South America.'

Patch suddenly looked every one of his sixty-plus years. 'Ro's not like Laura, Seb. She's kinder, smarter, less self-involved.' Patch dipped his paddle into the water and launched a stream of water into Seb's face. 'Go on—get out of here.'

CHAPTER FIVE

WHEN HE WALKED into his kitchen forty minutes later—sweat-slicked and puffing—and saw Rowan bending over the kitchen sink, eating a juicy peach, he knew that Patch was right about his brain not being in control.

In fact it pretty much dissolved as he watched her from outside the door. Juice dripped down her chin and down her toned, tanned arms. She'd pulled her hair up into a messy knot and wore a lumo-purple bikini, the bottom half of which was covered by a thin multi-coloured wrap. Thanks to the afternoon sun pouring into the kitchen he could see the outline of her legs beneath the wrap, the shape of her hips, the rounded perfection of her butt. Sunlight on her back illuminated her spine, the soft skin between her jaw and neck, the slope of her thin shoulders.

Unaware that he stood there, she groaned as she bit into the peach again and more juice dripped.

He didn't—couldn't—think. His feet moved of their own accord, his hand whipped out to grab her hips and spin her around, and his mouth slammed onto hers. Peach juice, warm and sweet, thundered over his tongue, quickly followed by the taste of Rowan, as sweet and a hundred times spicier. He thought he heard—felt?—her squeak of surprise, but he didn't care; all he needed was to taste her, to feel her breasts flattened against his chest, her pelvis lifting into his to ride his erection.

Seb hooked his hand around her thigh and yanked her leg upwards, mentally cursed when her thigh encountered the barrier of her wrap. Without leaving her mouth—how could he?—he dropped his hands and fumbled at the loose knot at her hips. He needed to feel her, taste her, consume her... This was madness and fiercely unstoppable.

Unable to undo the knot, he pushed his thumbs between the fabric and her hips and shimmied it down so that it fell into a rainbow at her feet. Plastering his hands on her back, on her butt, he yanked her even closer until he doubted they could slip a piece of paper between them.

And, miracle of miracles, she was as into the kiss as he was. Little nips here. A long slide of her tongue there. Small hands were exploring his bare chest, down his ribcage, over his obliques and around to his back. She linked her arms around his neck and he was dimly aware that she still held the half-eaten peach in her hand, the juice from which was dripping down his back.

She could lick it off... She could lick anywhere she wanted to. Hopefully the thought would occur to her...

It was like being caught up in a hot, sexy, whippy storm, Rowan thought. One moment she'd had a peach in her hands and mouth, the next moment they were filled with a hard, sweaty, sexy man.

With the peach still in her hand she made a sticky path of juice across his shoulder, down his pec and over a flat nipple, lightly covered in blond hair. Dropping her head, she watched a bead of juice hit that nubby surface and shot her tongue out and licked it up, sighing as she tasted the saltiness of his skin, felt his muscles contract under her tongue.

'What's good for the goose...' Seb muttered, pulling the half-eaten fruit from her hand.

Rowan's eyes clouded over as he pulled the triangle of fabric covering her right breast away and touched her with the tips of his fingers, tanned against her much lighter skin. Her eyes watched his intense concentration as he played with her breast, running the wet peach over her distended nipple, alternating with subtle brushes of his thumb.

'To hell with this.'

Seb tossed the peach onto the floor, wrapped one strong arm around her bottom and, with the other arm, lifted her onto the dining room table, yanking the chair out of his way. Rowan barely noticed that the chair had toppled over and clattered to the floor because Seb's warm tongue was curled around her nipple and his other hand was burrowing into the back of her bikini pants, tracing erotic patterns on her butt.

He claimed her mouth again in a kiss that flew past heated and went straight to molten. Her legs, operating independently, hooked themselves around his waist and she scooted closer to him to feel that hard ridge against her mound.

Nothing else was important but to feel Seb, taste him, know him.

Seb pulled his mouth away and his hands, still on her breast and her butt, stilled. 'Point of no return, Ro. Yes or no?'

Like she had a choice, Ro thought, dazed. There was only one answer and her body was screaming it. 'Yes. Now.'

'Here?' Seb demanded.

She couldn't wait—had no patience to climb the stairs to a bedroom, to spare the couple of minutes that would take. 'Here. Now. Please.'

Seb muttered a curse and tried to step away. Rowan slapped a hand against the back of his neck and dragged him into a kiss that caused their feet to curl.

Seb yanked his mouth away and held up his hands. 'Ro, one sec...condom.'

Rowan bounced on the dining room table, her body one

long electrical current. 'If you have to go upstairs for one I'm coming with you,' she told him, deadly serious.

'There's a deal.' Seb picked up his wallet from the counter near the door and cards and cash were scattered over the floor. 'There should be one in here. Bingo.'

He held it up in his fingers as he stood between her legs again. 'You going to do the honours or must I?'

Rowan smiled slow and deep as she pulled the little packet from his fingers. 'Oh, I think I will. Why don't you make yourself useful and get me naked?'

Seb nipped the corner of her mouth as she pushed his running shorts over his erection, down his hips. 'That's a hell of an offer, Brat.'

Rowan sighed as her fingers whispered the latex over him, encircling all that masculine strength in her fist. 'I'm a hell of a girl, Hollis. Now, why don't we slide your Part A into my Plot B and see if we fit?'

The luminous hands on the bedside clock informed Rowan that it was past midnight as she rolled over onto her stomach to watch Seb walk into his *en-suite* bathroom. She'd been in Seb's arms, in his bed, for more than six hours. Six hours of intense, bone-dissolving, earth-spinning pleasure. She was one gooey, sexy mess and she wanted nothing more than to roll over and drift off to sleep.

Instead, she forced herself to sit up, then stand... Ooh, wobbly legs. The nearest garment was one of Seb's T-shirts and she pulled it over her head, unable to stop herself from sniffing the collar for that special combination of soap and cologne that she couldn't get enough of.

Just as she couldn't get enough of his kisses, of the feel of his hard muscles under her hands, the way she felt... *complete* when he slid inside her.

In between their lovemaking they'd dozed, before one

of them reached out for another kiss, another stroke, and they fell into passion again...

It was time to face reality. She didn't want to, but she had to.

She didn't know how to do this. She didn't do this... Well, she had—but not enough to feel comfortable waking up naked in his bed, with his room looking as if a hurricane had hit it after them rolling around like maniacs and bouncing off the furniture. She didn't want to stay but she couldn't just leave.

She really, really needed to polish up on her one-night stand etiquette.

And a one-night stand was all it was—all it could ever be. She had to be sensible about this... This was sex. Nothing more. They had acted on impulse, had used each other's bodies for brief, intense pleasure. It wasn't anything more—could never be anything more...

Rowan placed the balls of her hands into her eyes and pushed. It was okay, she told herself. She was allowed to have sex with a single man. The world hadn't stopped spinning. Wasn't free choice high on her list of values? She hadn't agreed to anything more than one night, to a casual hook-up, a night of pleasure.

It didn't change anything... In a couple of weeks her parents would be back. She'd say hello and how are you doing, make nice, and then she'd borrow that money from Seb and fly away. Because that was what she did best: she flew, caught trains, ox-carts, buses... That was how she lived her life. She didn't stay in one place, in one house, couldn't imagine a steady life with one man.

Staying still, coming face to face and heart to heart with a man terrified her. Mostly because she'd been disappointing people all her life and she'd have to love a man very much to stay still. The thought of losing her freedom—so hard earned—caused a cold, hard ball of something *icky* to form in her stomach.

She should leave, go back to her own room…take some time to regain her equilibrium.

'God, you look like someone shot your favourite dog,' Seb said from the doorway of the *en-suite* bathroom.

Rowan's eyes shot up and met his. Earlier they'd been warm with desire, laughter. Now they were cool and flat, and his expression was guarded and remote. Ah, so she wasn't the only one in the room having second—or third—thoughts.

Good to know.

'Ah… I was just…' Rowan placed her hands on her hips and looked around.

'Leaving?'

Since she was clear across the room and two feet from the door, what was the point in lying? 'Yeah…'

Was it her imagination or did she see his face harden? It was hard to tell in the dim light spilling from the bathroom.

'No cuddling required? After-dinner pillow-talk?'

Oh, that was sarcastic, and it blew any of her few remaining warm and fuzzies away. The problem was that there was a part of her that would have loved a cuddle, a gentle hand down her back, listening to his heartbeat under her ear, drifting off to the sound of him breathing next to her…

Because she felt weak and vulnerable—girly—she gave herself a mental slap and straightened her spine.

'Do you need pillow-talk and cuddling?' Rowan demanded, equally facetious.

'Of course I don't,' Seb ground out, walking naked back into the room.

There was no point in feeling embarrassed, Rowan realised, since she'd explored most, if not all of that luscious body. He had a swimmer's build, broad shoulders, slim hips, muscular thighs.

Rowan felt she should say something to dissipate the heavy, soggy blanket of emotional tension in the room. 'Look, Seb, you don't need to get all weirded out by this… I'm not going to get all hearts and flowers over you.'

'Oh, goody.'

Sarcastic again. He did it so well. 'For someone who is anti-commitment, and who doesn't do emotional connections, I would've thought that me leaving and getting out of your face would be the perfect scenario for you.'

'Yep, you'd think,' Seb said, in that bland voice that made her itch to smack him.

Rowan threw up her hands. 'How can we be so great in bed but so pathetically useless at actual talking?'

'Beats me.'

'You're ticked because your big brain is running at warp speed, trying to rationalise this, trying to intellectualise what just happened. You're frustrated because you don't understand how you can have mind-blowing sex with a woman you're not sure you like and who has driven you nuts your entire life.'

'I am not doing anything of the sort!' Seb retorted.

But Rowan caught the flicker of guilt in his eyes. Of course he was. She sighed. It was what Seb did. When something caught him off guard he put his extraordinary intellect to work and tried to figure it out on a cerebral level. Hadn't she watched him do exactly that growing up? She and Callie would wail and whine when things went wrong. Seb and her brother Peter would ignore the emotion and look for the cause and effect.

Men are from Mars, indeed…

'Your brain is going to explode. Attraction and lust can't be measured, analysed, categorised. It just *is*—like some things just are,' Rowan said softly. 'It was just sex, Seb, not quantum physics.'

'Yeah, whatever.'

Seb made a production out of yawning, pulled back the covers on his bed and flicked her a quick glance before climbing into bed.

'I'm going to sleep. Night.'

Rowan narrowed her eyes at him as he punched the pillows before rolling over and snuggling down. No *Thanks for a fun time*? No *See you in the morning*? He couldn't be more clinical about it if he left a couple of notes on the dresser table...

No—*no!*—that wasn't fair.

Be honest, here, Dunn. You were the one who set the tone for the way this ended... You were heading out of the door when he returned to the room. You were running scared and saying that you didn't need the mushy stuff...

And you don't.

You don't need anything but to research your netsuke, gather some cash, say a brief hello to your folks and hightail it back to...where? London? Canada? South America?

You need to be free, on the road, responsible to no one but yourself.

Rowan sent Seb one more look—was that snoring she heard? Really?—and half banged, half slammed his bedroom door closed.

Tangling with him had been fun physically, but mentally—huh! A toxic spill...

His brain, when blood finally reached it, was red-lining, Seb decided as the door banged shut behind Rowan and his eyes flew open. He was doing exactly what she'd said: intellectualising, categorising, analysing. He didn't understand what had happened earlier—that tsunami of want and need and pure animal instinct. He was a rational and stable guy. He didn't get caught up in the moment or swept away by passion.

He needed to understand why it had happened tonight

with Ro. He had to understand. Because if he could comprehend it then he would regain control of the situation. It was his modus operandi—the way he approached and dealt with life, with his problems. When his mum had left he'd expected her home within a month, then three, then six. The only way for him to deal with the slow-dawning reality that he and Callie had been essentially abandoned by the person who was supposed to love them most had been to rationalise it, to find a plausible—though mostly improbable—explanation.

She was ill and couldn't come home. She'd been kidnapped by Colombian drug lords and/or an alien space ship. She was an international spy.

He'd think it through, dissect the problem, and in that way he could subdue the bubbling, unpredictable mess emotions generated.

He didn't cope well with unpredictable and messy emotions.

And Rowan was five-foot-four of unpredictable and messy.

And why on earth did he feel ticked because Rowan didn't want to spend the rest of the night in his bed? Didn't want to be held? Her reaction should have him slipping off to sleep guilt-free, with a satisfied body and a huge smile on his face. Instead he was lying here like a freaking moron wanting...*what?* He cursed. Was he actually considering wading into messy and unpredictable?

Was that what had sent his brain into hyper-drive?

It couldn't possibly be, he decided. *You don't do emotional and you don't do connections, Butt-face.* And, really, if he decided that was something he suddenly wanted— through alien possession or a punch to his head—why would he choose a world-wanderer who couldn't stay in one place for more than a heartbeat? Choose a connection with someone who, when the thrill of those first couple of weeks wore off and the excitement of great sex started to fade away, would be on the first plane…

Oh, wait…he was going to lend her the money to do that anyway!

Seb stood up and walked back into the bathroom, gripped the edge of the counter. It shouldn't be this way, he thought. He should be glad that she'd walked out through that door and left him alone—instead of feeling as if he wanted to go to her, pull her back to his bed, fall asleep and wake her up by making love to her again. Again…why was he wondering whether they could connect on some sort of intellectual level as well as they did in the sack?

It didn't matter… Bottom line, he shouldn't be thinking about her this way. She'd been a good way to spend the night—an exceptional way to spend the night.

His junk twitched and pulsed at the memory of her… under him, over him…her hair brushing his chest, her warmth enclosing him like a warm, wet perfect glove…

Oh, hell, now he was never going to get to sleep with those thoughts rattling around in his head.

Seb walked back into his room and saw the shadows of his computers sitting in the far corner of his room.

Okay, well…he might as well give his big brain some work to do.

The following evening Seb stood just outside his front door and watched as Rowan, standing in front of the antique mirror in the hallway, tugged at the short white T-shirt that showed an inch of her waist above black low-slung jeans. Good grief, she looked hot!

They hadn't seen each other since their awkward goodbye last night and, thanks to having to jump on the super-early flight to Durban this morning, he hadn't had a moment to touch base with her.

He'd thought that the meeting in Durban would be a

morning affair, but he'd run into some serious challenges—
his clients had been more paranoid than normal and had
required a lot of reassurance that their precious information was safe in his hands—and the entire day had been a
nightmare, with suits peering over his shoulder, checking
and rechecking his progress.

Blerch.

And Rowan hadn't reached out to make contact. Then
again, neither had he... Should he have? He didn't have
the faintest clue—mostly because women always chased
him. It was what they did. They normally followed up with
a BBM, an SMS, a hello-how-are-you-doing e-mail. But
Rowan? Nothing.

He was equally intrigued and annoyed...and didn't *that*
make him sound like an egotistical jerk? He'd thought about
calling to check up on her but he hadn't been sure what
to say.

He hadn't slept much and he rubbed his eyes with his
thumbs. Why was he still so wigged out about the way the
evening had panned out? Maybe it was because Rowan
had blown every perception he'd had about women and
sex out of the window.

He'd thought that most women needed some kind of
emotional connection to have sex—that they needed to talk
before and after. Rowan hadn't required before-sex cajoling
or after-sex reassurance and she'd approached the whole
experience like a guy would. Like he did.

It was a blessing in disguise that she hadn't needed him
to talk, because thanks to that damned peach and the see-
through wrap his tongue wouldn't have been able to form
the words.

She was keeping him at an emotional distance, they'd
had sex and practically no conversation—which he normally considered the ideal relationship—and it bugged the
crap out of him.

Could he say hypocritical and bastard and then put them together in a sentence?

Rowan jumped as he stepped into the hall. Dropping his laptop and briefcase onto the old yellow wood table, he pulled off his wire-rimmed glasses, tossed them down and raised his eyebrows at Rowan. 'Going somewhere?'

To keep from tugging her shirt down, Rowan shoved her hands into the pockets of her jeans and rocked on her heels. 'Hi. You're…back.'

'It is Friday night,' Seb pointed out. And it was his house.

'I thought you might have plans—like a date,' Rowan said to his back as he disappeared down the passage.

He was back in under a minute, a bottle of beer in his hand. A date? He'd slept with her last night and she had him already trawling for another woman?

He didn't know whether to be ticked or flattered that she thought him to be such a player. Seb thought for a moment; nah, he was definitely POed.

'My plans? Nothing more strenuous than a burger, a beer and an early night. It's the Fish and Fern tomorrow.'

Rowan wrinkled her nose. 'The what?'

Seb gave her a long look before emptying his pockets, placing his mobile, keys and a thin wallet on the table. 'The triathlon race. The one on the fridge. Swimming, running, biking?'

'Oh, right. What time do you think you'll be home?'

Seb shrugged. 'Eight-ish, I suppose. There's a barbecue after the prize-giving and I'll probably stay for that. Problem?'

'No.'

Rowan tugged the shirt down but it sprang up her tummy with all the obstinacy of stretched cotton. He clocked her tousled but elaborate hairdo, the subtle make-up, the bangles at her wrist and the beaded earrings. She looked as if *she* was going on a date… Was that why she'd asked him whether he had plans? Because she did?

Hell, no. That wasn't happening.

'So, what are *you* up to tonight? That's one heck of an outfit, by the way.'

Rowan responded to the thinly disguised annoyance in his tone by raising her chin. 'What's wrong with my outfit?'

'Tight low-rise jeans, short top, fixed hair. Wherever you're going, you are going to get hit on all night.' The beer was not doing the trick of relaxing him; Rowan changing and staying at home would.

'Don't be ridiculous.'

'I'm a guy and I know exactly what *I'd* read into your outfit.'

'Guys would read sex into a nun's habit.'

He noticed that she still hadn't told him where she was going. What was the big deal? His temper, on a low simmer all day, started to heat. He shrugged out of his jacket and threw it over the newel post of the staircase. He yanked his pale green dress shirt out of his black pants and sat on the bottom stair to pull off his shoes.

Seb rested his elbows on the stair above, took a long sip of his beer and picked up a shovel to dig his own grave. 'So, where are you going? And who are you going with?'

'I'm going to a bar.'

'A bar?'

'You make it sound as if I am about to do a deal with the local meth supplier! I feel like I've been catapulted back to my teenage years with my over-protective parents. I'm not sixteen any more, Seb. What is your problem?' Rowan demanded when he just looked past her in stony silence. 'Why are you acting like this?'

Fair question.

'I didn't expect to come home to…' Seb rubbed his temple '…this.'

'This?' Rowan felt the bubbles of her temper rise to the surface and pop. '"This" being jeans and a tee?'

'"This" being you dressed up and looking hot.'

'I did my hair and put on some make-up…this is pretty normal!'

'Nothing about you is normal!' Seb sprang up, his eyes tired and sparking. 'Do you know how sexy you look? You'll have every male tongue dropping to the floor in that bar. You were mine last night and the thought of you going out and being someone else's is making me want to punch something.'

As soon as the words left his mouth and their meaning sank in Seb knew that he'd made a crucial mistake—that he'd been a total tool. Her eyes shimmered with hurt and she bit her lip to keep it from wobbling. He *never* spoke without thinking, but those words had just bubbled up, over and out…

Seb swore at himself and ran an agitated hand through his hair.

'Excuse me?'

Oh, crap. She'd kicked 'hurt' into the back seat and now she was seriously ticked. Wonderful. And could he blame her?

Seb twisted his lips and thought he'd attempt to explain. 'Okay, look, that came out wrong…'

'You think I am so easy that I could jump from your bed to someone else's?' Rowan laughed and the sound didn't hold a teaspoonful of mirth. She held up a hand. 'No, don't answer that, because I'm very close to smacking you silly! What a joke!'

If it was, he failed to see it.

Rowan shook her head, snapped a set of car keys off the hall table and picked up the bag that she'd hung on the coat stand. She walked towards the door.

Seb was thinking of how to keep her in the room when

she turned around abruptly and looked at him with blazing eyes. 'No, I'm not going to do this again.'

'Do what?'

'Leave you to your assumptions. I think that's a mistake I keep making over and over with you and my family. I allow you to jump to these crazy assumptions about me because…because of habit, maybe. Pride, maybe. But this—you thinking that I treat sex casually just because we had a great time in the sack—I can't let this ride. The reason we had great sex is because we obviously—who knows why?—have amazing chemistry. Why we have this chemistry when I think you have the personality and charm of a horse's ass is a mystery for another day.'

'I—'

'My turn.' Rowan cut him off with a sharp wave of her hand. 'As for my sexual history—do you know how hard it is, as a female travelling on her own, to get laid?'

She looked as if she was waiting for a response so Seb thought it was safe to say: 'Uh…no?'

Rowan looked momentarily triumphant. 'Hah! Of course you don't. You just assume that it's what we travellers do.' Her chest rose and fell with temper. 'Every man I meet— all the time—is a stranger. I don't know him. I'm not given the time to know him. I can think he's cute, but psychos come cute as well. Now, say I decide to take a chance… I have to get into a room with him—because, you know, I like a bit of privacy with my sex. That means I put myself in danger every time. And do you want to know how many times I've done that?'

Seb, now feeling like a first-prize fool, shrugged.

'None, Seb. I've *never* done it. I've had a couple of relationships over the years with guys I've known for a long time. I don't do hook-ups. It's a dangerous and stupid thing to do when you don't have any friends or family to rescue you if something goes horribly wrong.'

Seb scrubbed his face with his hands, feeling equally relieved and foolish.

'And, just so that I'm very clear about this, *we* rocked it because you have a heck of a bod and you arc a good kisser and I haven't had any for a while.'

Okay, how deep was that hole he'd dug for himself and when could he throw himself into it?

But Rowan wasn't quite finished; she still had another layer of skin to strip off him. 'And I'm not going *to* a bar, you moron. I've got a job *tending* bar so that I can make some cash to pay you back and get out of your stupid, judgmental face!'

With that last verbal slap—which he so deserved— Rowan turned on her heel and walked out of his house.

CHAPTER SIX

ROWAN, EXHAUSTED AND smelling of beer and bar, walked back into the hall of Awelfor shortly after twelve-thirty and sighed when she saw Seb standing in the doorway to the small TV lounge, dressed in casual track pants and a loose-fitting T-shirt.

She was still feeling raw, hurt and angry that Seb—smart, smart Seb, who apparently had the emotional intelligence of an amoeba—had assumed that she was back-packing baggage with the morals of an alley cat. She was exhausted from not sleeping much last night, from career-ing around Cape Town today picking up all the equipment she needed—haybales, paint guns, food—for the party the next day, and she was depressed that she hadn't had a sec-ond to research the netsuke and that she'd been reduced to serving beers and martinis again. Dammit, she was twenty-eight years old—not nineteen.

'I don't want to fight, Seb.' Rowan dropped her bag to the floor and rubbed the back of her neck. 'If you're going to take any more shots at me, can I ask that you do it in the morning? I'm wiped out.'

'Come in here for a moment.'

Rowan cursed silently as he walked away without waiting for her response. *Let's just get this over with,* she thought, following him into the messy room. A large screen, big boys' TV dominated one wall and dark choco-

late leather couches, long and wide enough to accommodate his large frame, were placed in an L-shape in front of
the screen. A wooden coffee table held a large laptop and
a bottle of red wine and two glasses.

Seb lifted the bottle and filled a glass, topping up his
own half-full glass after he did so. He handed her the glass
and nodded to the couch. Rowan, figuring that it was easier just to take the glass and sit down rather than argue
with him, dropped to the couch and sighed as the pressure
eased off her feet. She had forgotten how hard bartending
was on the feet.

Seb sat down on the coffee table in front of her, his knees
brushing hers. He held his wine glass between his knees
and stared at the brown and cream carpet beneath him.

'I owe you the biggest apology.'

Okay, she knew she was tired, but was she really hearing Seb correctly? He was apologising? Seriously?

'Saying what I did earlier was…unkind and ugly and…
Sorry. I really didn't mean it. It was a stupid off-the-cuff-
comment that slipped out because I was annoyed and tired
and not thinking.'

'Now, there's a first—you not thinking,' Rowan teased,
and Seb's face was transformed by a relieved smile.

Seb dropped a casual hand onto her knee. 'Friends?'

'Can we possibly be?' Rowan asked him, cocking her
head and looking into those dark blue eyes.

Seb tugged on his bottom lip, placed his glass on the
table next to his powerful thigh and put his elbows on his
knees. 'Your verbal slap about making assumptions also hit
home. Although I never believed those drugs were yours,
I *did* think that you were reckless and rebellious and irresponsible as a kid.'

'I *was* reckless and rebellious and irresponsible as a kid,'
Rowan pointed out.

'But I carried on assuming that. I didn't think that you

had changed, that you'd grown up. There's so much that I—we—all of us—don't know about you. I don't know you and I wonder if I ever did.'

Rowan felt her throat tighten. Finally. Finally someone from her past was looking at her differently, trying to see her and not the person they wanted her to be. Rowan put her fist to her lips and nibbled at the skin on her index finger. And, in fairness, how much did she know about *him*? About any of them? Surface stuff. Social media stuff. And how much of that was the truth?

She had to have some preconceived ideas about him and her family that weren't based in reality either.

'So, how about we try to get to know the grown-up versions of ourselves?' Seb suggested.

There was nothing she wanted more. Acceptance and understanding. While she craved her freedom, she also wanted the freedom to be herself in this place where she'd always felt she could never be that.

Rowan dropped her hand and picked up her glass with a shaky hand. 'I'd like that, but...'

'But?'

'But what about the other thing? The last night thing?'

'Sex?' Seb lifted his glass, drained half its contents and tapped his finger against the crystal. 'Let's not make this any more complicated than it has to be. What if we just put that onto the back burner for now and try to be friends?'

Rowan's smile was wide and true. 'Okay, let's try that.'

'Good.' Seb placed his hands on the table behind him and leaned back. 'And, as your friend, I'm going to ask you something.'

Rowan groaned theatrically. 'Oh, no.'

'Why haven't you been home? Why haven't you popped your head through the fence, looked at your house, walked through the gardens? Said hello to the dogs?'

'New dogs. They don't know me.'

'Hedging, Ro.'

'The house is occupied, Seb. I can't just go wandering through.'

'Hedging. I told the occupiers that you were home and not to worry if they saw you hovering around. They were cool about it. So, again, hedging...'

She was, and she didn't know what to say. She'd been avoiding going home because that way she could avoid thinking about her parents, about what she'd say to them when she saw them again, what they would say to her. And the truth was seeing the house made her remember how unhappy—no, not unhappy, just how excluded she'd felt from her family. Her parents and brother had been so close, sharing the same interests, the same quest for knowledge and mental improvement.

It made her feel eighteen again and all at sea.

'Were you so miserable at home, Ro?'

'Miserable? No.' Rowan looked around. 'But I always felt so much more at home here in Awelfor. Here I could dance and sing and laugh loudly...home was so quiet.'

Seb smiled. 'And you were the most lively child we knew.'

'I suppose I should take a look at the house... I can't avoid it for ever.' Rowan brushed her hair back. 'I don't know what I'm going to say to my parents, Seb. Should I apologise for living my own life? For not coming back for so long?'

'Did you want to?'

Rowan shook her head. 'No, I wasn't ready to come home. Didn't feel strong enough.'

'Then don't apologise, Ro.' Seb leaned forward and rested his elbows on his knees. 'I've been listening to your folks—mostly your dad—moaning about your travelling for years, but tonight for the first time I looked at it from another angle. Your parents are wealthy enough to travel and you've always returned to London. They could've met you there, or anywhere else, quite a few times during the last decade.'

'I've thought about that often,' Rowan admitted in a whisper. 'Why didn't they do that?'

'Because they didn't want you there; they wanted you here. Because it would have given you their tacit approval of your travelling, for choosing your own way of life, if they did that.' Seb grimaced. 'I like your parents, Ro. They were good to me growing up. But I could engage them on an intellectual level. As Patch said, you were always way too emotional for them.'

'Patch said that? I love that man.'

'I do too. He's been the best dad—apart from his habit of dating too-young, too-stupid-to-live gold-diggers.'

Rowan laughed, loosely linked one arm around Seb's neck and placed her cheek to his. 'I like this—talking to you. I think it's the first proper conversation we've had.'

'And I'm pretty sure that it's snowing in hell.' Seb ran his hand down Rowan's back before pulling away. 'You need to go home, Ro. Take a look. Confront those demons. They aren't as big as you think. And you need to go to bed— because if you don't I'm going to become very unfriendly and kiss you stupid.'

Rowan pulled her head back and her eyes were smoky with passion. 'I was thinking exactly the same thing.' She stood up and scooted around his legs. 'Sleep well, Seb.'

'You too, Brat.'

Rowan handed out the last goodie bag, ruffled the last head and placed her hands on her hips as she watched the last expensive car—this one was a Bentley—cruise away.

Thank God, thank God, thank God! Rowan felt almost dizzy with relief. Hauling the envelope out of her back pocket, she took out the cash and nearly did a happy dance in the middle of the driveway. Annie's son and daughter-in-law, although taken aback by their very muddy, very happy boy, had instantly recognised by his jabbering, excited conversation that his party had been a huge success. His father, his neck pulled forward by the rope-thick gold chain around his neck, had added a bonus of five hundred to the highway robbery price Annie had already paid her.

Three other mummies, obviously in awe of Seb's property, had asked for her business card. Not having one, she'd hastily scribbled her contact details on a serviette.

Professional, she was not.

But the cake had been perfect, and the mini-quadbikes and paintball shooting had been fun. She'd had her own gun and was supposed to be treated like Switzerland—but all that meant was that the rug-rats had had a common enemy and had shot at her whenever the opportunity arose. She had a bright purple paint mark on her neck and her T-shirt, jeans and legs were multi-coloured blotches.

Looking towards the paddock, she noticed that the hay-bales and used car tyres that had formed the track for the mini-quadbikes, as well as Seb's white fence poles, were splattered as well. Nothing that a hosepipe or a good thunderstorm couldn't fix… Rowan looked up at the sky and cursed the lack of clouds. She was exhausted already, and she had the kitchen to clean up. She didn't feel like hosing down the poles as well.

Crab-fishing in the stream at the bottom of the property had been another highlight of the day. It had been a bit of a problem finding enough branches to make adequate poles, and she had sacrificed a nice piece of fillet steak she'd found in the fridge to use as bait, but they had pulled up a lot of the unwelcome creatures that populated the small stream.

None of the kids had got hurt, lost or even cried. They'd had enough sugar to put them on a high for days, had a whole lot of fun, and if their parents had to throw away their mud-and paint-stained designer clothes Rowan was pretty sure they could afford to buy more. She had some cash in her pocket and she felt a sense of accomplishment that was different from buying and selling.

It was being around innocence, having fun doing the simple things she'd done with Callie, feeding off the kids' joyous energy. She'd run, skipped, hopped, climbed and crawled, and she'd frequently thought that she couldn't believe she was getting paid to have this much fun.

Kids. Not having had much to do with them, she would never have believed that she would enjoy them so much.

Rowan grimaced as she sank onto the bottom of the four steps that led to the wide veranda. She rubbed her lower back—she'd tumbled backwards off a stack of hay-bales and was now paying the price—and rested her aching head against the stone wall. She'd had minimal sleep over the past few days—sleeping with Seb and bartending had both translated into very late nights—and she'd been up with the sparrows this morning to get everything done before the kids arrived.

She shouldn't have stopped, shouldn't have sat down. Now that she knew how tired she was she didn't think she could find the energy to get up, never mind clear up the mess that the kids had made and the disaster area that was the kitchen. She'd just sit here for a minute with her eyes closed and try to recharge her batteries...

When Seb shook her awake the sun was dipping behind the mountains and she felt slightly chilly. She yawned as she glanced up at him, still dressed in his exercise gear, although he'd pulled on a hooded sweatshirt. Seb held out his hand and pulled her to her feet.

'I've made tea,' he said, leading her by the hand to the kitchen.

'You hate tea,' Rowan said on a smothered yawn.

'Not for me, for you.' Seb pulled out a chair from the table and shoved her into it.

As her eyes focused Rowan noticed that, instead of looking as if a nuclear bomb had exploded in it, the kitchen was tidy, all the surfaces were clean, the chip and sweet packets were packed away and the remains of the cake were in a big plastic container.

'You cleaned up.' Rowan took the cup he held out and wrapped her hands around it. 'You shouldn't have. I was going to.'

'Anyone who could fall asleep against a stone pillar for an hour was not up to cleaning up.' Seb held a cup of coffee in one hand, his fingers curled around the mug.

Rowan wished, passionately, that they were curled around something attached to her.

'So, that was your function?'

'Mmm. My stupid way to make some money.'

'If it's legal, there is no stupid way to make money,' Seb responded. 'Was it worth it?'

Rowan nodded. 'Yes, it was. Do you mind your property being invaded by a horde of kids? They didn't come into the house, by the way, except to use the downstairs bathroom.'

'No, of course I don't mind,' Seb said, and shook his head at her puzzled look. When he spoke again, he sounded frustrated. 'Ro, you could fill this place with a hundred kids and I wouldn't mind. I *do* mind you working so hard that you fall asleep with your head on the wall as soon as you sit down. You coming home is supposed to give you some space to sort your life out, but you're bartending and arranging kids' parties and you're exhausted. You don't need to do this...'

'I need to earn some money, Seb. Quickly. I hate being...'

Seb waited through her silence, then added his own words. 'Beholden? In my debt? That's such crap, Ro. You're sleeping in a bed that isn't being used, you don't eat enough to feed a mouse, and you are housekeeping…'

Rowan looked around at the neat kitchen. 'I pack the dishwasher and I throw a load of laundry into the machine…it's hardly housekeeping.'

'True; any chance of you actually mopping anything?'

'Maybe.' Rowan blew a tendril of hair away from her mouth and stared down into her strong tea. 'Worse than feeling in your debt is feeling that I'm trapped. That I'm in this city, this place, this house, and I can't leave. It makes me feel…panicky.'

Seb pulled out a chair and sat down opposite her, wincing as he did so. 'Why? Why is being here so difficult for you?'

'Because I am so free out there, and when I am free I'm happy. Being here just makes me remember how controlling and protective my folks were, and…'

'They were trying to protect you, Rowan. From yourself, mostly.'

Rowan sighed. 'You always defend them…' She held up her hand to hold off his hot reply. 'I don't want to argue with you, Seb. I know that you think that they were good parents because yours—'

'Mine weren't. Well, Patch was okay. My mother was a train wreck.'

'Patch gave you freedom to move, to explore. I was never allowed beyond the walls of our two houses.'

'They—'

Rowan interrupted him. 'My point is that whether the ties that bind are silk scarves or barbed wire you still can't move, and I've always had the need to be unconstrained, unfettered…free.' Rowan sipped her tea. 'That makes me jittery, but coming home broke just makes me mad. I wanted to show them that I am successful, together…responsible. Not in their way but in *my* way. Now they are going to hear that I'm broke and homeless, they'll roll their eyes and launch into one of their what-did-we-do-wrong? speeches.' Sadness swept across her face. 'Do you think I could've been adopted and they never told me?'

'Considering the fact that you look exactly like your mum, I'd say the chances are slim,' Seb said, his tone bone-dry.

'It's just that I couldn't be more different to them if I tried.'

Seb stroked a hand over her head. 'Different isn't bad, Ro, it's just different. I'd like to believe that they'd like to be part of your life but have no idea how to achieve that—especially since you hop around the world like a schizoid bunny.'

Rowan glared at him.

'Have you ever thought about how scary your life must be to them? To them, going to London was a massive challenge: the crowds, the congestion, the unfamiliarity of a new city. You do that all the time. They would be terrified to live your type of life. They are not as brave as you, Ro.'

She'd never thought about her parents from that angle and she realised that Seb was right. Her parents thought that going to their timeshare unit up the coast was a mammoth undertaking, so going to London would be equivalent to going to the moon. Doing what she did would be, to them, inconceivable.

She understood that. But why couldn't *they* understand that while they needed to stay in their cocoon she needed to be free.

'Why did they go? I haven't even asked.'

'Your dad was asked to present a paper at some conference and Peter was going to meet them in the UK.' Seb wriggled in his chair, winced again, and Rowan frowned.

'What have you done to yourself?' she demanded.

'Tumbled down a hill on the trail run.' Seb took a sip

of his coffee and stood up. Taking a bread knife from the
drawer, he lifted the lid off the container holding the cake
and cut two healthy slices. Putting them onto the lid of the
container, he carried it back to the table and slid the lid
between them. Sitting again, he snapped off a square and
shoved it into his mouth. 'Yasmeen's chocolate cake. God,
that tastes good. Who made it?'

'How do you know I didn't make it, using her recipe?'
Rowan asked indignantly.

'Because I've tasted enough of your disastrous cakes
to last me a lifetime. I don't think you ever made one that
tasted like...well, like cake.'

'You're right. I didn't make it. I found a lovely lady who
makes cakes, gave her a copy of Yas's recipe—'

'If she finds out, you'll hang,' Seb told her.

'Are you going to rat me out?' Rowan asked indignantly.

Seb smiled. 'She'll find out. She always does. None of
us have ever been able to sneak anything past her.'

'I'll be out of the country by then,' Rowan replied, relieved.

'You poor, naïve, deluded child. You think that mat-
ters? If I could harness her powers I could rule the world.'

'I'll change my name and she won't find me. Anyway,
if I do more parties I'll use this woman again.'

'More parties? You want to do it again?'

'Strangely, I enjoyed it.' Rowan lowered her cup. 'And
it's really good money, Seb. Two of today's mummies said
that they'd call me because they have parties they need to
arrange. If they want them done in the next two weeks or
so I'll do it.' Rowan forced herself to meet his eyes. 'Will
you let me have them here?'

Seb stared down at the cake in his hand for the longest
time. 'I'd like to say no, but I know that won't stop you.
You'll just find another venue. So I'll say yes—with certain conditions attached.'

Rowan bit the inside of her lip and waited for his words.

'Do the parties, Ro, but with help. There is no way that you can keep an eye on thirty kids by yourself. And that blonde who was hanging around was as much help as a corkscrew in a bottle-free desert. I mean proper help. Someone who can lift chairs and move tables and carry stuff, run after the kids if necessary,' Seb said, his tone serious. 'No help, no party. Deal?'

'But where would I find someone to help?' Rowan demanded.

'There are lots of kids in the area looking for casual work,' Seb replied, breaking off another piece of cake. 'Or me.'

Rowan hooted with laughter. '*You'd* help?'

'If you needed me. It wouldn't be my first choice on how to spend my time, but if you needed my help I'd give it.'

And he would—of course he would. 'Okay, thanks. *If* I get another party and *if* I need help I'll ask for it.'

'Good.' Seb's face softened as he handed her a piece of cake. 'Eat.'

Rowan placed it on her saucer and shook her head. 'Yank down your track pants.'

'I thought we discussed this? We were going to be friends...'

'Stop being a jerk and let me see your injury,' Rowan stated patiently. 'Anyway, I've seen all you have, so it's a bit late for modesty.'

'Why?'

'Because you're in pain and I want to see what is causing it.'

'And congratulate it?' Seb grumbled.

'Of course. I live to see you hurting!' Rowan replied, her voice chock-full of sarcasm. 'Seb, you know how stubborn I can be, and I'm going to nag you until I get to see it.'

She *was* stubborn and she *would* nag.

Seb tipped his head back in frustration, thinking about the foot-and-a-half-long graze that ran from his buttock to his knee. His elbow also displayed the results of connecting with the ground at speed. After fifteen years of doing trail runs and triathlons he should know better than to hurtle down a mountainous track with his mind somewhere else—like in bed with Rowan.

It also burned that he'd been lying fourth at the time, feeling strong, with a good chance of catching the front runners. If he had seen that loose gravel right in front of his nose he would have finished the race—except that he'd broken the front joint on his bike as he'd tipped head over heels and had to retire. He hated not finishing a race almost as much as he hated not doing well.

He made the mistake of looking at Rowan, who was watching him...and waiting. For the love of God...

He pushed his track pants over his hips, stepped out of them and pulled up the back of his running shorts. He knew it looked bad when Rowan said nothing for a long time.

'It needs to be cleaned, and you can't reach to do it properly. Where's the first aid kit?'

Seb shook his head. 'If you think I'm going to let you come within a mile of me with a bottle of peroxide, you're mad.'

'First aid kit?'

'Ro, you're a better baker than you are a nurse!'

Rowan just folded her arms and tapped her foot and waited. Then she waited some more. Stubborn, obstinate and wilful; she gave a deeper meaning to those three words.

Giving in, with very bad grace, he stomped to the cupboard and lifted the first aid box from the top shelf. Banging it onto the kitchen table, he scowled at Rowan. 'Try not to kill me, Nurse Ratched.'

Rowan pulled her tongue at him before ordering him to

lie with his chest on the table and his legs stretched out. Doing as he was told, he felt like an idiot.

When nothing happened, Seb turned around to see her inspecting his leg. 'What's the problem?'

'Small pieces of stone and gravel are imbedded in the skin,' Rowan replied as she reached for the tweezers, the cotton wool and the peroxide bottle.

Seb gritted his teeth as she picked out pieces of stone and gravel. Taking a peroxide-wet cotton ball, she dabbed it over the spot and Seb swore viciously.

Rowan used the tweezers and dabbed again. Seb repeated the words.

He kept up his litany of swear words as Rowan tweezed the bigger pieces out.

A little while later he heard Rowan's stomach rumbling. 'So, any ideas about supper? I'm starving,' she said.

'Steak, potatoes and a green salad? Bloody hell, Ro!' Seb shouted, clenching every muscle in his body in pain as she worked on the area directly behind his knee.

Rowan stopped, glanced towards the fridge and pulled a face. 'Is that fillet steak?'

'Yes. Can you get a move on, please?' Seb demanded through a red haze of pain.

Rowan peered at the graze, and when she dropped the tweezers Seb realised that she was finally satisfied that he was stone-and-dirt-free.

'Problem. I used your fillet steak to bait the hooks for crab-fishing.'

Seb turned his head and glared at her.

'Sorry,' Rowan responded, dousing another cotton ball in peroxide and swabbing it across his elbow this time.

Seb flew up, ripped the ball from her hand and launched it in the direction of the dustbin. 'You're having a bit too much fun at my expense, Rowan.'

Rowan met his hot eyes and clearly saw the mixture

of desire, frustration and amusement bubbling there. She licked her lips and risked lifting her hand to touch his cheek. 'Not fun, exactly. Maybe a tiny little bit of revenge for all those times you were so mean to me growing up.'

'You deserved everything I ever gave you,' Seb muttered, his gaze on her luscious mouth, wishing he could bend his head and cover it with his. He still wanted her... didn't think he'd ever stop wanting her.

Rowan, surprisingly, made the first move. Standing on her tiptoes, she brushed her lips against his, her tongue darting out to lick his bottom lip. His mouth softened as his hands gripped her upper arms. He started to pull her forward, to deepen the kiss...

Dammit! He couldn't do this—couldn't start something neither of them could finish. Seb placed his hands on her waist, lifted her up and away—as far away from him as possible—and dumped her, bottom first, on the kitchen table. He reached past her to pick up his mobile, which he slapped into her hand.

'What's this for?' she asked, puzzled and annoyed.

'Pizza. Order it. You can pay, since you fed my steak to the crabs. And no girly stuff like capers and asparagus!'

The past week of living with Rowan had been like living within a twister, Seb decided as he strolled into the kitchen. He'd had a tough day at work and his kitchen held Patch, an attractive blonde around Patch's age and Rowan, and they were all stuffing brightly coloured bags with sweets.

'Seb, do you know where I can hire a boat?' Rowan demanded.

'Hello to you too,' Seb said pointedly, and looked at Annie, his face quizzical.

'Seb, this is Annie—my friend. She hired me to organise the party last weekend. Annie, this is Seb, Patch's son,' Rowan gabbled, grabbing a handful of sour worms.

'Hi, Annie. Speaking of that party, the paddock poles still have paint splotches on them,' Seb pointed out.

'I'll get to it. Now, do you know where I can hire a boat?'

'A Hobie? A catamaran? An ocean liner?' Seb asked as he shook hands with Annie. He took the beer Rowan pulled from the fridge for him and twisted off the top.

Rowan wrinkled her nose. 'Something that can accommodate ten teenage girls for a sunset cruise around the harbour.'

Seb, who thought he had a reasonably fast mind, was battling to keep up. 'What are you talking about, Brat?'

Rowan sent him a try-to-keep-up look. 'I had an enquiry about a boat party: food, drink, sunset cruise. I need a boat.'

Seb took a long sip of his beer and rested the neck between his eyes. 'Was she always this exhausting?' he asked Patch.

'Pretty much. Rowan has always only had two speeds: fast and super-fast,' Patch replied, sliding a look at Annie.

Annie smiled slowly, dropped her eyes and lifted them again in a look that was all seduction. Oh, wow, Patch was flirting with a woman his own age. *His own age!*

Seb felt like looking out of the window to see if a pig was flying past. He leaned against the far counter and crossed his legs at the ankles. 'And these bags are for another party you're organising?'

'Yep, for tomorrow.' Rowan flashed him a grin. 'Not here, though. The mummy wanted it at her house, but she didn't want to take the time out from her business to organise the details. So she's paying me an insane amount to set out snacks, organise a magician and a Slip and Slide and to make party bags.' Rowan looked at her watch. 'And Patch and Annie are helping me because I need to get to the bar later.'

As he'd said—a twister. He'd barely seen her this past week. She'd dashed in and out of the house like a woman possessed. He'd tried to get her to stop for a glass of wine, a meal, a conversation. She'd brushed him off, saying that she didn't have time to do anything, and it had annoyed the crap out of him. He'd never been put in the position of running after someone, waiting for someone to give him a minute of their time, and it wasn't fun. Was this how his previous girlfriends felt? Was this a touch of karma?

Karma? Jeez, he sounded like a hippy girl... *Get a grip, dude! You're just freakin' miserable and, frankly, ticked off because you're horny.*

He switched gears fast. 'And your netsukes? Have you done any research yet?'

Rowan pulled a face. 'Not really. I've been so busy...'

'You have a shedload of money tied up in those statues and you're messing around with children's parties?'

Rowan's shoulders stiffened as she sent him a cool look. 'I thought that if I could earn some money I could get back to London and take them to the experts there. That would save me the hassle of trawling the net.'

The reluctance in her voice as she said 'trawling the net' had him shaking his head. 'You don't know where to start, do you?'

Rowan wouldn't meet his eyes. 'Not really.'

'And you couldn't ask me for help? Ro, what do I do for a living?'

Annie's and Patch's eyes played ping-pong as they bounced off their faces.

'It's just that you are busy...'

'That's an asinine excuse! You just didn't want to ask for help—again! I thought we'd talked about your stupid independent streak?'

Rowan launched a sweet at his chest. 'Don't you dare call me stupid!'

Seb snatched the sweet out of the air. 'I never said you were stupid. I said you had a stupid independent streak!'

Patch sighed and looked at Annie. 'I feel like I've been transported back to their childhood. This could go on for a while, so what do you say to leaving them to argue and coming to have a glass of wine at my place?'

And that reminded him... When was his father going to move out of the cottage and back into his own house? Seb opened his mouth to ask, then snapped it closed again. Finish one argument first.

He waited for Patch and Annie to leave—Patch's hand was very low on Annie's back...definitely something happening there—and then banged his bottle down on the counter. He looked at Rowan, who was still packing bags, and rubbed his hands across his face. It annoyed the pants off him that she was living in his house and yet he hardly saw her, that she was so damn close—across the hall from him—yet might as well be in China in terms of being available. He wanted to spend time with her, get to know her, but she was never in the bloody building!

And that felt strange—very bizarre. He'd never actively wanted to seek out a woman's company before, had never wanted to deepen the connection between him and his lovers.

Yet here he was, wanting to spend time with a woman he wasn't sleeping with. It didn't make any sense.

Look at her, Seb thought. Sexiness on steroids. She wore her hair up in a high ponytail and a tank top revealed the curves of the tops of her breasts. It skimmed her long, slim torso and ended an inch above the waistband of her white cotton shorts. Endless slim legs ended in bare feet tipped with fire-red nails. Rowan turned away, bent over to pick up a sweet that had fallen to the floor, and he saw the thin string of the top of her thong, a little red heart on the cross of the white T.

His saliva disappeared as his eyes slid over the rounded

curve of her ass, the knobs of her spine under that thin shirt.
The band of her bra, the slim column of her neck.

He took two steps to reach her, and his arm banded
around her waist as he hauled her back against him, his
hand low on her stomach, pushing her into his throbbing
erection.

Rowan spun round and her hips slammed into his. Her
eyes were on his mouth as her hands went up to his neck
and she mashed her chest against his. Then her mouth
slammed against his and she yanked him into a kiss that
set his blood on fire.

Rowan was poised for a moment on the edge of that
precipice and then she tumbled into kissing Seb. She'd been
thinking of this, dreaming about being in his arms again, all
week—a mess of sexual frustration—and she'd kept herself
super-busy to keep her mind off jumping him again. But
now, as his hand grabbed her butt and yanked her up and
into him, she could indulge in her need to rediscover those
strong muscles, the heat of his skin, his talented hands, his
sexy mouth.

Rowan yanked at his shirt and pulled it up his chest,
her lips kissing the skin it revealed. Seb pulled the shirt
over his head with one hand and Rowan placed her lips on
the edge of the fabulous geometric tattoo that covered his
shoulder and his bicep.

'I love this,' she murmured against his inked skin. 'So
hot, so sexy.'

'I love the way you smell,' Seb replied, his words blowing warm air against her neck. 'Of sunshine and flowers.'

The tip of Rowan's tongue swirled against his collarbone. 'I thought we weren't going to do this...that we were
going to get to know each other.'

'I know that you are a brat and that you kiss like a
dream,' Seb replied, his hand curling around her breast

and his thumb swiping her nipple. 'So I'm good, knowledge-wise, for now.'

Rowan's breath caught in her throat. 'And I know that nobody spikes my temper like you do and that you make my blood boil when you touch me like that. That's all I need to know right now.'

'Bed?' Seb demanded, clasping her face in his hands.

Rowan licked her lips. 'Bed, couch, floor. Take your pick.'

Seb grinned. 'I really like the way you think.'

CHAPTER SEVEN

'ONE OF THESE days we are going to have a post-coital conversation,' Seb muttered as Rowan bounded from his bed and headed into his *en-suite* bathroom.

She grinned as she shoved her hand into the shower and flipped on the taps to boiling. She popped her head around the doorway and smiled again. Seb lay face down on the bed, his head turned in her direction. 'Poor baby, are you feeling neglected?' she teased. 'Do you need me to act like your girlfriend?'

His eyes narrowed. 'I've never needed my actual girlfriends to act like my girlfriend so…no. You're exhausting. You never stay still for a second.'

He was right. She didn't. Staying still gave her too much time to think about things she'd rather not think about—needs that had gone unrecognised for far too long. Like affection and friendship, a sense of belonging, a house to come home to. Since they were too high a price to pay for losing her freedom she pushed them away and refused to think about them.

'One of these days I'm going to tie you to this bed with silk scarves and keep you here.'

Rowan flushed at the thought of being at his mercy, being under his control. Instead of making her feel panicky she felt excitement and…lust. Excitement? Good grief.

But she'd ignore the silk scarves portion of that sentence for a minute…

'Does that mean that you want us to carry on sleeping together?' Rowan demanded, ignoring the pounding shower.

'Since I spend so much time thinking about sleeping with you I might as well just have sex with you.'

'Ooh, don't stop. I just love it when you say such sexy, sweet things,' Rowan drawled.

Seb winced, turned over, and pushed himself up on his elbows. 'Sorry, that sounded churlish.'

Rowan folded her arms against the towel she'd wrapped around her torso. 'Churlish is the least of it.'

Seb rubbed his hand over his head and scowled. 'Dammit, Ro…this situation is going to bite me—us—in the butt, yet I can't stop wanting you. Sleep with you…don't sleep with you. Either way my ass is on the line to get chomped. I look at you and my control flies out of the window.'

Seb had looked as if he was passing a kidney stone as he'd said that, Rowan thought on an internal hiccupped laugh. Still, he was trying to express himself and she appreciated the effort, even if it was clumsy and ass-related. And, really, didn't she feel exactly the same way? She was leaving soon, and had no intention of letting Seb get under her skin, yet here she was, newborn-naked in his room, wishing he'd get out of bed and join her in the shower. And if they did this—continued to sleep together—they had to be very careful about what they were jumping into.

'If we're going to do this then we need to be very sure of what we are doing.' Rowan repeated her thought. 'I'll lay my cards on the table… I like you, and I love sleeping with you, but I *am* going to leave.'

Seb nodded, his gorgeous eyes holding hers. 'I *love* sleeping with you, I like you, and I don't want you to stay.'

Why did that sting? Rowan asked herself. It shouldn't—

couldn't. He was saying what she wanted him to say! Stupid, stupid girl…

'But…'

Rowan tipped her head at his hard tone, his intractable face.

'While we *are* sleeping together we're together. There's only me and you. No one else. No colouring outside the lines.'

She could live with that—wouldn't actually accept anything else. Rowan pushed her shoulders back and tossed her hair. 'Just so you know, I won't act like your girlfriend.'

'Good. I won't act like yours…boyfriend, that is.' Seb pulled a face. 'That's such a juvenile term. How come the word boyfriend sounds so much worse than girlfriend?'

'It's a moot point, since we're not either,' Rowan said firmly as Seb swung his legs off the bed, stood up and walked over to her, all long, lean, masculine grace.

'What time will you be home from your shift at the bar?' he asked, running a possessive hand down her arm.

'My shift ends at twelve. So around half past twelve,' Rowan replied as he put his hands on her hips and backed her into the steaming shower.

He bent his head to her breast and tongued her nipple.

'That sounded remarkably like a question a boyfriend would ask, Hollis,' Rowan said, streaking her hands over his broad shoulders.

Seb picked up his head and sent her a wicked look that had her toes curling.

'Nope, just trying to work out how much time I have to buy some more condoms.' A foil packet appeared as if by magic between his thumb and finger. 'This is the last one. Shower sex?'

Rowan sighed. She was definitely going to have to buy herself a toy when she left… Then she'd be able to drift back to memories of what Seb was doing to her. And why did that thought make her feel instinctively sad?

'Ro?' Seb lifted his head and his hand stilled on her breast. 'You okay to go again?'

She needed to make as many memories as she could. 'Yes, please.'

It was past three in the morning when Rowan parked her car—Yas's car—in the carport next to the three-car garage. Seb's hog sat in one spot, Patch's Jag in the other and his SUV in the last space. Poor little car, Rowan thought, left out in the cold. She glanced up at the house and saw that the light was off in Seb's room. Rowan considered slipping quietly into bed with him, snuggling down for the night, with his back warm against her chest, her legs tucked in behind his knees. And if he woke up so much the better...

No! Rowan shook her head. That would be a girlfriendy thing to do, and she wasn't going to act like that. She and Seb were having sex, for a defined period, then she was leaving and he was staying. Getting cosy was a sure way to get her heart involved, and that would be a disaster of magnificent proportions! Leaving would be so much harder than it needed to be, and settling back into her transient life would take more effort than normal.

Was that why she'd accepted the offer from a couple of the pub's regulars to accompany them into the city and listen to a blues band in a late-night café? Because it was an impulsive decision? Because it was something that she'd do if she was on her own...accept a random invitation from strangers to try something different?

She sometimes felt that she was too comfortable in Seb's house—in his bed, his arms.

She couldn't afford to get too attached to him, to his house or this city, Rowan told herself as she climbed out of the car and headed towards the front door. She had a little over a ten days left here; her parents were due back at the end of next week and she'd spend the weekend with them. Hopefully, if she could land the boat party gig, she'd have enough money to feed and house herself when she got back to London.

Of course if she actually did some work researching those netsukes she could be out of here sooner. She knew Grayson wanted them, and she suspected that, judging by his increasingly frequent e-mails on the subject, and as long as she could prove that they weren't stolen, he might buy them unseen. At the very least she'd recover the cash she'd laid out and then she could go anywhere she wanted to…

She should start with researching the Laughing Buddha—the miniature she'd spotted first in the shop, instantly recognising that it was the stand-out piece of the collection—so why wasn't she carving out some time to research the wretched thing? Sure, it would take a bite out of her money-collecting time, but she wasn't a total numpty on the computer, as she'd made herself out to be to Seb.

Did she want to keep it? Or could it be—dammit—because she was feeling slightly sentimental? A tad grateful to that tiny little object that it had been the catalyst to her coming home?

Home. There—she'd said it. And it was time she acknowledged that, no matter what had transpired before, this *was* home. This house,—*not* the house next door… *This* was home.

Whoomph!

Rowan let out a high-pitched squeal and cannoned into a hard shape as she pushed open the door to Awelfor. Familiar arms grabbed her before she toppled over and her heart steadied as she realised that she'd run into Seb.

'You scared my breath out of me!' She wheezed as she placed a hand on her chest. 'Jeez, Seb!'

Seb flicked on the hall light and Rowan blinked at the

brightness. When the black dots receded she turned to Seb, and her smile faded when she saw that he was dressed in jeans and an old T-shirt and held his car keys in his hands.

'Where are you going at three in morning?' she asked, puzzled.

'To bloody look for you!'

Rowan took a step back as his roar washed over her. Then she saw his wild eyes, his dishevelled hair and his inside-out T-shirt. He was in a complete tizzy and it was fairly obvious that *she* was the cause of it.

'You said that you would be home around half-twelve!' Seb paced the hallway, tension bunching every muscle in his body. 'At twelve-forty-five I was worried. At one-fifteen I was concerned enough to call you on your mobile and I've been calling every ten minutes since then. Why don't you bloody well answer your phone?'

Rowan pulled the mobile out of her bag and checked the display. *Oh, yeah...* She'd missed more than a couple of calls...like fifteen.... 'I'd put my mobile on silent...I didn't think to change it back.'

'And doesn't that just explain a whole lot?' Seb shouted. 'You don't *think*, Rowan. Where on earth have you been?'

Crap. She hadn't seen Seb this mad since she'd chirped him about his ex-fiancée. And he'd passed that level of anger five minutes ago. 'I went to a late-night blues café in Simon's Town.'

'You *what*?'

Rowan thought that she saw the chandelier tremble. 'Whoa, hold on a sec! I thought you'd be sleeping—'

'Like I could *sleep* until I knew you were home safely!'

'Seb, the pub is five minutes away.'

'And I expected you home fifteen minutes or so after the pub closed. And I know it closed at one because I called there too!' Seb shoved his hands into his hair. 'I've been imagining you stabbed or raped or driven off the road—'

'Oh, come on, Seb! You're overreacting!' Rowan retorted. When his eyes lightened she knew that she'd made an tactical error. His anger had just deepened and his eyes had gone cold.

'You know, I *get* that you have this free-spirit, answer-to-no-one gig going on, and I know you well enough to choose my battles with you,' Seb said, his voice colder than an Arctic breeze. 'So I'm prepared to let the little things go… But when you roll in at three in the morning, after saying that you'll be home a lot earlier, I get to yell at you!'

'I'm not a child, and you're not allowed to place restrictions on me!' Rowan snapped, going on the defensive because she suspected that she'd crossed a rather big line.

'You keep telling me that you're not a child, but you're acting like one. A responsible, thoughtful grown-up would've picked up the phone and called me, told me not to worry.'

Seb rubbed the back of his neck with his hand. His anger had faded and she could see disappointment and resignation on his face. She could fight anger. The other two were like acid on her soul.

'Rowan, you're free to come and go as you please. I can't and won't ask you to be something you are not. But I do expect you to think, occasionally, about other people. I was worried. I had a right to be. If not as your lover, then as a man who has known you all your life.' Seb twisted his lips. 'And if you can't see that then you are even more screwed up than any of us thought.'

Seb's words hovered in the air as he walked up the stairs and a minute later she heard his bedroom door close. Rowan sank to the third step of the staircase and dropped her head to her knees. He was right and she couldn't run away from it. She had been selfish and thoughtless and she didn't like being either.

Why couldn't people understand—and why couldn't she explain?—that restrictions felt like chains to her? That rules felt like the bars of that long-ago jail cell and that she couldn't trust anyone not to change the rules on her to suit their needs better?

She knew that he had a point—a really valid point. She knew she should apologise, ask for forgiveness for being thoughtless, but the words were stuck in her throat. Why did she feel that if she apologised she would also be apologising for her lifestyle? For being impulsive, freedom-seeking, for being who she was?

She was at fault and she knew that she should admit it—just go up those steps and say sorry. Wake him up if she had to... But saying *I'm sorry* had become incredibly difficult for her. Maybe it was because she hadn't had anybody in her life for so long to say sorry to—or was it because she'd apologised constantly as a child and a teenager for her high spirits and impulsive behaviour? Back then her apology had always been followed by more lectures, more disappointment, more opportunities to throw her indiscretions back in her face.

By seventeen she'd stopped saying sorry—mostly because nobody had heard her any more. They certainly hadn't believed she was remorseful, and no one except for Callie—God, she loved that woman—had ever attempted to understand why she felt the need to push the barriers, to taste, touch, experience life.

Geez, she sounded like a whiny, childish...victim. *Damn*, she sounded like a *victim*? Did she subconsciously see herself that way? As a casualty of her parents' narrow-minded world view, Joe's deception?

Maybe she did.

And she didn't like it.

So, she could sit on these stairs and think about how misunderstood she was, justify why she should brush this incident under the carpet, but then she'd feel guilty and dreadful—especially since it was pure pride standing in the way of her saying sorry.

Seb would probably give her another lecture on thoughtlessness and selfishness, but she was a big girl. She'd take it, say goodnight and go back to her own room. She could do this—she *had* to do this! If only to prove to him that she had grown up...

Rowan dragged herself up the stairs, hesitated outside Seb's door. When she saw the sliver of light under the door she gently knocked. She heard his 'Come in' and when she entered saw that he was in bed, a computer on his knees. His face was blank when he looked at her.

Rowan put her hands behind her back and gripped the doorframe behind her. 'Sorry. That was selfish and thoughtless of me.'

Seb's face remained inscrutable while he closed his computer and placed it on the bedside table. Rowan shifted from foot to foot while she waited for him to say something.

'Okay. Come here.'

Rowan stepped closer to the bed and wondered what else was coming. When he just looked at her, a small smile on his face, she frowned. 'That's it? No more lectures?'

Seb smiled slightly as he pulled the covers back and shifted across the bed. 'Nope. Hop in.'

Rowan plucked at her T-shirt and shook her head. 'Seb, I can't. I smell of beer and booze. I'm exhausted. I'm going to take a shower and head back to my room.'

'Take a shower and head back here,' Seb said.

His face and voice were calm. Steady. God, she loved his steady.

His bed...it was tempting. So tempting. But so...*girl-friendy*. 'I—I shouldn't.'

'You really should. Come on, Ro, the world won't stop

if you simply sleep in the same bed as me. Besides, I never got to buy those condoms, so you're safe from me...tonight.'

Those eyes were dreamy again. That hard body was relaxed, his face sleepy. He was as tired as she was and she knew that it would now take a cattle prod to get her to go back to her room. 'Okay, I'll just take a quick shower.'

'Mmm, okay. Hurry up,' Seb murmured, his head on the pillow and his eyes closed.

Rowan kept his sleepy face in her mind as she rushed through the shower and brushing her teeth. When she came back into the room, dressed in the T-shirt Seb had been wearing earlier, he was fast asleep. She slid under the covers next to him and felt his arm slide around her waist. She snapped the light off and Seb snuggled closer. She felt his lips in her hair.

'You scared me, Ro. Don't do it again, okay?' he whispered.

'I'll try not to,' Rowan whispered back into the darkness. And she *would* try—but she couldn't guarantee it.

Five days later it was early morning and Rowan sat in the cushioned area of Seb's bay window. She stared over the hedge to the windows of her old bedroom, with Seb's gentle breathing the soundtrack to her thoughts.

She still hadn't gone home—still hadn't managed to slip through the gate and walk around her mum's prize rose garden, or sit on the bench outside, where her father had always used to read the Sunday papers in the winter sun.

They were due home in less than a week and she still hadn't wrapped her head around how she was going to approach them, deal with them. Should she e-mail them and tell them that she was home and staying with Seb? Should she just wait and rock up on their doorstep? How would they react? What would they say, feel, want from her?

Would they be able to see her as a grown woman who

made her own decisions and lived with the consequences thereof? Would she receive any respect from them for doing that? Any understanding? She no longer required them to be supportive of her, of her lifestyle, but she didn't want to listen to them nag her about settling down, studying further, about her clothes and her hair and her inability to make good choices...

Seb rolled over in his sleep and Rowan watched him for a moment. How would her parents react when they found out about her and Seb? Because find out they would. They weren't completely oblivious to everything around them, and she and Seb gave off enough heat to generate a nuclear reaction. They wouldn't understand the concept of a short-term, mutually satisfying sexual relationship. They'd been childhood sweethearts and hadn't, as far as she knew—and she probably didn't, because her parents were about as talk-ative as clams—dated anyone else.

They'd probably worry more about Seb than they would about her. Seb was a part of their lives, a constant presence, while she was their erratic and eccentric wayward daughter.

'Ro? You okay?' Seb asked from his massive double bed, leaning back on his elbows, his hair rumpled from sleep.

Gorgeous man, Rowan thought.

'Mmm, just wrapping my head around visiting the old house.'

'You still haven't been over?'

Rowan shrugged. 'I really should. It's funny—funny ironic, not ha-ha—that I can walk into a slum in Bombay or a yurt in Mongolia but I haven't managed to screw up the courage to go home. Every time I think about going over I feel like I'm eighteen again. Lost, alone, scared. I don't like feeling like that, Seb.'

'Understandable. Want me to go with you?' Seb asked, sitting up and crossing his legs. 'And then if you feel like you're eighteen you can tell me and I'll kiss you, or touch you, and remind you that you're all woman.'

'Generous of you.' How did he always manage to make her smile when she was feeling blue? Rowan bundled her hair up, held it on top of her head for thirty seconds before allowing it to fall again.

'Okay, we'll go over later. Tell me about your travelling.'

Rowan turned to face him, her back to the window. 'That's a pretty broad subject. Narrow it down...'

Seb thought for a moment. 'Tell me what you love about travelling.'

'The colour, the wonderful local people, their tolerance; the differences that are wonderful, the similarities that are universal. Buildings, bazaars, street food.'

'And what do you most hate about it?'

'Practically? Dirty kitchens and cheap hostel dorm rooms. The constant partying all around. The same questions all the time. "Where do you come from?" "How much of the world have you seen?" "How long have you been travelling for?" "Where to next?" Boring conversations, over and over and over again...' Rowan hesitated.

'Tell me, Ro.'

Rowan gestured to the bed. 'This...'

'This?' Seb looked puzzled. He looked at the bed and then turned his gaze back to hers. 'What?'

'One of the worst things about travelling is relationships: finding them, keeping them, losing them. I have said goodbye far too many times, Seb. Far more than any person should. Ever. I can go for weeks without meeting another traveller, depending on where I'm staying, because I don't want to...don't want to get to know them and then have to wave them off.'

'Are we talking about friendships or lovers?'

'Either. Both,' Rowan said. 'Saying goodbye always hurts.'

And it will hurt so much more when I have to say good-bye to you, Rowan thought, holding his intense gaze. She knew from talking to other backpackers and from her couple of failed relationships that a relationship limited by time, like hers and Seb's, was always more passionate than a normal, run-of-the-mill romance in the real world. They both knew that it had to end some time soon, so they had to make every moment count.

It wasn't real. Or maybe it was too real. It just wasn't built to last.

It would end with another goodbye. And she already knew that it would be absolutely the hardest goodbye she'd ever have to say.

Seb ran his hand through his very short hair and then over his stubbled jaw. He looked as if he wanted to say something, pursue the subject, but then she saw him retreat. Was he running from the emotion in her voice? From the sentimentality of her words? She knew that he'd never been good at dealing with raw emotion. He preferred to find a rational explanation behind every decision or action. She envied him that ability to be so clear-thinking, so sensible.

She couldn't be like that… She felt everything. Twice.

'Oh, hey…I've been meaning to ask you. Do you want to come with me to a cocktail party tomorrow night? It would be nice to go with someone.'

Rowan blinked at the change of subject, thought for a moment, and then said, 'I'd love to, but I don't have anything that could even vaguely pass as a cocktail dress.' She held up her hand to stop Seb from talking. 'And, no, you are *not* going to buy me a dress and shoes for one evening! What a waste! So, sorry—no can do.'

'Oh, come on, Ro. It's just money.' Seb rolled out of bed and walked over to her, his sleeping shorts riding low on his hips. He bent down, brushed his lips across hers and pulled her to her feet.

'It's money I would have to pay you back. I'm already in debt to you for the airfare from Jo'burg to here, for the airfare when I leave—though maybe I might be able to pay for some of that...'

'Then get your ass onto a computer and do something about your netsukes,' Seb complained, his hands loose on her hips. He looked down at her, assessing her. 'I have a feeling that you don't want to sell them.'

Rowan wrinkled her nose, thought about denying it and shrugged. 'I really don't want to sell the Laughing Buddha. But I have to sell the others. I can't afford a twelve-thousand-pound indulgence—especially when I owe you money.'

Seb rested his forehead against hers. 'I can understand why you want to keep it. It's stunning. As for owing me money...it's not important.'

Rowan stroked the side of his neck. 'It's important to me. I can't take your money, Seb.'

'You could give lessons in stubborn to mules, Brat,' Seb muttered.

'I know...' Rowan dug her fingers into the light smattering of his chest hair. 'Listen, are those massive chests still up in the attic?'

'As far as I know.' Seb sat back, looking puzzled at her change of subject. 'Why?'

'Callie and I used to play dress-up with your grandmother's dresses. If I remember right she was quite a socialite in her day.'

Seb—smart guy—immediately made the connection.

'Ro, you cannot possibly wear a sixty, seventy-year-old dress! Fish moths! Dust!'

'Dry cleaners! And Yas banished fish moths a hundred years ago. Haven't you ever heard of vintage dresses? I think there were shoes up there too.'

'You're nuts.'

Rowan raised an eyebrow. 'Do you want me to go with you or not?'

'Oh, okay. We'll take a look. If we don't find anything, then I'll buy you a dress and no arguments—okay?'

'Maybe.'

Seb kissed her nose. 'So, plan of action for the day... Sex, breakfast, a quick visit to the War Room for me, a tour of your old place for both of us and then up to the attic. Then sex again. And then sex later.'

'And maybe sex for pudding,' Rowan said dryly.

Seb laughed. 'You catch on quick.'

Limited time, maximum pleasure, Rowan thought as he swept her into a kiss that had her toes curling. And, yeah, saying goodbye to him was going to sting.

CHAPTER EIGHT

SEB, NOT FINDING Rowan in any of the rooms downstairs, jogged up the stairs to the main floor. Instead of turning left, as he usually did, he took the second flight set of stairs, passing the closed doors to the smaller rooms that hadn't been used since his grandparents' day—such a waste of space—and heading for the narrow stairs that led up to the attic.

He wondered when last he'd been up here. Fifteen, twenty years? Callie and Rowan had used to play up here all the time when he'd been glued to his computer.

Some things never changed, he thought sourly. He'd planned to spend most of this day with Ro, but his staff had run into sophisticated firewalls on a site they needed to crack—today—and it had taken all their combined strategy skills to climb over, under and around them. As a result he'd spent most of the day in the War Room and hadn't seen Ro since breakfast.

He wondered if she'd gone next door, but doubted it.

Seb poked his head into the attic and looked around. Instead of being dark and poky the attic was filled with natural light, courtesy of the skylights in the roof. The usual detritus filled the space directly in front of him—boxes that were labelled 'Christmas decorations', old computers, a set of water skis, and a pile of life jackets lay on top of more stacked cardboard boxes.

He really needed to toss some of this rubbish out.

'Ro?'

'To your left, Seb,' Rowan called.

Seb turned and followed her voice, walking around a wooden partition, and blinked in surprise. Thick, old-fashioned oak chests spilled garments over the rough blankets Rowan had placed on the floor, and in the centre of the clothes-spill Rowan stood in front of an antique full-length mirror framed in oak, dressed in a sleek black gown and three-inch heels. Even with her hair in a messy ponytail and a make-up-free face she looked stunning.

'What do you think?'

'That's a hell of a dress. Did you spray paint it on?'

'Ha-ha. Your gran was slightly skinnier than I am.'

His grandmother... He'd never known her, but he'd like to know how anyone could have so many clothes. He stepped over a pile of coats and looked down at the garments closest to his feet. Jeans, a thigh-length leather jacket, a velvet trenchcoat, a white linen suit.

'These are too modern to be my grandmother's clothes.'

'I think they're your mum's—what she left behind. There are a couple of nice dresses... Do you mind?'

Seb felt his throat clench and forced himself to shrug carelessly. 'Knock yourself out. She left them here, didn't she?'

Rowan looked at him with sympathetic eyes and he hoped that she wouldn't say anything. He didn't discuss his mother—ever. The longest discussion he'd had about her had been with his father a week or so ago.

Rowan ran her hands over her hips and turned back to the mirror. 'What do you think of this dress?'

Seb looked at her properly, felt the saliva disappearing from his mouth and swallowed several times. Hot, hot, *hot*. He couldn't find the words...

'Uh...' he grunted as his brain shut down.

Rowan looked at her reflection and tipped her head. 'You're right. I never liked this shade of black.'

How could she possibly take his silence to mean that he didn't like the dress? Was she mad? It was figure-hugging, cleavage-revealing, backless and strapless.

It sent every blood corpuscle heading south.

Seb smacked the ball of his hand against his temple to reboot his speech function. 'I love the dress, And black is black…isn't it?'

Rowan sent him a pitying look. The kind women reserved for those moments when they thought men had the understanding of a two-year-old. 'Of course there are shades of black. Obsidian, peppercorn, domino, raven, ebony…'

Seb felt as if he'd fallen into an alternative universe. 'Peppercorn is a shade of black?'

'There are many shades of red—fire engine, cherry, scarlet—why can't there be shades of black?'

'I have no idea what you're talking about. And I really don't care.' *All I want to do is get you out of that dress*. To distract himself from that thought, he looked around again. 'Good God, look at these clothes! I never knew there was so much still up here.'

Rowan's eyes were shining with pleasure. 'They're fabulous. I've seen six cocktail dresses I want to try on.'

'I like that one you have on,' Seb said gruffly. 'Wear that.'

Rowan shook her head. 'This is a ballgown—too much for a cocktail party. I just couldn't resist trying it on.'

'Aren't they out of fashion?' Seb asked, toeing a froth of purple silk.

'Designer dresses like these are never out of fashion.' Rowan disappeared behind a screen in the corner. 'And it seems like your gran's taste ran to classic, timeless outfits.'

Good for Gran, Seb thought as he walked to the centre

of the room and sat on the dusty floor, crossing his legs
at the ankles.

'What do you think?'

Seb glanced up and swallowed his tongue. The dress
was red, a shocking slap to the senses, low-cut, and with
what seemed like a million tassels falling to just under her
backside. 'It's red. And short.'

'It's raspberry, and I'm decent underneath.'

Rowan twirled, the tassels whirled, and Seb saw the
high-cut shorts underneath in the same shade.

'It's a heart attack dress,' Seb said. 'A bit too much for
a corporate do.'

Rowan looked at herself in the mirror. 'Mmm, maybe
you're right.'

Seb removed his smartphone from the back pocket of
his jeans and checked his e-mails while Rowan changed
again. Why she had to disappear each time to change was
a puzzle for another day. He'd seen—and tasted—every
inch of her, quite a few times.

'Ready for the next one?' Rowan asked cheerfully.

Seb grinned. 'Hit me.'

Seb leaned back on his elbow and almost choked at
the puffball that sashayed across the wooden floor. It was
orange, it was ruffled, and it was hideous. He searched for
something to say and decided that no words could describe
the awfulness of the dress.

'That bad, huh?' Rowan arched an eyebrow, turned
to look in the mirror and laughed. 'Oh, *yuk*! I look like
orange icing.'

Seb laughed. 'I think the proper shade is cosmic carrot.
Take it off, please, and we'll burn it!'

'Not a bad idea,' Rowan agreed.

Seb watched as the gown got thrown out towards the
chest and imagined her next to naked behind that screen. It

took all his will-power to stay where he was, and the front of his jeans was growing tighter by the second.

The next three dresses were all black, sexy and sophisticated. Seb used the orange monstrosity for a pillow and spread out on the floor, lazy in the diffused sunlight that drifted through the skylights. He could think of worse ways to spend a lazy late afternoon than watching a sexy woman model slinky dresses for him.

'This is it,' Rowan declared. 'If this one isn't suitable, then I give up. I want a glass of wine.'

'Let's see it.'

Seb turned his head and his heart bumped in his chest. He slowly sat up and looked at Rowan, who was looking at herself in the mirror. The dress was a colour somewhere between blue and silver, low-cut, and a concoction of lace and fine ruffles. He could see glimpses of her fine skin through the lace and his saliva disappeared.

He remembered that dress—remembered his mother wearing it to a party some time shortly before she'd left for good. She'd grabbed him as she walked out through the door, pulling his reluctant twelve-year-old self into a hug that he'd professed to hate and secretly adored.

Mostly because her hugs had been so rare and infrequent. Laura had not been affectionate or spontaneous, and gestures like those were imprinted on his memory. She'd smelled of vanilla and she'd worn her blonde hair piled up onto her head.

Two weeks after wearing that dress out she'd been gone. For ever.

'I love this…love the lace…' Rowan bubbled, turning in front of the mirror.

When he didn't respond, she turned to look at him. She crouched down in front of him, her cool hands on his face.

'Seb? What's wrong?'

Seb tried to shake off his sadness. The hurt that he normally kept so deeply buried was frying his soul. He attempted a smile but knew that it didn't come close.

'Please, please talk to me,' Rowan begged.

Seb reached out and touched the fabric that draped her knees. 'This was my mum's.'

'Oh, sweetie. I'm sorry.' Rowan rested her head on his. 'I'll take it off, find something else to wear.'

'Actually, it's a happy memory. I remember her wearing it just before she left. She hugged me, called me her computer geek, said something about…' He tried to recall her exact words but they were lost in time. 'Um, how someone like her had managed to produce someone as bright as me. Or something like that.'

'I remember her vaguely.'

'So does Callie. You were—what?—seven when she left?'

'I was seven. Cal was six.' Rowan pulled the dress above her knees and sat down on the blanket next to Seb.

'I still feel crap that Callie didn't have a mother growing up.'

'Neither did you, Seb. Cal didn't feel the effects of her leaving as much as you did, sweetie. She had Yas…we both had Yas. My mother was so involved in Peter's life and his studies and her music that she didn't have much energy or time left over for me. So when we needed a hug, comfort, or to talk to someone we turned to each other or to Yas. Grumpy, spinsterish, with a tongue that can slice metal. It's strange without her here in Awelfor.'

Seb ran his hand down her calf, knowing that she was trying to lighten his mood. 'If she was here you wouldn't be sleeping in my bed.'

Rowan laughed and quoted one of Yasmeen's favourite expressions. '"You want the milk, buy the cow!"'

Seb grinned, and then his smile faded as he looked at the dress again. He was silent for a long time before stating quietly, 'She's in Brazil, in Salvador. Low on funds. She was in the hospital a couple of months ago with a burst appendix.'

Why had he told her that? Why did he want her to know? This wasn't like him, Seb thought, regretting the words that he'd let fly out of his mouth. He didn't have this type of conversation with the women he was sleeping with—didn't have this type of conversation at all.

What was it about Rowan that made him want to open up to her? To let her see behind the steel-plated armour he'd so carefully constructed? Was it because he'd always known her? Because she was Callie's friend and now his too? Was it those deep black sympathetic eyes that held understanding but no pity?

'When did you find out where she is?'

'I've always known where she is,' Seb said, his voice harsh.

'How?'

Seb lifted his eyebrows at her. 'What do I do for a living, Ro?'

'Oh,' Rowan whispered, connecting the dots.

Seb rubbed the material between his fingers again. 'I found her when I was about sixteen. She was in Prague. I managed to get hold of an e-mail address and I sent her a couple of letters…angry, vicious letters…demanding to know why she'd left and then, in the next breath, begging that she come home.'

'Did she ever reply?'

Seb shook his head. 'She changed her e-mail address and I lost track of her for a while. I'd tell myself that I didn't give a damn and wouldn't look for her. Then something would happen and I'd start again. But I never sent her another e-mail. I just need to know…you know…that she's alive. And okay. Not in trouble…'

'But you send her money.'

Seb's eyes flew up to meet hers and Rowan shook her head at him.

'You do send her money. Oh, Seb, you...'

'Sucker? Chump? Idiot?'

Rowan placed her fingers over his lips. 'You're putting words into my mouth. I was going to say you shouldn't.'

He felt his cheeks flush. 'She's often broke. What can I do? It's just money. I don't know why everyone gets all heated up about it. Money is easy...'

Rowan nodded her head. It was. Of course it was. To him. Money was black and white, no shades of grey, clearly defined. It held no emotion, no grudge, didn't waver or prevaricate. He understood money. People, with all their flaws and craziness and ups and downs, flummoxed him.

'What am I supposed to do, Ro? Not send her cash? Let her suffer because we suffered?' he demanded.

Rowan saw the decades of pain buried deep and bit back her protective response—the one that made her want to snap, *Yeah! You should let her climb out of the hole she's dug herself into!* Instead she bit her tongue and knew that he needed to talk to her, to someone, about his mum. Even tough guys, seemingly unemotional guys, needed to unload occasionally.

Rowan suspected that Seb was long overdue.

'How many times have you sent money?' she asked in her most neutral voice.

'A couple of times a year for the past few years,' Seb admitted reluctantly. 'Before that she seemed to be okay for funds.'

'And, if I know you, you probably sent a lump sum every time?'

'It was always an anonymous deposit. There is no way she can trace who it came from.'

Rowan sucked in her cheeks and gazed at the floor, literally swallowing the angry words at the back of her throat.

His mother was many things, but she wasn't stupid, and she had to at the very least suspect that it was Seb. How many people would she have met and had a big enough impact on for them to make anonymous, generous ongoing deposits into her bank account? Who else would it be other than her computer genius son? And she'd never sent him an e-mail to say thank you, to acknowledge him…

Oooh, that was rough.

Rowan looked down at her hands, vibrating with tension. Good grief, families were complicated. Parent-child relationships could be crazy. The ways to mess up your children were infinite, she decided.

Seb still held the hem of her dress—his mum's dress—between his fingers and Rowan looked at his bent head, at the masculine planes of his face, the tiny tick of tension in that single dimple in his cheek. Her tough guy, smart guy, good guy. So strong, so alpha, so damn attractive in his complexity. She'd known him for ever but she felt that she could spend another lifetime discovering all the nuances of his personality; he was that layered, that interesting.

That intriguing.

Ugh, pull up those reins, cowgirl. Your horse is bolting away from you… You're not going to get sappy and sentimental. You can't afford to, and you know this!

Rowan stood up, grabbed the edges of the hem of the dress and pulled it up and over her head. Seb gaped as she stood in front of him in just a brief pair of white panties and silver heels. No bra.

His eyes clouded over and Rowan smiled a tiny smile of feminine satisfaction. So sue her. She could make this hot guy salivate, and as a bonus banish the sadness from his eyes.

She looked at the dress in her hand. 'I love this dress… but I understand if you don't want me to wear it.'

Seb bit the inside of his lip. 'I want to say yes but…
Maybe some day. Just…'

'Not today.' Rowan nodded her understanding. She
looked at the pile of discarded dresses on the floor. 'Okay,
black it is, then. Which one?'

Seb pulled a face. 'Ugh. Come on, Ro, let me take you
shopping. One dress, one pair of shoes… Consider it as
nine years' worth of Christmas and birthday presents I
never got to buy.'

He needs to do this, Rowan realised. *He needs to spoil
me—wants to do something for me that is outside of the
crazy little deals we've struck to work around my pride and
independence.* Could she allow him to do that, or would
her stiff neck and habitual self-reliance spoil it for him?

It was hard. She couldn't lie. But seeing the pleasure
on his face when she finally nodded her agreement was
worth the risk.

He scooted up, dropped a kiss on her nose and grabbed
her hand. 'Okay, let's go. Now.'

'Good grief, Hollis, I'm still half naked!' Rowan protested. 'Pass me my clothes, Einstein.'

Seb picked up her pink T-shirt from the floor next to his
foot and Rowan saw that he did it with great reluctance.
His eyes were firmly on her breasts.

She grabbed his chin and forced him to look in her eyes.
'Get your head out of bed, Seb. We're going shopping. For
a dress. And shoes. Cocktail dresses and shoes are expensive, by the way.'

Seb grinned. 'I'm pretty sure my credit card can stand it.'

Rowan let him go, stepped away and picked up her
shorts. She pulled them up, zipped, and placed her hands
on her hips. 'Seb?'

'Yeah?'

'Your mum's failings are hers, not yours. You didn't do

or say anything that made her leave. That was on her and not on you.'

Seb pulled her close and buried his face in her hair. Just stood with her in his arms. She didn't know where those words had come from. She just knew, soul-deep, that he'd needed to hear them.

Just as she knew that all she had to do right then was hold him.

And when he pulled away to let go she pretended that the moment *hadn't* been charged with all those pesky emotions he tried so damn hard to ignore.

She did it because quite simply he needed her to.

'I need an ice cream,' Seb whined theatrically, and Rowan rolled her eyes at him.

What a lightweight, she thought. They'd only done one level of the mall and there were three more to go. She still hadn't found a dress that was both within the budget she'd set in her head—she didn't care how flexible Seb's credit card was; she was *not* going to pay a fortune for a dress she'd only wear once!—and nice enough to wear.

'Or a beer. Actually, I definitely need a beer,' Seb added as she pulled him into a tiny boutique that looked interesting.

'This was your idea,' Rowan told him, unsympathetic, and headed for a rail of dresses at the back of the shop.

Black, black, red… She pulled a coral chiffon cocktail dress off a hanger and held it up to look at it. Oh, it was pretty, she admitted as she held it against her and looked in the full-length mirror against the wall. It was sleeveless with a dropped waist and a multi-tiered skirt that fell to mid-thigh.

Take me home, it whispered urgently.

'That's the one,' Seb stated, jamming his hands into the

pockets of his shorts while Rowan looked for a price tag. 'Go try it on.'

No tag, Rowan thought, and knew that it would cost a bomb. She had an eye for picking out quality. She sighed. In clothes and in *objets d'art*.

Rowan shook her head and replaced the hanger on the rail. 'We'll look for something else.'

Seb tugged it off the rail and thrust it at her. 'Try it on.'

'It's the perfect colour for you,' the shop assistant stated, and Rowan narrowed her eyes at her.

'Stop being stubborn and try the bloody thing on.' Seb pushed her towards the discreet dressing room. He turned to the shop assistant. 'Shoes?'

'Silver diamante sandals. I have the perfect pair. Size seven?'

'Of course you do,' Rowan muttered as she stepped into the dressing room. She raised her voice so that it could be heard above the partition. 'Size six.'

Rowan slipped her clothes off, carefully undid the discreet zip and slid the dress over her head. *Yeah, this is the dress,* she thought; it was a pity she couldn't have it.

'Does it fit?' Seb demanded.

'Yes. Beautifully. It's a fairytale dress.'

And she was living in a fairytale at the moment. She had the run of a gorgeous house she'd always loved and was sleeping with a super-hot, sometimes not-so-charming prince.

She was loving every second of it.

But it wasn't real life, Rowan reminded herself. She—no, they were *both* enthralled by their sexual chemistry, and it was colouring how they saw each other. When the dust settled, they'd start to argue, and then they'd start to fight, and soon—as per usual—they wouldn't be able to stand each other.

Because the best predictor of future behaviour was past

behaviour, and neither of them had a very good track record at playing nice for extended periods.

Then why did she feel so settled, living in Seb's house, living with Seb? Was a part of her yearning for the stability of living in one place with one man? At twenty-eight was her biological clock starting to tick? Was it just being in Seb's home, waking up in Seb's arms, that had her wanting to believe that she could be happy with the picket fence and the two point four kids and the Labrador and...?

You're being ridiculous, she told herself. *The grass always looks greener on the other side.* She knew this—heck, she knew this well.

Before coming home she had never had a serious thought about settling down, about relationships and children and suburbia. Okay, that was a lie—of course she had—but only little, non-serious thoughts. Even *she* knew she was capable of being seduced by the idea of *what-if,* of thinking that a wonderful experience could translate into a wonderful life in that place. Hadn't she gone through something similar in Bali, where she'd thought she'd buy a little house and stay for ever? And when she'd first seen the Teton mountain range, and that gorgeous little cake shop that had been for sale in the Cotswolds? She'd imagined herself living and working in all those places, but the urge to move on had always come—as it would here as well.

'Rowan? You lost in there?'

Seb's voice pulled her out of her reverie.

'Coming.' Rowan pulled on her clothes, stepped out of the room and handed the assistant the dress. 'Thanks, but we'll keep looking.'

The assistant looked at Seb, eyebrows raised, as she slipped the dress into an expensive cover.

'I've already paid for it. Shoes too.' Seb took the covered dress, slung it over his shoulder and grabbed the bag holding her shoes. 'Can we please get a beer now?'

'You paid for it?' Rowan asked in a icy voice. 'What on earth…?'

'You said it fitted beautifully, it's your colour, and I could see that you love it,' Seb replied, puzzled. 'I'm not seeing the problem here.'

'The problem is that it costs a fortune!' Rowan grabbed the bag and peered inside at the shoe box. 'And the shoes are *designer*!'

'Geez, you're boring when you rattle on and on about money.' Seb yawned. 'You agreed that I could buy you a dress and shoes. I've bought you a dress and shoes. Can we move on to the next subject for the love of God? Please?'

Rowan sent him a dirty look, turned on her heel and stomped out of the shop. Outplayed and outmanoeuvred, she thought, and she didn't like it.

Yes, he was on-fire hot, and he was really good company, but she had to remember that Seb could be sneaky sharp when he wanted to be.

'Beer… Food…' Seb breathed in her ear, before grabbing her hand, tugging her around and pushing her in the opposite direction. 'The food court is this way.'

CHAPTER NINE

SEB SNAGGED AN outside table belonging to a funky-looking bistro, draped Rowan's dress on the third chair and grinned at her sulky face. She still wasn't happy about the dress... No, she loved the dress, but she didn't like the idea of him buying it for her.

She took independence to stupid heights, he thought. So the dress was expensive? So were his computers and the technology he loved to spend money on.

His last computer had cost him three times what he'd paid for the dress...

'Stop sulking and order a drink,' he told her, and grinned as her pert nose lifted in the air. He smiled up at the red-headed waitress, placed their orders and leaned back in his chair.

'Thank you for the dress,' she said primly, politeness on a knife-edge. 'And the shoes.'

'I can't wait to get you out of it,' he said, just to rattle her cage.

'Your chances of doing so are diminishing rapidly,' Rowan retorted, but her lips twitched with humour. 'Do you really like the dress or did you just want to stop shopping?'

'Both,' Seb admitted, funeral-director-mournful. 'The things you make me do, Brat.'

'Talking of that...' Rowan gestured to the huge electronic advertising board to the left of them. 'I saw a sign advertising an antiques fair and night market in Scarborough tonight. We could go take a look when we're finished eating.'

'Yeah…no. I'd rather eat jellyfish. Besides, I have a houseful of antiques and you're broke.' Seb took the beer the waitress had placed on the table and drained half the glass in one swallow.

'Thanks for reminding me,' Rowan grumbled. 'And I'm not broke. I'm financially constrained. Asset-rich and cash-poor. We don't have to buy—we could just look.'

Seb mimed putting a gun to his head and pulling the trigger and Rowan laughed.

They sat and sipped their drinks in a comfortable silence before Seb asked, 'By the way, what happened to the boat party you were organising?'

'Ah, the sixteen-year-old birthday girl changed her mind. Now she wants to go to a Justin Bieber concert instead.'

Seb shuddered.

'I'm getting party enquiries all the time, but I don't want to take on anything I can't deliver in the next week or so. You said that my parents should be home on Sunday—four days from now—and I have to be in London by the following weekend to meet Grayson, so there's no point in trying to get too involved. Pity, because it's good money.'

'So you'll be gone in a week or so?' Seb asked in a very even voice that hid all the emotion in his voice.

'That's the plan,' Rowan said lightly as her heart contracted violently. A week? Was that all they had? Where had the last two weeks gone? She wanted them back, dammit.

'God…' Seb muttered into his drink.

It would be another goodbye and the hardest one that she'd ever have to say. Harder even than that first one, when she'd run away to find herself, to find out what made sense to her. When had he become so important? So hard to leave?

'Did you go next door this afternoon?' Seb asked, changing the subject.

Rowan nodded.

'And...?'

She shrugged. 'It's just a house. They haven't changed much.'

'Your parents don't do change.'

'But I do, and maybe now I can look at them differently.' Rowan took a sip of wine and looked thoughtful. 'I did a great deal of thinking this afternoon, so maybe it was a good thing that you got tied up at work.'

'I want to hear about it, but maybe we should order first.' Seb beckoned the waitress over, asked for two gourmet burgers and another round of drinks. When the waitress had left, he gestured to Rowan with his glass. 'Talk.'

'How come you just expect me to spill my guts but you don't?'

'Because you're the emotional one and I'm not,' Seb replied.

Except that she was beginning to realise that Seb was far more emotional than anyone knew. He just had years of hiding it.

'I'm starting to think that Fate had a hand in me coming home—that it's telling me that I need to pull my head out of the sand and start dealing with all those old hurts and grievances. If I hadn't bought those netsukes, run out of cash and been flagged by Oz immigration I wouldn't be here.'

'Having amazing sex with your arch enemy?' Seb interjected.

'Having amazing sex with my old friend,' Rowan corrected, and saw the flare of appreciation, of attraction... fondness?...in his eyes. *No emotion, my ass.*

'I need to see my parents, deal with my issues around my mother, reconcile with them—her. Mostly her.' Rowan sighed. 'Maybe I'm finally starting to understand that we are very different people. I wasn't the daughter she needed and she didn't understand what I needed—especially that night I got arrested—but…but my childhood is over. I need to find a new "normal" with them.'

Seb folded his arms and placed them on the table. He linked his fingers in hers and stared down at their hands. 'I never understood why you ran. You were always a fighter. You always came out of the corner ready to fight.'

Rowan nibbled her lip. 'I got knocked down one too many times, resulting in emotional concussion.'

'That's a new one… Who knocked you down?'

'My parents—my mum especially. Peter, Joe Clark…'

'Your dipstick ex? What did he do…exactly? Apart from frame you?'

'When did you realise he had?'

'I think I've probably always known. What else did he do?'

Rowan blew out her breath and held his eye. It was time she told him—time she told someone the whole truth of that evening.

'I fell in love with him. He was kind and sweet and said all the right things to get me into bed. I kept him waiting because…you know…he was my first, and I wanted to make sure he was the right one. Someone who really loved me and not someone who was using me… Ha-ha, what a joke!'

Seb's face hardened. 'So he took your virginity…?'

'Yeah, we made love three hours before we got to the club. The policeman knew the drugs weren't mine—he even admitted it to me—but they were on me and he had to arrest me. Joe told me while he was laughing at me for getting arrested that he'd just wanted to bag and bed "the virgin rebel". That's what he called me.'

Seb swore, low and slow. 'I swear I'm going to rearrange his face.'

'I'm over it—over him. I really am.' Rowan managed a

small smile. 'But it wasn't the best night of my life. I was reeling. I'd had my heart kicked around by the boy who had just taken me to bed—the whole experience of which, sadly, was not nearly as brilliant as I thought it would be—'

'Bad?'

Trust a man to get distracted by sex, Rowan thought as she rocked her hand in the air. 'Meh…'

'Meh?'

'Not good, not bad—and I am *not* discussing my first sexual experience with you, Hollis. Jeez! Do you want to hear this or not?'

'Keep your panties on… So you went off to jail…'

'I had been there for a day or so and I was so scared, terrified. Another young girl had been arrested for something—I can't remember what. Her mother came to the jail, and when they wouldn't release this girl her mother came into the cell with her and just held her until she *could* be released. I wanted that like I've never wanted anything in my life.'

Rowan swallowed and took a deep slug of her wine.

'I just wanted my mother to love me, to support me, to hold me while I sat in that corner. And I knew that she wouldn't. Ever. That hurt more than anything else. So when I got home I thought I would test my theory; how far could I push her until I got a reaction out of her? I never got much of one. My dad screamed and raged and tried to lay down the law but my mum switched off. Until the day I wrote my finals. I came home and she and I had a…discussion.'

'About…?'

Okay, so this was something that she'd never told anybody. Not even Callie. 'My life, my plans. I told her I wanted to go overseas and she immediately agreed. Said it was the first sensible sentence I'd uttered all year.'

'What the…?'

'She said that it would be good for all of us—mainly

her, I think—that I went. I heard the subtext in her speech; she'd had enough of me and her life would be that much easier if I were out of her face. So I packed my stuff, took the money she offered—she was the one who cashed in those unit trusts of my grandmother's—and caught the first plane I could.'

'God, Ro…'

Seb ran his hand over his face and felt sick. They'd all known that Ro and her mum bumped heads, known that Peter was her obvious favourite, but they'd never believed—not for a second—that their relationship had been that broken. Okay, his mother wasn't a saint, and she'd left and it sucked, but she hadn't constantly been there, physically present but emotionally unavailable.

Rowan's staying away from Cape Town made a lot more sense now.

'I'm so sorry,' he muttered, knowing his words were inadequate and stupid after so much time.

But he didn't know what else to say—how to convey how angry and…sad he felt. Because, unlike him, Rowan had needed to be nurtured and shown affection, to be bolstered and boosted. She'd needed affection and love and affirmation.

Bile roiled in his stomach as the waitress placed their burgers in front of them. 'I should take you home…let me take you home.'

Then he felt Rowan's hand cover his, her touch comforting him when he should be comforting her.

'Your mind is going into overdrive, Seb. I'm fine now and I've learnt to live with it. I'm way over Joe Clark and him screwing me—figuratively and literally. As for my mum…she is what she is. I've grown up…'

'But you'd still like a relationship with her?'

'I'd love a relationship with her. So I'll see her, say my sorrys if that's what she needs to hear, and try again.'

He turned and stared down into her face. Oh, dear God, he could fall for her; tumble for this brave, beautiful woman with midnight in her eyes.

Seb shook his head, trying to replace emotion with rational thought. He was just feeling sorry for her, feeling guilty because he hadn't pushed hard enough, dug deep enough to find out the truth about her before this. He'd always known that there was more to Rowan's story, more to Rowan.

Besides she was leaving...*soon*. And he had no intention of letting anyone else leave with his heart again.

Mothers...jeez. The million and two ways they could screw you up.

Rowan popped a chip in her mouth and chewed thoughtfully. 'I really want to go to that antiques market, Seb.'

Seb picked up his knife and fork, looked at his food, and put them down again. He really didn't feel like eating.

'What?' he asked, his mind still reeling. He digested her words, understood them and frowned. 'Are you playing me?' he demanded, innately suspicious of her cajoling face. 'Are you making me feel sorry for you to get what you want?'

Rowan chuckled. 'It's what we woman do. You're smart enough not to fall for it.'

'Brat.'

'Let me try something else.' Rowan batted her eyelashes at him. 'If you take me I'll let you charm me out of that dress.'

Seb looked her up and down and slowly grinned. 'I'm going to charm you out of that dress anyway, so no deal.'

Rowan twisted her lips to hide her grin. 'I *can* resist you, you know.'

Laughter chased the shadows out of Seb's eyes. 'No, you can't. I can't resist you either. Eat—you're going to need the energy.'

'Is that a threat?' Rowan asked silkily.

Seb picked up her hand, turned it over and placed an open-mouthed kiss into the palm of her hand. Rowan shuddered and lust ran up and down her spine when he touched the tip of his tongue to her palm.

'Absolutely it's a threat,' Seb said, before attacking his burger.

Seb cast another look at Rowan as they walked down the steps to his car, parked by the front door earlier, and thought about walking into that cocktail party with her hand in his. Her dress would be enough to have the older men choking on their drinks, their wives raising an over-plucked eyebrow and any man below sixty sending approving looks at her stunning legs, from thigh to the two-inch silver heels she had absolutely no problem rocking.

She was gorgeous, with her wild hair pulled back into a casual roll, minimal make-up and a coral lipstick that perfectly matched the red of her dress. She looked fresh and sexy and he was already anticipating the end of the evening, when he could strip it off her as he'd promised. Which was insane, since they'd made love just over an hour ago and again this morning. And twice last night after they'd got back from visiting that antiques market, where Rowan had tried to persuade him to buy a silver cigarette case he didn't like and certainly didn't need.

'It's old and it's valuable. You could double your money,' he remembered her insisting.

'It might be old but it's ugly,' he'd replied, not telling her that he earned more money in fifteen minutes than he'd make on the hideous case.

He'd offended Rowan's horse-trader instincts for about a minute—until another pretty object had caught her attention and their brief argument had been totally forgotten as she'd engaged stallholder after stallholder in conversation.

It had taken them for ever to visit every stall—which

she'd had to do. She was so charming, easily drawing people into conversation and melting the sternest or shyest
heart there. She had a natural warmth that just pulled people
to her, he thought as he drove down the driveway.

'You look…God…amazing, Ro,' he said, turning left
into the road.

'Thanks. You don't look too shabby yourself. I like that
suit.'

Rowan placed her hand on his thigh and he could feel her
warmth through the fabric of his black suit. He'd teamed it
with a white shirt—no-brainer—but Rowan had swapped
the tie he'd chosen—black—for a deep blue one he'd never
worn in his life which, according to his sexy date, deepened the blue in his eyes.

He'd liked her choosing his tie… Seb sighed and reminded himself yet again to get a grip, catch a clue.

She. Was. Leaving.

As in bye-bye, birdy.

Next week.

And he was getting goofy because she was picking out
his ties.

Get over yourself, already, Hollis.

Rowan's fingers dug into his thigh. 'Seb, stop!'

He slammed on the brakes. 'What? Jeez!' He looked
past Rowan, down her parents' driveway, and saw Heidi
and Stan standing in the driveway, pulling bags out of their
sedate sedan.

'Oh, crap. Your parents are back.'

'Looks like it.' Rowan bit her lip and lifted her hand as
her parents swivelled around to see who was idling at the
bottom of their driveway. She turned and looked at Seb,
her heart in her eyes. 'It would be so much easier if you
just drove on.'

Seb touched her cheek with his thumb. 'I'm right behind you, babe.'

'Well, at least I'm looking my best,' Rowan quipped in a small voice as he turned off the engine.

'You look fantastic,' Seb said as he left the car, walked around and opened the passenger door for Rowan.

Heidi and Stan walked down the driveway to greet them.

'Seb, hello!' Heidi called as Seb took Rowan's icy hand in his. 'We're back—as you can see.'

'Stan…Heidi.' He placed his hand on Rowan's back and pushed her forward. 'So is Rowan.'

'Mum…hi, Dad.' Rowan stepped closer, reached up and brushed her father's cheek with her lips, leaned in for a small hug and then turned to her mum. Seb clenched his fist when Heidi pulled back and Rowan's lips brushed the air about two inches from her cheek. She couldn't even kiss her, hold her, after nine years apart?

What the…?

Who *was* this woman? Had he ever really known her? Had he been so blinded by the fact that she was there every day that he thought she was marvellous for that alone? No, he'd seen her interact with Peter—loving, kind, affectionate.

His heart clenched for Rowan as she stood back and straightened her shoulders. 'You're both looking well.'

'How long have you been home?' Her father took her hand, held it tight. 'It's so good to see you. You look beautiful—so grown-up.'

Rowan smiled. 'Seb and I are going to a party. I arrived about two weeks ago…I needed to come home unexpectedly. Seb's been helping me out.'

Heidi lifted her eyebrows and pursed her lips at Seb's hand, resting on her hip. 'Seems like he's been doing more than helping you out. Strange, since you could never stand each other before.'

Seb started to speak, but Rowan gripped the hand on her hip and he got the message. *Shut up, dude.*

'I've grown up, Mum.'

Heidi looked her up and down. 'Your skirts certainly haven't.'

'Mum! Nine years away and all you can do is gripe about my clothes?' Rowan snapped.

'Well, I think you look gorgeous, Ro.' Stan jumped into the conversational bloodbath. 'Absolutely terrific.'

'Well…' Heidi folded her arms. 'I'm tired, and you two are going to be late for wherever you are going. Maybe you should be on your way.'

'Heidi!' Stan protested, and Seb's temper simmered.

'We'll see her again,' Heidi said. 'Tomorrow. Maybe.'

Stan sent Rowan an apologetic look and Rowan stepped into his arms and gave him a longer hug. A hug Seb was pleased to see that he returned. He kissed her head before they stepped apart. 'I'll see you in the morning, Ro. It's good to have you back, darling.'

Rowan nodded and held onto Seb's hand with a death grip. 'See you then, Dad. And it's good to be back. Night, Mum.'

'Goodnight, Rowan. Sebastian.'

Seb pulled Rowan back to the car and opened the passenger door for her, helped her in. When he was back in his seat he placed his hand on the back of her neck. 'You okay, Ro?'

'Sure.' Rowan shrugged, her eyes on her parents, who were walking into their house. 'Situation normal. My mum cool and uninterested; my dad the buffer between the two of us.'

'She called me Sebastian. She's never called me that.'

Rowan managed a smile. 'It's because you're sleeping with me. She thinks you can do better.'

'Then she's an idiot.' Seb dropped his hand and started the engine. 'I need a drink. A couple of them.'

'Me too. Lead me into temptation, *Sebastian*.'

'Buzz off, Brat,' Seb shot back, but he kept his hand on her knee the whole way up the coast to the cocktail party.

In Seb's bedroom, much later that evening, Rowan slipped off her dangly silver earrings and dropped them onto Seb's credenza, next to his wallet and keys. 'Jeez, who would've thought I would run into Joe this evening at the cocktail party? I mean, heck, this is a big city. What were the chances?'

'Fairly good, I'd say, since he's reputed to be one of the most up-and-coming young businessmen in the city and it was a Chamber of Commerce function.'

'Up and coming dipstick, more like it,' Rowan muttered. 'Thanks, by the way.'

'For…?'

Seb shrugged off his jacket and Rowan could see the residual annoyance in his eyes. She knew that Seb had wanted to clock Joe, but he'd just cut him off at the knees with one burning look when he'd tried to engage them—her—in conversation.

'For sticking close…for not letting him near me.'

'My absolute pleasure,' Seb muttered, taking a step towards her. 'Why are we talking about him and why aren't you kissing me?'

'An epic fail on my part,' Rowan admitted, putting her hands on his waist.

'Damn straight,' Seb replied.

Rowan lifted her mouth to his, touching those surprisingly soft lips that could kiss her so tenderly but could also utter soft, deadly words that could strip hide. But he was only tender, only affectionate with her. He tasted of the whisky he'd sipped earlier, and as he opened his mouth to allow her to explore further she sensed a change in him.

This wasn't just about sex and pleasure any more, about maximising the moment. This kiss and the lovemaking that would follow were about making memories, capturing tastes and feelings that would sustain them when they separated.

Seb lifted his head and his deep, sombre eyes held hers as his hand travelled down the back of her neck to the zip of her dress. He pulled it down, one tantalising inch at a time, his fingers touching the skin beneath until the fabric gaped open to her buttocks. Using one finger, he pushed the fabric off one shoulder and then the other, until the dress fell in a frothy puddle over her feet.

Seb shoved his fingers in her hair and gently pulled the pins out, winding her curls around his hand before allowing the weight of her hair to fall down her back. Bending down in front of her, still fully dressed except for his jacket, he lifted one foot and deftly undid the ankle straps of her shoes. His fingers lightly caressed her ankles before he sat back on his heels and allowed his hands to drift up her calves, to explore the backs of her knees, the tops of her thighs.

'You are so beautiful,' Seb said, placing his forehead against her thigh.

Rowan frowned as she stroked his head. He sounded sad, she thought. Scared. As if this was just becoming a bit too much for him, a little too intense.

No, that was how *she* was feeling...

'Seb? Are you okay?'

'Fine,' Seb said, his words muffled.

He placed an open-mouthed kiss on her right knee and Rowan felt the familiar rush of heat, the tightening of her chest. How much longer would she feel like this? The intensity of their lovemaking couldn't last for ever—it never did. Then again, they didn't *have* for ever. They only had next week and then she would be gone. But she would enjoy every nerve-tightening second while she had the chance. She owed it to herself to do that.

Rowan stepped back, reached down and lifted Seb's tie, pulling it apart and allowing it to hang against his white shirt. Her fingers slipped between his neck and his collar and she snapped open the top button and then the next. Sinking to her knees, she placed her mouth on that masculine triangle at the bottom of his throat and inhaled deeply. God, she loved his smell.

Her fingers opened the rest of the buttons, and she shook her head when he tried to undo the clasp of her lacy bra.

'No, not yet,' she whispered. 'Let me play. I need to touch you, know you, taste you…'

'Why?' Seb demanded hoarsely.

Rowan bit her bottom lip as their eyes collided. 'So that I can remember every detail of you.'

'We could do this for a while yet, Ro. Nobody is making you go.'

Rowan shook her head as her hands slid over the bare skin of his sides. 'That's just sex talking, Seb. We both know that this can't last—won't last. You don't want a full-time lover and I can't stay in one place. We know this, Seb.'

'I just can't imagine not doing this any more,' Seb muttered, his face in her neck.

'Right now, I can't imagine going.'

Rowan pushed the shirt off his shoulders, stood up and pulled him to his feet. Small hands undid the snap of his suit pants and pushed the fabric off him, so that he stood naked in front of her, his erection hard and proud. Rowan ran her thumbnail down him and he jumped in reflex.

'Sit on the bed,' Rowan told him.

Rowan sat on the edge of his knees and her hands flowed over his broad shoulders, explored his tattoo and ran over the ridges of his stomach. 'I'm going to miss you when I go. I didn't think I would, but I know that I will. Lean back on your hands.'

Seb obeyed and tipped his head back. He stared at the

ceiling, his chest rising and falling rapidly. 'Don't just slip away without telling me,' he said, his voice vibrating. 'When you say goodbye, say goodbye. Don't sneak out.'

Like your mother did, Rowan thought. 'I promise. When I know I'm going, so will you. I promise to say goodbye properly.'

Rowan stroked her hand over his lower abdomen, moving her hand into his thatch of hair, down his penis and around to cup his balls. She felt him tense, relax, then groan.

'You're driving me crazy, Ro.'

Rowan was enjoying the power she was wielding, having this fantastically smart, sexy man under her control. It made her feel immensely potent to feel his reaction to her, to know that he was surrendering to her, trusting her to take care of him.

'I need to be inside you,' Seb groaned, launching himself upwards.

Rowan slipped off him and knelt in front of him, her fist encircling him, hard, warm, pulsing madly.

'Ro, don't. I won't be able to stop. I need you so much as it is,' Seb begged, his eyes wide in the dim light of the room. 'I won't be able to wait for you.'

'You can owe me...' Rowan smiled wickedly before her lips encircled him. She knew she'd won when his hand burrowed into her hair and his back bent over her head...

Was it so bad that she wanted him to keep a few erotic memories of her as well? Rowan certainly didn't think so.

CHAPTER TEN

'WELL, WELL, WELL…look what the cat has dragged in.'

Rowan thought she was still dreaming when she heard the gravelly voice—thought she was having a hallucination from too much sex and too little sleep when she saw Callie sitting at the dining table in the kitchen at Awelfor, blonde hair in a ponytail and her bare feet up on the corner of the table.

Callie?

'Callie!' Rowan screamed.

'Ro!' Callie shouted back as Rowan bounced forward and flung her arms around her best friend's neck, nearly toppling her off the chair.

Callie's arms wrapped around Rowan's back to return the hug, but when Callie's hand landed on her bottom Rowan lifted her eyebrows, then her head, and looked into Callie's green eyes.

'Are you copping a feel? Because if you are I have to tell you that you're not my type,' Rowan said, leaning her butt on the table, where Callie still had her feet.

'Just checking that you're wearing panties and haven't turned into a total slag while you've being bonking my brother.'

Callie grinned and Rowan's heart turned over. She and Seb shared that same smile—why had she never realised that until now?

'Coffee. I need coffee.' Rowan hoisted her bum off the table and wandered over to the coffee machine. She stared at it helplessly. 'Dammit, I hate this thing!'

As Rowan reached for the instant coffee she felt Callie shoulder her aside. 'Hasn't His Majesty shown you how it works?'

Rowan shrugged. 'He normally makes it for me himself; if he's not here I settle for instant.'

'It's not rocket science, BB.' Callie showed her what to do, and within a minute Rowan had made herself her first cappuccino.

'Awesome.' Rowan sipped and headed back for the table, sitting down before she started peppering Callie with questions. 'Why are you back? What happened to your Yank lover? Your appointments in LA and Vancouver?'

Callie quickly answered and then flipped the attention back to Rowan. Placing her face in her hands, she eyed her. 'You're glowing. I've never seen you glow.'

'Good sex.'

'I have good sex all the time and I never glow.' Callie's eyes radiated concern. 'What are you doing, Ro? Have you thought this through? Has Seb thought this through?'

Rowan sipped her coffee before sighing. 'I don't know... I can't speak for Seb—you know that he doesn't wear his heart on his sleeve. As for me... I went into this thinking it was just about sex, that I could control this...craziness I feel for him.'

'And can you? Did you? Have you?'

Rowan stared into her cup and wondered what to say. 'I have to, Cal. I can't do anything else but control it. I'm leaving. I have to leave.'

'Why?'

Rowan frowned at her. 'What?'

'Why do you have to leave? Who says that's the rule?

You've never been swayed by arguments about what one is "supposed" to do. So why do you now have to leave?'

Callie's verbal punch landed in her stomach. But if there was anyone she could be totally honest with it was Callie. 'Because staying is far too scary.'

'Why, sweetie?'

Rowan took a deep breath as her eyes filled with tears. 'Because I could love him, Cal. Really love him. But I don't know if I could love him enough to stay, to give up my freedom.'

'You'll never know if you don't try,' Callie pointed out.

'I'll never hurt him, or myself, if I leave before this takes on a life of its own,' Rowan said. 'I can leave now, but if this goes any deeper—if I fall in love with him—I'll be ripped apart when it ends. And it always ends, Cal.'

'Just don't leave without explaining to Seb exactly what you're doing,' Callie warned her, and Rowan remembered her promise to Seb the night before.

'I won't, Cal.' Rowan ran her finger around the rim of her cup and blew air into her cheeks. 'So that's where I am—emotionally, mentally. But I have no idea what Seb is thinking. He's probably not interested in anything more than what we have.'

'You guys really should talk more and bonk less,' Callie grumbled. 'Where *is* His Wonderfulness?'

'Still sleeping.' Rowan looked self-satisfied. 'I kind of wiped him out last night.'

'*Blerch.*' Callie shoved her fingers in her ears. 'Too much information.'

'Then I don't suppose you want to know about the lady kissing your dad on the cottage balcony at the moment?'

Callie slapped her hands over her eyes. 'No! What is *wrong* with you people?' She spread her fingers and looked at Rowan. 'Please tell me that she's older than us for a change.'

'A little older.' Rowan laughed. 'Okay, a lot older.'

Callie slowly lowered her hands. 'How much older? Five years? Ten?' she asked hopefully.

'Try thirty.' Rowan grinned.

Callie turned around and through the kitchen window looked at Annie, who was standing in Patch's arms and laughing up at him. In the morning sunlight they could see the fine lines around her eyes, the lack of tone in her arms. But her face was radiant and Patch's face reflected her happiness.

They looked like happy-ever-after.

'Oh, my, I think I'm going to cry,' Callie said, her words soaked with emotion. 'I think my daddy might be in love.'

'Crap on a stick,' Seb said from the doorway. 'That's all I need to hear. I'm going back to bed.'

Callie jumped up, snaked her arms around Seb's waist and squeezed. 'If I have to watch them play tonsil hockey so do you. Hey, big bro'.'

Seb dropped a kiss on her blonde head as he tucked her under his arm. His two favourite women in the room, and Ro was making him coffee. At least he hoped she was—though he thought that he needed it intravenously injected for the caffeine to have any effect soon.

Rowan walked to the fridge to grab a carton of milk and Seb had to hold Callie tighter to keep from reaching for her. Not necessarily to start anything—he was wiped!—but he just wanted to touch her, connect with her.

This was ridiculous, he thought. He'd never wanted to be close to someone before, had never sought out female company, yet he wanted to be closer to Rowan, needed to spend time with her outside the bedroom. He wanted more than sex. He needed...*time*, he decided. He just wanted more time.

Her parents were back and, judging by the looks she was sending towards their house, he could see that she was nervous about a repeat of last night's dismal performance. Seb stepped away from Callie and took the cup Rowan held out to him. He wanted to discuss her parents with her, see where she was mentally, and reassure her that he would go next door with her if she needed him to.

'Any chance of breakfast?' Callie asked brightly.

'Pancakes and bacon?' Rowan quickly responded with the suggestion of their favourite childhood meal—the only one that they could ever cook with any success.

'Whoop!' Callie bounced up again—Tigger on speed—and yanked open the freezer, looking for bacon.

'Top left?' Seb suggested, dropping into a chair and placing his bare feet up onto the seat next to him. *Coffee, kick in, please.*

He watched in resignation as Callie and Rowan fell into conversation as if they had seen each other yesterday, and tuned out automatically when they started discussing Callie's latest boyfriend in case he heard something he'd rather not…

Like the fact that Callie was having sex. Which he did not need to know. *Ever.*

Seb sighed into his coffee. He loved his sister, but he cursed her returning to Cape Town right now. He was selfish enough to want Rowan to himself for the little time she was in the country.

'Anyway, he was spectacular in the sack, but he couldn't hold a conversation with a stump.'

He saw the look Rowan sent his way, caught the teasing glint in her eyes because she knew how uncomfortable he felt hearing this stuff.

'Spectacular in the sack? Tell me more.'

'If you do, I'll beat you,' Seb interrupted, and changed the subject before they ganged up on him. 'Have you done any work on your netsukes, Ro? Anything?'

'Some.'

'Hallelujah.'

'There's no need to be snarky.' Rowan gently smacked the back of his head.

'You took two weeks to find out information I could probably have found in an hour. If that,' Seb retorted. 'I think snarky is called for.'

'I hate a bragger.' Rowan flicked his shoulder and Seb caught her finger and tugged her closer.

'That's not what you said last night,' Seb said, his voice silky as his brain started to fire on all cylinders.

Callie cracked an egg into a bowl and pulled a face. '*Eeew!* Gross! TMI, thank you. Tell me about these net-sukes so that I can push the thought of you two out of my head.'

Seb kissed Rowan's finger before letting her go.

Rowan wrinkled her nose as she opened the bacon. 'Well, they definitely aren't stolen. I found out that much. The four netsukes stolen from that gallery aren't anything like the ones I have, except for the subject matter.'

'Well, that's a relief.' Seb leaned back in his chair. 'So, what's the next step?'

Rowan pushed her hair behind her ears. 'I spoke to Grayson again, and he's scheduled a trip to London in ten days. If I can meet him in London he'll look at them and make me an offer.'

Seb fought to keep the dismay off his face and out of his voice. Ten days. She'd be out of his life in ten days. No, that didn't sound right.

Rowan carried on speaking and he forced himself to concentrate.

'I've some money to contribute to the airfare back to London, but—' she picked up a dishcloth and pulled it through her fingers in agitation '—I'd have to pay you the balance when I get to London, after Grayson has paid me. Is that okay with you?'

Seb managed to nod. Nothing was okay about this situation. Wanting to get closer to her, not wanting her to go, imagining her in his bed, in his life, for many more days, weeks—years, a lifetime... *Dammit!*

Seb watched her fry the bacon and thought it was deeply ironic that he'd been so on guard with his previous girlfriends, constantly batting off their attempts to get closer, and yet Rowan had pulled him in without making any effort at all.

He wanted to be with her and it was all self-imposed; he wanted to be with her, spend time with her, purely because he thought she was so damn wonderful. By not putting any pressure on him she'd untied the knots—the fear and concern over commitment—little by little by herself.

Was this what love felt like? He didn't think so. Who fell in love in two weeks? That was crazy! But he had had to admit that he was ass-deep in something. Something beyond lust, beyond attraction.

You just need some time alone to think this through, to be logical and practical, he insisted to himself. When she gave him some time to catch his breath he'd work it through, put the various components of what he was thinking into their proper boxes and he'd understand.

He needed to understand.

Seb tipped his head back and stared at the ceiling. She had to go. She would run because she needed to be free...

His heart wanted to flop at her feet and beg her to stay.

His brain told him he'd be okay—that things would go back to normal, that he'd plug the holes she'd made. Eventually. Maybe.

'Hey, you lovebirds! Stop snogging!'

Seb jumped at Callie's yell and saw his sister leaning across the sink, her face to the open window. 'You guys want pancakes? And, Dad, is she going be my new *mummee*?'

Rowan's eyes brimmed with mirth as she turned to look at him and his breath caught in his throat.

'Your sister—so shy, so bashful. She really should learn to put herself forward more.'

Rowan, her head reeling, carried the dinner dishes from the formal dining room to the kitchen and placed them on the counter for Seb to pack them into the dishwasher.

She'd had coffee with her father the morning after they'd returned home and then she'd waited two days for the invitation to dinner that her father had assured her was forthcoming. When it had never materialised, she'd bitten the bullet, called her dad and asked whether they'd like to have Sunday brunch with her and Seb.

It had been an unmitigated disaster.

Rowan felt Seb's arms around her waist, felt his solid frame against her chest, and the tears that she'd ruthlessly suppressed floated up her throat. 'I'm not sure whether to laugh or cry,' she said, her voice wobbly.

'At which part?' Seb asked, his lips just above her ear. 'There were many highlights. Your lack of a formal education, the fact that you are no better than a vagrant, your criminal past...'

'I'd heard all those before.' Rowan pushed her hair out of her eyes. 'What I *didn't* know was that they are putting the house on the market and moving to the UK to be closer to Peter when he goes there. I thought that Peter was planning to remain in Bahrain. Did you know that he was moving? He's your friend.'

Seb's arms dropped as she wiggled out of them. 'We don't talk that often, Ro. A bi-annual call to catch up— that's it. So, no, I didn't know about his move to the UK.'

'And his girlfriend? Did you know that she's six months pregnant?' Rowan heard the shrill demand in her voice and knew that she was not going to be unable to keep back the tide of emotion that was threatening to engulf her.

'No, I didn't know.'

Rowan moved a pile of plates from one stack to another, dumped the cutlery in an oven pan. 'Well, if that's not a huge bloody clue that they no longer consider me a part of this family then I don't know what is. I never thought it could still hurt this much.'

'What, Ro?'

'Knowing that I am, categorically, on my own,' Rowan whispered.

She'd always had this little dream — one she took out only occasionally and let it fly—that she was the beloved daughter, the fun sister, that she would have a relationship with her mother that was normal, loving…involved.

Well, their prosaic announcement earlier had detonated that fantasy into a million bloody shards. Every one of which was embedded in her heart.

'You're not on your own. You're part of us. You've always been part of us,' Seb stated, his voice calm and reasonable. Steady.

God, she wished she could climb into his steady and rest awhile. But she couldn't—wouldn't. Whatever they'd had was at an end. Her ties were cut with her parents and she should cut them with Seb as well. While she could.

They would be friends, would some day look back on the madness that had been their affair and smile, knowing that it had been a marvellous interlude in time that was pure fantasy.

'You are part of us,' Seb repeated.

Rowan shook her head. She wasn't—couldn't be. If she couldn't be accepted by her own family, how could she expect to be part of theirs? Especially after being away for so long. And what would that mean while she was on the road? The occasional call to Seb? To Patch? E-mails? Facebook?

It didn't work. She knew this.

Seb's hand drifted over her hair, a touch of pure comfort, and she jerked her head away. She had to start stepping back, start preparing herself to leave.

Practically she needed to get London to sell the netsukes, to bolster her bank account. To repay Seb.

Emotionally she had to pull away, to put some distance between them before he did. She couldn't bear it if he rejected her too—and he would. He'd made it very clear that what they had was a brief fling. He'd said nothing to make her believe that he wanted her to stay.

The realisation that a big part of her really wanted to stay terrified her.

'Oh, I took a call for you earlier, while you were in the shower,' Seb said, stepping away from her and leaning against the opposite kitchen counter.

'From..?'

'Melanie? Melissa?'

'Merle?'

'That's it. She said that you spoke to her the other day about organising her wedding?' Seb picked up an orange from the fruit basket and dug his fingers into the skin, pulling the peel away.

'She's Annie's niece and she wants a Moroccan-themed wedding. Since I've been to Morocco, Annie thought I could do it.' Rowan closed her eyes. 'I'd love to do it; I have all these ideas running through my head.'

'When is it?' Seb made a pile of peel on the dining room table.

'Three months' time.'

'So do it,' he suggested blandly.

Rowan blinked as she tried to process his words. Stay here for another three months? Was he insane? 'What are you suggesting?'

'Stay here with me. Do the wedding.' Seb pulled a seg-ment from the orange and popped it into his mouth.

'Are you mad? That's the most illogical, impractical, stupid suggestion you have ever made!' Rowan's voice climbed with every decibel. 'I have to get to London to sell the netsukes!'

'Planes go both ways,' Seb pointed out in his cool, prac-tical voice. 'Go to London. Come back.'

'I need to travel,—to keep moving, Sebastian. To be free!' Rowan shouted. 'I can't stay here.'

'Have I put a ring on your finger? Asked you to stay for ever? No. I've suggested that you stay for another three months, to do something you obviously want to do and obviously enjoy. I thought that you could stay here with me, which you seem to enjoy as well. Or am I wrong about that?'

'I thought that this was a fling...'

'And I thought you were good at change!' Seb snapped back. 'If you were anywhere else in the world would you stay?'

'Yes, but—'

'Then why can't you stay here? For a little while longer?'

'Because you haven't thought this out! Because you're feeling sorry for me, wanting to protect me, wanting to help me out of another jam! This is an impulsive offer that you are going to regret when you've thought it through and you'll wish that you'd never opened your big mouth. I don't want to be something you regret, Seb!'

'You wouldn't be.'

'Of course I would, Seb! I'm great for a fling but I'd drive you mad long-term. I can't stick to anything. I'll waft from job to job, get involved in one project and then go off at a tangent to explore something else. I'd pick up stray people and stray animals and bring them home. I'd fill your home with crazy objects that you'd hate and colourful fabrics that would hurt your eyes. I'd turn this place upside down! Drive you nuts.'

'Just leave the War Room alone.'

Rowan didn't hear him, so intent on listing every reason why she couldn't stay. 'And I'd feel hemmed-in, constrained. I'd feel frustrated and then I'd get bitchy—and then I'd start planning trips and then I'd get depressed because I'd know that I couldn't leave you like—'

'Like my mother did.'

Seb's eyes had hardened and Rowan swallowed. Dammit, why had she compared her leaving to his mother's? If he could survive that, it would be easy to wave *her* goodbye.

Just tell me that you love me, Rowan silently begged him, *that this is something more than just sex and I'll be prepared to take the risk. Tell me that I am important to you, that I mean...something. Throw me a bone here, Seb. Persuade me to stay.*

Seb didn't say a damn word.

Rowan scrubbed her hands over her face. 'I'm going to get some air. This is going nowhere.'

'Good idea. But while you're out there think of this.' Seb dropped the orange, placed sticky fingers and hands onto her face and held her head still while he ransacked her mouth.

Tongues clashed and collided—frustration and fury combined with lust and confusion. His hand on her butt pushed her into him, so that she could feel the long, solid, pulsing length of him against her stomach, and under her hands his heart thumped and rolled.

Seb yanked his mouth away from hers and looked at her with wild eyes. 'Yeah, think of that, Rowan. And then tell me you can just walk away from it.'

Rowan held her fingers to her lips, still tasting him there as he stormed out of the kitchen. She heard him thunder up the stairs and the door to his bedroom slam shut.

She would think about that—of course she would!—
but she knew that thousand-degree kisses and fantastic sex
wasn't enough long-term. Because falling in love with him
properly would kill her if he didn't feel anything more than
fierce attraction for her. She didn't know if she could pick
up the pieces of her life again when he told her that he was
tired of her, that it wasn't working, that he'd had enough.

She'd been the second best child, the not-up-to-par
daughter, and she wasn't prepared to be the almost-good-
enough-but-not-quite, good-for-the-short-term lover.

She wasn't prepared to play guessing games with her
heart.

CHAPTER ELEVEN

ROWAN, NOT KNOWING where else to go, slipped through the gate into her parents' garden and headed to the north-east corner, to the mini-orchard, overgrown and neglected. In this place, between the peach and apricot trees, she and Callie had played, out of sight of both houses. It was a place where they could pretend, talk, wish, dream. Well, Callie had talked and she had dreamt.

God, she wished Callie was here. Callie would help her sort through her confusion.

'Rowan?'

Rowan spun around and hastily brushed the tears off her face. Her mum stood in front of her, looking deeply uncomfortable. Rowan held up her hands in defeat. 'Mum. What now? Why are you here?'

'I saw you streaking across the lawn, knew where you were going.' Heidi ran her hand through her still-black hair. 'Your father just tore into me, said that I was cruel to you.'

Yeah. Well. Duh.

'He thought I'd told you about Peter, about selling, moving. He thinks that we correspond regularly.'

Rowan tipped her head. 'Why did you let him think that?'

Heidi shrugged. 'I wanted to avoid an argument. I don't like arguing, conflict, trouble.'

'And I was trouble from the day I was born,' Rowan said bitterly.

Heidi didn't argue and Rowan cursed as pain slashed through her.

'Just go, Mum. I can't deal with you now.'

'When you were so sick, when you nearly died, I thought I would die too.'

Heidi's voice cracked and Rowan thought that she'd never heard her mum's voice so saturated with emotion.

'I was so scared… I don't think I've ever prayed so hard and so much. I loved you with every fibre in my being and the thought of losing you was too much for me to bear.'

What the heck…?

'When you recovered I suppose I…I retreated from you. I vowed to protect you, but I didn't think I could go through that again so I pulled back.'

Heidi must have seen something on Rowan's face because her lips twisted.

'I'm not good with emotion like you are, Rowan. I can't embrace it. I'm steadier when it's at a distance, when I am in control. Peter didn't demand that from me. You did.'

'So you pushed me away?' Rowan said, her voice flat.

Heidi nodded. 'People like us—me, your father, Peter, even Seb—we're intellectuals. We are brain-based not feelings-based. You were—*are*—all feelings. All the time. You need to touch, taste, experience.'

That was true, Rowan admitted.

Heidi nodded. 'I know you think I was cruel, encouraging you to go overseas, but I knew that you needed to. To taste, experience. Though I did think you'd come home in a year or two, settle down into a degree, get it out of your system.'

'Don't start,' Rowan warned her.

'I didn't think it would take you nine years to come home.' Heidi twisted her hands together. 'It's easier when you're not here. I can push the guilt away. But looking at you, so beautiful…'

'Mum.' Rowan placed her hand over her mouth.

Heidi straightened her shoulders and tossed her head. 'As for this…thing…with Seb…'

Oh, jeez, she really didn't want her mum commentating on her love-life. 'Mum, I don't feel like I want to hear—'

Heidi interrupted her. 'You need to leave. Because the two of you—'

Rowan growled in frustration. *Stop.* Maybe she did want to hear what she had to say. 'What, Mum?'

'The two of you spark off each other,' Heidi said, flustered. 'Anybody with half a brain can see that. But you're going to hurt each other. You are too different, worlds apart. It's not built for long-term… Love isn't enough.'

We're not in love, Rowan wanted to tell her. *Not quite. Not yet.*

Heidi kicked a branch at her foot. 'I suppose we'll have to get this area cleared if we want to sell.'

'Mum! We were talking about Seb and I! Tell me why you think we could never work.'

'Because you are too irrational, too impulsive for him to live with long-term, and his inability to be spontaneous would drive you mad. He wants someone steady and settled and you want someone exciting and unstructured. You'd kill each other.'

'So you don't believe in the theory that opposites attract? That love can conquer all?'

Heidi shook her head. 'It doesn't—not in real life. In books and in the movies, maybe, but this is your life—his life—and it's not a movie and it's not a book. Save yourselves the heartache, Rowan. I know you and I know Seb. This will blow up in your faces. You'll get hurt. And, believe it or not, I actually think you've been hurt enough.'

Rowan, reeling from having such an intense conversation with her mother, sucked in her breath. 'Why are you telling me this now?'

'Because I have failed you in so many ways, so many times. I should've tried to understand you better, loved you more, held you more. Drawn you closer instead of pushing you away. I failed you. But—' Heidi's voice cracked. 'But if I can save you some heartache, some pain, maybe you can start to forgive me. Maybe I can start to forgive myself.'

Heidi wrapped her arms around her middle and Rowan saw that her eyes were wet. She couldn't believe that her mother, who never cried, was crying over *her*.

She was nearly out of earshot when Rowan finally forced the word through her own tear-clogged throat. 'Mum?'

Heidi turned.

'I'm often in London. I have a house that I'm renovating there. Maybe we can meet, just you and I? Have tea, some time together. Maybe we can find a way back to each other?'

Heidi took a long time to answer and Rowan thought that she'd lost her. Again.

'I'd like that, Ro. I'd really like that.'

Rowan was relieved that Seb's bedroom was empty when she reached it. She immediately went to the spare room, dragged her backpack out of the cupboard and hauled it back to his room.

Somehow her clothes had found their way into his walk-in closet. Panties in his sock drawer, shorts next to his T-shirts. When had they migrated there? Who'd placed them there? Seb…? Seb had put the washing away. Hell, she'd been so busy bartending and arranging parties that she'd never got around to doing much laundry anyway. Seb had just done it quietly, with no fuss.

Shirts, shorts, jeans. Shoes? Red cowboy boots, trainers, pumps, flats. They all stood on the shelves in his shoe cupboard, along with her sparkly silver sandals. Rowan bit her lip as she traced the design on the front of one shoe; she loved these shoes but she wouldn't take them. Like the coral dress, like Seb, she had to leave them behind.

The box containing her netsukes sat on an open shelf above the shoes and Rowan stretched up and pulled it down. She lifted the lid and furiously unwrapped the little statues until she found the one she was looking for—the one of the Laughing Buddha with mischief in his eyes.

She wouldn't be selling this one—wouldn't take it with her. This was Seb's—her gift to him. She'd planned on keeping it herself but, like her, he'd fallen in love with it the first time he'd held it. It didn't matter that it was probably the oldest and most valuable of the collection. Nothing much mattered now. She placed it on the shelf next to a pile of his T-shirts, where she knew he would see it.

She was leaving and she had a new life to make. Her mum was right. They would eventually decimate each other. While she had the right to take chances with her own heart, she didn't have the right to play fast and loose with his. With anyone's. It was better to be on her own, responsible for only herself...

No risk of being hurt. Of hurting him.

'Running again, Brat?'

Rowan turned and looked at Seb, who had one shoulder plastered against the wall, his eyes shuttered.

'Packing.' Rowan kept her voice even. 'We both knew that I'd be leaving once I saw my folks.'

'Yeah, but neither of us thought that we'd be burning up the sheets a day later. That changes things, Rowan.'

'It's just sex, Seb. You can find it anywhere.'

Rowan yelped when Seb streaked across the room, gripped her arms and glared at her.

'It is not just sex! Get it?'

'Then what is it?' Rowan demanded. 'And let me go. You're hurting me.'

Tell me. Tell me that you need me to stay. Give me something to work with, to take a risk on.

Seb dropped his hands and then threw them up. 'It's something! I don't know what it is, exactly, but we'll never find out if you don't stop running!'

Something? Something wasn't enough. Not nearly enough.

'I'm leaving. I'm not running!' Rowan shouted. 'And I never said I'd stay! Besides, what would I be staying for? Another couple of months of sex? What do you want from me, Seb? Can you tell me?'

Seb raked his hand through his hair. 'No. Maybe. Not yet. I haven't thought it through.'

'You see, that's the essential difference between you and me. It has to make intellectual sense to you and it just has to feel right to me.' Rowan sat on the edge of the bed.

'Does it feel right for you to stay?' Seb asked quietly.

'Yes! But the problem is...'

'What?'

Rowan lifted pain-saturated eyes to his. 'This time I know that it's smart to leave. That, no matter how right it feels to stay, I have to listen to my brain. Because this time I can't trust my heart.'

'Why?'

'Because you'll break it. And I'll break yours. We have the ability to do that to each other,' Rowan said in a quiet, determined voice. 'If I walk—run—leave now, we can avoid that. You can't give me enough of what I need for me to consider staying. I don't want to hurt you, and God knows I don't want you to hurt me. Let me go, Seb, please. It's for the best. You know it is.'

'All I know—*feel*, dammit!—is that you are running as fast and as far away from me as possible. But I've never begged a woman for anything in my life and I'm not going to start now.'

Seb walked over to his desk, shoved the chair so hard that it skidded across the floor and bent over his computer. His fingers skipped over the keys and ten minutes later—the longest ten minutes of her life—he turned back to face her.

His face and voice were completely devoid of emotion. 'I've booked you on a flight to London, leaving tonight. I've ordered you a taxi. It will be here in an hour. I'm sure you won't mind spending the afternoon in the airport. It's what you do, isn't it?'

'Seb, I'm doing what I think is best for us,' Rowan protested, trying once more to get him to understand.

'And where does what I want, what I need, what I think is best, come into it? All I'm asking is for some time, Rowan! A slice of your time so that we can work out what we want to do. We've been together for nearly three weeks! We're adults. Adults don't make snap decisions about the rest of their lives, about whether they're going to get hurt or not. I want time with you—time that you seem to be able to give to mountains and monasteries, temples, sights and cities but not to me!' Seb roared. 'So, really, take your excuses about doing what is best for us and get the hell out of my life.'

Seb slammed the lid of his computer closed, sent her another fulminating, furious look and walked out of the room. Instead of slamming the door, as she knew he wanted to do, he closed it quietly. Its snick was the soundtrack to her heart cracking and snapping.

Crap; she was *so* screwed.

'You look awful, darling.' Grayson Darling looked at her across the table in the English tea room and then at an original artwork just beyond her head. 'Love that painting.'

'Gray, I've drunk the tea, eaten the scones…can we talk netsukes now?' Rowan demanded, in a thoroughly bad mood. Then again, she'd been in a bad mood since she'd left Cape Town two weeks ago and it was steadily getting worse. Having to spend two hours with Grayson, making small talk over high tea, was just making her feel even more cranky—which she hadn't believed was possible.

She needed to do this deal with Grayson; the money she'd made arranging those parties and bartending was almost finished and she was sick of sleeping on a friend's pull-out couch.

She needed money. Fast. She'd played this song to death; hopefully after today she wouldn't have to hear it again.

Grayson wiped his fingers on a snow-white cloth serviette and sighed dramatically as he pulled the box towards him. 'Where is the charming Rowan I enjoyed so much?'

Back in Cape Town, with her heart. With Seb. Seb… Her heart clenched. She missed him so much—missed her heart, which had remained behind with him. Without it she was just existing, just skating.

She didn't skate. She didn't exist. She *lived*. It was what she did. But no longer. Not any more. Not without Seb. She'd thought that she'd been so clever, leaving Cape Town before she fell in love with him. But love, she realised, didn't stop to count the miles between them and had snuck inside her anyway.

'Oh, Rowan, these are wonderful,' Grayson said, appreciation in every syllable as he lined up the netsukes between them. 'Fantastic composition, brilliant condition. But you're missing one… Where's the Laughing Buddha?'

'It's not for sale.'

'Of course it's for sale; it's the jewel of the collection.' Grayson looked at her in horror. 'It's the one I want.'

Seb's the one I want… Okay, stop being a complete drip, Dunn, and concentrate. 'Sorry, Grayson. I gave it away.'

Grayson closed his eyes and shook his head. 'Dear God, you are a basket case. Get it back.'

'It's gone. Move on. Make me an offer on these,' Rowan demanded, exhausted.

She watched as Grayson examined the netsukes again and allowed her mind to wander. She recognised the light of acquisition in his eyes and knew that within a day she'd be a couple of thousand pounds richer than she had been when she'd emptied her bank account a month ago. Good grief, had it only been a month? How could so much have happened in so short a time?

Forcing her mind away from the path it travelled far too frequently straight back to Seb, she tried to make plans on where to go from here. Back to Thailand or west to Canada? Or home to Cape Town.

Every cell in her body reacted when she thought of Cape Town. She didn't want to go anywhere else. She wanted to go home, to Seb.

Being deported and being broke had catapulted her into a situation where she'd had to slow down, move beyond the good-time surface and come face to face, heart to heart, with another person. With Seb. And she'd loved what she'd found. She'd resisted it, resisted love, with everything she had, and it was hard to admit that freedom didn't stand a chance against not having Seb in her life.

She loved him. Just loved him with every atom in her body. He was her freedom, the next world she had to discover, understand. He was what had been missing from her life, what she'd been searching for all over the world.

And he was right. She ran when she most needed to stand and fight.

'Fifty thousand and not a penny more for all of them,' Grayson said.

Rowan blinked, smiled and held out her hand. 'Deal. When can I have the money?'

Grayson looked horrified. 'Rowan, dammit, you are supposed to negotiate! Haven't I taught you *anything*?'

'I know you're low-balling me, Gray—' Well, she did now. 'But I don't have the time to argue with you. How much do you have on you?'

'Ten thousand. Okay, I'll give you sixty,' Grayson muttered. 'I'd feel like I was robbing you if you took less.'

Rowan held out her hand. 'I'll take the ten and you can transfer the balance into my account as per normal. Maybe by then you'll realise that you are still screwing me and up the offer again.'

Grayson sent the netsukes a greedy look before pulling out a money clip from his jacket pocket. 'It's entirely possible.'

Rowan took the cash from his hand, stood up and dropped a kiss on the balding crown of his head. 'Thanks. Enjoy.'

'If you ever want to sell the Laughing Buddha I'm your man.'

Rowan shook her head. 'I'll tell the new owner, but he won't sell it.'

'Gave it away…sacrilege.' Grayson gestured to the pile of food still on the table. 'Where are you shooting off to in such a hurry? We've hardly made a dent in the food.'

Rowan grinned at him. 'Home. I'm going home.'

Dusk was falling and it looked as if someone was randomly sprinkling lights over Scarborough as the sea darkened to cobalt and then to midnight-blue. It was Seb's favourite time of the day and, pre-Ro, he had often spent this half-hour at his desk, whisky in his hand, just watching the transition from night to day. With all the lights in his office off, his staff, who were still at their stations in the War Room, knew better than to disturb him.

Seb took a sip of his whisky, felt the burn and was grateful he could feel anything.

Since Rowan had left he'd felt numb. And that was when he wasn't feeling lost and sad and crap. He was feeling opposed to thinking and he didn't like it at all. This was why he didn't get emotionally involved; this was why he kept his distance.

He was a walking, talking cliché. Drinking too much, thinking too much, wishing too much. Finding things to do so that he didn't go to sleep, because she was there in his dreams and it hurt too damn much when he woke up, rolled over and realised—again—that she wasn't there.

He just hurt. Full-stop.

The lights flashed on overhead and he lifted his hand against the glare. 'What the...? Dad?'

'Drinking in the dark is a new low, even for you,' Patch said cheerfully, sitting in the chair on the opposite side of the desk. He gestured towards his half-full glass. 'Got another of those for your old man?'

Seb pushed the glass across the desk. 'Take this one. I'm going to hit the gym and try and work out my frustration.'

'Horny?' Patch joked, but his eyes were serious.

Seb couldn't find the energy to pretend. 'Just sad.'

'You do have it bad. Have *her* bad.' Patch sipped the whisky, put his ankle over his knee and looked at his son. 'I thought she'd be the one to get hurt, yet you are taking a pounding.'

'Yeah.' That summed it up.

'I'm going to marry Annie,' Patch said, and Seb's head snapped up.

He was wallowing and his father was getting married? What the—?

'She doesn't know, and I haven't said anything, but she's the one. I just want to be with her for ever. I know it in here.'

He thumped his heart. 'So do you, if you'd stop thinking so much and take a chance.'

Jeez, he'd tried. His father didn't know that he was the one who'd asked her to stay, to give them some time, so he briefly explained the situation.

Patch sent him a pitying look. 'So you asked her to stay... what did *that* mean?'

'Excuse me?'

'Did you tell her that you love her? That you want to be with her?' Patch demanded.

'No. I just asked her to stay, to give me time to think. I just wanted time to figure it out,' Seb protested.

'And if she'd given you that time and you'd decided that you didn't love her? What then? Where would she have been then?' Patch demanded. 'What reason did you give her to stay? Why would she stick around, running the risk of getting closer to you, when she knew she could get heart-slammed at the end of it?'

Seb dropped an F-bomb and his head. 'I didn't think about it like that.'

'What is the one thing Rowan has been looking for all her life, Seb?'

'Uh...'

'Love, acceptance, a place and a person she can belong to. How can somebody as smart as you not know this?'

He wasn't smart with people. He never had been.

'So, what are you going to do about it, Seb? Are you going to track her around the world like you do your mum? Never making contact and making yourself miserable? Or are you going to reach out and try and make this work?'

Seb felt the slap of Patch's words. 'What? Whoa, back up! Do you think I *should* contact my mum?'

Patch sighed. 'I think that you either have to or let her go. Callie and I, we're reconciled to the fact that she is out of our lives. We're over it—over her. You? Not so much. I think it would be healthier if you either had a relationship with her or if you cut ties completely. No man's land is no place to operate from. Same with Rowan. Either take a chance or let her go. Don't be half-assed about it.'

'Jeez, Dad. Why don't you just let it rip, huh?'

'I'm trying. Get Rowan back, Seb, or get a grip! Just, for all our sakes, stop moping!'

And that was his dad's verbal boot up the ass, Seb thought. He took a deep breath and ran his hand over his head. 'I don't know where she is. I presume she is still in London.'

Patch rolled his eyes. 'You've been tracking Laura since you were sixteen and you're telling me you don't know where Rowan is? That you can't find out where she is going? What do you do every day, Seb? Get on that bloody machine and found out!'

Seb grinned, jumped to his feet and headed for the computer across the room. Within minutes he'd plugged in the necessary code and the result flashed up on the screen.

Holy hell… Were his eyes playing cruel tricks on him?

He felt Patch at his elbow. 'What? What's the problem?'

Seb pointed to a line on the screen. 'Do you believe this? Am I seeing things?'

Patch's hand gripped his shaking shoulder to steady him. 'No, bud, I don't think that you are.'

Rowan cleared Customs and Immigration and stood in the middle of the arrivals hall, staring at the mobile in her hand. *Seb Hollis*, it said. *Seb Hollis. Dial me, dial me. Just push the green button.*

She'd thought that asking him for a favour all those weeks ago would be hard, but it was nothing—*nothing!*—compared to the terror she felt now.

Please love me. Please keep me.

Yeah, as if she was going to come right out and say that!

No, she'd figured this all out. She was going to be rational and unemotional; she'd say that they had something worth exploring, that she would stay if he wanted her to, give them time to work it out.

She would not be the gibberish-spewing, sobbing, crazy, wildly-in-love person she knew herself to be. She would be sensible if it killed her—which it probably would, if the terror didn't get her first.

What if he refused to come and get her? What if she had to bang down his door to see him? What if…?

She was driving herself over the edge. *Just dial the damn number!*

Seb took five rings to answer. 'Seb? It's me.'

'Rowan.'

Rowan heard the tension in his voice and felt her stomach swoop to her toes. Oh, this was much, much harder than anything she'd ever done before. *Courage, Dunn. This is your do-over, your second chance. You're going to regret not doing this, so do it!* 'I need a favour.'

'Another one?'

'It's the last one, I promise.'

'Uh huh.'

Before her vocal cords seized up she forced her words out. 'Can you come pick me up? I'm back and I'm at the airport. And I need to talk to you.'

'Yeah. Okay. Stay where you are. Sexy jeans, by the way,' he said, before abruptly disconnecting.

What the…? She was taking the biggest chance of her life and he was commentating on her jeans? How would he know what she was wearing anyway? How *could* he know…?

'Really sexy jeans. I like the way they hug your butt.'

Rowan spun around and there he was…large, solid, *there*…right in front of her. Dear Lord, he was there. Rowan lifted her fist to her mouth and bit her knuckle hard. The

pain reassured her that he wasn't a figment of her imagination, that he was real.

So damn real. As real as the hand that now covered the
side of her face.

'Breathe, Ro.'

Tears that she'd sworn weren't going to fall ran down
her face. 'You're here.'

'I'll always be here, if you let me,' Seb told her, his eyes
radiating emotion.

'How did you know…? How? My flight? I only decided
yesterday to come back…to come home.' Ro gripped his
shirt and hung on. As long as she held him he couldn't disappear on her. 'How?'

'I keep telling you that I could track you on the moon if I
wanted to. When are you going to believe me?' Seb placed
his hand on her hip and pulled her closer. 'Come here. I
need to touch you—all of you.'

Rowan burrowed her face into his neck, inhaling his
scent, trying to climb inside him. One strong hand held
her head there, another wrapped around her lower back,
pulling her as close as possible. They stood there for many
minutes, just holding on.

Maybe, just maybe, he'd missed her as much as she'd
missed him.

'Can I come home, Seb? Can I come back?' Rowan
asked when she eventually lifted her head, forcing herself
to meet his eyes.

Seb placed a gentle kiss on her mouth before pushing a
curl behind her ear. He stroked the pad of his thumb across
her cheekbone before dropping his hand back to her hip.

'You *are* home. You *are* back,' Seb replied. 'And,
frankly, it's about bloody time.'

They didn't speak much on the way home, but Seb's hand
on her knee reassured her that they would—that they would

find a way to move forward. She placed her fingers on top of his and her heart turned over when he smiled at her. Was that love she saw in his eyes, on his face, or was she just imagining it?

She was probably just imagining it... Yes, he was happy that she was back, but there was no point in jumping to conclusions. She was just setting herself up for a fall. It was enough—it should be enough—to know that that she loved him, that she was home, that she had to take every day as it came and treasure the time she had with him.

She felt Seb's fingers widen under hers, stretch, and then he patted her knee. 'You were gripping my hand so hard I lost all feeling. Relax, Ro, we'll sort this out.'

'We will?'

Seb sent her his cocky grin. 'Damn straight. I'm not letting you go again without a fight.'

Rowan looked puzzled. 'I thought that *was* a fight.'

'That wasn't even close,' Seb assured her. 'Now, put your hand back on mine, try not to stop the blood, and relax. We're going to get home, have a glass of wine and talk it through. Like adults. In a reasonable, mature fashion...'

They had crazy monkey sex instead. On the stairs...

They walked into the house and Seb closed the front door behind him and dropped her rucksack to the floor. 'I'll take this upstairs later. Do you want a glass of wine?'

Rowan shook her head. She didn't want anything. She just wanted that mouth on hers, that skin under her hands, him inside her.

'Ro? Water? Juice? Food?'

Rowan shook her head again and Seb looked at her, puzzled. 'Okay. What *do* you want?'

'You. Just you. Right now. Right here,' Rowan whispered.

And, while she craved his touch, she didn't expect him

to immediately back her into the wall, his mouth covering hers and his hands everywhere. On her breasts, on her butt, her thighs, skimming her face, in her hair. It was as if he was rediscovering her, re-exploring her, touching her for the first time.

And she needed him to feed off her as she was feeding off him. She shoved her hands up and under his T-shirt, pulling it over his head so that she could touch his stomach without the barrier of cotton, run her hands over his chest, up his neck.

'Do you have any particular attachment to this shirt?' Seb demanded, his voice hoarse in her ear.

'Uh? What? No.'

'Good.' Seb grabbed each side of her shirt and ripped it open, scattering buttons over the floor. 'Much better,' he muttered, shoving the sleeves down her arms and letting it fall to the floor.

A finger hooked the cup of her bra away and his mouth covered her nipple as lust swirled and whirled, hot and fast.

Underneath love quivered and sighed, hoped and dreamt.

'I missed you so much,' Rowan said as he unhooked her bra and threw it over his shoulder.

'This place was like a morgue without you. Get those jeans off,' he muttered, his fingers busy pleasuring her breasts.

'Get yours off too,' Rowan retorted as she wiggled the fabric down her legs.

'For you? Any time.' Seb shucked his jeans along with his boxers and stared down at her, his heart in his eyes. 'You are so beautiful, Ro. I'm so glad you're home.'

'Me too.' Rowan sighed, placing her fingers on his cheek. 'Now, why don't you show me how glad you are by—?'

Seb's mouth cut off her words as one hand hoisted her thigh, his other hand pulled aside her panties and he thrust into her, hard and deep, filling her body, her mind and heart.

Seb. There was only Seb—would only be Seb.

'Ah, *now* I'm home,' Seb said into her mouth. 'You're my home, Ro. Only you.'

Later, after they'd made love again in his bed, Rowan sat on the love seat in the window of Seb's room and was thankful that he'd said that he needed to run downstairs for a minute.

She needed that minute. She needed more than a minute. To catch her breath, to allow her brain to catch up with her body.

She was trying to be brave, trying not to worry, but her brain was now in hyper-drive, red-lining with worry. Had nothing changed while she was away? Were they just going to fall back into what they'd had? When were they going to talk, work this out, as Seb had suggested in the car?

And what, exactly, did his 'working it out' entail?

Rowan released her bottom lip from between her teeth as Seb walked back into the room, carrying a large tray. His boxer shorts rode low on his hips and his 6-pack rippled as he walked over to her.

'Stop looking at me like that or you'll be back on that bed so fast your head will spin,' Seb said as he placed the tray on the cushions next to her.

'Promises, promises,' Rowan replied, and frowned when she looked down at the tray. A bottle of champagne she could understand, and the two glasses, but the set of keys that looked like a carbon copy of his house set and a keyless car remote had her puzzled. There was also a red jewellery box on the tray...

A jewellery box? Oh, dear God...

'You're not proposing, are you?' she asked, in a very high, very nervous voice.

Seb laughed. 'Not today.'

Phew!

'Then what's all this?' Rowan asked as Seb sat down, keeping the tray between them.

'We'll get to the box eventually, but first...it's time to work it out, Ro,' Seb said, popping the cork on the champagne and pouring her a glass.

He handed it over and poured his own glass.

'Why did you come home?' he asked her bluntly.

Rowan licked her lips. 'I missed you.'

'I missed you too. And...?'

Rowan stared at the bubbles in her glass. If she said these next words she could never take them back. They would be out there for ever...and she was okay with that.

'I love you. I do... I never expected to, never wanted to, but I do. So I thought I'd come home, tell you that and see how you feel about it.'

Seb just looked at her, his glass halfway to his mouth.

The moisture in Rowan's mouth dried up and she swirled some champagne around her tongue to get it to work. 'Feel free to give me a reaction, here, Hollis.'

'I feel pretty good about it. I thought I'd have to drag those words out of you with pliers but you've astounded me again.' Seb reached across the tray, kissed her gently and ran his thumb across her trembling bottom lip. 'I love you too, by the way. In every way possible and in lot of ways I thought were impossible.'

Ah... *Aaaahhhhh!* Rowan's shoulders fell down from her ears and her cheeks deepened. Relief, hot and strong, pulsed through her.

'Good to know... My mum says that we will destroy each other. That we are too different, diametrically opposed.' Rowan thought it was important to tell him that her mother rated their chances as less than nil.

'Your mother talks a lot of crap,' Seb said mildly, play-

ing with her fingers as he sipped his champagne. 'We'll be
fine. Yes, you'll turn my life upside down, but as long as
you leave the War Room and my hackers alone you can do
whatever you want. And if you go too crazy I'll pull you
back in. In the same way, if I get too stuck in my head,
you'll bully me out of it. We're good for each other precisely because we are so different.'

'I've been independent for so long and I'm worried that
I'll get restless, feel hemmed-in.' Rowan also felt it was
important to warn him. Maybe staying in one place would
be enough for her, being with him would be enough, but
there might come a day that she needed to fly, just to know
that she could…

'I know.' Seb gestured to the tray. 'I've thought about
that. So, first things first.' He held up the set of keys. 'Keys
to your house—this house. I don't want to hear any more
of this "your bedroom" and "your house" rubbish. This
house is as much yours as it is mine. Replace the furniture, paint the walls—do whatever you want; just treat it
as yours, okay?'

'It's not mine.'

'Rowan…!' Seb warned.

'Or yours, or Patch's. It's Yas's, as we all know. And
whatever I do I'll have to put up with Yas yapping on about
it, so I'll think long and hard before I go mad. You might
not care, but she will.' Rowan took the keys and bounced
them in her hand.

Seb grinned. 'All true, but I'll back you if comes down
to a fight.' He lifted up the credit-card-type key. 'Keyless
car key. We'll share the Quattro until I get you something
else to drive.'

'You can't buy me a car!' Rowan squeaked. 'I have
money. I can buy my own car. I sold the netsukes.'

'Thanks for mine, by the way. I love it. It's kept me from
going insane these past couple of weeks.' Seb tossed the

key card into her lap. 'Are we going to argue about money and stuff for the rest of our lives?'

'Are you going to love me that long?' Rowan asked, her hands on his knees.

'Planning on it.'

Seb picked up the jewellery box and tossed it from hand to hand. Rowan saw fear flash in his eyes.

'Giving you this is hard for me, but I know that it's necessary.'

Rowan frowned, took the box, flipped open the lid and saw that it was a credit card. He was giving her a credit card? What on earth…?

'There's enough money there to buy you ticket anywhere in the world, any time you want to go. Enough for you to book into any hotel you want to, buy what you want to. It has a heck of a limit in that it doesn't *have* a limit.'

'Seb. Why are you giving me a credit card? I don't understand.'

Seb licked his lips. 'It comes with a couple of conditions.'

'I'm listening.'

'I'll pay for everything, but you have to promise to say goodbye, to tell me that you're going. No walking out. And you can't use it after we've had a fight. You have to give us—me—a chance to work it out before you run.'

Tears tumbled. That was fair. God, that was so fair. She nodded furiously. 'Okay.'

'And you have to promise me that you'll always come back, because if you don't I swear I'll find you and drag you back home. I love you. It took me nine years to find you and I am not letting you go again.'

'Oh, Seb.' Rowan used the heels of her hands to swipe away her tears. It was such an enormous gift, such a demonstration of how well he knew her, how much he trusted her.

'Is that a deal, Brat?'

Rowan nodded. 'Deal.'

'Good. I told you we could work this out. Do you love me?'

'So much!'

'And I love you.' Seb's eyes brimmed with all the emotion he usually tried so hard to suppress. 'So explain to me—again—why you aren't over here, kissing me stupid?'

Rowan sighed as she moved into his arms. 'Another very epic fail on my part. Must try harder.'

* * * * *

'Sean Beresford. I am the acting manager of the Beresford Hotel, Richmond Square. Pleased to meet you, Miss Flynn.'

'Richmond Square?' she replied, trying to keep the panic out of her voice. 'That's the hotel where I booked a conference room for early February and…'

Then her brain caught up with the name he had given her, and she inhaled through her nose as his fingers slid away from hers and rested lightly on the counter.

'Did you just say Beresford? As in the Beresford family of hotel-owners?'

A smile flickered across his lips, which instantly drew her gaze, and her stupid little heart skipped a beat at the transformation in this man's face that one simple smile made.

Lord, he was gorgeous. Riveting.

Oh, smile at me again and make my blood soar. Please?

And now she was ogling. How pathetic. Just because she was within touching distance of a real, live Beresford it did not mean that she had to go to pieces in front of him.

He gestured towards the nearest table and chairs.

'You may need to sit down, Miss Flynn.'

Dear Reader

Tea.

My favourite hot drink.

Working from home means that I enjoy way too many cups of hot black tea with just a spoonful of whole milk than are probably good for me, but I couldn't do without it.

Coffee is a definite second best!

And I am so picky when it comes to the type of tea I drink.

Yes, I am the girl who always takes my favourite tea bags with me whenever I go on holiday or to a hotel.

At one time tea was one of the most exotic and valuable trade goods, but we take it so much for granted in our modern world, where tea in every possible form and variety is so widely available.

It was a joy to be able to share my love of all things tea with my heroine, Dee Flynn, tea-lover extraordinaire and wannabe tea importer.

Dee is not afraid to share her love of black, green and even pure unroasted white tea with the uninitiated—especially when Sean Beresford is holding her tea festival in one of his hotels.

Sean might understand the hotel business, and he's used to dealing with awkward customers. But a woman like Dee Flynn...? That is entirely different! They come from different worlds. But the one thing that unites them is their passion for what they do, for the people who love them—and for one another.

I loved following Dee and Sean on their journey to love and I hope that you do too.

And here is one more treat to look forward to.

Dee's friend Lottie and Sean's brother Rob may both be chefs but they come from completely different worlds. Would they be willing to risk everything for love? Watch out for my next foodie romance book which will be coming your way soon.

I am always delighted to hear from my readers, and you can get in touch via my website at: www.NinaHarrington.com

Every best wish

Nina

TROUBLE
ON HER DOORSTEP

BY
NINA HARRINGTON

MILLS &
BOON

Published in Great Britain 2014
by Mills & Boon, an imprint of Harlequin (UK) Limited,
Eton House, 18-24 Paradise Road, Richmond, Surrey, TW9 1SR

© 2014 Nina Harrington

ISBN: 978 0 263 91084 1

Harlequin (UK) Limited's policy is to use papers that are natural,
renewable and recyclable products and made from wood grown in
sustainable forests. The logging and manufacturing processes conform
to the legal environmental regulations of the country of origin.

Printed and bound in Spain
by Blackprint CPI, Barcelona

Nina Harrington grew up in rural Northumberland, England, and decided at the age of eleven that she was going to be a librarian—because then she could read *all* of the books in the public library whenever she wanted! Since then she has been a shop assistant, community pharmacist, technical writer, university lecturer, volcano walker and industrial scientist, before taking a career break to realise her dream of being a fiction writer. When she is not creating stories which make her readers smile, her hobbies are cooking, eating, enjoying good wine—and talking, for which she has had specialist training.

CHAPTER ONE

Tea, glorious tea. A celebration of teas from around the world.
There is no better way to lift your spirits than a steaming hot cup of builders' brew. Two sugars, lots of milk. White china beaker. Blend of Kenyan and Indian leaf tea. Brewed in a pot. Because one cup is never enough.

From *Flynn's Phantasmagoria of Tea*

Tuesday

'LADIES, LADIES, LADIES. No squabbling, please. Yes, I know that he was totally out of order but those are the rules. What happens in the Bake and Bitch club…?'

Dee Flynn lifted her right hand and waved it towards the women clustered about the cake display as though she was conducting a concert orchestra.

The women put down their tea cups, glanced at one another, shrugged their shoulders and raised their right hands.

'Stays in the Bake and Bitch club,' a chorus of sing-song voices replied, a second before they burst into laughter and sank back into their chairs around the long pine table.

'Okay. I might not be able to snitch, but I still cannot

believe that the faker tried to pass that sponge cake off as his own work,' Gloria sniggered as she poured another cup of Darjeeling and dunked in a homemade hazelnut biscotti. 'Every woman at the junior school bake sale knew that it was Lottie's triple-decker angel drool cake and you can hardly mistake that icing. We all know how hard it is to make, after last week's efforts.'

'Hey! Don't be so hard on yourself,' Lottie replied. 'That was one of my best recipes and chiffon sponge is not the easiest to get right. You never know; I might have become one dad's inspiration to greater things.'

A chorus of 'Boo,' and 'Not likely,' echoed around the table.

'Well, never mind about dads wanting to show off at the school bake sale in front of the other fabulous baked creations you gals create. We have five more minutes before your cakes come out of the oven so there is just enough time for you to taste my latest recipe for a February special. This is the cake I am going to demonstrate next week.'

With a flourish reserved for the finest award-winning restaurants where she and Dee had trained, Lottie Rosemount waited until every one of the girls had stopped talking and was looking at the cake plate at the centre of the table, before whipping away the central metal dome and revelling in the gasp of appreciation.

'Individual cupcakes. Dark chocolate and raspberry with white-chocolate hearts. And just in time for Valentine's Day. What do you think?'

'Think?' Dee coughed and took a long drink of tea. 'I am thinking that I have a week to come up with the perfect blend of tea to complement chocolate and raspberries.'

'Tea? Are you joking?' Gloria squealed. 'Hell no. Those cupcakes are not meant to be washed down with tea around the kitchen table. No chance. Those are after-dinner bedroom dessert cakes. No doubt about it. If I am lucky, I might get to eat half of one before my Valentine's Day dinner date gets really sweet—if you know what I mean. Girl, I want me some of those. Right now.'

A roar of laughter rippled like a wave around the room as Gloria snatched up a cupcake and bit into it with deep groans of pleasure, before licking her fingers. 'Lottie Rosemount, you are a temptation. If I made those cupcakes I know that I would get lucky, and just this once I would not think about the risk of chocolate icing on the bedclothes.'

Dee sniggered and had just pulled down a tea caddy of a particularly fragrant pomegranate infusion when she heard the distinctive sound of the antique doorbell at the front door of the tea rooms.

Lottie looked up from serving the cupcakes. 'Who can that be? We've been closed for hours.'

'Not to worry. I'll get it. But save one of those for me, can you? You never know—my luck might change and a handsome new boyfriend might turn up out of the blue just in time for Valentine's Day. Miracles can happen.'

Dee skipped out of the kitchen across the smooth wooden floorboards in her flat ballet pumps, and in three strides was inside the tea rooms. She flicked on the lights and instantly the long room was flooded with warm natural light which bounced back from the pistachio-and-mocha painted walls and pale wood fittings.

Lottie's Cake Shop and Tea Rooms had only been open a few months and Dee never got tired of simply walking up and down between the square tables and comfy chairs, scarcely able to believe that this was her space. Well, Lottie and Dee's space. They had each put up half of the money to get the business started. But they were partners sharing everything: tea and cake; both crazy, both working at the thing they loved best. Both willing to invest everything they had in this mad idea and take a risk that it would work.

Big risk.

A shiver ran across Dee's shoulders and she inhaled sharply. She needed this tea shop to work and work brilliantly if she had any hope of becoming a tea merchant in her own right. This was her last chance—her only chance—of creating some sort of financial future for herself and for her retired parents.

But suddenly the ringing bell was replaced by a hard rapping on the front door and she looked up towards the entrance. 'Hello? Is someone there?' A male voice called out from the street in a posh English accent.

A tall dark figure was standing on the pavement on the other side of the door with his hands cupped over his forehead, peering at her through the frosted glass of the half-glazed door.

What a cheek! It was almost nine o'clock at night. He must be desperate. And it was lashing down with rain.

She took a step forward then paused and sniffed just once before striding on.

After a lifetime of travel she was not scared of a stranger knocking on her door. This was a London high street, for goodness' sake, not the middle of some jungle or tropical rain forest.

With a lift of her chin and a spring in her step, Dee turned the key in the lock in one smooth movement and pulled the front door sharply towards her.

A little too sharply, as it turned out.

Everything from that moment seemed to happen in slow motion—like in some freeze-framed DVD where you could scarcely believe what had happened, so you played the same scene over and over again in jerky steps, just to make sure that your memory was not playing tricks on you.

Because as she flung open the door, the very tall man just raised his arm to knock again and, in that split second he leant forward, he found the door was missing.

But his body carried on moving, carrying him forward into the tea room. And directly towards Dee, who had stepped backward to see who was knocking so loudly.

A pair of very startled blue-grey eyes widened as he tumbled towards her, the bright light almost blinding him after the gloomy dark street outside.

What happened next was Dee's fault. *All of it.*

Either time slowed down or her brain went into overdrive, because suddenly she had visions of lawyers claiming compensation for broken noses and bruised elbows. Or worse.

Which meant that she could not, dared not, simply leap out of the way and let this man, whoever he was, fall forward, flat on his face and hurt himself.

So she did the only thing she could think of in that split second.

She swept his legs out from under him.

It seemed to make perfect sense at the time.

Her left leg stepped forward to his left side as she reached up and grabbed hold of the soggy right sleeve of his rather elegant long dark-wool coat and pulled him towards her.

Then she swept her right leg out, hooked her ballet pump behind his left ankle and flipped him over sideways. By keeping a tight hold on his coat sleeve, even though it was wet and slimy, she took his weight so that instead of falling flat on his back his besuited bottom hit the wooden floor instead.

It was actually a rather good side judo foot sweep, which broke his fall and took his weight at the same time. Result!

Her old martial arts tutor would have been proud.

Shame that the two middle buttons on what she could now see was a very smart cashmere coat popped open with the strain and went spinning off onto the floor under one of the tables. But it was worth it. Instead of flying across the floor to join them, her male visitor sat down in a long, heavy slow slump instead. No apparent harm done.

Dee's fingers slowly slid away from the moist fabric of his coat sleeve and his arm flopped down onto his knees.

She closed the front door and then sat back on her ankles on the floor so that she could look at him from about the same height.

And then look again.

Oh, my. Those blue-grey eyes were not the only thing that was startling. For a start he seemed to be wearing the kind of business suit she had last seen on the bank manager who had grudgingly agreed to give the bank loan on the tea room. Only softer and shinier and much, much more expensive. Not that she had much experience of men in suits, but she knew fabric.

And then there was the hair. The sleet had turned to a cold drizzle and his short dark-brown hair was curled into moist waves around his ears and onto his collar. Bringing into sharp focus a face which might have come from a Renaissance painting: all dark shadows and sharp cheekbones. Although the baggy tired eyes could probably use some of her special home-sewn tea bags to compensate for his late nights in the office.

Blimey! She had just swept the legs out from under the best looking man she had seen in a long time and that included the boys from the gym across the street, who stoked up on serious amounts of carbs before hitting the body-sculpting classes.

Men like this did not normally knock on her door.... ever. Maybe her luck *had* finally changed for once.

A smile slid across Dee's mouth, before the sensible part of her brain which was not bedazzled by a handsome face decided to make an appearance.

So what was he doing here? And who was he?

Why not ask him and find out?

'Hello,' she said, peering into his face and telling her hormones to sit down. 'Sorry about that, but I was worried that you might hurt yourself when you fell into the shop. How are you doing down there?'

How was he doing?

Sean Beresford pushed himself up on one elbow and took a few seconds to gather his wits and refocus on what looked like a smart café or bistro, although it was hard to tell since he was sitting on the floor.

Looking straight ahead of him, Sean could see cake stands, teapots and a blackboard which told him that the all-day special was cheese-and-leek quiche followed by an organic dark-chocolate brownie and as much Assam tea as he could drink.

Sean stared at the board and chuckled out loud. He could use some of that quiche and tea.

This was turning out to be quite a day.

It had started out in Melbourne what felt like a lifetime ago, followed by a very long flight, where he had probably managed three or four hours of sleep. And then there had been the joy of a manic hour at Heathrow airport where it soon became blindingly obvious that he had boarded the plane, but his luggage had not.

One more reason why he did not want to be sitting on this floor wearing the only suit of clothes that he possessed until the airline tracked down his bag.

Sean shuffled to a sitting position using the back of

a very hard wooden chair for support, knees up, back straight, exhaled slowly and lifted his head.

And stared into two of the most startling pale-green eyes that he had ever seen.

So green that they dominated a small oval face framed by short dark-brown hair which was pushed behind neat ears. At this distance he could see that her creamy skin was flawless apart from what looked like cake crumbs which were stuck to the side of a smiling mouth.

A mouth meant to appease and please. A mouth which was so used to smiling that she had laughter lines on either side, even though she couldn't be over twenty-five.

What the hell had just happened?

He shuffled his bottom a little and stretched out his legs. Nothing broken or hurting. That was a surprise.

'Anything I can get you?' The brunette asked in a light, fun voice. 'Blanket? Cocktail?'

Sean sighed out loud and shook his head at how totally ridiculous he must look at that moment.

So much for being a top hotel executive!

He was lucky that the hotel staff relying on him to sort out the disaster he had just walked into straight from the airport could not see him now.

They might think twice about putting their faith in Tom Beresford's son.

'Not at the moment, thank you,' he murmured with a short nod.

Her eyebrows squeezed tight together. She bent forward a little and pressed the palm of one hand onto his forehead, and her gaze seemed to scan his face.

Her fingers were warm and soft and the sensation of that simple contact of her skin against his forehead was so startling and unexpected that Sean's breath caught in his throat at the reaction of his body at that simple connection.

Her voice was even warmer, with a definite accent that told him that she has spent a lot of time in Asia.

'You don't seem to have a temperature. But it is cold outside. Don't worry. You'll soon warm up.'

It he did not have a temperature now, he soon would have, judging by the amount of cleavage this girl was flashing him as she leant closer.

Her chest was only inches away from his face and he sat back a little to more fully appreciate the view. She was wearing one of those strange slinky sweaters that his sister Annika liked to wear on her rare weekend visits. Only Annika wore a T-shirt underneath so that when it slithered off one shoulder she had something to cover her modesty.

This girl was not wearing a T-shirt and a tiny strip of purple lace seemed to be all that was holding up her generously proportioned assets. At another time and definitely another place he might have been tempted to linger on that curving expanse of skin between the top of the slinky forest-green knit and the sharp collar bones and enjoy the moment, but she tilted her head slightly and his gaze locked onto far too many inches of a delicious-looking neckline.

It had been a while since he had been so very up close and personal to a girl with such a fantastic figure and it took a few seconds before what was left of the logical part of his brain clicked back into place. He dragged his focus a little higher.

'Nice top,' he grinned and pressed his hands against the floor to steady his body. 'Bit cold for the time of year.'

'Oh, do you like it?' She smiled and then looked down and gasped a little. In one quick movement she slid back and tugged at her top before squinting at him through narrow eyes. Clearly not too happy that he had been enjoying the view while she was checking his temperature.

'Cheeky,' she tutted. 'Is this how you normally behave in public? I'm surprised that they let you out unsupervised.'

A short cough burst out of Sean's throat. After sixteen years in the hotel trade he had been called many things by many people but he had never once been accused of being cheeky.

The second son of the founder of the Beresford hotel chain did not go around doing anything that even remotely fell into the 'cheeky' category.

This was truly a first. In more ways than one.

'Did you just deck me?' he asked in a low, questioning voice and watched her stand up in one single, smooth motion and lean against the table opposite. She was wearing floral patterned leggings which clung to long, slender legs which seemed to go on for ever and only ended where the oversized sweater came down to her thighs. Combined with the green top, she looked like a walking abstract painting of a spring garden. He had never seen anything quite like it before.

'Me?' She pressed one hand to her chest and shook her head before looking down at him. 'Not at all. I stopped you from falling flat on your face and causing serious damage to that cute nose. You should be thanking me. It could have been a nasty fall, the way you burst in like that. This really is your lucky day.'

'Thank you?' he spluttered in outrage. Apparently he had a cute nose.

'You are welcome,' she chuckled in a sing-song voice. 'It is not often that I have a chance to show off my judo skills but it comes in handy now and then.'

'Judo. Right. I'll take your word for it,' Sean replied and looked from side to side around the room. 'What is this place?'

'Our tea rooms,' she replied, and peered at him. 'But

you knew that, because you were hammering at our door.'
She flicked a hand towards the entrance. 'The shop is
closed, you know. No cake. No tea. So if you are expecting to be fed you are out of luck.'

'You can say that again,' Sean whispered, then held up
one hand when she looked as though she might reply. 'But
please don't. Tea and cakes are the last thing I came looking for, I can assure you.'

'So why were you hammering on the door, wearing a
business suit at nine on a Tuesday evening? You have obviously come here for a reason. Are you planning to sit on my
floor and keep me in suspense for the rest of the evening?'

His green-eyed assailant was just about to say something else when the sound of female laughter drifted out
from the back of the room.

'Ah,' she winced and nodded. 'Of course. You must be
here to pick up one of the girls from the Bake and Bit…
Banter club. But those ladies won't be ready for at least
another half-hour.' One hand gestured towards the back
of the room where he could hear the faint sound of female
voices and music. 'The cakes are still in the oven.' Her
lovely shoulders lifted in an apologetic shrug. 'We were
late getting started. Too much bit…chatting and not enough
baking. But I can tell someone you are here, if you like.
Who exactly are you waiting for?'

Who was he waiting for? He wasn't waiting for anyone. He was here on a different kind of mission. Tonight
he was very much a messenger boy.

Sean reached into the inside breast pocket of his suit
jacket and checked the address on the piece of lilac writing paper he had found inside the envelope marked
'D S Flynn contact details' lying at the bottom of the conference room booking file. It had been handwritten in dark-

green ink in very thin letters his father would instantly have dismissed as spider writing.

Well, he certainly had the right street and, according to the built-in GPS in his phone, he was within three metres of the address of his suspiciously elusive client who had booked a conference room at the hotel and apparently paid the deposit without leaving a telephone number or an email address. Which was not just inconvenient but infuriating.

'Sorry to disappoint you, but I am not here to pick up anyone from your baking club. Far from it. I need to track someone down in a hurry.'

He waved the envelope in the air and instantly saw something in the way she lifted her chin that suggested that she recognized the envelope, but she covered it up with a quizzical look.

That seemed to startle her and he could almost feel the intensity of her gaze as it moved slowly from his smart, black lace-up business brogues to the crispness of his shirt collar and silk tie. There was something else going on behind those green eyes, because she glanced back towards the entrance just once and then swung around towards the back of the room, before turning her attention on him again.

And when she spoke there was the faintest hint of concern in her voice which she was trying hard to conceal and failing miserably.

'Perhaps I could help if you told me who you were looking for,' she replied.

Sean looked up into her face and decided that it was time to get this over with so he could get back to the penthouse apartment at the hotel and collapse.

In one short, sharp movement he pushed himself sideways with one hand, curled his knees and effortlessly got back onto his feet, brushing down his coat and trousers with one hand. So that, when he replied, his words were more directed towards the floor than the girl standing watching him so intently.

'I certainly hope so. Does a Mr D S Flynn live here? Because, if he does, I really need to speak to him. And the sooner the better.'

CHAPTER TWO

*Tea, glorious tea. A celebration of teas from around
the world.*
'A woman is like a tea bag: you never know how
strong it is until it's in hot water.' Eleanor Roosevelt.
From *Flynn's Phantasmagoria of Tea*

'WHAT WAS THAT name again?' Dee asked, holding on to
the edge of the counter for support, in a voice that was
trembling way too much for her liking. 'Mr Deesasflin.
Was that what you said? Sounds more like a rash cream.
It is rather unusual.'

A low sigh of intense exasperation came from deep inside his chest and he stopped patting down his clothes and
stretched out tall. As in, very tall. As in well over six feet
tall in his smart shoes which, for a girl who was as ver-
tically challenged as she was, as Lottie called it, seemed
really tall.

Worse.

He was holding the envelope that she had given to the
hotel manager the first time she had visited the lovely,
posh, boutique hotel to suss out the conference facilities.

They had gone through everything in such detail and
double-checked the numbers when she had paid the deposit on the conference room in October.

So why was this man, this stranger, holding that envelope?

Dee racked her brains. Things had been pretty mad ever since Christmas but she would have remembered a letter or call from the hotel telling her that it had been taken over or they had appointed a new manager.

Who made house calls.

Oh no, she groaned inside. This was the last thing she needed. Not now. *Please tell me that everything to do with the tea festival is still going to plan...please?* She had staked her reputation and her career in the tea trade on organizing this festival. And the last of her savings. Things had to be okay with the venue or she would be toast.

'Flynn. D. S.' His voice echoed out across the empty tea room, each letter crisp, perfectly enunciated and positively oozing with annoyance. 'This letter was all that I could find in the booking system. No name or telephone number or email address. Just an address, a surname and two initials.'

What? All that he could find?

Great. Well, that answered that question: he was from the hotel.

She was looking at her gorgeous but grumpy new hotel manager or conference organizer.

Who she had just sideswiped.

Splendid. This was getting better and better.

The only good news was that he seemed to think that his client was a man, so she could find out the reason for his obvious grumpiness without getting her legs swiped from under her. With a bit of luck.

As far as he knew, she was just a girl in a cake shop. Maybe she could keep up the pretence a little longer and find out more before revealing her true credentials.

'You don't seem very pleased with this Mr Flynn person.' She smiled, suddenly desperate to appear as though she was just an outside party making conversation. 'They must have done something seriously outrageous to make you come out on a wet night in February to track them down.'

Ouch. That was such a horrible expression. The idea that he had made it as far as the tea rooms and was actually hunting her was enough to give her an icy cold feeling in the pit of her stomach which was going to take a serious amount of hot tea to thaw out.

From the determined expression on his face, right down to the very official business suit and smart haircut, this man spelt 'serious'.

As serious as all of the finance people who had tried their hardest to crush her confidence and convince her that her dream was a foolish illusion. She had been turned down over and over again, despite the brilliant business plan she had worked on for weeks, and all the connections in the tea trade that she could ever need.

The message was always the same: they could not see the feasibility of a new tea import business in the current economy. All of the statistics about the British obsession with tea and everything connected with it had seemed to fly over their heads. Not enough profit. Too risky. Not viable.

Was it any wonder that she had gone out on a limb and offered to organize the tea festival so that she could launch her import business at the same time?

Lottie had been her saviour in the end and had pulled in a few favours so that the private bank her parents used was aware that it was a joint business with the lovely, seriously wealthy and connected Miss Rosemount as well as the equally lovely but seriously broke Miss Flynn.

Come to think of it, the banker had been a girl in a suit. But a suit all the same.

'On the contrary, Mr Flynn has not done anything. But I do need to speak to him as soon as possible.'

'May I take a message?' she asked in her best 'innocent bystander' voice, and smiled.

He paused for a second and she thought that he was going to slide over to her counter but he was simply straightening his back. Oh lord. Another two inches taller.

'I am sorry but this is a confidential business matter for my client. If you know where I can find him, it is important that we talk on a very urgent matter about his booking.'

A cold, icy pit started to form in the base of Dee's stomach and something close to panic flitted up like a bucket of cold water splashed over her face.

She blinked, lifted her chin and stuck out her hand. 'That's me. Dervla Skylark Flynn. Otherwise known as Dee. Dee S Flynn. Tea supplier to the stars. I'm the person you are looking for, Mr…?'

He took two long steps to cross the room and shake her hand. A real handshake. His long, slender fingers wrapped around her hand which Dee suddenly realized must be quite sticky from dispensing cake and biscuits and clearing away bowls covered in cake batter.

His gaze was locked on her face as he spoke, and she could almost see the clever cogs interconnecting behind those blue eyes as he processed her little announcement, took her word that she was who she said she was and went for it without pause.

Clever. *She liked clever.*

'Sean Beresford. I am the acting manager of the Beresford Hotel, Richmond Square. Pleased to meet you, Miss Flynn.'

'Richmond Square?' She replied, trying to keep the

panic out of her voice. 'That's the hotel where I booked a conference room for February. And…'

Then her brain caught up with the name he had given her and she inhaled through her nose as his fingers slid away from hers and rested lightly on the counter.

'Did you just say Beresford? As in the Beresford family of hotel owners?'

A smile flickered across his lips which instantly drew her gaze, and her stupid little heart just skipped a beat at the transformation in this man's face that one simple smile made.

Lord, he was gorgeous. Riveting.

Oh, smile at me again and make my blood soar. Please?

And now she was ogling. How pathetic. Just because she was within touching distance of a real, live Beresford did not mean that she had to go to pieces in front of him.

So what if this man came from one of the most famous hotel-owning families in the world? A Beresford hotel was a name splashed across the broadsheet newspapers and celebrity magazines, not *Cake Shop and Tea Room Weekly*.

This made it even more gut-clenching that he had just been in close and personal contact with her floorboards.

'Guilty as charged,' he replied and touched his forehead with two closed fingers in salute. 'I am in London for a few months and the Richmond Square hotel is one of my special projects.'

'You're feeling guilty?' she retorted with a cough. 'What about me? You almost had an accident here tonight. And I could have dropped you. Oh, that is so not good. Especially when you have come all the way from the centre of London late in the evening to see me.'

Then she shook her head, sucked in a long breath and carried on before he had a chance to say anything. 'Speaking of which, now we have the introductions sorted out, I think you had best tell me what the problem is. Because I am starting to get scared about this special project you need to see me about so very urgently.'

He gestured towards the nearest table and chairs.

'You may need to sit down, Miss Flynn.'

A lump the size of Scotland formed in her throat, making speech impossible, so she replied with a brief shake of the head and a half-smile and gestured to one of the bar stools next to the tea bar.

She watched in silence as he unbuttoned his coat, scowled at the missing buttons then sat down on the stool and turned to face her, one elbow resting on the bar.

Nightmare visions flitted through her brain of having to tell the tea trade officials that the London Festival of Tea was going to going to be cancelled because she had messed up booking the venue, but she fought them back.

Not going to happen. That tea festival was going ahead even if she had to rent the damp and dusty local community centre and cancel the bingo night.

She had begged the tea trade organization to give her the responsibility for organizing the event and it had taken weeks to convince the hardened professionals that she could coordinate a major London event.

Everything she had worked for rested on this event being a total success. *Everything*.

Suddenly the room started to feel very warm and she dragged over a bar stool and perched on it to stop her wobbly legs from giving way under her.

Focus, Dee. Focus. It might not be as bad as she was thinking.

'I only took over the running of the hotel today so it has taken me a while to go through all of the paperwork. That's why I only started working through the conference-booking system this afternoon. I apologize for not calling in earlier but there has been a lot of catching up to do and I didn't have any contact details.'

She swallowed down her anxiety. 'But what happened to the other manager? Frank Evans? He was taking care of all my arrangements in person and seemed very organized. I must have filled in at least three separate forms before I paid the deposit. Surely he has my contact details?'

'Frank decided to take up a job offer with another hotel company last Friday. Without notice. That's why I came in to sort out the emergency situation at Richmond Square and get things back on track.'

She gasped and grabbed his arm. 'What kind of emergency do you have?' Then she gulped. 'Has something happened? I mean, has the hotel flooded or—' she suddenly felt faint '—burnt down? Gas explosion? Water damage?'

'Flooded?' he replied, then tilted his head a tiny fraction of an inch. 'No. The hotel is absolutely fine. In fact, I went there straight from the airport and it is as lovely as ever. Business as usual.'

'Then please stop scaring the living daylights out of me like that. I don't understand. Why is there a problem with the booking?'

'So you met Frank Evans? The previous manager?'

She nodded. 'Twice in person, then I spoke to him several times over the phone. Frank insisted on taking personal responsibility for my tea festival and we went over the room plans in detail. Then we had lunch at the hotel just before Christmas to make sure that everything was going to plan. And it was. Going to plan.'

'In any of those meetings, did you see him recording any of your details on a diary or paper planner? Anything like that?

'Paper? No. Now that you mention it, I don't remember him taking any notes on paper. It was all on his notebook computer. He showed the photos of the layout on the screen. Is that a problem? I mean, isn't everything loaded onto computers these days?'

There was just enough of a pause from the man looking at her to send a shiver across Dee's shoulders.

'Okay; I get the picture. How bad is it?' she whispered. 'Just tell me now and put me out of my misery.'

'Frank may have taken your details but he didn't load them onto the hotel booking system. If he had, Frank would have found out that we were already double-booked for the whole weekend with a company client who had booked a year in advance. So you see, he should never have accepted your booking in the first place. I am sorry, Miss Flynn, I have to cancel your booking and refund your deposit... Miss Flynn?'

But Dee was already on her feet.

'Stay right where you are. I need serious cake washed down with strong, sugary tea. And I need it now. Because there is no way on this planet that I am going to cancel that booking. No way at all. Are we clear? Good. Now, what can I get you?'

'I don't understand it. Frank seemed so confident and in control,' Dee said in a low voice. 'And he loved my oolong special leaf tea and was all excited about the conference. What happened?'

Sean was siting opposite and she watched him sip the fragrant Earl Grey that Dee had made for him. Then took another sip.

'This is really very good,' Sean whispered, and wrapped his fingers around the china beaker.

'Thank you. I have a wonderful supplier in Shanghai. Fifth-generation blender. And you still haven't answered my question. Is it a computer problem? It was, wasn't it?

Some crazy, fancy booking system that only works if you have a degree in higher mathematics?'

She waved the remains of a very large piece of Victoria sandwich cake through the air. 'My parents were right all along: I should never trust a man who did not carry paper and pen.'

She paused with her cake half between her mouth and her plate and licked her lips.

'Do you have paper and a pen, Mr Beresford?'

He reached into the inside pocket of his suit jacket and pulled out a state-of-the-art smart phone.

'Everything I type is automatically synched with the hotel systems and my personal diary. That way, nothing gets lost or overlooked. Which makes it better than a paper notepad which could be misplaced.'

Dee peered at the glossy black device covered with tiny coloured squares and then shook her head. 'Frank didn't have one of those. I would have remembered.'

'Actually, he did. But he chose not to use it.' Sean sighed. 'I found it still in the original packaging in his office desk this afternoon.'

'Ah ha. Black mark for Team Beresford Hotels. Time for some staff training, methinks.'

'That's why I am back in London, Miss Flynn.' Sean bristled and put away his phone and started refastening his remaining coat buttons. 'To make sure that this sort of mistake does not happen again. I will personally arrange to have your deposit refunded tomorrow so you can organize a replacement venue at your convenience.'

She looked at him for a second then took another swig of very dark tea before lowering her large china beaker to the table. Then she stood up, stretched and folded her arms.

'Which part of "I am not cancelling" did you not understand? I don't want my deposit back. I want my conference suite. No, that's not quite right.' Her eyebrows squeezed tight together. 'I *need* my conference room. And you...' she smiled up at him and fluttered her eyelashes outrageously '...are going to make sure I get it.'

Sean sighed, long and low. 'I thought that I had made it clear. The conference facilities at the Richmond Square had already been reserved for over a year before Frank accepted your booking. There are four hundred and fifty business leaders arriving from all over the world for one of the most prestigious environmental strategy think-tank meetings outside Davos. Four days of high-intensity, high-profile work.'

'Double-booked. Yes. I understand. But here is the thing, Sean; you don't mind if I call you Sean, do you? Excellent. The lovely Frank made my copies of all of those forms I signed on his very handy hotel photocopier and, as far as I know, my contract is with the Beresford hotel group. And that means that you have to find me an alternative venue.'

'But that is quite impossible at this short notice.'

And then he did it.

He looked at her with the same kind of condescending and exasperated expression on his face as her high school headmistress had used when she'd turned up for her first big school experience in London after spending the first fifteen years of her life travelling around tea-growing estates in India with her parents.

'Poor child,' she had heard the teacher whisper to her assistant. 'She doesn't understand the complicated words that we are using. Shame that she has no chance in the modern educational system. It's far too late for her to catch up now and get the qualifications she needs. *What a pity she has no future.*'

A cold shiver ran down Dee's back just at the memory of those words. If only that teacher knew that she had lit a fire inside her belly to prove just how wrong she had been to write her off as a hopeless case just because she had been outside the formal school system. And that fire was still burning bright. In fact, at this particular moment it was hot enough to warm half the city and certainly hot enough to burn this man's fingers if he even tried to get in her way.

This man who had fallen into her tea rooms uninvited was treating her like a child who had to be tolerated, patted on the head and told to keep quiet while the grown-ups decided what was going to happen to her without bothering to ask her opinion.

This handsome man in a suit didn't realize that he was doing it.

And the hair on the back of her neck flicked up in righteous annoyance.

She had never asked to come to London. Far from it. And what had been her reward for being uprooted from the only country that she had called home?

Oh yes. Being ridiculed on a daily basis by the other pupils because of her strange clothes and her Anglo-Indian accent, and then humiliated by the teachers because she had no clue about exam curricula and timetables and how to use the school desktop computers. Why should she have? That had never been her life.

And of course she hadn't been able to complain to her lovely parents. They were just as miserable and had believed that they were doing the right thing, coming back to Britain for the big promotion and sending her to the local high school.

Well, that was then and this was now.

The fifteen-year-old Dee had been helpless to do anything about it but work hard and try to get through each day as best as she could.

But she certainly did not have to take it now. She had come

a long way from that quiet, awkward teenager and worked so very hard to put up with anything less than respect.

Maybe that was why she stepped forward and glared up into his face so that he had to look down at her before he could reply.

'Exactly. There is no way that I could find another hotel that can cope with three hundred international tea specialists less than two weeks before the festival. Everywhere will be booked well ahead, even in February.'

She lifted her cute little chin and stared him out. 'Here is a question for you: would you mind reminding me exactly how many hotels the Beresford hotel group runs in London? Because they seem to be popping up everywhere I look.'

'Five,' he replied in a low voice.

'Five? Really? That many? Congratulations. Well, in that case it shouldn't be any trouble for you to find me a replacement conference room in one of the four other hotels in our fine city. Should it?' she said in a low, hoarse voice, her eyes locked onto his. And this time she had no intention of looking away first.

The air between them was so thick with electricity that she could have cut it with a cake knife. Time seemed to stretch and she could see the muscles in the side of his face twitching with suppressed energy, as though he could hardly believe that she was challenging him.

Because she had no intention whatsoever of giving in.

No way was she going to allow Sean Used-to-having-his-own-way Beresford to treat her like a second-class citizen.

And the sooner he realized that, the better!

Sean felt the cold ferocity of those pale-green eyes burn like frostbite onto his cheeks, and was just about to tell her what an impossible task that was when there was an explosion of noise and movement from behind his back. What seemed like a coach party of women of all shapes and ages burst out into the tea rooms, laughing like trains, gossiping and competing with one another in volume and pitch to make their voices heard above the uproar.

It felt like a tsunami of women was bearing down on him.

All carrying huge bags bursting with what looked like cake tins and mystery utensils and binders. Sean stepped back and practically squeezed himself against one wall to let the wall of female baking power sweep past him towards the entrance and out into the street.

'Ah, Lottie. There you are!' Dee Flynn cried out and grabbed the sleeve of a very pretty slim blonde dressed in a matching navy T-shirt and trousers. 'Sorry I did not get back to serve more tea. Come and meet Sean. The London Festival of Tea is going to have a new exciting venue and Sean here is the man who is in charge of finding the perfect location. And he is not going to rest until he has found the perfect replacement.'

She grinned at him with an expression of pure delight, with an added twist of evil. 'Aren't you, Sean?'

CHAPTER THREE

Tea, glorious tea. A celebration of teas from around the world.
There are many different kinds of tea, but they are all derived from just one type of plant: *Camellia sinensis*. The colour and variety of the tea (green, black, white and oolong) depends on the way the leaves are treated once they are picked.

From *Flynn's Phantasmagoria of Tea*

Wednesday

'So HOW ARE you enjoying being back in London?' Rob Beresford's voice echoed out from the computer screen in his usual nonchalant manner. His eyebrows lifted. 'Same old madness?'

'Nothing that boring.' Sean snorted and pointed to the bags under his eyes. 'Still shattered. Still jet-lagged. Still wading through the mess Frank Evans got himself into at Richmond Square. I still can't believe that the man we trusted to run our hotel just took off and left this disaster for someone else to sort out.'

Sean's half-brother sat back in his chair and gave a low cough. 'Now, who does that remind me of? Oh yes, your ex-girlfriend. I caught up with the lovely Sasha at the catering-strategy forum last week. She asked me to say hi, by the way. Now, wasn't that sweet? Considering that she dumped you with zero notice. I could almost dislike her if it wasn't for her fantastic figure.' Rob gave a low, rough sigh. 'And that tan… She's looking good, brother. The Barbados hotel seems to be suiting her very nicely and the clients love her.'

'Thanks for the update.' Sean coughed and then squinted towards the computer screen. 'And she did not dump me. It simply wasn't working out for either of us. Trying to co-ordinate our diaries so that we were in the same time zone for more than a few days had stopped being funny a long time before we called it a day. You know what chaos it was last year! You were there, working the same hours as I was.'

Sean turned back to shuffling through a file on the desk. Sasha had been on the fast-track Beresford Hotels management programme and he had been working so hard that he hadn't even noticed that they barely saw one another face to face any more.

Until he'd come back to her apartment at one a.m., exhausted after two weeks on the road solving all the teething problems for a hotel opening, to find Sasha sitting waiting for him.

He had just missed her birthday dinner, the one he had promised that he would be there for. Not even the private jet could fly in tropical storms.

It was a pity that it hadn't been the first time that he'd missed her birthday. They had both worked like crazy over the Christmas and New Year holiday, but February should have been down time. Until the new hotel they were opening in Mexico had flooded only days before the grand opening and a holiday became a distant memory.

They had talked through the night but in the end there had been no escaping the truth. He was the operations troubleshooter and Tom Beresford's son. It was his job to be on stand-by and cope with emergencies. No matter what else was happening in his life. Or who. And she'd wanted more than he was prepared to give her.

It had been crunch time. He could either decide to give her the commitment she needed and deserved or they could walk away as friends who had enjoyed a fun and light hearted relationship and leave it like that.

He had not even bothered to unpack.

'Ah, but I still managed to find the time to enjoy the company of a few lovely ladies,' Robert replied. 'Unlike some people. But that's past history. So last year! Come on; you were in Australia for six weeks scouting for new locations! You must have spent some time at the beach.'

Robert Beresford sat back with his hands clasped behind his head. 'I am having visions of lovely ladies in very small bikinis on golden sands and surf boards. Classy. You have just made my day.'

'I know. I can see you drooling from here,' Sean shook his head. 'That was the plan. Two glorious weeks in Melbourne in February. Two weeks to sleep, soak up the sun and generally have some down time before starting the Paris assignment.'

He waved the conference-booking file at the screen. 'That *was* the plan. And now I am in London instead. Remind me again why I am the one who gets called in to pick up the pieces when the brown stuff hits the fan?'

'Who else is the old man going to call? I am only interested in the food and drink side of this crazy business, remember? There has to be someone in the family who can squeeze into a super-hero costume and fly in to save the day and Annika is way too stylish to wear underpants over her tights.'

Sean laughed out loud and flicked open the event files.

'Now, that is just being mean. I caught those last restaurant reviews. The food critics are crazy about that new fusion franchise you brought in. Kudos.'

Rob saluted him with a hat-tip. 'I'll tell you all about it when we meet up for the conference on Friday. Right? And try and relax. You'll have that mess sorted out by then. You always do. Shame that you can't take some down time before starting the new job. But you never know. You might find some sweet distraction while you are in London.'

Then Sean's gaze caught the lilac envelope that he had popped onto his desk to be filed. He quickly stole a glance at the file he had updated the minute he had got back to his hotel room the previous evening. Complete with the photo of Dee he had clipped from a London newspaper article from the previous October about the opening of Lottie's Cake Shop and Tea Rooms.

The two girls were standing outside the cake shop in what looked to be a cold autumn day.

Dee grinned out to the photographer with a beaming smile which was a lot warmer than the one he had been on the receiving end of. But her colour scheme was just as alarming.

She was wearing a short, pleated green skirt in a loud check-pattern tweed and a knitted top in fire-engine red partly covered with a pretty floral apron. Her blonde friend, Lottie, was in navy trousers and top with the same apron and compared to Dee looked elegant, sedate and in control while Dee looked…like a breath of fresh air. Animated, excited and alive.

That was the strange thing. Even in a digital scan from a newspaper this girl's energy and passion seemed to reach out from the flat screen, grab him and hold him tight in her grasp. She was looking at him right in the eyes. Just as she had in the flesh. No flinching or nervous sideways glances. Just single-minded focus, with eyes the colour of spring-green leaves; it was quite impossible to look away.

But not cold. Just the opposite, in fact. Even when she'd been challenging him to come up with a replacement venue that sexy smile was warm enough to turn up the heat on a cold winter's evening. Or was it that slippery one-shoulder sweater that she had been almost wearing?

He had vowed never to get involved in another relationship after Sasha, and no amount of bar crawling with Rob had persuaded him to change his mind. But there was something about Dee that seemed to get under his skin and he couldn't shake it off.

Maybe it was getting very up close to a client when he had no clue who she was?

It was usual practice in Beresford hotels for the conference manager to take a photo of their client so that the team could recognize who they were dealing with.

Sean blinked and cricked back his neck, which was stiff from stress and lack of sleep. Jet lag. That was it. He had a workload which was not funny and two weeks in London before heading to his new job in Paris. He didn't have time to sort out double bookings and track down conference space in the London hotels.

If only Frank had followed procedures!

'You wouldn't be calling me Superman if you had seen me last night,' he chuckled, then blinked and looked up at the monitor, where Rob was tapping his pen and looking at him with a curious expression.

'Do tell.'

'A girl with green eyes and a wicked judo throw brought me to my knees. That's all I am going to say.'

Rob snorted and sat forward with his elbows on the desk, and that gleam in his eyes which had got both of them into trouble on more than one occasion. 'Now that really is being mean. I need facts, a photograph and vital statistics. Sounds like the kind of girl I would like to meet. In fact, here is an idea—free, gratis and no charge. Bring this green-eyed fiend to the management dinner on Friday night. If you think you can handle it? Or should I have security on standby?'

'What…so you can ogle the poor girl all evening? No way.'

'Then give me something to report back to Annika in the way of gossip. You know she is always trying to set me up with her pals. It's about time our sister focused on you for a change. Are you planning on seeing this girl again?'

Sean checked the clock on the computer screen.

'As a matter of fact, I am meeting up with her this morning. Our latest client has given me a mission and I have a feeling that this lady is not going to fobbed off with anything but the best. In fact, come to think of it, I might need that super-hero costume after all.'

'How about this one?' Dee called out as Lottie swept by with a tray of vanilla-cream pastry slices. '"Flynn's Phantasmagorian Emporium of Tea".'

Then she leant back and peered at the words she had just written in chalk on the 'daily specials' blackboard next to the tea and coffee station.

'It has a certain ring to it and I can just see it on a poster. Maybe dressed up in a Steampunk theme. I like it!'

Lottie gave two short coughs, continued filling up the tiered cake stand on the counter then waved to two of their favourite breakfast customers as they strolled out onto the street.

'You also liked "Flynn's Special Tea Time Fantasies", until I pointed out that some folks might get the wrong idea and think you are selling a different kind of afternoon fantasy experience where you are not wearing much in the way of clothing. And I don't know about you, but I am not quite that desperate to sell your leaf teas.'

'Only people with that kind of mind.' Dee tutted. 'Shame on a nice well-brought-up girl like you for thinking such things.'

'Just trying to keep you out of mischief. Again.'

Dee felt the weight of an unexpected extra layer of guilt settle on her shoulders and she slipped off her stool and gave Lottie a one-armed hug. She had been so focused on organizing the festival that Lottie had done a lot more work than she should have done in the shop. 'Thanks for putting up with me. I know I can be a tad obsessive now and then. I don't know what I would have done without you these past months. Organizing this tea festival has already taken so much of my time; I'm sure that you have done more than your fair share in the shop.'

'That's okay.' Lottie grinned and hugged her back. 'It takes one obsessive to know one, right? Why else do you think I came to you the minute I had the idea for a cake shop? I needed someone who loved tea.'

Lottie stood back and nodded towards the blackboard with the daily specials. 'Tea. Cake. Gotta be a winner.' Then she turned back to the cake stand. 'Turns out that I was right.'

'Any chance that you could sprinkle some of that business-fairy dust in this direction? I am going to need something to give my own special blend of afternoon tea that special oomph, or I'll never make any money out of the tea festival.'

Dee slumped down on her stool and stared out at the breakfast customers who were slurping down her English breakfast tea with Lottie's almond croissants and ham and cheese paninis.

Lottie strolled over and sat down next to her before replying. 'I know that I promised not to get involved, because we agreed that it is important that you do this on your own, but what about all of the exhibitors who will be selling their teas and chinaware and teapots and special tea kettles and the like? Surely they're giving you a fee or a cut in any sales they make on the day?'

'They are. But it's just enough to cover the money I spent on the deposit for the hotel. Beresford is really expensive, even for one day. But I thought that a big international hotel chain like Beresford wouldn't let me down, so it was worth paying for the extra security just to make that there wouldn't be any last minute hassles with the venue. Hah! Wrong again.'

Dee started tapping her tea spoon on the counter. 'After Mr B left I called Gloria to ask if the church hall might be available. The ladies' lunch club loved my last demonstration on tea tasting. I thought that Gloria could put a good word in for me and I might even get it for free. But do you know what? Even the church hall is fully booked for the rest of the month.'

'I thought you said that it was damp and there were mouse droppings in the kitchen,' Lottie replied as she cut two large slices from a coffee-walnut layer cake and tastefully arranged them on the cake stand.

'Yes and yes. Small details. But that settles it; Sean Beresford is going to have to find me a mega replacement venue. Whether he likes it or not.'

'Well, you did have one bonus. The lovely Sean. In the flesh. I didn't think that the millionaire heirs to the Beresford hotel chain turned up in person to break bad news, so he scores a few points on the Rosemount approval board. And, oh my—tall, dark and handsome does not come close.

And he seemed very interested in you. I think that you might be on to a winner there.'

The memory of a pair of sparkling blue eyes smiling down at her tugged at the warm and cuddly part of Dee's mind and her traitorous heart gave just enough of a flutter to make her cover up her smirk with a quick sniff.

Dee pressed her lips together and shook her head. 'Charlotte Rosemount, you are such a total romantic. Can I remind you where that has taken us in the past? I lost track of the number of frogs we had to kiss back at catering college before you finally admitted that not one of those boys was a prince. And then you had the cheek to set me up with Josh last year.'

'It was a simple process of elimination!' Lottie grinned and then twisted her face into a grimace. 'I did get it wrong about Josh, though. He looked so good on paper! His dad was even a director at the tea company and he had the looks to die for. But sheesh, what a loser he turned out to be.'

'Exactly!' Dee nodded. 'And it took me six months to find out that all he wanted was a stand-in girl until someone more suitable came along. No, Lottie. Handsome hotel owners do not date girls who deck them. Well-known fact. Especially girls who give them extra work and refuse to go along with their get-rid-of-the-annoyance-as-quickly-as-possible schemes.'

'Perhaps he likes a girl who can stand up him. You are a change from all of the gold diggers who hit on him on a daily basis. And he liked your Earl Grey.'

'Please. Did you see him? That suit cost more than my last shipment of Oolong. That is a man who fuels up on espressos and wouldn't let carbs pass his lips. He will pass the problem on to someone else to sort out, you wait and see. Big fish, small pond. Passing through on the way to greater things. Just like Josh. I think he only turned up to tell me so that he could tick me off his to-do list.'

'But he is trying to find you a replacement venue. Isn't he?'

'His assistant is probably run off her feet at this minute calling every hotel in London which is still available on a Saturday two weeks before the event. The list will be small and the hotels grotty. And he is not getting away with it. I need a high-class venue and nothing else will do.'

Lottie was just about to reply when the telephone rang on the wall behind them and the theme song for *The Teddy Bears' Picnic* chimed out. She scowled at Dee, who shrugged as though she had not been responsible for changing the ring tone. Again.

'Lottie's Cake Shop and Tea Rooms,' Lottie answered in her best professional voice, and then she reached out and grabbed Dee by the sleeve, tugging hard to make sure that she had her full attention. 'Good morning to you, too, Sean. Why yes, you are in luck, she is right here. I'll just get Dee for you.'

Lottie opened her mouth wide, baring her very white teeth, and held out the telephone towards Dee, who took it from her as Lottie picked up a menu and fanned her face. The message was only too clear: hot.

Dee looked at the caller ID on the phone for second longer than necessary and lifted her chin before speaking.

Time to get this game of charades started the way she wanted.

'Good morning, Flynn's Phantasmagorian Emporium of Tea. Dee speaking.'

There was a definite pause on the other end of the phone before a deep male voice replied. *Excellent*. She had put him off his stride and victory was hers.

Shame that when he replied that deep voice was resonant, disgracefully measured, slow and confident. It seemed to vibrate inside her skull so that each syllable was stressed and important.

'That's quite a name. I am impressed. Good morning to you, Miss Flynn.'

The way he pronounced the end of her name was quite delicious. 'I have just made it up, and that's the idea. And how are you feeling this morning, eh? I hope that there is no bruising or delayed mental trauma from your exciting trip to the tea rooms yesterday evening. I wouldn't like to be responsible for any lasting damage.'

She almost caught the sound of a low chuckle before he choked it. 'Not at all,' Sean replied in a voice that was as smooth as the hot chocolate sauce Lottie made to pour over her cream-filled profiteroles.

'Excellent news.' Dee smiled and winked at Lottie, who was leaning against her shoulder so that she could hear every word. 'So, does that mean you have found me a superb replacement venue that will meet my every exacting need?'

'Before I answer that, I have a question for you. Are you free to join me for a breakfast meeting this morning?'

Dee held out the phone and glanced at Lottie, who rolled her eyes with a cheeky grin, stifled a laugh and headed off into the kitchen, leaving Dee to stare at the innocent handset as though it were toxic.

'Breakfast? Ah, thank you, but the bakery opens at six-thirty, so Lottie and I have already had our breakfast.'

'Ah,' he replied in a low voice. 'Misunderstanding. I didn't mean eating breakfast together, delightful as that would be. But it would be useful to have an early morning meeting to go through your list of exhibitors and put a detailed profile together, so that my team can work on the details with the venue you decide on. Pastries and coffee on the house.'

Dee squeezed her eyes tightly shut with embarrassment and mentally kicked the chair.

Sean Beresford had not only made her toss and turn most of the night, worrying about whether the event was going to happen, but apparently those blue-grey eyes had snuck in and robbed her of the one thing that was going to get her through the next two weeks: the ability to think straight.

Of course, a breakfast meeting wasn't about bacon butties and wake-up brews of tea that would stain your teeth. She knew that. Even if she had never been to one in person.

How did he do it? How did he discombobulate her with a few words? Make her feel that she was totally out of her depth in a world that she did not understand?

It was as though he could see through the surface barriers she had built up and see straight through to the awkward teenager in the hot-weather cotton clothes on her first day in a London high school. In November.

She had known from the first second she had stepped inside that narrow off-grey school corridor that she was never going to fit in and that she was going to have to start her life from scratch all over again. She was always going to be the outsider. The nobody. The second best. The girl who had to fight to be taken seriously in anything she did.

But how did Sean see that? Did she have a sign painted in the air above her head?

This had never happened to her before with any man. *Ever.* Normally she just laughed it off and things usually turned out okay in the end.

Usually.

Dee inhaled a deep breath then exhaled slowly. Very slowly.

Focus. She needed to focus on what was needed. That was it. Concentrate on the job. Her entire reputation and future in the tea-selling business was dependent on it. She couldn't let a flash boy in a suit distract her, no matter how much she needed him to make her dream become a reality.

Dee looked out of the tea-room window onto the busy high street; the first sign of pale winter sunshine filtered through the half-frosted glass. The sleet had stopped in the night and the forecast was for a much brighter day.

Suddenly the urge to feel fresh air on her face and a cool breeze in her hair spiralled through her brain. She quickly glanced at the wall clock above the counter. It was just after nine. Swallowing down her concerns, Dee raised the phone to her mouth.

'I can be available for a briefing meeting. But pastries and coffee? That's blasphemy. Do I need to bring my own emergency supply of tea?'

'Better than that. Following our meeting, I have set up appointments for you at three Beresford hotels this morning. And they all serve tea.'

Dee caught her breath in the back of her throat. Three hotels? Wow. But then her brain caught up with what he was saying. He had set up appointments for *her*. Not *them*.

Oh no. She was not going to let him get away with that trick.

'Ah no, that won't work. You see, I still don't feel that the Beresford management team is fully committed to fixing the problem they have created. It would be so reassuring if one of the directors of the company would act as my personal guide to each of the three venues. In person. Don't you agree, Sean? Now, where shall I meet you?'

CHAPTER FOUR

Tea, glorious tea. A celebration of teas from around the world.

Do you add the milk to your tea? About two-thirds of tea drinkers add the milk to the cup before pouring in the hot tea. Apparently this is an old tradition from the early days of tea drinking, when fine porcelain was being imported from China and the ladies were terrified the hot tea would crack the very expensive fragile china.

From *Flynn's Phantasmagoria of Tea*

Wednesday

DEE STEPPED DOWN from the red London bus and darted under the narrow shelter of the nearest bus stop. The showers that had held off all morning had suddenly appeared to thwart her. Heavy February rain pounded onto the thin plastic shelter above her head in rapid fire and bounced off the pavement of the smart city street in the business area of London.

Typical! Just when she was determined to make a good impression on Sean Beresford and prove that she was totally in control and calling the shots.

She peered out between the pedestrians scurrying for

cover until her gaze settled on a very swish glass-plate entrance of an impressive three-storey building directly across the road from her bus stop. The words Beresford Hotel were engraved on a marble portico in large letters.

Well, at least she had found the hotel where Sean had asked her to meet him. Now all she had to do was step inside those pristine glass doors and get past the snooty concierge. Today she was a special guest of the hotel management, so she might be permitted entry.

What nonsense.

She hated that sort of false pretension and snobbery. In India she had met with some of the richest men and women in the land whose ancestors had once ruled a continent. Most of the stunning palaces had been converted into hotels for tourists but they still had class. Real class.

She could handle a few London suits with delusions of grandeur.

Dee took another look and sighed out loud as the rain faded and she could see the exterior more clearly.

This was one part of town she didn't know at all well. Lottie's Cake Shop and Tea Rooms were in smart west London and she rarely went further east than the theatres around Soho and Covent Garden. The financial and banking part of the City of London past St Paul's Cathedral was a mystery to her.

At first sight the outside of the hotel looked so industrial. Metal pipework ran up one side of the wall; the lift was made of glass and looked as though the architects had glued it to the outside of the stone block building.

There was nothing welcoming or friendly about the entrance at all.

Just the opposite, in fact. It was imposing. Cold. Austere. Slippery and grey in the icy rain.

Where was the connection to that warm and communal spirit that came with the ritual of making tea for people to enjoy?

It was precisely the kind of building she avoided whenever possible. In fact, it gave her the shivers. Or was that the water dripping down onto her jacket from the back of the bus shelter?

Dee closed her eyes and, ignoring the two other ladies waiting at the bus stop, exhaled slowly, bringing her hands down from her cheeks to her sides in one slow, calm, continuous motion.

If there was ever a time to be centred, this was it.

This had been her decision. She was the one who had volunteered to organize the London Festival of Tea. Nobody had forced her to take on all of the admin and co-ordination that came with pulling together dozens of exhibitors, tea growers and tea importers looking for any excuse to show and sell their goods.

But there was one thing that Dee knew for certain.

This was her big chance, and maybe even her only chance, to launch her own business importing tea in bulk from the wonderful tea estates that she knew and understood so well, and the passionate people who ran them.

This was her opportunity to show the small world of the tea trade that Dee Flynn was her father's daughter and had learnt a thing or two after spending the first fifteen years of her life travelling the world from tea plantation to tea plantation. Peter Flynn might have retired from the world of tea importing, but his little girl was right up there, ready to take over and make a name for herself as an importer.

Just because her parents had found out the hard way that there was a big difference between importing tea other growers had produced and running your own tea plantation, it did not mean to say that she was incapable of running a business.

And she was determined to prove it.

Of course, that had been last summer while she'd been working for a big tea-packaging company. Before Lottie had asked her to help her run the tea rooms in her cake shop. Her life had certainly been a lot simpler then.

But she had done it. No backing out. No giving in. No staying put in a nice, safe job in the back room of the tea importers while her so-called boyfriend Josh took the credit for the work she had done.

Josh had been so kind and attentive that her good nature had stepped in the first time he had struggled over a technical report. He really did not have a clue about the tea and had really appreciated her help. For a few months Dee had actually believed that they could have a future together, and the sex had been amazing.

Pity that it had turned out that Josh was waiting for his real girlfriend to come back from her gap year travelling in nice four-star hotels. Walking in on the two of them in bed last August had not been her finest moment.

Past history. Done and dusted. No going back now. And good luck to them both. They were going to need it.

Dee blinked her eyes open and smiled across the street as the rain shower drifted away and she could see patches of blue in the sky above the hotel roof.

Idiot! She was overreacting.

As usual.

This was probably where Sean had his office. There was no way that he could offer her a conference room in a hotel this swanky. This was a five-star hotel for bankers and stockbrokers, not rough and ready tea growers and importers who were likely to drop wet tealeaves on the no-doubt pristine hand-woven carpet.

She was just been silly and she was exhausted from the worry.

Time to find out just what Sean had come up with.

With a quick laugh, Dee shook the rain from the sleeves of her jacket and dashed out onto the pavement in a lull in the traffic as the lights turned to red and the queue of people at the crossing ran across the busy road.

In an instant she was with them, her boots hitting the puddles and taking the splashes, but she made it.

Taking a breath, Dee lifted her chin, chest out, and rolled back her shoulders as she stepped up to the hotel entrance. For the next few hours she would be D S Flynn, tea importer, not Dee from the cake shop.

Stand back and hear me roar.

She flashed a smile at the doorman, who held the heavy glass door open for her, but the frosty look he gave her almost sent her scurrying back outside, where it would be warmer.

With one bound she was inside the impressive building. Shaking off the rain, she looked up and froze, rocking back on her heels, trying to take in what she was looking at.

White marble flooring. Black marble pillars. Tall white orchids in white ceramic bowls shaped like something from a hospital ward. And, in the centre of the reception area, a large sculpture fabricated from steel wire and white plastic hoops hung from the ceiling like an enormous deformed stalactite.

Well, that was one spot she wouldn't be walking under. If that monstrosity fell on her head, the tea festival would be the least of her problems.

Ha. So the interior *did* match the outside.

The only warmth in this room was the hot air blasting out from vents high in the walls.

Dee gazed around the reception area, from the black leather sofas in the corner to the curved white polymer reception desk.

There was no sign of Sean, but she was five minutes early.

Dee started to stroll over to the reception desk but changed her mind. The rail-thin receptionist with the stretched-back, shiny, straight ponytail and plain black fitted suit was collecting something from a large printer on the other side of the desk and probably had not even noticed her coming in.

It might be more interesting to watch Sean work from this side of the desk. As a hotel guest. People-watching was one of her favourite pastimes. And free!

Dee strode over to a black high-back chair and slid as gracefully as she could onto the narrow seat. The stainless-steel legs were about the same thickness as the heels on some of Lottie's designer shoes and she didn't entirely trust the chair to take her weight.

Comfort had clearly not been one of the design specifications for this place.

She stroked the skirt of her cotton dress down over her warm leggings and neatly clasped her hands in her lap.

A butterfly feeling of nerves fluttered across her stomach and into her throat as the heat from the vents started to blow on her shoulders.

Memories of sitting on a hard bench at a railway station at a tiny Indian stop waiting for her parents to come and collect her flitted through her brain. Those had been the days before mobile phones, and her parents would not have used one even if they could, so all she'd been able to do was sit there and wait with her luggage and presents. And wait, worrying that something had happened to them, alone in the heat and crush of the ladies' waiting room, for long hour after hour before the kindly station master had offered to phone the tea estate for her.

It turned out that her dad had been working on a problem with one of the shipping agents and had forgotten that she was flying back from London to spend Christmas with them and that they had agreed that she should take the train to the nearest station that day.

Work had always come first.

Even for those who loved her best in this world.

It had been two years since she had last seen them. She couldn't afford the air fare when she needed every penny for the tea rooms and they certainly couldn't spare any cash to fly back to see her now they were retired.

But it would have been fun to have them here for the tea festival at a Beresford hotel of all places. They would have found this all very grand, and probably have been a bit intimidated, but she had promised to send them photos of the event and write a long letter telling them how it had gone.

And they certainly would have been impressed with Sean Beresford. Now, there was a man with a good work ethic! Her dad would like that.

With those good looks and all the money he wanted, Sean would have pre-booked dinner-and-drinks dates already scheduled into his electronic diary to share with his no-doubt lovely girlfriend.

In fact that might be her now, at the reception desk. All polished and groomed; pretty and eloquent. A perfect choice for the second in line to the Beresford hotel fortune.

Sean would probably be astonished that Dee had taken the trouble to look him up on the Internet. For research purposes, of course.

It was amazing the amount of celebrity gossip his father Tom and brother Rob featured in, but Sean? Sean was mostly photographed shaking hands with some official or other at the opening ceremony of the newest Beresford hotel.

Perhaps he did have some hidden talents.

Dee shuffled out of her padded jacket and picked up a brochure about the hotel spa treatments. She was just considering having hot rocks placed on certain parts of a girl's body which were not supposed to have hot rocks on them when there was a blast of cool air from the front entrance and she shivered in her thin dress as she turned to see who had let the cold in.

It was Sean.

Only not the Sean who had sat on her floor the previous evening. This version of Sean was a different kind of man completely.

He stood just inside the entrance shaking the water droplets from a long, navy waterproof raincoat—a different one from last night, but just as elegant. She could tell because the smiling doorman was helping his boss out of his damp coat and she caught a glimpse of a pale-blue silk lining with a dark-blue tartan stripe. Very stylish. Classy. Smart. A perfect match for the man who wore it.

Sean's face was glowing from the cold wind and rain and he ruffled his hair back with his right hand like a male fashion model on a photo-shoot. The master of the ship. Lord of all he surveyed.

He looked taller somehow. More in control. Last night he had invaded the tea rooms and entered a foreign territory with strange new customs and practices. But here and now the difference shone out. This was his space. His world. His domain. Confidence and authority seemed to emanate out from him like some magical force-field.

No wonder the doorman was happy to take his coat; there was absolutely no mistaking that he was the boss.

She envied him that confidence and physical presence that came from a wealthy family background and the education to match. He had probably never known what it was like to be ignored and sidelined and made to feel second rate. It was as if they were from different worlds.

Sean rolled back his shoulders, picked up his briefcase and strode out towards the reception desk. And as he turned away Dee sucked in the breath that had been frozen in her lungs.

The fine navy cloth of his superbly cut business suit defined the line of his broad shoulders. From the way his legs moved inside those trousers, she wouldn't be in the least bit surprised if Sean made regular use of the gym facilities she had just been reading about in the hotel magazine.

That confident stride matched his voice: rich, confident and so very self-assured of his identity. He knew who he was and liked it.

This version of Sean could have graced the cover of any business magazine. He was the personification of a city boy. A man used to being in authority and calling the shots.

The second son and heir.

A man who would never know what it felt like to have to cash in his pension fund and savings to pay the staff wages.

A lump formed in Dee's throat and she turned her gaze onto what passed for the floral display on the coffee table.

Her sweet, kind father had been too soft-hearted to cut the wages for the estate workers when it had become obvious that his dream tea plantation on Sri Lanka was not able to pay for itself. Those wages paid for health care and made it possible for the workers' children to go to school. How could he take that away from them? How could he be responsible for ruining so many people's lives? But, even when they were selling their possessions, her parents had kept reassuring her that she shouldn't worry, they would get their savings back. It would all work out for the best in the end.

Dee exhaled very, very slowly and focused on the pattern of the marble floor tiles beneath her boots.

Past history.

And it was not—*not*—going to happen to her.

History was not going to repeat itself.

She was not going to lose her tea shop or let her dream slip away. With her contacts and experience, she had the technical ability to go right to the top. Now all she had to do was make it happen. No matter how scared she was.

She had worked so hard to get to this point, she could not afford to let her foolish pride get in the way.

Even if it meant asking for help now and then.

A rustle of activity across the room broke the hushed silence of the reception area and she looked up just as Sean turned away from the desk and saw her.

There must have been something about her that amused him, because she felt those blue eyes scan her entire body in a flash, from the toes of her practical red boots to the top of her head, before they slid down to her face. His gaze seemed to lock onto hers and stay there, unmoving, as though he was trying to decide about something.

Whatever it was, the corner of his mouth slid into a lazy smile which reached his eyes as they locked with hers and held them tight.

The heat of that smile warmed the air between them faster than the hot-air vent behind her legs.

The few hotel guests and staff milling around disappeared and all Dee could see was the handsome man in a suit and tie standing at the reception desk.

It was as though they were the only people in the room.

Dee had often wondered what it would feel like to be the star of the show and the centre of attention. To have people adore you and admire you because you are so very special.

Well, now she knew.

It felt…wonderful.

Instead of squirming away into a corner out of embarrassment, she stretched her head high and stared right back at Sean.

Her blood was thumping in her veins, filling every cell of her body with confidence and life.

And something else. Because, the longer he smiled at her, the more she recognized that tell-tale glint of animal attraction in his eyes. Attraction which had nothing to do with the suit and everything to do with the man wearing it.

Elemental. Raw. Alive.

A look that was flicking switches she had locked down into an off position ever since she'd found Josh in bed with a pretty blonde and decided to focus on her career plans and put herself first for once.

How did he do that? How did he make her want to flick her hair, run out to the nearest department store and buy the entire lingerie department and latest beauty products?

Was there an executive training course for that? Or did it come naturally?

One thing was for certain: this hotel was looking better by the minute.

Sean could not resist smiling as he crossed the floor to where Dee was sitting. She was sitting looking up at him with a look of total innocence and sweet charm. As though she had not planned her outfit today with one single purpose in mind: to knock any chance of sensible thought out of his brain.

A printed floral dress above grey leggings which seemed to have tiny hearts embroidered on them. And her hair? Short, cropped into a pixie style. Textured into a mass of tight brunette curls which any man within a thousand feet would want to run his fingers through and tousle up a bit.

But it was her eyes that captivated him.

Who was he kidding? Those pale-green eyes reached out, grabbed him by the man-parts and tugged him to her with a steel cable that just got tighter and tighter the closer he came.

After Sasha he had set his female-resistance setting on high. But there was something about Dee that was simply irresistible.

She looked like a bright spring flower against the monochrome hotel design scheme. And just as fragile. Slender and small. A greenhouse blossom which could be knocked over in the slightest cold breeze.

No way. This tiny girl was the one who had stopped him falling flat on his face last night. Then had beaten him up verbally.

'Fragile' was not how he would describe her.

Interesting was more like it. Intriguing. Enchanting.

Who was she? Apart from a tea fanatic?

'Good morning, Miss Flynn.' He smiled and stepped forward and held out his hand. 'I am so sorry to have kept you waiting.'

'Actually, I was early,' she replied and her long slender fingers wrapped around his with a firm positive grip before sliding away. 'Couldn't wait to hear what you have lined up for me.'

Completely inappropriate images of what those fingers would feel like on other parts of his body flicked like a video show through Sean's mind and he gave a low cough and took a tighter hold of his briefcase.

He pointed the flat of his right hand towards the office suite. 'I have booked one of the breakout rooms. Shall we?'

'Breakout rooms?' Dee laughed as she got to her feet

and flung her coat over one arm. 'That sounds ominous. Is that where your hotel guests organize the escape committee?'

'Just the conference delegates.' Sean smiled. 'And only when they have had enough of the speakers. Most of the business meetings we hold here need separate rooms where they can hold workshops and seminars away from the main group. It works well.'

'Workshops,' Dee repeated and followed him down a wide corridor fitted with an oatmeal carpet. 'Right. I don't think that I shall be needing any of those.'

'Understood.' Sean nodded and held open the white polymer door to the only small meeting room that was available for the next hour on a busy week day. 'After you.'

Her reply was a quick nod as he stood back, waited for her to step inside, then turned and followed her in.

Only Dee could not have taken more than two steps into the room when she whirled around to face him so quickly that he had to lean back slightly to stop her from swinging her bag into his chest.

Her eyes were wild, flashing green and he could see her breathing fast and light, the pulse throbbing in her neck.

They were so close that he could have reached out and touched her face, or fastened up the top button on her cotton dress which was gaping open slightly as it stretched taut from her coat and bag, revealing that same creamy, clear skin that he had seen last night when she'd worn the one-strap jumper.

'Is something wrong?' Sean asked and looked over her shoulder at the perfectly orderly and clean meeting room with its cluster of tables and chairs.

Dee took one step closer and pressed both hands against the front of his shirt. He inhaled a heady mix of bakery sweetness and spice blended with a spicy floral perfume with a touch of musk which surprised him by being so girly. Sweet. Aromatic. Personal.

She smelt wonderful, but when she lifted her head to reply her gaze darted from side to side with alarm and there was just enough of a quiver in her voice for his every nerve to stand to attention.

'There are no windows in this room. Not one. I can't stay here. No way. No how. No discussion. Borderline claustrophobia. Had it for years. Nothing I can do.'

Then she shuddered and his hands automatically reached out and rested on her hips to steady her, hold her, warm her and sooth away whatever problem was causing her such clear distress.

'Sean, I am really sorry, but I hate this hotel. Do you have another one? Because I have to get out of here. Right now.'

CHAPTER FIVE

Tea, glorious tea. A celebration of teas from around the world.
On a cold winter's day? A piping-hot infusion of ginger and lemon will do the trick. Fruit and flower combinations are brilliant at lifting the spirits.

From *Flynn's Phantasmagoria of Tea*

Wednesday

SEAN ALMOST HAD to snatch his raincoat from the hotel doorman before dashing out onto the pavement. But it was worth it, because Dee was still waiting to cross the busy road, her attention focused on shrugging into her duvet jacket, her bag clenched tight between her knees.

'Dee. Wait a moment. What about our meeting?'

Her head swivelled back towards him and she looked from side to side for a moment before she realized who was calling out. Instantly her shoulders seemed to slump and she fastened up her jacket and slung her bag over one shoulder.

'Meeting? Can we do it over the phone? I really don't want to go back inside.'

She shrugged her shoulder bag higher and sighed out

loud. 'I think that I've embarrassed myself enough for one morning. Don't you?'

Then she pulled a dark-green and gold knitted cap out of her jacket pocket and pulled it down over her pixie cut. 'Right now I am far more interested in finding the nearest piece of park, grass, garden, anything in fact, that will make me forget the white holding cell that I have just been in. Okay?'

Then she noticed the crossing light had turned green and she turned on the heels of her ankle boots and strode forward, her cotton dress swinging from side to side above the grey-patterned leggings.

Her outfit was the perfect match for her personality: stylish, modern and surprisingly sexy. Just like the woman wearing them. The ankle boots were just short enough to display a finely turned ankle and toned calf muscles.

And just like that his libido switched up another level.

What had he told Rob? That he had missed his two weeks in the sun? Well, maybe he could find some of that life and colour right here in London in the shape of Dee Flynn.

He rarely met women outside work, and never dated guests or his employees, so his social life had been pretty static ever since the disaster with Sasha.

But there was something about this girl that screamed out that her open, friendly manner was real. Genuine. And totally, totally original. Which in his world was a first.

She knew exactly who she was and she knew what she wanted. Yet she was prepared to tell him that she had a problem with closed, windowless spaces and she had to change the rules to deal with it.

Sexy and confident inside her own skin.

And she was totally unaware of how rare a thing that was, especially in the hotel business, where most people had hidden agendas. Her goal was simple: she had placed her trust in the hotel and they had let her down. And she needed him to put that right. Because it was personal. Very personal.

Was that why he had taken time out today to meet her when his conference team were perfectly capable of finding a replacement venue in one of the other Beresford hotels in this city?

She marched ahead, then stopped and looked up at the street names high on the wall of the buildings on either side, hesitant and unsure.

'Looking for somewhere in particular, or will any stretches of grass do?'

Dee whirled around to face him, her eyebrows squeezed together, her hands planted firmly on her hips. 'I have no clue where I am. Seriously. I left my street map back at the shop and was too frazzled to jump on the next bus. I would probably end up even more lost. And shouldn't you be back doing your hotel management thing?'

She waggled her fingers in the direction of the hotel with a dismissive sniff.

'What? And leave my special client lost in a strange part of the city? Tut tut. That would be a terrible dereliction of my duties. Please. Allow me to be your tour guide.'

He closed the gap between them on the narrow pavement outside the smart row of shops and waved his right hand in the air. 'As it happens, I know this area very well even without a map. And you wouldn't want to see me get into trouble with the senior management, would you?'

'Is this all part of the Beresford hotel's five-star service?' She asked with just enough of an uplift in her voice to tell him that she was struggling not to laugh.

'What do you think?' he asked, and was rewarded with

a knowing smile before she squeezed her lips together, a faint blush glowing on her neck.

Her gaze scanned his face, hesitant at first, but the longer she looked at him, the more her features seemed to relax and she lifted her chin before replying in a low, soft voice which to his ears was like the rustle of new leaves in the trees that lined the street. The relentless noise of the buses, taxis and road traffic faded away until all he could focus on was the sound of her words. 'I think I would like to see the river. Do you know how to get there?'

Sean nodded, and soon they were walking side by side along the wide, grey stone pavement that ran along beside the river Thames.

'Okay, what was it that made you hate my hotel so much that we had to dash out into the rain?' Sean asked.

Dee winced. 'Do you really want to know? Because I am famous for being a tad blunt with my opinions when asked questions like that.'

He coughed low in his throat and took a tighter grip on his briefcase. 'I noticed. And, yes, I do want to know.' Then he glanced over at her and gave a small shrug. 'It's my job to keep the guests happy and coming back for more. So fire away; I can take it.'

Dee stopped walking and dropped her head back, eyes closed. Her chest lifted and fell inside her padded jacket a couple of times.

'I'm so glad that the rain stopped. I like rain. Rain is good. Snow too. But cold sleet and grey skies? Not so much.'

Then she opened her eyes and looked up at him. 'What were you like when you were fifteen years old?'

The question rocked Sean a little and he took a second before replying. 'Fifteen? Living in London, going to school then working in the kitchens at my dad's first hotel: loading dishwashers, peeling veg, helping to clean the rooms. My brother and sister did the same. We are a very hands-on family and there was no special treatment for any of us. We had to learn the hotel business from the bottom up. Those were the rules. And why do you want to know that?'

'I was born in north-east India. At a tea plantation where my dad was the general manager. He worked for a big firm of Scottish tea importers who owned most of the tea gardens in that district of Assam. And don't look at me like that. I am simply answering your question the long way round.'

'Are you always so curious about other people's lives?' Sean asked.

'Always, especially when I can see the worry on your face. No doubt you have some terribly important business meeting that you should be attending at this very minute instead of putting up with me. As a matter of interest, how long had you given me in your whizzy electronic diary this morning? Just for future reference?'

Sean lifted both hands in the air and gave a low chuckle. 'A whole fifty minutes. So we are still on the clock. Please, carry on. Your delightful childhood in sunny India. That must have been very special.'

She grinned, shook her head, then carried on walking. 'You have no idea. Both of my parents were working estate managers so I was left with my nanny and the other kids to run feral across a huge farm most of the time outside school. It was paradise. I only went down with serious diseases twice and grew up speaking more of the many local languages than English. I loved it.'

'When did you leave?'

'We moved four times to different estates in fifteen years and that was tough. But they all had the same problems and my dad had a remarkable talent for turning the businesses around. He seemed to have a knack for dealing with people and helping them with what they needed. Mostly better education for their children and health care.' Then her voice faded away and she looked out over the wide, grey river in a daze. 'They respected him for that. I'm sure of it.'

'Did you come back to England for your education?' Sean asked and stepped closer to avoid a couple of joggers.

Dee stopped and turned back to face him, and her eyebrows squeezed together as she focused on his question. 'Partly. But mainly because the firm promoted my dad to be a tea broker. We came back to London when I was fifteen.' Then she exhaled and blew out hard. 'Total culture shock. I had been here for holidays many times, but living here? Different thing.'

Then she paused and licked her lower lip. 'That was when I realized how much I had taken the outdoor life for granted. Being cooped up in a classroom with only a couple of small windows to let in air and light started to be a real problem, and my schoolwork suffered. I found that the only lessons where I could relax were the cookery and art classes where we were taught in a lovely sunlit studio extension at the back of the school.'

She looked up at him through her eyelashes, which he realized were not black but more of an intense dark brown.

'I was okay there. Big open patio doors. Lots of space. And colour; lots of colour. The gardens were planted out in wonderful displays of flowering shrubs and plants. Tubs and hanging baskets. Planters everywhere.'

Then she pressed her lips together tight. 'In fact, that studio was just about as opposite as you could get to that windowless, airless cube of a white room we have just escaped from.'

She titled her head to one side and blinked. 'Human
beings are not supposed to be in spaces like that meeting
room of yours. Seriously. What was the designer thinking? Monochrome, hard surfaces. No colour or texture. No
living plants. If I was a business person, it would be the
last place on the planet where I would want to go to work.'

Then she winced and flashed him a glance. 'Sorry, but
you did ask. And I am sure that the bedrooms are very
nice and cozy.'

'Actually, they are exactly the same. We market the
style as minimalist couture. No pictures on the walls and
all-white polymer surfaces and sealed tiling.'

'What about the food?' Dee asked in a low, incredu-
lous voice.

'Micronutrients, hand-harvested seafood and baby organic vegetables. It is very popular with the ladies who
lunch.'

'Not the same ladies who come into our tea rooms.
Those girls can eat! We are run off our feet keeping up
with the demand. But I am starting to get the picture. Oh,
Sean! I don't envy you that job. How do you survive? Oh
no—I've just had a horrible thought. Wait. Wait just one
minute.'

Sean stopped walking and Dee stomped up to him, close
enough that she had to look up into his face.

'Please tell me that this other hotel is not the same! I'm
not sure that I could stand another minimalist venue. Forget
the breakfast meeting. All I want is a replacement venue,
Sean.' And she clutched hold of the lapels of his raincoat.
'Somewhere with windows and light and air where people can enjoy tea. Because you have to understand, that's
what tea is all about. Having fun and sharing a drink with
friends and family. The ceremony and the rituals are optional extras. And you can't do that in a cement basement

garage. Please give me some light and space. Is that too much to ask?'

Her bright eyes were shining. Her hands were on his coat, so it made perfect sense for his right hand to rest lightly on her hip.

'As it happens, this hotel is the first one on my list of options. They have a vacancy a week Saturday and can easily fit the numbers you gave on the booking form.'

He flicked his head over his right shoulder. Dec's stunning green eyes widened in surprise and she took a small gasp of astonishment.

'This was the first of the Beresford luxury five-star hotels. Art deco. Original stained glass. Plenty of natural light, and the conference suite opens up onto the lawns leading down to the river. It's also the same place where I cut my teeth as a junior manager so I think I know it pretty well. And not a minimalist detail in sight. In fact, I would go as far as to say it is old school. So. What do you think?'

'Think? I am too stunned to think. Wow. You can officially consider yourself forgiven.'

And, without asking permission or forgiveness, she leant up on the tips of her shoes and tugged his lapels down towards her so that he was powerless to pull back even if he wanted to.

The quick flutter of her warm breath on his cold cheek happened so fast that, when her soft and warm lips pressed against his skin, the fragile sensation of that tender, sweet kiss was like liquid fire burning her brand onto his skin and in a direct line to his heart.

To Dee it was probably nothing more than a quick, friendly peck on the cheek but when Sean looked into those smiling green eyes he saw his world reflected back at him.

He should have looked away. Made a joke, stepped back and pointed out some of the famous London landmarks that were on the other side of the Thames. But for the first time since Sasha the only thing Sean was interested in was the warm glow and welcome that a pair of captivating green eyes held out to him.

Tantalizing. Alluring. He was held tight in their grasp and that suited him just fine. Forget the cold wind. Forget that they were on a public footpath. Forget that she was a client.

All that he could think about was the red glow on her cheeks, and when she tilted her face to one side the first real smile of the day creased the corners of her mouth and lingered there for a moment before reaching her eyes.

Sean lifted his hand and popped a stray strand of hair back under her knitted hat with one finger. He made sure that the knuckles of that hand traced a feather-light track along cheekbones which were so defined and yet so soft that his skin ached to do it again to make sure that he had not mistaken the sensation.

Instantly her head lifted just a little and those eyes recognized a shift in the electricity in the air between them. It had that same power as the energy bolt he had felt when he first saw her in the hotel, but here it was magnified a hundred times.

It seemed only natural to drop his briefcase to the floor, slip both hands behind the back of Dee's head and cradle her skull. When he bent down and pressed his cheek against her temple, he could feel her breath on his skin, and each breath he took was warmed by the scent of the woman he was holding so close to his chest.

His mouth slid slowly down to her lips, making her take a sharp gasp that told him everything he needed to know.

This was a woman designed for pleasure, and given the chance he wanted to be the one to show her just how good that pleasure could be.

Shame that two cyclists just happened to be speed-racing past them at that very second, laughing loudly, followed by a woman on a mobile phone with a tiny yapping dog on a lead.

Perhaps this was not the place. Dee certainly thought so; she let him go so quickly that he almost overbalanced but held it together by keeping a tighter grip on her waist.

Dee grinned back at him, and suddenly it was as if the sunlight in the break in the clouds above their heads was focused on the genuine warmth of her delight. The grey was gone, replaced by an infectious smile which seemed to reach down inside his very being and twist by several hitches that steel wire of attraction that bound them together.

Irrepressible, fun, real. His sunshine on a grey day.

This was what he wanted. This was what he needed in his life.

This was probably why he stepped back, slid his hand from her hip and held his elbow out towards her.

'May I have the pleasure of being your personal hotel guide on this fine February morning, Miss Flynn?'

Dee looked at his elbow, eyebrows high, as though she was getting ready to give him her very best snarky remark, then flashed him a blushing half-smile.

'Well, if you can stand the scurrilous gossip this will create, I may be prepared to risk it,' she replied and threaded her hand through the crook of his elbow. 'Although, there is something you should know.'

'You have a jealous boyfriend at home who is going to track me down and sort me out if I make a move?' Sean chuckled as they strolled up the path away from the river, Dee leaning slightly into his shoulder because of the height difference.

'Hah! Very amusing. Not a bit. No boyfriend, jealous or

otherwise. I am working on my master plan to take over the tea trade one festival at a time. No time for boyfriends; hell, no. They are far too distracting to a lady entrepreneur like myself.'

'Of course. I completely understand. Today Lottie's Cake Shop and Tea Rooms, tomorrow the world. I can see it now. And a great idea for a franchise.'

'I know. But the tea shop is only one of my many talents.' Dee coughed dismissively. 'I was quite serious this morning when I answered the shop phone. The tea-import business is at the very early stages and I am taking my time to think about the name of the company and how to brand myself. So important, don't you agree?'

Sean opened his mouth to answer then looked down at this girl who was capable of rendering him silent.

Then he looked at her again in silence before replying. She was serious. Totally, totally serious.

And his interest in her just ramped up another notch.

'I do agree. The right name and brand are crucial for creating the perfect image for your company. It has to be unique, creative but easy to recall. Not easy. Which is why there are a lot of companies making serious money working for clients who have exactly that problem.'

His reward was a short nod. 'I had a feeling that you would appreciate my business sense, which is why I plan to launch my new company at the tea festival. That way I get the perfect feedback direct from the experts in the trade. It's an ideal opportunity.'

Then she looked up at him with a sly glance.

'Ah. So this is not just about the tea. Now I understand; you are taking a chance. That's quite something. Brave.'

'Daft more like,' she replied and flashed him a light, quizzical glance though her eyelashes. 'As a matter of interest… Were you…planning to make a move? Just curious.'

'Might be. Miss Curious.'

'Not Miss Anything. The name is Dee, but my friends call me Dee.'

Then she bumped her head against his side. 'Dee.'

Sean slid his hand down his side and clasped hold of her fingers. 'My friends call me Sean. Conventional, but I like it.'

'Sean,' she whispered and the sound was carried away in the breeze like the sound of the wind in the trees. 'I like it too.'

He grinned and took a tighter hold of her fingers. 'Let me show you my hotel. Somehow, I think it might be a perfect match. Ready to find out?'

'Prakash! What on earth are you doing here?'

A slim, elegantly dressed man with a Beresford hotel name-pin on his lapel and a lively open smile turned towards them in the foyer of the stunning hotel. But he did not have a chance to reply because Dee squealed and practically pounced on him, pressing her chest against his suit before pecking his cheek.

Then she stood back and covered her mouth with her hand.

'Oh no, you're working here. Sorry, Prakash. Especially since your boss is right here with me. Do you know Sean?'

Sean stepped forward and in an instant scanned the employee name-badge and mentally made the connections.

'Prakash.' He nodded. 'Of course.' They exchanged a hearty handshake. 'Haven't you just graduated from the management academy? I know my father was very impressed with the whole team.'

'Thank you, Mr Beresford. It was tough but I learnt a huge amount.'

'But what are you doing here?' Dee pressed, looking into her friend's startled face as she grabbed his arm. 'Last time I saw you was when we graduated from catering college and you were all set to run your parents' chain of family restaurants.'

Ah. So they'd been at catering college together. That would explain why Prakash Mohna was looking shell-shocked. He was probably terrified that Dee was going to start sharing some scandalous student prank that they had got up to.

As though a hidden sensor in the back of Dee's head had detected that Sean was thinking of her, when she turned his way her face twisted into an expression that screamed out: *go on, say something snarky about students.*

'Actually, I am the new conference manager. Started yesterday,' Prakash blustered.

'Conference manager.' Dee laughed and thumped him on the shoulder. 'That's brilliant news. Because I, Miss Dee Flynn of Flynn's Phantasmagorian Tea Emporium, need a conference room. In a hurry. Sean here—' she flicked her head over her shoulder in his direction '—found out that I had been double-booked at another Beresford hotel. And several hundred tea lovers are going to descend on London looking for a tea festival a week on Saturday. Do you think that you can help me out? Because otherwise we'll be setting up the stall in this gorgeous foyer.'

Her college friend flashed Sean a look of sheer panic before licking his lips and waving down a hallway. 'Why don't we check the booking system and find out?'

'Is it computerized?' Dee winced.

'Well, yes, but we also have the printed booking sheet as back-up,' Prakash replied, obviously confused, then he nodded. 'Don't tell me that you are still a complete technophobe? Dee!'

She held up both hands in protest. 'Not a bit. I have a laptop. Lottie has set it up for me and I run my world-class tea empire from the comforts of my own home. Progress has been made.'

Then she turned and opened her mouth to say something with that glint in her eye which told Sean that she couldn't resist giving him a sly dig, but Sean saw it coming and cut it off.

'Human error caused the double booking at Richmond Square, so we are going to have to convince Dee that our systems can handle it.'

Sean looked up at Prakash who had pressed a finger to his lips as though he was finding the fact that his boss and his pal from catering college were on first-name terms very amusing.

'I checked the system this morning, Prakash, and we had a cancellation which might fit the bill. Why don't I leave you to look after Dee and sort out the details while I take care of some other business? I'll be just over here if you need me.'

Sean looked up from the reception desk as Dee's laughter echoed out across the marble foyer. She was strolling out of the main conference room with her arm looped around Prakash's elbow.

Right now Prakash seemed to be doing a fine job of charming their latest client and keeping her entertained.

Strange that every time he looked up Dee just happened to glance in his direction and then instantly turn away. With just enough of a blush on the back of her neck to tell him she was only too aware that they were sharing the same breathing space.

Sean paused. For a moment there he thought... Yes, he was right. They were chatting away in what sounded like Hindi.

Of course. She had grown up in India. Nevertheless, it was still impressive.

Dee Flynn was certainly an unusual girl. In more ways than one.

He had made a mistake when he'd walked into the cake shop last night and taken her for a baker or shop assistant.

This girl was a self-employed tea entrepreneur who was organizing what sounded like a very impressive festival on her own.

That took some doing.

She couldn't be a lot older than his half-sister Annika, who had grown into a lovely and talented photo-journalist. But when it came to organisation? Not one of her strengths, and Annika was happy to admit that, even to him.

Even their father had been impressed with how the shy little blonde girl had blossomed into a lovely teenager and confident, beautiful woman with straight As, and a first-class honours degree from a famous university under her belt.

It was an education designed to open doors. And it had.

He loved Annika and was the first to admit that she had achieved her success by working as hard as he had to make it happen. Yet he did wonder sometimes how things would have turned out for them all if their father had not been there to pay for the private education, with a solid back-up plan and financial edge to give them the support they needed.

Things might have been different for all of them if his father had not insisted that all of his children should grow up together: same school, same house most weekends and holidays.

Three children with three different mothers living in the same house had not always been easy—especially for his stepmother—and they had fought and bickered and had vicious pillow fights just like any other children. But Tom Beresford had forged them into a family and he had done it through love and making sure that each one of them knew that he would always be there for them. The one constant in each of the children's lives.

For that, he was prepared to forgive his dad's womanising ways. Rob never stopped teasing him that his little brother was letting the side down by staying faithful to every one of the lovely women who had agreed to put up with a light and fun relationship with him while it lasted.

Sean Beresford did not do long-term commitment. He had seen first-hand the fallout from that kind of life when you were working twenty-four-seven, and he was determined to learn from his father's mistakes.

But to succeed on your own? With parents who worked overseas? That took a different skill set.

Dee was definitely a one-off.

Suddenly aware that he had been totally focused on Prakash and Dee, Sean bent his head over the conference-centre booking system and one thing was only too obvious: Prakash was not going to be very busy for the next few weeks. Far from it. Compared to the previous year, bookings over the winter had fallen by over forty per cent and were only picking up now for spring weddings and business meetings. Summer was busy most weeks but the autumn was a disaster.

Something was badly wrong here. The recession had hit some London businesses more than others, and large conferences were a luxury many companies could no longer afford. Events booked a year in advance were regularly being cancelled.

Sean stretched up and ran his fingers along the back of his neck, anxious not to make a fool of himself. But the girl in the flowery cotton dress and leggings distracted him by strolling across through to the other room, totally confident and completely at ease, with Prakash and his assistant making notes as they walked.

Their half-whispered words tickled the back of his neck and Sean yearned to drop everything and join in the conversation instead of focusing on the work.

Well, at least they would have one happy customer.

The conference centre at this luxury hotel was in a different league from the facilities at Beresford Richmond Square, which was designed for large seminar groups. Most of the time companies booked the whole hotel for the event and organized special catering and personalized planning.

That did not happen too often in a hotel this size... Maybe that was something he could look at?

Sean quickly checked the hotel brochure. Conference delegates could have a ten per cent discount if they stayed here. At Richmond Square it was fifty per cent. And he already knew that this hotel was never fully booked. Ever.

Perhaps he should be thanking Dee for giving him an idea.

He looked up as the door to one of the ground-floor meeting rooms opened and a stream of hotel guests walked past him towards the sumptuous buffet he had already spotted being laid out.

Slipping in right behind them, Dee smiled back at him over one shoulder and waltzed into the dining room with Prakash leaving Sean to stare after her. And the way her dress lifted in the air conditioning as her hips swayed as she walked.

Suddenly light-headed, Sean blinked. Food. Now, that was an idea.

Sean stood in silence as the chatting, smiling strangers filled the space his newest client had left in her wake, and watched as Dee looked over her shoulder with a wry smile, shrugged her shoulders, then turned to laugh at something Prakash said, before they were swallowed up by the businessmen who were clearly desperate for brunch after a hard morning.

The last thing he saw was the slight tilt of her head and a flash of floral cotton as she sashayed elegantly away from him. Every movement of every muscle in her body was magnified, as though a searchlight was picking her out in the crowd for him alone.

This was a girl whom he had only met in person for the first time yesterday.

Strange that he was even now reliving the moment when her body had been pressed against his arm.

Strange how he was still standing in the same spot five minutes later, watching the space where she had last stood. Waiting. Just in case he could catch a glimpse of her again.

The prettiest woman in the room.

And a very, very tantalising distraction.

Sean breathed out slowly through his nose and turned away.

Before Sasha, the old Sean would have already flown in his lady and made dinner reservations, or drinks that would stretch out into the evening with a long, slow languorous seduction as a nightcap.

But now? Now long-term relationships were for men who stayed longer in one place than a few days or weeks at most. Men who were willing to commit fully to one woman and mean it.

His gaze flicked up to the place where Dee had just been and lingered there longer than it should have.

They were different people in so many ways, yet there was something about Dee that made him want to know her better. A lot better.

He would love to have the luxury of being able to take personal time in London, but that was impossible if he wanted to get his job done before leaving for Paris. Even if that temptation came in the shape of a tea-mad beauty who was different from any other girl that he had met for a long time.

A cluster of older men in suits burst into the reception area, blasting away his idle thoughts in a powerful rush of financial chatter and cold air.

Sean gave a low cough and straightened his back as he nodded to the guests.

Nothing had changed. The work had to come first.

He owed it to his father and the family who were relying on him to get things back on track. There was no way that he could let them down. Not now. Not ever.

Not after all that his father had done for him. For all of them.

Sean looked up at the screensaver on the computer: *The Beresford Riverside. A Beresford Family Hotel.*

There it was. The Beresford family. His rock when things had collapsed around him when his mother had been taken ill. His rock when his father had remarried but kept the children together, making sure that they all felt loved and cherished.

His family was all he had. And he was not going to let them down.

Dee was a lovely girl and a new client. He had been friendly and gone beyond the call of duty. The last thing either of them needed was a long-distance relationship which

was bound to end in heartbreak and tears—at both ends
of the telephone. From now on he had to keep his guard.

His family had to come first.

It was time to get back to work.

CHAPTER SIX

Tea, glorious tea. A celebration of teas from around the world.
You can't have a cup of tea without something to go with it: from tiny fairy cakes and English cucumber-and-salmon sandwiches to seafood accompanied by warm green tea in Japan. Tea and food are perfect partners.

From *Flynn's Phantasmagoria of Tea*

Wednesday

DEE GAVE PRAKASH a quick finger-wave and then stood on tiptoe and peered over the top of the frosted glass barrier which separated guests from hotel staff.

Sean was sitting in exactly the same position as she had left him well over an hour ago. A plate with the remains of a sandwich sat next to his keyboard, an empty coffee cup on the other.

'You missed a great meal,' she said, but Sean's focus did not waver from the computer monitor. 'In fact, I am officially impressed. So much so, that I have just come to a momentous decision.'

He flashed her a quick glance, eyebrows high. And

those blue eyes seemed backlit with cobalt and silver. Jewel-bright.

'Okay, Mr B. You win,' Dee whispered in a high musical voice. 'You have pulled out the big guns and wowed me with the most fantastic hotel that I have ever stepped into in my entire life. And the conference suite is light, airy and opens out onto the gorgeous grounds. I am powerless to resist.'

Dee lifted her head and pushed out her chest so that she could make the formal pronouncement with the maximum splendour. 'I accept your offer. The Beresford Riverside *is* going to be the new home of the annual London Tea Festival. Congratulations.'

Then she chuckled and gave a little shoulder dance. 'It is actually happening. I can't wait. Can*not* wait. Just can't. Because this festival is going to be so mega, and everyone is going to have the best time.' Then she clasped her fingers around the top of the barrier and dropped her chin onto the back of her hands so that Sean's desk was practically illuminated by the power of her beaming grin.

Sean replied by sitting back in his swivel chair and peering at her with one side of his mouth twisted up into a smirk. 'Let me guess—Prakash introduced you to the famous Beresford dessert buffet in the atrium restaurant.'

'He did.' Dee grinned then blinked. 'And it is spectacular. But how did you know that?'

He shook his head then pointed the flat of his hand towards her and pulled the trigger with his thumb before sliding forwards again. 'The last time I saw someone so high on sugar and artificial colours was at my sister Annika's fourth birthday party. And I know that you don't drink coffee, so it can't be a caffeine rush. How many of the desserts did you sample?'

Dee pushed out her lower lip. 'It seemed rude not to

have a morsel of all of them. And they are so good. Lottie would be in heaven here. In fact, I might insist that she comes back with me and tries them all for research purposes.'

'Better give me some warning in advance so I can tell the dessert chef to work some overtime,' Sean muttered.

Then he stood up and stretched out his hand over the top of the glass. 'Welcome to the Beresford Riverside, Miss Flynn. We are delighted to have your custom.'

Dee took Sean's hand and gave it a single, firm shake. 'Mega.' She smiled and clutched onto the edge of the conference brochure tight with both hands. 'Righty. Now the room is sorted, we can get started on the rest of the organization.'

'Don't worry about that,' Sean replied and walked around to her side of the barrier. He reached into the breast pocket of his suit jacket, pulled out a business card and held it out towards her. 'Prakash will make sure that you have a great event. I wish you the very best of luck, Dee. If there is anything else you need, please get in touch.'

Dee glanced at the business card, then up into Sean's face, then back at the card.

And just like that, the joyous emotional rush of finding this fabulous venue and knowing that her fears had been unfounded was swept away in one spectacular avalanche that left her bereft and mourning the loss.

This was it.

She was being dismissed. Passed off. Discarded.

So that was how it worked? She'd been given the personal attention and star treatment by one of the Beresford family for just as long as it took to get her booking sorted out. Then she was back in line with all of the other hotel guests. Business as usual. Fuss and bother all sorted out.

She was being discarded as not important enough to invest any more time on.

Just as her parents had been.

She had been forced to stand back and watch her parents lose their tea gardens when the money had run out and the powers that be had refused to wait until the tea could be harvested and sold before pulling the plug.

A one-family tea-growing business had not been a priority customer. Not worth their time. Not worth their money. Not worth spending time to get to know who they were and how they had invested everything they had in that tea garden.

She had been a teenager back then and struggling to cope with the relentless exhaustion of training in a professional kitchen after she'd left catering college, powerless to do anything to help the people she loved most.

Her parents had come through it. They had survived. But their dreams had been shattered and scattered to the winds.

Well, history was definitely not going to repeat itself when it came to her life.

Nope. Not going to happen. Not when she was around.

What made it even worse was that it was Sean who was giving her the big brush-off. What had happened to the man who'd been happy to give her a cuddle only a few hours ago after listening to her life story? Now that same Sean was only too willing to pass her off onto an underling to deal with, so that he could get rid of her and get back to his real job.

No doubt there was some terribly important business meeting that required his attention and he could not possibly waste any more time with the simple matter of a conference booking.

It was such a shame. Because, standing there in his fitted suit, pristine shirt and those cheekbones—lord, those cheekbones—he looked delicious enough to eat with a spoon and a dollop of ice-cream on the side.

Shame or no shame, she recognized the signs only too well. And if he thought for one second that he could get rid of her that easily, he was badly mistaken.

'Oh no,' Dee said in a loud voice which echoed around the reception area, making several of the men in suits glance in their direction. 'Big misunderstanding. I obviously have not made myself clear. No business card; I am not going down that route.'

Then she tilted her head slightly to one side and shrugged before carrying on in a low, more intimate voice, confident that she now had his full attention.

'You screwed up. Big time. So now I have to reprint all of my promotional materials and contact loads of exhibitors to let them know about the new venue. Posters, flyers, postcards to tea merchants and tea fanatics. All have to be done again. Then I have to go back to all of the tea shops and online tea clubs with the new details with only a week or so to go. That's a lot of work to get through, and I have a full-time job at Lottie's.'

She pressed her lips together and shook her head. 'Prakash is a pal, but he does not have the level of authority to spend the cash and resources to make all of those things happen and happen fast. It seems to me to point one way. I am going to need that five-star Beresford service from the man at the top.'

Dee fluttered her eyelashes at his shocked face and there was a certain glint in those blue eyes that was definitely more grey than azure. 'You are not off the hook yet, Mr B. In fact, I would say that this is only the start of the project. Now, here is an idea. Shall we talk though the next steps on the way back to your office? You must be very excited about this opportunity to demonstrate your commitment to customer service. And there is an added bonus: we will be working together even longer! Now, isn't that exciting?'

Sean shrugged into his coat and double-checked the long string of emails before popping his smart phone into his pocket. Apparently the Beresford hotels around the world did not have anything so urgent that he needed to jump on a plane and take off at a minute's notice. So, no excuse. He glanced back towards the conference centre.

Dee was still talking to the scariest office manager in the company, and from the laughter coming out of her office they were getting on like a house on fire.

It was first time he had ever heard Madge laugh.

Almost six feet tall and built like a professional rugby player, his very well-paid, über-efficient and organized manager terrorised the reception areas on a daily basis, ruthlessly checking every guest bill, and even his brother Rob had been known to hide when he heard that Madge was chasing up his expenses.

This was turning out to be one hell of a day of firsts and it was not over yet.

Of course, he had tried to convince Dee that he was already committed to making her event a success.

Sean had introduced Dee to three of the full-time conference organizers who took care of event management, and both of the office admin ladies who provided the VIP business concierge service. They had demonstrated their fax and photocopying equipment; their digital scanners and super-fast laser colour printers; their spreadsheets and floor plans; their menu cards and delegate stationery.

And Dee had smiled, thanked them for their time, promised each of them free tea samples and refused to budge one inch.

In fact, if anything the list of items she had written out in her spidery handwriting on the conference pad she had snatched from his desk was getting longer and longer by the minute.

Madge would sort it out, he had no doubt about that, and he had already asked her to make it her top priority.

But there was no getting away from the fact that Dee Flynn was not a girl who gave up easily.

Sean chuckled low in his throat and shook his head. He could not help but admire her for having the strength to stand up and demand what she believed he owed her.

Problem was, from everything he had seen so far, she had no intention of making his life any easier. At all.

In any way.

Because, every time he looked up and saw her with Prakash or one of the team, his brain automatically retuned to the sound of her musical voice and the way she jiggled her shoulders when she got excited. Which was often.

And when those mesmerising eyes turned his way?

Knockout.

Of course, Dee was not the only reason he found it difficult to settle at the Riverside.

It was always strange coming back to this hotel where he had found out the hard way that washing frying pans and loading dishwashers in a kitchen that could serve four hundred hot meals was not for wimps.

Rob's fault, of course. From the very moment that his older half-brother Rob had announced that he wanted to follow his passion and learn to cook professionally, their father had insisted that he should learn his trade from the bottom up, starting in the hotel kitchens and going to the local catering college. No free rides. No special favours or dispensations from the award-winning chefs the Beresford hotels employed, who had learnt their trade through the classic apprentice system, working their way through gruelling long hours at kitchens run by serious taskmasters.

If that was what his eldest son and heir truly wanted to do, then their father had said he would support Rob all the way. But he was going to have to prove it in a baptism of fire. And, where Rob had gone, his little brother Sean had wanted to follow.

Somewhere in the London house their father had a photograph of Rob in his kitchen whites, standing at a huge stainless-steel sink sharpening a knife on a steel, with his brother Sean at his side scrubbing out a pan as though his life depended on it. Rob could not have been more than nineteen at the time, but he looked so deadly serious. Skinny, unshaven and intense. There were only a few years between them in age but sometimes it felt a lot more.

They had both come a long way since then. A very long way.

The sound of a woman's laugh rang out from the office and his body automatically turned as Dee and Madge strolled down the corridor together.

Now, there was a killer team. Dee was probably five feet and a few inches tall in her boots, but looked tiny compared to Madge, who towered above her in smart heels.

Amazing. Madge even smiled at him after shaking Dee's hand and waving her off as though they were best pals who had known one another for years.

Dee seemed to accept this sort of miraculous behaviour as completely normal, and a few minutes later she had found her jacket and they were outside the hotel and heading for the taxi rank.

Only, before the doorman could hail a black cab, Dee rested her hand on Sean's coat sleeve and asked, 'Do you mind if we walk? The rain has stopped, the sun is coming out and I am so busy in the tea rooms I just know that I'll be cooped up for the rest of the day.'

Sean made a point of checking his wristwatch. 'Only if we go a different route this time. I make it a rule not to go the same way twice if I can avoid it.'

'Fair enough,' Dee replied, shuffling deeper into her jacket. 'And, since you're my tour guide, I shall rely on you completely.'

'You didn't give me a lot of choice,' he muttered, but she heard him well enough.

'You can stop pretending that you are put out by my outrageous request for personal attention. You love it! And I love your hotel. It is gorgeous. Lucky girl; that's me.'

Sean nodded. 'You were very lucky to find the two-day slot you wanted at this much notice. That is certainly true.' He gestured to a side street and they turned away from the busy street down a two-way road lined with stately white-painted Regency houses. 'But, as a matter of interest, what was your back-up plan in case of some emergency? Your Plan B?'

Dee chuckled and shook her head. 'I didn't have one. There is no Plan B. No rescue mission. No back door. No get-out clause. No security exit.'

Sean blew out hard. 'I don't know whether that is brave or positive thinking.'

'Neither,' she replied with a short laugh. 'I don't have anything left in the piggy bank to pay for a back-up plan. Everything I have is in the tea rooms and this event. And I mean everything. If this festival doesn't bring in a re-turn, I shall be explaining to the bank why they won't be receiving their repayment any time soon. And that is not a conversation I want to have.'

Then she threw her hands in the air with a flourish. 'That's why I was having a mini melt-down last night.

But no longer. Problem solved. I only hope that Prakash enjoys his job long enough to stay around.'

'What do you mean?'

'I was only talking to Prakash for a fairly short time, but it's obvious that he feels like a tiny cog in a big machine where nobody knows his name or what he wants from the job. It seems to me that you and your dad and brother have created a training system which is incredibly impersonal and cold.'

Then she paused and twisted one hand into the air. 'Not deliberately. I don't mean that. But you are all so busy.'

Dee gave a small shrug. 'Maybe you could take a few tips from a small business and talk to Prakash and the new graduates one to one, find out what they need. It would make a change from a big, flashy presentation in a huge, impersonal lecture theatre. It might work.'

'That's an incredibly sweet idea, Dee, and maybe it would work in a cake shop, but we have hundreds of trainees. It would take weeks of work to get around all of them and then process the responses. It is simply not doable. I wish it was. But that's business.'

'No, Sean. You can talk to your graduates for days and give the all of the motivational speeches you like but when they are back in their jobs they have to want to do their best work and be inspired by you and your family. Because you motivate them. Not because they feel they have to perform to bring in a pay cheque. Totally different.'

Then Dee shrugged with a casual smile that left him speechless. 'And who would have guessed that your Madge is a total tea addict? And that girl knows her leaves! Only the finest white tea for her. I am impressed. And I hope you don't mind, but I did give her a voucher for a free cream tea if she came to Lottie's.'

'Mind? Why should I mind if you give away free samples?' Sean replied as he dodged a kamikaze cyclist who served around them. 'But you should try our traditional afternoon tea. It is very popular with the guests—and you seemed to enjoy our desserts.'

'Oh, the food would be amazing. That's not the problem. It's the tea you serve.' She winced as though there was an unpleasant odour. 'It's very nice—and I know the warehouse where you buy it from, because I used to work there—but for a five-star hotel? I have to tell you that you have been fobbed off with stale old tea that has been sitting in those boxes for a very long time. It's certainly not up to the standard I expected. Why are you looking at me like that?'

'Fobbed off? Is that what you said?' Sean replied, coming to a dead halt.

'Now, don't get upset. I just thought that I should point it out. For future reference.'

'Anything else you would like to mention?' Sean asked in a voice of disbelief. 'I would hate for all that great free advice to be burning up inside without an outlet. Please; don't hold back. Fire away.'

He ignored her tutting and tugged out his smart phone; his fingers moved over the keys for a second. 'There. The food and beverages director has been alerted to your concerns. And Rob Beresford is not a man who lets standards slip. What?'

Dee was standing looking at him with her mouth half hanging open. 'Wait a minute. Beresford; of course. I never made the connection. Are you talking about the celebrity chef Rob Beresford? The one who runs that TV programme sorting out rundown restaurants in need of a makeover?'

'One and the same. And it's even worse than that. He is my half-brother. And the man may look laid-back, but underneath that slick exterior he is obsessed with the quality of everything we serve and as sharp as a blade.'

A ping of reply echoed out from the phone. Sean snorted and held the phone out to Dee, who looked at it as if he were offering her a small thermonuclear device. 'I thought that might push his buttons. He needs your mobile number. Expect a call very soon.'

Dee stared at the phone and shook her head very slowly. 'I don't have a mobile phone. Never had one. No clue how to use one.' Then she looked up at Sean and chuckled. 'I could give him the number for the cake shop, but Lottie would probably put the phone down on him thinking it was a prank call. Would email be okay?'

Sean stood in silence for a few seconds.

'No mobile phone?'

She shook her head again. 'I live above the shop and rarely travel. My friends know where I live. No need.'

'Tablet computer? Or some sort of palm top?' She rolled her eyes and mouthed the word 'no'.

Sean took back his phone and fired off a quick message, then laughed out loud when the reply came whizzing back.

'Have I said something to amuse you? My life's mission is now complete,' Dee whispered and looked up and down the street as Sean bent over his phone as though she were not there. Then she spotted something out of the corner of her eye just around the next corner, glanced back once to check that Sean was fully occupied and took off without looking back.

Sean did not even notice that she had walked off until he had exchanged a couple of messages with Rob, who thought that the whole thing had to be one huge practical joke, and couldn't believe that a girl who was willing to criticize his tea supplier didn't have a phone. So he came up with another idea instead.

An idea so outrageous that Sean was sure Dee would turn him down in a flash, but hey, it was worth a try.

'Well, it seems that you were right, it really is your lucky day. I have a rather unusual request from my brother. Rob is flying in on Friday for… Dee?'

Sean turned from side to side.

She had gone. Vanished. Taken off. Left him standing there, talking to himself like an idiot. What was all that about?

The girl was a mirage. A mirage who he knew had not retraced her steps to the hotel—he would have spotted that—so she must have gone ahead.

One more thing to add to his new client's list of credentials: impatient. As well as a technophobe.

Sean strolled down the street, and had only been gone a few minutes when he turned the corner and walked straight into one of the local street markets that were famous in the area. Once a week stallholders selling all kinds of handmade goods, food, clothing, books, ornaments, paintings and everything else they had found in the attic laid out their goods on wooden tables.

A smile crept unbidden across Sean's face.

His mother used to love coming to these markets and he used to spend hours every Saturday trailing behind her as she scoured the stalls for what she called 'treasures'. Her collections: postcards of London; Victorian hand-painted tiles; antique dolls with porcelain faces; handbags covered with beads and sequins, most of them missing; cupboards-full of old white linen bedding which had always felt cold and scratchy when he was a boy. But to her eyes, glorious items which were simply in need of a good wash and a good home.

Each item had its own story. A silver snuff-box must have been owned by someone important like Sherlock

Holmes, while a chipped tin car had once been the treasured toy of a refugee who had been forced to leave everything behind when his family had fled. Just as she had done when she'd escaped persecution when she'd been a small girl, arriving in London with her journalist parents and only a small suitcase between them. Simply glad to be safe from the political persecution from the new regime in their corner of Eastern Europe.

The horror of being forced to flee from your home to avoid arrest was one thing. But to start again and make your life a success in a new country was something special. Sean admired his mother and his grandparents more than he could say. They had taught him that hard work was the only way to make sure that you were never poor or hungry again. To build a legacy that nobody could take away from you.

No wonder his dad had adored her.

His dad usually had been working all hours of the day and night at one or another of the hotels, but if he was home when they got back, carrying their bags of assorted 'treasures', he'd used to laugh like a train and go through every single one and pretend to love it.

Happy days.

Happier days.

Sean inhaled a couple of sharp breaths.

It had been years since he had been to a street market and even longer since he had thought about coming here with his mother as a boy. Most of the time he would much rather have been playing football with his mates from school. But now? Now they were treasured memories.

Long years filled with good times and bad. Hard, physical work had helped to block out the bad. Long years when he'd usually been so exhausted that he collapsed into bed at night without the luxury of dreams.

Not much had changed there. He was still working so hard that sometimes the days just melted together into one huge blur.

When was the last time he had walked anywhere? He always caught a black cab or had a limo waiting to take him to some airport. There was no down time. There couldn't be. His work demanded his full attention and he didn't know how to give anything else but his best.

He had paid the price for the hugely successful company expansion.

Only, at moments like this, he wondered if maybe the cost was too high.

Sasha had been the last of a long line of short-term relationships. His friends had stopped calling because there was always some excellent reason why he couldn't make their dinner or meet up for drinks.

All he had left was his family.

Sean stood in silence, overwhelmed by the sights, sounds and smells of the street market, and allowed all of those happy memories to come flooding back.

The sun broke through the clouds and filled the space with light and a little warmth. The birds were singing in the London plane trees which lined the street and, for the first time in months, he felt a sense of contentment well up inside him.

Shockingly new. Depressingly rare.

But for once he did not over-analyze how he felt or push it away.

He simply gave in to the sensation and enjoyed the moment. Each breath of the heady air seemed to invigorate him. The long-standing stiffness in his neck and shoulders simply drifted away. Gone.

He felt engaged and buoyant at the same time.

He shook his head and sighed. Maybe there was something to be said for leaving the hotel now and again.

And he knew precisely who to blame.

The girl who was strolling down between the market stalls, oblivious to the world, a grin on her face and a skip in her steps. Living in the moment and loving it.

Gorgeous, astonishing and totally pushing all of his buttons.

Dee Flynn was turning out to be the best thing that had happened to him in quite a while.

Forget the rules. Forget over-analyzing his schedule and responding to every email that came in. Time to take some of that personal time he was due and had never taken. And he knew who he wanted to share it with.

Dee dropped her head back and felt the sun on her face.

Oh, that felt so good.

Okay, it was a pale imitation of the sun she had grown up with, but right now she would take whatever sun she could get.

'Sunbathing already? Does this mean that you plan to strip off any time soon? Because if you do I can sell tickets and talk up the tea festival at the same time.'

Dee chuckled from deep in her chest.

Sean. His voice was deep, slow and as smooth as fine chocolate. Unmistakable.

She couldn't be angry with this man. Not when the sun was shining and she had a new venue which was ten times more impressive that the Richmond Square hotel—not that she would tell him that, of course.

She lifted her head and turned to face him. And blinked.

Sean was smiling at her with his hands behind his back and a look on his face that made the hairs on the back of her neck stand on end. Tiny alarm bells started to sound inside her head, and as he stepped closer she fought the sudden urge to buy something from the haberdashery stall. Buttons. Ribbons. Anything.

He had something on his mind and she knew before he opened his mouth that it would involve her stepping outside her comfort zone in a serious way.

This must be how antelopes felt before the lion pounced.

'Sorry I spent so long on the phone. Rob had come up with a few ideas about how to make the best use of your advice,' Sean said and then paused.

One more step and he had closed the distance between them, but before she could respond his hand whipped out from behind his back. He was holding the most enormous bunch of tulips that she had ever seen. And he was holding them out towards her.

No—make that bunch*es*. Lipstick-red tulips that called out to be sniffed; yellow tulips still in bud; and her favourite tulip: stripy parrot blossoms in glorious shades of white and red with splashes of orange and flame. All set off by swords of dark-green leaves with pristine, clean-cut edges.

Without a moment's hesitation she clutched the flowers from his fingers and gathered them into her arms and up to her face.

It was spring in a bouquet.

It was heaven.

'I thought that you might like them,' Sean said with a smile in his voice.

She blinked up into his face, and was totally embarrassed to find that she could hardly speak through the closed sore throat that came with the tears that ran down her cheek.

'Hey,' he said in a voice so warm and gentle that it only

made her cry more. 'It's okay. If you don't like them, the flower stall has a great selection of daffodils.'

He ran his hand up and down her arm and bent lower to look into her face. His blue eyes showed such concern that she sniffed away her stupid tears and blinked a couple of times.

'I love them. Thank you. It's just that…'

'Yes. Go on,' he replied, his gaze never leaving her face.

'This is the first time anyone has bought me flowers. Ever. And it is a bit overwhelming.'

Sean looked at her with an expression of complete bewilderment. 'Please tell me that you are joking. Never? Not one boyfriend? Impossible.'

'Never.' She nodded, reached into her pocket for a tissue and blew her nose in a most unladylike fashion.

'Well, that is totally unacceptable,' Sean said and stood back up to his full height. 'You've clearly been treated most shamefully and, as one of the many single men who would love to buy you flowers on a regular basis, I apologize for the oversight.'

Then he smiled with a smile that could have melted ice at fifty paces and which reached his eyes before he opened his mouth.

'Perhaps we can help you to feel more appreciated. Are you doing anything this Friday evening?'

Dee reared back a little and tried to reconnect her brain. 'No. I don't think so. Why?'

'Prakash and the other management graduates are meeting the hotel managers at a company dinner on Friday. Rob is flying in from New York and would love to meet you and talk tea.'

Then Sean lifted her hand that was not busy with the flowers, turned it over and ran his lips across the inside of her wrist, sending all chance of sensible thought from her brain.

'And I...' he kissed her wrist again, his hot breath tingling on the tiny hairs on the back of her hand, his gaze never leaving her face '...would love you to be my date for the evening.'

He folded her fingers into her palm but held her hand tight against his coat, forcing her to look into those blue eyes.

And she fell in and drowned.

'Say yes, Dee. You know that you want to. It's going to be a very special night.'

Words were impossible. But somehow she managed a quick nod.

That was all it took, because the next thing she knew she was walking down past the market stall in the afternoon sunshine with one arm full of tulips. And Sean Beresford was holding her hand.

It was turning out to be quite a day.

CHAPTER SEVEN

Tea, glorious tea. A celebration of teas from around the world.
Visualize a hot summer afternoon. Birds are singing and there is a warm breeze on your face. Scones and jam (no wasps allowed) and refreshing, delicious green tea in a floral-pattern china cup. Bliss.

From *Flynn's Phantasmagoria of Tea*

Thursday

'I DON'T UNDERSTAND the panic. So you're going on a date. With a multi-millionaire. To a management dinner, where all the Beresford hotel bosses will be lined up to kiss Sean's father's feet.' Lottie nodded slowly. 'That makes perfect sense to me. There was bound to be some intelligent man out there who could recognize a goddess when he saw one.'

Lottie waggled the plastic spatula she was holding over the bowl of blueberry-muffin batter in front of Dee's floral-print slimline trousers and canary-yellow long-sleeved top. 'Goddess. Obviously.'

Then she went back to folding in the vanilla and almond extracts and extra fresh blueberries for a few seconds before lifting her head and adding, in a dreamy, faraway voice, 'Why, yes, I did know Miss Flynn before she became the tea consultant to the international hotel chains around the world. But we both knew even then that she was destined for greatness. She had that spark, you see. Special. And she still sends me a Christmas card every year from her Caribbean tax haven. Just for old times' sake.'

Dee gave Lottie a squinty look as she packed napkins into the dispensers on the tables. 'Very funny. Laugh all you like. I'm having a screaming panic attack here. See these bags under my eyes? Haven't slept a wink.'

'I'm not laughing, I'm celebrating,' Lottie retorted as she spooned the batter into paper cases in the muffin tin. 'Sean obviously likes a girl who knows what she wants and can stand up for herself. I know these management types from my old job. They are always looking for something or someone to give them a buzz. You will be fine.'

'A buzz?' Dee groaned. 'I am not trained to give anyone a buzz. Ever. All I know about is tea!'

'Well, for a start that's not totally not true,' Lottie replied as she sprinkled cinnamon and crystallized brown sugar mixed with chopped pecans over the tops of the muffins. 'Who was the star of the celebration-cake contest? And your eggs Benedict are the best. I can only dream of making a hollandaise sauce that good. Remember what I told you when I called you at the tea warehouse and asked if I could buy you lunch? Universities do not award first-class degrees just for turning up. If I am going to set up a business with someone, I only work with the best.'

'True. Three first-class degrees in a class of forty-two.'

'Damn right,' Lottie said as she popped the muffin trays into the oven and set the timer. 'You, me and Luca Calavardi.' She stood up and pressed a sugary hand to her chest. 'Oh, my. Now you've done it. Reminded me about the lovely Luca.'

'Oh, stop. He was fifty-six, happily married with children and grandchildren, and only came on the course because he was fed up with being a sous chef all his life. That man had forty years of catering experience under his belt and we had four months.'

'All the more reason to feel proud of what we achieved. Right? Sean is a lucky man, and you are going to knock their socks off. You wait and see. And in the meantime...' Lottie grinned and looked over Dee's shoulder as the doorbell chimed. 'We have our first customer of the morning. They will probably want tea and plenty of it. Go to it, girl. Show them what you can do.'

Dee popped the last napkin holder onto the tray with a snort and walked out of the kitchen and into the tea rooms. But, instead of her usual customers, a short man in a biker's jacket with a motorcycle helmet over one arm was standing at the counter.

'Delivery for—' he glanced at the screen of a palm top computer '—Miss D Flynn. Have I got the right address?'

'That's me. You have come to the right place.' Dee smiled and leant on the counter with both elbows. 'What delights do you have in your bag today?'

The courier flashed Dee a withering glance, then dived into his rucksack and pulled out a small package the size of a book which he passed onto the counter. Dee barely had time to scratch her name with the stylus onto the computer screen before he was out of the door.

'And thank you and goodbye to you too,' Dee said as she turned the box from side to side. Too small for tea samples or festival flyers. Too large for a personal letter.

Intriguing.

A small, sharp knife and a whole bag of foam curls later, Dee stood in silence, peering at an oblong box. It was covered in fluorescent-pink gift paper with a dark-blue ribbon tied in an elaborate bow on the top. There was a small pink envelope tucked into the ribbon and she hesitated for a moment before opening it up and reading the note.

With thanks for a lovely morning. Operating instructions are included and my personal number is number one on the list.
Prakash is next.
Have fun.
Sean.

Dee had a suspicion she knew exactly what was inside the gift box but she tugged away the ribbon and peeked inside anyway.

Staring back at her from a whole pack of scary accessories and manuals was a very shiny, very elegant version of the smart phone that Sean had been using yesterday. But with pastel-coloured flowers in shades of pink and cream printed onto the silver cover.

'Oh my,' Lottie whispered over her shoulder. 'Please excuse my drool. Your boy has very good taste in toys. Am I allowed to be jealous?'

Dee shook her head. 'I know. And it would be churlish to send it back. But...I'm not sure how I feel about Sean sending me personal gifts. I've only known him two days.'

'Think of it this way—it gives him pleasure to send you a phone, and you need one to keep in touch with the hotel if you are out and about doing your organizing thing. It's a winner. Go on, have a play.'

Lottie finished drying her hands and pointed to the shiny silver button. 'That's the power button.' Then she stood back and smiled before giving Dee a quick one-armed hug. 'There you are. He took your photo yesterday when you hit the streets. You look so sweet carrying those tulips.'

Then Lottie gave a quick chuckle. 'Might have guessed. Dee, darling, I hate to state the obvious but that boy is smitten with you. Totally, totally smitten. And, the sooner you get used to the idea that you are being wooed, the better!'

'Wooed! Have you been sniffing the brandy bottles again? I haven't got the time be wooed by a Beresford. I have a tea festival to organize.'

'Wooed. Whether you like it or not. And, actually, I kind of like it. Sean and Dee. Dee and Sean. Oh yes. And that's my oven timer. Have fun with your phone.'

Dee watched Lottie jog back into the kitchen and waited until her back was turned before picking up Sean's note and reading through it again with a silly grin on her face. He had written it himself, using a pen on paper. That must have been a change for him. The man seemed to live for his technology.

Her foolish and very well hidden girly heart leapt a few beats as she scanned down to the photo he had taken when she'd stopped at one of the market stalls to look at the antique silver teapots.

The girl smiling back at her with her arms full of tulips looked happy and pretty.

Was that how Sean saw her? Or as a girl who had a problem with enclosed spaces who could deck him any time of the day or night?

Her finger hovered over the menu button. She was so tempted so call him right there and then and spend five minutes of easy, relaxed chatter like they had enjoyed the day before. Talking about their lives and how much he missed London sometimes, just as she missed warm weather and the mountains.

Two normal people enjoying a sunny winter's morning. Getting to know one another.

How had that happened?

Dee licked her lips and was just about to ring when a group of women swooped in and headed straight towards her. Customers!

Perhaps Lottie was right. Perhaps she was being wooed. Strange how much she rather liked that idea.

Sean looked out over the London skyline from the penthouse apartment at the Beresford hotel Richmond Square and watched the planted arrangements of ferns and grasses thrash about in the winds that buffeted his high-rise balcony.

No spring flowers or tulips here. Not on a cold evening three storeys above the street level where he had strolled with Dee the previous day.

But she was still with him, and not only in a photo on his phone.

No matter where he went in the Beresford Riverside he could almost hear the sound of laughter and easy chatter. Even Madge had smiled as he'd passed her office.

But it was more than that. Sean felt as though he had been infected with the Dee virus which coloured everything he did and made him see it in a new light.

He had spent the day getting to know the new hotel management trainees. They were a great group of young and not so young graduates: bright, keen and eager to learn. The future lifeblood of Beresford hotels.

It had been a pleasure to take them through some of the Beresford training materials, materials written and tested by experts in the hospitality industry and used in the hotels around the world. And yet, the more time he'd spent standing at the front of the minimalist meeting room at Beresford City, working through the elegant presentation materials while the graduates had scribbled away taking notes, the more his brain had reworked what she had said to him.

Was it really the best way to engage with his staff and motivate them?

Frank Evans was not the only hotel manager who had left Beresford hotels in the last twelve months, and they needed to do something different to keep the staff that were crucial to any hotel business. And it was not just the investment the family made in their training and development; it was that precious connection between the manager, his staff and the hotel guests. That kind of connection took years to build up and could transform customer service.

But it had to come from the top.

Perhaps that was that why he had turned off the projector after a couple of hours and herded these intelligent adults out onto the footpath to the Riverside hotel. He'd let them talk and chatter away as they'd walked, and he'd listened.

It was a revelation. A twenty-minute stroll had given him enough material to completely change his view on how to retain these enthusiastic new employees and make them feel engaged and respected.

The rest of the afternoon had been amazing. He had felt a real buzz and everyone in the room had headed back to their hotels exhausted and dizzy with new ideas and bursting with positivity.

He couldn't wait to tell Dee all about it.

He couldn't wait to see Dee and share her laughter. Up close and personal.

Sean flicked open his notebook computer and smiled at the new screensaver he had loaded that morning.

Dee's sweet, warm smile lit up the penthouse. Her green eyes sparkled in the faint spring sunshine under that silly knitted hat as she clasped the red and yellow tulips to her chest.

She was life, energy and drive all in one medium height package.

The kind of girl who would enjoy travelling on rickety old railways, and always be able to find something interesting to do or someone fascinating to talk to when their flight was delayed. Dee was perfectly happy to spend her days serving tea to real people with real lives and real problems.

She was content to work towards her goal with next to nothing in the way of backing or support, making her dream come true by her own hard work.

His mouth curved up into a smile. He hadn't forgotten the hit in his gut the first time that he had looked into those eyes only a couple of days ago. The touch of her hand in his as they'd walked along the London streets like old friends, chatting away.

Sean turned his screen off, got up, walked over to the window and looked out over the city where he had grown up.

Where was his passion? He was a Beresford and proud to be part of the family who meant everything to him. There had hardy been a day in his life when he had not been working on something connected to the hotels.

Sasha had accused him of putting his work before everything else in his life, blaming him for not having time for a relationship.

But she had been wrong. Sasha had never understood that it was not the work that drove him. It was the love for his family, and especially his commitment to his father.

That was the fuel that fed the engine. Not money or power or success. They came with the job.

When his mother had died of cancer a few short months after that first visit to the doctor, he had shut down, blocking out the world, so that he could grieve alone and in silence. His father was the only person who had been able to get through to him and prove that he had a home and a stable base where he was loved unconditionally, no matter what happened or what he chose to do.

The family would be there for him. His father and his half-brother Rob: Team Beresford.

Damn right. His father might have remarried when he'd gone to university, and he had a teenaged sister on the team now, but that had only made it stronger.

So why was his mind filled with images of Dee, her smile, the way her hair curled around her ears and the small brown beauty spot on her chin? The curve of her neck and the way she moved her hands when she talked?

Magic.

Sean ran his hands over his face.

Was it a mistake inviting Dee to the management dinner and introducing her to the family?

Paris was a short train ride from central London and Dee would love it there.

Maybe he could take a chance and add one more person to Team Beresford?

Only this time it would be for totally selfish reasons. *His own.*

Dee locked the front door, turned the lights off one by one and then slowly climbed the stairs to the studio apartment where she lived above the tea rooms.

What a day!

She never thought that she would be complaining about the tea rooms being busy but they had been going flat out. It was as if the rays of sunshine had encouraged half the tea-drinking and cake-eating population of London out of their winter hibernation in time for a huge sale at a local department store. And they all wanted sustenance, and wanted it now.

The breakfast crew had scarcely had time to munch through their paninis and almond croissants before the first round of sales-mad shoppers had arrived, looking for a carb rush before they got down to the serious shopping, and the crush had not stopped since.

Ending with the Thursday evening young mums' club who held their weekly get-together in the tea rooms between seven and nine p.m. while their partners took care of the kids. And those girls could eat!

Lottie had gone into overdrive and a production line of cakes, muffins and scones had been emerging from the tiny kitchen all day. The girl was a baking machine in the shape of a blonde in whites.

And the tea! Lord, the tea: white; green; fruit infusions; Indian extra-strong. Pots. Beakers. And, in one case, a dog dish for a guide dog. She must have hand-washed at least sixty tea cups and saucers by hand because the dishwasher had been way too busy coping with the baking equipment.

They had never stopped.

But there were some compensations.

Whenever she had a moment it only took one quick glance at the huge display of bright tulips which Lottie had moved onto the serving counter to put the smile back on her face. Sean!

Dee padded through the small sitting room into her bedroom, unbuttoning her top as she went, and collapsed down on her single bed.

She slipped off her espadrilles and dropped her trousers and top into the laundry basket before flopping back onto the bed cover, arms outstretched.

Bliss! The bedroom might be small but Lottie had agreed to a rent which was more than affordable. And it was hers. All hers. No need to share with a nanny or friend or relative, as she'd had to for most of her life growing up. This was her private space and she treasured it.

She bent forwards and was rubbing some life back into her crushed toes when the sound of Indian sitar music echoed around the room and made her almost jump out of her skin.

Dee scrabbled frantically from side to side trying to work out where the song was coming from for a few seconds, before she realized it was bellowing out from the phone that Sean had sent over that morning.

Dee picked it up and peered at it before pressing the most obvious buttons and held it to her ear. 'Hello. This is Dee. And I should have known that you would set my ringtone to something mad.'

'Hello, this is Sean,' a deep, very male voice replied with a smile in his voice. The same male voice that had kept her awake most of the previous night, reliving the way it had felt to saunter down the streets with Sean holding her hand.

Which was so pathetic it was untrue.

It was her choice not to have a boyfriend. And just because he had asked her to be his date at a company dinner did not mean that they were dating. Not real dating. His brother wanted to talk to her about tea. It was a business meeting.

She had tried that line on Lottie, who had still been laughing and muttering something about her being delusional when she'd staggered home.

'I was wondering how you were getting on with your new phone. Do you like it?'

She snuggled back against the headboard and smiled. 'I do like it. It was one of those unexpected gifts that take you by surprise and then make you smile. Thank you. Sorry I haven't had time to call. We have been really busy.'

'No problem. And you can change the ringtone to anything you like. There are several to choose from on the special options menu.'

Dee held the phone at arm's length and made a scowl before holding it closer. Suddenly she felt as though she was being asked to sit an exam and she had not had time to study the subject.

'Sean. It is flowery and shiny, and there are so many touch-screen buttons that working out which one to use is going to take me the rest of the day. If I can stay awake that long. I'm long past the tired stage.'

'I know what that feels like.' He breathed out hot and fast. Then his voice faded away until he was speaking in little more than a whisper that reached down the phone and sent tendrils of temptation into her mind, mesmerizing, tantalizing and delicious. 'So here is an idea—have dinner with me tonight. I know a few restaurants in your part of town and we can have a great meal and a glass of wine while I squeeze in a master class on how to use your phone.'

Just the way he breathed out the word 'squeeze' was so suggestive that Dee almost dropped her new phone.

Dinner?

Oh, that sounded good.

But she was shattered and full of cake.

And not sure that she could sit opposite Sean Beresford without pouncing on him, which would be bad news for both of them.

'That sounds great, Sean, but work has been mad and I ate earlier. And now you have made me feel extra guilty for not calling to thank you.'

'No need. This is the first real break that I've taken all day. And if anything I should be thanking you.'

'Why? Talk to me. After all, that's why you sent me this phone. Wasn't it?'

A gentle laugh echoed down the phone that warmed her in places that even her best hot tea could not reach. It was a laugh designed to tantalize any female within earshot and make her skin prickle with awareness. Right down to her toes. Pity that it was a sensation she liked more than she would ever be willing to confess to a man like Sean. He would enjoy that far too much.

'I was giving a presentation to our new group of trainee hotel managers this morning and after thirty minutes in the all-white holding cell, as you described it so delightfully, I began to understand what you meant by an airless, windowless room. So do you know what I did?'

'You went to the park and sat on benches and fed the ducks.' Dee smiled. 'The wannabe managers had to train the ducks to race for the food and the trainee with the fastest duck got the best job in the hotel chain. Was that how it worked?'

'Ah. Duck training and Pooh sticks are only used in the advanced management courses. These were first-year students. If it had not been raining, I might have given them a treasure map to follow around London, but that option was out. So I decided to take your advice instead and I moved the whole group to the conservatory room at the Riverside, opened every door to the lawns and turned the presentation into a discussion about hotel design and meeting customer expectations. It was fascinating. And useful. Every one of those trainees seemed to come to life in the conservatory. They were transformed from sitting in total silence to being open and chatty and much more relaxed. You should have seen their faces when I told them why we had moved.'

Dee sucked in a breath. 'Did you mention my name so that they could pin it to a dart board for target practice?'

'Not specifically.' He laughed. 'You were a valued event planner who gave me feedback on the repressive feeling of the breakout rooms. But they totally got it, in a way that I couldn't have predicted. Instead of telling them about the impact of room design, they described how they felt in the two spaces and worked it out for themselves. It was brilliant. Thanks.'

'Ah. So that is the real reason for this call. It's confession time. What you really want to say is that you listened to my whining about how intelligent people shouldn't be packed into closed box rooms and then pretended that you had come up with the idea all by yourself. Is that right?'

'Drat, you have seen through my evil plans,' Sean replied in a low, hoarse voice which sent shivers down her back. She imagined him sitting in his office in the minimalist hotel surrounded by all-white marble and smooth, plastic surfaces, and instinctively pulled the silky cover over her legs.

'Are you still at work?' she asked, daring to take the first move.

'I just got back to the penthouse at Richmond Square. The view from up here is fantastic. Pity you aren't here to share it with me. Floor-to-ceiling windows. Breathtaking skyline. I have a feeling you might enjoy it.'

Dee closed her eyes to visualize how that might look and took a couple of breaths before replying. 'Sorry to disappoint you, but I would hate to be one of those girls who only suck up to you because they want to share the view from the penthouse over breakfast.'

The second the words were out of her lips, she winced in

embarrassment. What was it about this man that caused apparently random sounds to emerge from her mouth which bypassed the brain?

'You could never disappoint me. And, as it happens, I know how to make breakfast without needing to call for room service.'

I bet you do.

'I told you that you were cheeky.' Dee smiled and nibbled at one corner of her little fingernail. 'But I may have been mistaken about that.'

'So you do make mistakes?' Sean hit right back across the net. 'And just when I thought that you had all of the answers.'

'Cheeky does not come close. Brazen might be a better description. Does this wonderful breakfast include tea?'

'Dee,' he replied in his rich, deep, sensual tone that reached down the phone and caressed her neck, 'for you, it would include anything you like. Anything at all.'

Suddenly she was glad that she was lying down because her legs seemed to turn to jelly and her throat went dry.

Closing her eyes should have helped but all she could hear was his lazy, slow breathing in her ear which did nothing at all to calm her frazzled brain.

A handsome man who she liked far more than she ought to was holding something out to her on a velvet cushion, gift-wrapped and sumptuous, and she already knew that it would be astonishing.

And terrifying. She was going to have to face him in less than twenty-four hours and somehow she had to get a hold on this out-of-control attraction before it spiralled away into something more elemental which could only ever be a short-term fling.

So she did what she always did when someone came

too close. She put a smile in her voice and hit him right back between the eyes.

'Would that be part of the Beresford five-star service or the VIP special?'

His open and carefree laughter was still ringing in her ear when she said, 'Goodnight, Sean. See you tomorrow.' And she pressed the red button then turned the phone off.

Goodnight, Sean. Sleep tight.

CHAPTER EIGHT

Tea, glorious tea. A celebration of teas from around the world.
Finding the perfect tea to drink with your meal is just as tricky as matching food and wine. One tip: green tea flavoured with jasmine is wonderful with Chinese food but serve it weak and in small cups, and add more hot water to the pot as you drink. And no hangover!

From Flynn's Phantasmagoria of Tea

Friday

IT WAS ALMOST six on the Friday evening before Dee was finally satisfied that all of the leaf-tea canisters were full, the tea pots were all washed and ready for the Saturday rush and that everything the tea rooms needed for an eight a.m. start was in place.

But she still insisted on helping Lottie load the dishwashers, then cleaned the floor and generally got in the way of the last-minute customers, until Lottie had to physically grab her shoulders and plop her into a chair with a steaming cup of chamomile until the closed sign was up on the door.

Whipping away her apron, Lottie poured a cup of

Assam and collapsed down opposite Dee with a low, long sigh before stretching out her legs.

Her fingers wrapped around the china cup and Lottie inhaled the aroma before taking a sip. Her shoulders instantly dropped several inches.

'Oh, I am so ready for this. When did Fridays get so mad?'

'When you decided to have a two-for-one offer on afternoon cream teas, that's when. I have never served so much Indian tea in one session. How many batches of scones did you end up making?'

Lottie snorted. 'Six. And four extra coffee-and-walnut cakes, and three chocolate. And I gave up counting the sandwiches. But the good news is…it worked. The till is full of loot which I will be taking to the bank before the lovely Sean picks up his princess to take her to the ball.'

'The ball? I'm not so sure that I would call a management dinner a "ball". But the food should be good and apparently all the Beresford clan will be there en masse to toast the staff. So there's a fair chance I will score a free glass of fizz.'

Lottie cradled the cup in both hands and sat back in her chair. 'Ah. So that's what the problem is,' she said, then blew on her tea before taking a long sip. 'For the next few hours you are going to be up close and personal with Sean's father and his swanky brother and sister, and you're feeling the pressure. I see.'

'Pressure? I don't know what you mean. Just because his dad founded a huge chain of luxury hotels, and Sean's older brother, Rob the celebrity chef, is flying in from New York especially for the occasion, it doesn't mean that the family will be snooty and look down their noses at me.' Dee flashed a glance at Lottie. 'Does it?'

'No, not at all. Why should they? And if my experience

of management meetings is anything to go by, the owners will be way too busy talking to the staff and making sure they feel the love to worry about extra guests.'

Then Lottie leant her elbows on the table and grinned. 'Think of it this way—you are going to a great night out in a lovely hotel on the arm of a handsome prince. You are a goddess! What can possibly go wrong?'

Dee choked on the tea that went down the wrong way and had to grab a couple of napkins to stop her from spraying Lottie with chamomile through her nose.

'Are you kidding me?' she spluttered. 'I have a long list of things that could go wrong, and the more I think about it the more opportunities I have to put my foot in it. Everything from what I am going to wear, which is a nightmare, right through to my total inability to control the words that spill out of my mouth.'

Her hands came up and made circles in the air. 'And, when it does all go wrong, I can wave goodbye to my free conference centre and any chance I have of finding a replacement venue at this short notice for the tea festival and—' she swallowed '—show Sean up at the same time. Now, isn't that something to look forward to?'

She slid her cup out of the way and dropped her head forward until it rested on the table. 'I am doomed.'

Lottie shook her head and smiled. 'What rubbish. Do you remember that first day we met in catering college? I had come straight out of the business world, had no clue what to expect and turned up to the first morning wearing a designer skirt-suit, four-inch heels and a silk blouse. I thought that the first morning would be paperwork and class schedules, just like university. Instead of which, I spent the whole day gutting fish and making white sauces.'

Dee put her head to one side and sniffed. 'It was a different look, I'll give you that.'

'So you said—right before you passed me your new chef's coat and trousers.'

'I had spares. You hadn't,' Dee replied, sitting up, her shoulders slumped. 'The funniest thing was when you had them bleached and starched at some posh dry cleaners overnight. It was hilarious.'

'It was kind of you to offer me them in the first place. Which is why it is time for me to return the favour. I cannot believe I am saying this, because I think all your clothes are brilliant and suit you perfectly, but if you're worried about not having a cocktail dress to impress Sean's family then I can probably help you out.'

'You're going to lend me one of your fancy posh frocks?' Dee asked in a quiet voice, eyebrows high.

Lottie nodded her head. Just once.

Dee propped her chin up with one finger and looked up at Lottie through her long, brown eyelashes.

'And the shoes and bag to match?'

'Natch!' Her friend slurped down the last of her tea and rolled her shoulders back. 'Good thing we take the same shoe size. Come on; we have a lot to do and not much time to do it in. You, my girl, are going to take time out and celebrate just how much you've achieved whether you like it or not. Let the makeover begin.'

An hour later Dee paced up and down on the bedroom carpet in bare feet, her hands on her hips as she moved from her bed to the wardrobe, then back to the bottom of her bed again.

It was quiet in her bedroom. A chilly, gentle breeze fluttered the edge of the heavy curtains, bringing with it the welcome sound of chatter and traffic from the street below. The sound of normal people living normal Friday-evening lives.

But inside the room the atmosphere was anything but calm.

She stretched out her hand to lift the black fitted cocktail dress from the hanger, then froze. *Again.*

She blinked at the dress hanging on the wardrobe door for several seconds, nodded, then slipped her feet into Lottie's favourite stiletto-heeled sandals and tried a few tenuous steps. Lottie had told her that she should practise walking in them in case she had to take the stairs in the hotel. Four-inch heels with a platform slab under the toes were going to take some getting used to.

Two steps. Three. Then her right foot toppled over sideways on the slippery couture leather and she had to grab hold of the wardrobe door before she almost twisted her ankle as it bent over.

These were not shoes! They were instruments of torture, which had clearly been designed by men who hated their mothers and were determined to make all women suffer as a result. That was the only possible explanation!

And it did not matter one bit if they had pristine red soles if she couldn't walk in them.

Her shoulders slumped and she rested her forehead on the waxed oak panel, not caring that she might destroy the make-up which had taken Lottie an hour to put on, wipe off, then put on again in a different way.

She was terrified that she was sending out the wrong message. Or was it the right message?

She had been aiming for elegant and attractive, while the girl who stared back at her from the mirror looked like a stranger. Some clone from a fashion magazine. Not her. Not Dee Flynn, the wannabe tea merchant.

This wasn't working.

She had been mad even to think that she was ready to

go out on a date with Sean Beresford. Even if it was for only one evening.

She tottered to her bed in one shoe, fell backwards and let her arms dangle over the sides.

She was just about to make herself a laughing stock in exchange for a few canapés and a glass of fizz in a luxury hotel.

Dee bit down on the inside of her lip. Deep inside, where she kept her dreams and most sacred wishes, she knew that she had every right to stride into that hotel in these high-heeled shoes with her head high and stun the lot of them, including Sean. Strong, and confident that she was the equal of anyone there.

She had worked for this success and deserved to be treated like a goddess.

Drat Sean for reminding her that she still had a long way to go.

Dee closed her eyes, her throat burning and tears stinging at the sides of her eyes.

She was pathetic.

This handsome and attentive man had chosen her to be his date for the evening. Which was so amazing that she still couldn't believe it.

The past few days had passed in a blur of activity and mad work.

Sean had kept his word, and Prakash and Madge were now her official best friends in the whole world. Nothing was too much trouble. Extra power points for the hot-water heaters? No problem. Portable kitchen equipment, refrigerators and study tables appeared out of nowhere like magic.

Apparently the word had come down from on high that, whatever Miss Flynn needed for her festival of tea, the team had to make sure happened.

Especially when the boss, the one and only Mr Sean

Beresford, had seemed to find his way into the conference area several times during the day, just to make sure that everything was on track.

Oh, it was on track. *In more ways than one.*

Strange how many times in the day he'd found a way to brush against her hand with his, or look over her shoulder at some suddenly vital piece of information on the floor plan.

She'd had to stop the tickling, of course. That had got completely out of hand and she'd had to scold him about being professional in front of his staff.

Of course, he had insisted on regular tea breaks. Just the two of them, sitting around an elegant table in the hotel dining room, chatting about her critique of the quite good tea the hotel served. And all the while he'd told her anecdotes about his work in the hotel trade which had her clutching her stomach with laughter, and family stories about the antics his brother and sisters got up to.

And maybe it was just as well that she had been kept busy. It had kept her mind from mulling over all of those intimate moments they had shared since he had walked into the tea rooms: the sly glances that set her pulse racing and the gentle touch of his hand on her back or arm. His kindness. His quiet compassion. His humour.

A girl could fall for a man like that.

Hell. She was already halfway there.

Then her smile faded. This evening was turning into a date with Sean when she should be focusing on taking her dream one step closer to being a reality.

And that sent a cold shiver across her shoulders.

She couldn't let the exhibitors down. Some of the tea merchants were coming a long way to show London what tea was all about.

And she couldn't let Sean down either.

No wonder she had the jitters.

Dee stole another glance at the dress hanging outside the wardrobe.

Lottie had done a fantastic job and the girl in the mirror looked every bit the type of sophisticated, elegant girl that Sean was used to having on his arm.

It was the world that Lottie had been born into. A world of luxury and privilege where eating dinner in a Beresford hotel costing hundreds of pounds was something her family did without thinking.

Lottie had her own problems to deal with, no doubt about that, but she could never truly understand what it felt like always to have been the new girl with the second-hand school uniform and the strange accent. Never feeling as though she fitted in. No matter what she did to change her clothes, her hair and the way she spoke, she was always going to be different. And her parents had loved that about her. Loved that she was unique.

Pity that as a teenaged girl going to a city high school the last thing the fifteen-year-old Dee Flynn had wanted to be was unique.

Strange. She thought that she had conquered that particular battle years ago when her flair for catering had taken her higher than she had ever expected.

But that was not the only reason for the jitters.

For the next few hours she would be dealing with Sean's father and his wife Ava, their daughter Annika and Sean's older brother Robert—the professional celebrity chef and current pin-up for a lot of trainee chefs at catering college. And Sean—the blue-eyed boy who had come to her rescue.

How was she going to make polite chit chat with Sean when they had become…what? Event planners? Friends? Or as close to it as you could be when you had spent half the week together.

Dee wrapped her arms around her bare waist, squeezed her eyes tightly shut and relived, once more, the sensuous pleasure of his gentle kiss in the park and the touch of his hand on the small of her back. All of those subtle moments where she had felt him next to her.

No matter that those thoughts had made for very little sleep the night before. In an hour or so she would be seeing him again. Holding him. Just being in the same room within touching distance.

Delicious.

Her eyes flicked half-open and she glanced across at the brightly coloured tulips which she had popped into a plain white milk-jug on her desk. She could smell their fragrance anywhere in the room, and just seeing the blossoms reminded her of Sean all over again.

His laugh. His smile. The expression of pure pleasure and delight on his face when he'd telephoned his brother the other day and talked to her about his family. They truly were the most precious people in the world to him. He loved his family. And they loved him right back.

It would be so special to be on the receiving end of that kind of devotion.

Had it only been a few days since Sean had walked into the tea room? It felt so much longer. And like the tulips he would fade and go out of her life. Back to his hotel chain, bottomless wallet and first-class everything. Back to the life she would never have.

A low groan of exasperation escaped her lips, and she would have wiped her eyes but Lottie had just spent her evening using make-up brushes Dee had not known existed to create the face that she was wearing. She dared not mess it up.

She dared not mess any of this evening up.

Too much was at stake. The tea festival was serious

business and people were relying on her to do the very best she could.

But why now? Of all the times she could have chosen to have a crush, why did it have to be now, and why, oh why, did it have to be on Sean Beresford—the big-city hotel executive with the shiny, shiny lifestyle and looks to die for? The man who was in line to run the Paris branch of the Beresford hotel empire?

Fate had certainly played her a blinder of a hand. And Sean was currently holding all of the aces.

Sean could make her laugh like no other man, and discombobulate her with equal ease. But she dared not tell him. Could not tell him. Letting him know how attracted she was would only lead to heartbreak, disaster and embarrassment on both sides. He had his life and she had hers, and never the twain would meet. Wasn't that how the poem went?

One evening—that was their deal. Sean had kept his side of the bargain. Now it was time for her to keep hers.

Shame it was so hard to remember that fact when he was so close.

She smiled and slipped off the bed.

Maybe Lottie was right—maybe it was time to celebrate everything that she had achieved and take time out to enjoy herself.

Why shouldn't she enjoy his company for this evening? He had asked her to be his date. And that was precisely what she was going to be.

His date. Yes. That was it. Tonight Sean would be her date who she could rely on not to let her down. Even if it did mean never letting him out of her sight.

Sean rang the doorbell of Lottie's Cake Shop and Tea Rooms. Twice. And heard the bell tinkle inside the shop.

There was a bustle of movement from behind the front door and he could see a dark shape slip forward; as he lifted his chin, the ornate half-glass door opened inwards.

A woman dressed in black was standing just a few feet away: slender, medium height and absolutely stunning.

So stunning that he had to do a double take for his brain to recognise who was standing in the doorway smiling at him with a quizzical look on her face.

It was Dee Flynn. Only not the hard working, tea-obsessed version of Dee he had half the week with.

She had been transformed into a completely different person.

This Dee was dressed in a black cocktail dress: sleeveless, with a high collar tied behind her neck with a ribbon. And a low-cut back. Totally hot.

Sean had seen enough French couture dresses, and had bought enough fashion for Sasha and Annika to know the real thing when he saw it.

The dress fitted her perfectly, the fabric draped close to her waist then flaring out over the slim hips to just above the knees.

Sheer black stockings covered long, slim but muscular legs.

Silk shoes with heels so high that for the first time during the week she came almost to his height.

In a flash he could suddenly feel the life force of this woman emanate towards him, and her energy sparkled like the jewels in the gold bracelet on her wrist. Intoxicating, invigorating and bursting with confidence.

She was effervescent, hot and so attractive he had to fight down that fizz of testosterone that clenched the muscles under his dress shirt and set his heart racing just at the sight of her.

'Hello,' he said, suddenly keen to break the silence and

stop the ogling. 'I thought it might be safer to stand out-side just in case you had your judo costume stashed behind the counter. Last time I barely made it out alive.' Then he grinned. 'You look amazing, by the way.'

'Why, thank you. You don't look too bad yourself.' She nodded with her head towards the counter. 'Do you want to come in out of the cold? I just need a minute to get my coat.'

'No problem; we have plenty of time. No need to rush.' He smiled and followed her into the warmth of the tea rooms. He was happy to be able to spend a few extra min-utes alone with Dee before they joined the noisy crush of hotel guests and the management team, who were prob-ably just hitting the bar back at the hotel.

Dee smiled back at him then swivelled towards the back of the room. Then, as he watched in horror, she flung both of her arms out into the air and launched herself towards the counter, as her right foot twisted over sideways and the girl literally fell off her shoe.

Sean leapt forward and grabbed her arm so that she wouldn't fall, and heard her slow hiss of pain as she winced and exhaled sharply.

'Are you okay?' he asked, looking into her face in concern.

Her response was an exasperated sigh followed by a sharp nod. 'Fine. Just dandy. My ankle will survive. Un-like my dignity.'

Then she turned her back on him, feeling stupid and humiliated, and scrabbled to slip the silly shoe back onto her foot and fasten the strap tighter. But her trembling fin-gers let her down and the shoe fell to the floor.

Before Dee could reach down to scoop it up, she sensed his presence seconds before a strong hand slid onto each side of her waist, holding her firm. Secure.

She breathed in a heady fragrance of fresh citrus aftershave and testosterone that was all Sean, which made it impossible for her to resist as he moved closer behind her until she could feel the length of his body from chest to groin pressed against her back.

His arms wrapped tighter around her waist, the fingers pressing oh, so gently into her rib cage and Dee closed her eyes, her pulse racing. It had been a long time. And he smelt fabulous. Felt fabulous.

Sean pressed his head into the side of her neck, his light stubble grazing against her skin, and her head dropped back slightly so that it was resting on his.

Bad head.

Bad heart.

Bad need for contact with his man.

Bad, full-stop.

One of his hands slid up the side of her dress and smoothed her hair away from her face so that he could press his lips against the back of her neck.

'Is there a rule somewhere that dictates that lovely ladies lose all sensible parts of their brain at the sight of shoes they can't actually walk in? Because it does seem to be a very common affliction. I see it everywhere I go. Sad, really.'

Dee tried to pretend that it was perfectly normal to have a conversation with her back pressed against the pristine dinner suit of the most handsome and desirable man she had ever met.

'Absolutely,' she whispered. 'They belong to Lottie, and she promised me that these were the latest thing in limo shoes. Dancing was out unless I wanted permanent disfigurement, but standing in one place could work. Would you mind holding me up here a little longer? I have a small problem standing up straight in Lottie's stilettos and talking at the same time, and you might not be there to break my fall when I try to make it as far as the car.'

He chuckled deep in his chest as though suppressing a smile, and the sound reverberated across her collarbone, down her spine and into regions which were previously closed to reverberations of any kind.

Sean continued to breathe into her neck, and one of his hands slid up from her waist to move in small circles on her shoulder. The room began to heat up at a remarkably rapid rate.

She clasped hold of the serving counter as Sean gently, slowly, slowly, slid down the length of her body until he could reach down and pick the sandal from the floor.

It was quite remarkable that he also needed to touch the inside of her leg with his fingertips as he did so, sending shivers up and down her spine, which made it seriously difficult to breathe, focus and talk at the same time.

'Over the years I have been dragged by the ladies in my family around every fashion shop and footwear retailer in London at one time or another so I could carry their loot home. And we never, ever, bought shoes which they didn't try on in the shop and at least totter a few steps in. Walking any distance—now, that was different.'

She slowly lifted one of Sean's hands from her waist, and pushed gently away from him, instantly sorry that she had broken the touch, but Sean had other ideas and held her even tighter this time as she turned to face him.

Without her shoes, her head came up to his chest and she leant back against the counter so that she could look into the smiling, quizzical, handsome face of a truly nice man.

His eyes never blinked or left hers, and her breathing seemed to match his; it was a few seconds before he broke the silence.

'Did I mention that I am a hotel manager? Yes? I did? Well, we have these terribly practical health and safety standards which mean that I cannot condone any footwear which is likely to lead to personal injury. Not in our hotels.'

He took a step back and held both of her arms out wide as his gaze stayed locked onto her wonky feet.

He flicked one hand in the air and tutted. 'My hands are tied. No choice—you can either slip your shoes off and go barefoot the whole evening, or you pop back inside and change into something you can walk in and stand in for several hours. What's it to be?'

CHAPTER NINE

*Tea, glorious tea. A celebration of teas from around
the world.*
The tea a person chooses to drink for pleasure is as
unique as their fingerprint. Personal and special. And
a true insight into their character.

From *Flynn's Phantasmagoria of Tea*

'I HOPE THAT you are not going to inspect the contents of
my entire wardrobe,' Dee snorted as Sean bounded up the
stairs from the tea shop to her apartment and followed her
along the narrow corridor. 'Because I'm going to tell you
now that my selection of footwear suitable for a conference dinner is rather limited.'

'Not at all.' Sean smiled, enjoying the view as Dee
skipped up the stairs in front of him and trying not to ogle
too blatantly. The memory of her judo training was still too
fresh to forget in a hurry. 'Your delightful choice of clothing has been inspired this week and I expect nothing less.'

Dee came to a dead stop outside a white-painted door
and he held onto the bannister as she looked down at him
with something close to nervousness in her eyes.

'What is it?' he asked with a smile. 'Worried that I will
reveal the terrors of your boudoir to the world?' He pressed
his right hand to his chest, lifted his head and said in a

clear voice, 'As a true gentleman, I promise that your se-crets are safe with me.'

Dee lifted both eyebrows high. 'No doubt. But that's not the problem. It's just that—' she coughed and Sean caught a shy blush at the base of her neck '—Lottie is the only person who has seen my bedroom before, and I am actually quite shy about showing my space to other people. In fact, I think it might be better if you wait downstairs. I shouldn't be too long.'

Sean shook his head very slowly. 'Not a chance. I'm not going anywhere.'

Dee sighed and folded her arms. 'Has anyone ever told you that you are annoyingly stubborn?'

'Frequently. It is one of my finer qualities,' he replied in a light, lilting voice. 'Once I make my mind up about how to do something or a particular plan—that's it. My plans are not for changing.'

She gazed at him for a few seconds before slowly un-folding her arms.

'This tea festival has a lot to answer for,' Sean heard her mutter, but she turned and opened her bedroom door, swinging her shoes in one hand.

Sean stood at the door and took a breath as he tried to take in what he was looking at.

For a small bedroom Dee had managed to squeeze in a wide pale-wood wardrobe and a table under the window. An upright bookcase stacked with papers, magazines and books of all sizes took up the rest of the wall as far as her bedside cabinet.

The walls had been painted in a warm shade of cream. All of the soft furnishings in the room were variations of shades of lavender and primrose yellow, including a cream quilted bed-cover embroidered with tiny blossoms.

The whole room was calm, orderly, clean, serene and

tranquil. Feminine without being over-the-top girly or pretty. It was the type of colour scheme and arrangement several of his interior designers had introduced for the new boutique-hotel range his sister was running.

Sean realized with a shock that it was the exact opposite of what he had been expecting. Shame on him for making judgements about the choices Dee would make in her home. Shame on him for judging her. Full-stop.

A smile crept up on him unannounced.

Dee Flynn was turning out to be one of the most astonishing people that he had ever met.

'You can come in if you promise not to touch anything or criticize,' Dee said as she lifted a silk kimono from the bed, swung open her wardrobe door and pulled out a hanger.

'Thank you. This is…a lovely room.'

She coughed and whirled around to face him.

'Don't sound so surprised. What exactly were you expecting? Did you think I had made a nest of straw from old wooden tea chests or something?'

Sean held up both hands. 'Not a bit. I simply didn't think that you would go for a Scandinavian colour scheme with an English twist. Most of your clothes seem bright and Far Eastern. I thought you might have chosen an ethnic style—something bright. That's all.'

'Ah, you were expecting to see rainbow colours and dark wood. I see what you mean. This must be really quite shocking. But you forget that this is where I come to relax at the end of the day. I need this quiet space to help me centre myself and calm down and focus. Otherwise, I think I really would go nuts with the chaos that is my daily life.'

'Well, I know what that feels like. Especially with jet lag,' Sean replied and squeezed past her and picked up a silver-framed photograph from her computer desk.

A tall, slender, grey-haired man in white tunic and trousers was standing with one hand resting on a wooden balcony, the other hand across the shoulders of a dark-haired woman wearing a bright azure top and wrap skirt. All around them was exuberant green foliage, and a riot of flowering plants of all shapes and colours spilled out from pots and planters.

'Are these your parents?' he asked, and gestured with his head towards the photo.

Dee put down a shoe box and came and stood next to him.

'Yup. That's Mum and Dad on the veranda of the house they are renting in Sri Lanka. They love it there and I certainly cannot see them coming back to the UK now that they are both retired, especially in winter. The lifestyle is so different for retired people in a hot climate. And they can make their pension go a long way.'

'Do you see them often?'

'Once a year I save up for a flight and set up some appointments at the tea plantations. It's an amazing treat, and tax deductible. Actually, the owner of the estate where my folks live will be at the tea festival next week. It will be nice to see him again, even if he is a tough negotiator when it comes to his best tea. Mum and Dad get on with him and he treats the estate workers very well.'

'So you only see them once a year? That must be tough. Do they have Internet?'

She threw back her head and laughed out loud. 'Oh please, don't make me laugh. It took Lottie an hour to put this make-up on and she will go mad if I wipe it all off. But in answer to your question...' she dabbed the corner of her eyes with a tissue '...my folks are anti-technology in a big way. That place they are renting has a generator which breaks down at regular intervals but they get by without it most of the time. So, no—no Internet, computer, mobile phone or anything close to what they think is the curse of western culture. But they do write lovely letters. And for that I am thankful.'

Then she paused. 'And I'm talking way too much and not looking for shoes and we have a deadline. Righty; how about these?'

Dee turned and was about to dive into the shoebox when Sean stepped closer and took a gentle hold of both of her arms and smiled. 'I would much rather listen to you talking about your parents all evening than face the trainee managers. My seminar on time management and productivity can wait until tomorrow. Because right now I have a much more pressing task. I owe you a huge apology, Miss Flynn.'

She cleared her throat and stared back at him wide-eyed. And blinked. Twice. Then waited in silence for him to finish.

'When I fell into the tea shop the other evening and you decked me so delightfully, I filed you neatly away into a box labelled "sexy baker lady" who was responsible for my undignified first view of the tea rooms sitting on my butt. Ah; don't tut at me like that, because as it happens my view has changed.'

He flashed her a quick wink. 'Not about the sexy—that's still up there—but I was temporarily blinded by the force of your exuberance into thinking that you might be exactly what you appear to be.'

Sean shook his head, looked around the bedroom and exhaled slowly as he moved his head from side to side. 'Wrong. A thousand times wrong. Every day this week you have turned up to work wearing a riot of colour and pattern which has livened up my life and that of everyone you have met. But I am starting to see that that is only one tiny part of who you are.'

Then he stepped closer, then closer still, until he was totally inside her personal space, their bodies almost touching, tantalizingly close. So close that there was scarcely enough room for his hands to slide lightly onto her hips.

'You fascinate me, Dee Flynn. How many sides to you are there? And, more importantly, why are you keeping them hidden? Tell me, because I would really love to know.'

'Why do I wear bright clothing? That's easy, Sean. It's human nature to judge a book by its cover. You look at the clothes people are wearing and you make an instant judgement about who they are and what they do and where they fit in this crazy world. Especially in Britain, where the class system rules whether we like it or not.'

Her gaze scanned his body from head to toe.

'Look at you—you go to work in a smart suit and shiny black shoes every day. I've never seen you in jeans and a T-shirt. Perhaps you don't own those things. Perhaps this is who you are. And that's fine. You own that suit; it's gorgeous. And it's your job.'

Dee gave a small shrug. 'But the rest of us? The rest of us are doing the best we can to build bridges with people and make connections. I designed most of my day clothes, and they are friendly, open and welcoming for when I am working in the tea rooms. I love wearing them and it gives me pleasure. Practical too. They fit my personality. They express who I am. They are honest and real.'

'So why are you wearing black this evening?'

Dee slid out of his arms, paced over to the window and drew back the curtain so that the cool night air played on her bare arms.

'Isn't it obvious, Sean?'

'Not to me. Talk to me, Dee. Why black?'

She seemed to hesitate for a few seconds before whirling back towards him, and he was shocked to see tears in the corners of her glistening eyes.

'I didn't want to show you up. There; that's it. Happy now?'

Each word hit him right between the eyes like a high-velocity ice cube that melted the second it reached his heart, which burned hot and angry.

No other woman had ever done that for him.

Wanted that for him.

She was not wearing this lovely couture outfit to impress the big cheeses—she was wearing it so that she did not embarrass him.

And it blew him away.

Sean ran his fingers along the slippery silk fabric of her silk kimono strewn on the bedcover. For once in his life, words were impossible.

He slipped his dinner jacket onto the back of the small desk-chair and took a second before turning back to face his amazing woman.

'Not many people surprise me, Dee,' he managed to say. 'Not after a lifetime working in the hotel trade.'

Then he smiled and tapped the end of her nose with his forefinger. 'You don't need a little black dress to make you feel special. You could wear an old bath towel and still be gorgeous. Look at you. No, don't pull away like that. I think that it's time that you saw yourself through my eyes.'

'What are you doing? We're going to be late,' Dee protested.

'Then we are going to be late. You are more important than a room full of hotel management any day of the week. Okay? Besides, you have already pointed out that I have that stubborn streak, remember? I am not leaving this room until you have changed out of this dress and put on something which you love. Something you have chosen. Something you feel wonderful and special in. Then I might help you to choose the shoes.'

'You want me to change? Into what? This dress was really expensive. I don't have anything in my wardrobe to match it.'

'I didn't ask for an expensive dress to keep me company this evening. I asked you—Dervla Skylark Flynn. Not some designer clone. In fact, here is a challenge. What's the one outfit you possess which is the exact opposite of a black designer dress? Come on, you must have one.'

She snorted and shook her head. 'You mean my sari? I can't wear that to a hotel dinner when all of your clan will be there.'

'Yes.' He smiled. 'You can.' And then he bit down on his lower lip and stepped in closer. So close that his chest was pressed against hers as he held her tight around the waist with both hands flat on her back.

'But first we have to get you out of this dress. And, since I am the one who is insisting on it, I feel that it is my duty to help you.' His lips brushed lightly across her forehead. 'Every...' he moved onto her temple '...inch...' then her neck, nuzzling into the space below her ear with his cheek '...of the way.'

Dee closed her eyes and revelled in the glorious sensation of his cheek against hers, the feeling of his hot breath on her neck, the gentle friction of his hair on her ear. Whatever cologne or aftershave he was wearing should have been labelled with a hazard code and stored away in a bomb-proof box, because her sensitive nose and palate were overwhelmed with the rich, aromatic aroma blended with a base note that was nothing to do with a chemical laboratory and everything to do with the man who was wearing it.

Of course, she could feel the sensation of his fingers moving on her back but pressed so tight against his body it was suddenly irrelevant—the only thing that mattered was Sean and this moment they were together. Future. Past. Nothing else mattered but this moment. It was glorious.

So when he slowly, slowly inched his head away from her it was a shock. She eased open her eyes to find that his breathing was as fast as hers and she could see the pulse of the blood in the vein in his neck. Those blue eyes were wide, and the pupils startling deep and dark pools. Dark water so deep that she knew that she could dive into them and never find the bottom.

The intensity of that look was almost overwhelming and so mesmerizing that she could not break away.

No other man had ever looked at her like this before but she recognized it for what it was, and her heart sang. *It was desire.*

Seduction burned in Sean's eyes. Hot and passionate and all-consuming.

His desire for her.

And it astonished her.

Astonished her so much that she forgot to be scared of all of the chaos that love, desire and passion could bring and focused on the joy instead.

He wanted her.

He wanted her badly.

And the huge red switch marked 'danger' that had been buried under a lifetime of disappointment and making do with second-hand love suddenly and instantly flicked up and turned green.

She wanted him right back. On her single bed. And wearing Lottie's posh frock. Forget slow, she wanted fast. She wanted it all and she wanted it now.

It was almost a relief to turn in the circle of his arms

so that she could not feel the burning heat of his intense gaze scorching her face.

But that was nothing compared to what she saw when she opened her eyes fully.

She was standing in front of her full-length bedroom mirror on the wardrobe door with Sean standing behind her.

Instinctively she lifted both hands and pressed them to her chest as Sean slid Lottie's black dress away from her shoulders on each side. He had unzipped it as she enjoyed him. Now it was free and all that was holding it up, and protecting her modesty, were her two hands.

Dee stared at the girl in the mirror. Her hair was messed up, her eyes and skin glowing, and there was a handsome man with tight curled brown hair kissing her naked neck and, oh lord, her shoulders.

It was getting very hard to breathe but she could not look away, dared not look away, from the view in the mirror.

Sean was looking at the back of her neck as though it was the most beautiful and fascinating thing that he had ever seen, his fingertips stroking her skin from the innermost curve of her neck and along her collarbone. She could feel the heat from his touch, and the sensation of those fingertips was almost too much for her to tolerate.

A shiver of delicious excitement ran across her back and she saw Sean smile back at her in the mirror.

Lottie Rosemount had a lot to answer for. The mocha lace bra and shorts-style pants she was wearing had been a Christmas present from her, but not even the lovely Lottie could have anticipated that they would be on display in this way when Dee had slipped into them straight out of the shower only an hour earlier.

Slowly Sean brought his hands to the front, laid them

over hers and whispered in her right ear in a voice that she could have spread on hot crumpets.

'I want you to see yourself the way I see you. You don't need the dress.'

Dee smiled back at the man in the mirror as he slowly unfurled one finger at a time until only her palms were holding the couture dress against her bra.

'Do you trust me, Dee?'

Speech was impossible but she hesitated. This was it. If she wanted a way out, this was the time to say something or do something to take back control. Instead of which her head lifted and fell in a simple yes, and she was rewarded by a truly filthy grin.

And just like that she grinned back and pulled her hands away so that the dress fell to the floor in a heap around her feet.

She would have bent down to pick it up but that would have meant bending down while Sean was still holding her tight around the waist.

Bad idea! Such a bad idea!

So instead she swallowed down a sea of doubt and looked back at the mirror and the girl who was standing there in her underwear, with Sean's arms around her waist and his chin resting on her shoulder.

'Tell me what you see,' he whispered.

Her head dropped back and she half-closed her eyes, surrendering her entire body to his hands as they moved in firm and gentle circles in a delicious blissful movement.

Dee dared to open her eyes and watch the scene in the mirror.

Sean stroked and caressed her breasts through the flimsy fabric of her bra, lifting up her left breast then the right. He was slow and gentle, as though he was not in the slightest rush and they had all night to explore one another's bodies.

She felt Sean unclip her bra but did nothing to stop him and leaned back against him, feeling her bare skin on the crisp, white dinner shirt and not caring that she was probably creasing it.

The window was still slightly open and the chilly breeze wafted in, making her nipples stand proud inside her bra, pushing against the lace.

Sean noticed. She could see his reaction, feel the rise and fall of his chest and the pressure against her back from his trousers.

But instead of going for her nipples the pads of his soft fingertips expertly stroked down from her collarbone down over the top of her cleavage, as though he knew instinctively that was the most sensitive part of her neck.

Then her breasts. Exposed to the air, the dark skin around her nipples was already raised and ready. His fingers stroked all along the length of the side of her breast, moving into a more circular pressure, but then he looked up into the mirror.

But then his fingers paused, and every inch of her skin screamed out for release as he wrapped his arms around her waist and rested his chin on her shoulder so that they were both staring into the mirror at the same time.

'We need to be somewhere. And I need to get some air. Cold air.'

He pressed his lips to her throat and grinned. 'The sacrifices I make for my family. Oh yes...' And with one last, long, shuddering sigh he slipped back, picked up his jacket and walked slowly out of the bedroom.

CHAPTER TEN

Tea, glorious tea. A celebration of teas from around the world.
Tea is a natural product, hand-picked and completely free from artificial colours and preservatives, but rich in minerals and antioxidants. And best of all? Calorie-free.
Perfect for when you need to slip into that little black dress.

From *Flynn's Phantasmagoria of Tea*

Friday

SEAN SAUNTERED CASUALLY into the white marble reception area of the most prestigious Beresford hotel in London, the flashguns lighting up his back.

He might be the youngest director in the family firm but this was the one time a year he was willing to put his Armani tux on show for the press and wear his family pride on his sleeve.

Glancing around the room, he gave a quick wave to the management training team who were already lining up the latest graduates to chat to his father, who was greeting the hundred or so specially invited guests in person, same as always.

Tom Beresford. Straight-backed, tall, dark and impressive. The poster boy for every self-made multi-millionaire who had learnt his trade the hard way. The company PR machine loved to repeat the story about the boy who had started work at fourteen, washing dishes in the kitchens where his mother was the head chef, his father serving in the army overseas. His wages had been a hot meal every day and enough cash to pay his bus fare to school.

The weird thing was, it was all true. Except for one thing: he had been thirteen when he'd started, and barely tall enough to stand at the sinks, but had told the hotel he was older to get the work.

By eighteen he'd been working for the hotel and studying at college and at twenty-one had his first job as deputy manager. The rest was history.

Of course, the PR experts did not go into quite so much detail when it came to his father's complicated personal life, which was way more tabloid fodder than inspirational reading for young managers. He had certainly enjoyed female company as a single man—and when he was not so single.

Not that he could get away with that now. His lovely third wife Ava had been by his side night after night for the past eighteen years, just as she was greeting the guests tonight, and Sean knew that his father adored her.

He was still the man who had read him bedtime stories every night all dressed up in his dinner suit before heading to the hotel to work.

'Hey, handsome. Feeling lonely?'

Sean laughed out loud as his teenage half-sister Annika hooked her arm around his elbow and leant closer to give him a hug.

He replied by lifting the back of her hand to his lips then glancing up and down her gorgeous aqua cocktail dress. 'Why look at you, pretty girl. All grown up and everything.'

He was rewarded with a soft kiss on the cheek.

'Charmer! But you scrub up nicely. New suit?'

'Had it for months. All ready for the Paris job. New dress?'

'Had it a day.' She sniffed and looked around. 'What have you done with Dee? I noticed that fabulous sari she was wearing when she came in with Rob and then she seemed to disappear. You were very brave, letting him escort your lady friend. Rob is a scamp.'

Then Annika's voice faded away and she gave a small cough. 'Oh my. I think I think you'd better go to the rescue. Don't you? See you later.' And with that she released his hand to move to the cluster of new arrivals who had packed the reception area behind him.

Sean followed the direction of Annika's gaze and stood there, chuckling.

Judging by the number of people clustered around the buffet table, there was obviously something exciting going on. Sean could see Rob's head in the crowd but Dee had emerged from the tea rooms wearing far more practical flat gold sandals. Practical, but it also meant that in a room of tall men she was the orchid shaded by the tall trees.

Except that this was one girl who would always stand out in a crowd.

Especially when she was wearing a gold silk sari, gold jewellery and an azure-and-gold bodice which revealed a tantalizing band of the same taut skin he had admired back in the bedroom.

She took his breath away.

This was no clone. This was a real woman showing that she could act the part when she needed to, and revealing yet another side to her personality that he could never have imagined existed.

He had spent the week learning about one side of Dee Flynn. The woman who had taken a risk with her friend and transformed a simple patisserie into something spectacular. Doing what she loved to do, capitalizing on her passion. On her own terms.

When had he last met a woman like that? Not often. Maybe never. Oh, he had met plenty of glossy-haired girls with high IQs who had claimed they were doing what they truly loved, but so few people knew what they wanted in their twenties that it was astonishingly rare.

He had known precisely what he wanted from the first day he'd walked into his dad's hotel. His career path had been as clear as a printed map. He was going to do exactly what his father had done, start at the bottom and work his way up, even if he was the son of the owner of the hotel chain.

Dee Flynn had done the same.

Maybe that was why he connected with the tiny woman he was looking at now.

They were different from other people.

Different and special.

He was in awe, and ready to admit that to anyone.

Sean stood in silence as the chatting, smiling men and women in business suits who worked for his family filled the space that separated them. But his gaze was locked on one person. And it was not Rob, who seemed to be holding court.

He could hear his brother's familiar roar of laughter warm the room, but Sean's ears were tuned only to Dee's sweet laugh which was like a hot shower.

His senses were razor-sharp. And, as the cluster broke up, he caught sight of her.

She was looking around the room. Looking for him.

She winked at him with a wry smile, shrugged her shoulders and then turned to laugh at something Rob said before they were swallowed up by the trainees and older managers enjoying the delicious food and drink, only too happy to meet the celebrity chef Rob Beresford in person.

The last thing he saw was the slight tilt of her head and a flash of gold silk as she sashayed elegantly away from him.

Dervla Flynn was turning out to be one of the most remarkable women he had ever met in his life, and the last ten minutes had only served to increase his admiration.

He was totally in awe.

Then she slipped out of view as Rob and the whole entourage joined his father in the dining area, leaving him alone with his thoughts.

Strange that he was even now reliving that moment when her body had been pressed against his arm.

Strange how he was still standing in the same spot five minutes later, watching the space where she had last stood. Waiting. Just in case he could catch a glimpse of her again, the most beautiful woman in the room.

For that he was prepared to wait a very long time.

It seemed like ten minutes had gone by, but when the sitar music sang out from the mobile phone in her embroidered bag Dee was shocked to see that she had been swept up with Rob and his dad, talking food and drink, for over an hour.

There was a text message on the screen:

Ready to escape the noise and crush and get some air? Meet you at the elevator in five minutes. Sean

Sean! She had been so engrossed that she had only spent ten minutes with her date the whole evening. Quickly gathering up her skirts, Dee excused herself and skipped up the steps, and instantly caught sight of Sean, who was beckoning to her.

In a moment he had drawn her into the lift and pressed a card into a slot on the lift button before giving her a quick hug.

'Do you remember that penthouse suite I was trying to talk you into? Well, I seem to recall that this hotel has a private penthouse worth seeing. If you are willing to risk it?'

'Risk it?'

'It's the eighteenth floor, which means a quick trip inside a lift,' he whispered, and grinned at her shocked reaction. 'But it does have a balcony.'

And what a balcony!

Dee stepped out onto a long, tiled terrace, and what she saw in front of her took her breath away.

The rain had cleared to leave a star-kissed, cool evening. And stretched out, in every direction, was London. Her city. Dressed and lit, bright, shiny and sparking with street lamps, advertisements and the lights from homes and offices.

It was like something from a movie or a wonderful painting. A moment so special that Dee knew instinctively that she would never forget it.

She grasped hold of the railing and looked out over London, her heart soaring, all doubt forgotten in the exuberant joy of the view.

It was almost a shock to feel a warm arm wrap a coat around her shoulders and she turned sideways to face Sean with a grin, clutching onto his sleeve.

'Have you seen this? It's astonishing. I love it.' Dee breathed.

'I know. I can see it on your face.'

Then he moved closer to her on the balcony, his left hand just touching the outstretched fingers of her right hand.

But Sean was looking up at the stars.

'Last February it was snowy and cloudy for the whole of the three weeks that I was back in London. But tonight? Tonight is perfect.'

'This is amazing. I had no idea that you could see skies like this in London. I thought the light pollution would block out the stars.'

And she followed his gaze just in time to see a shooting star streak across the sky directly above their heads, and then another, smaller this time, then another.

'A meteor shower. *Sean! Look!*'

'What is it, Dee?' he asked, his mouth somewhere in the vicinity of her hair. 'Have you made a wish on a shooting star? What does your heart yearn to do that you haven't done yet?'

'Me? Oh, I had such great plans when I was a teenager and the whole world seemed to be an open door to whatever I wanted. My parents loved their work, and I was so happy for them when they decided to retire and run their own tea gardens. Warmth. Sunshine. They could not have been happier.'

She wrapped her arms tight around her body. 'But then the hard reality of running a business in a recession where tea prices are falling hit. And they lost it. They lost everything they had dreamt of. And it was so hard to see them in pain, Sean. So very hard.'

'But they stayed. Didn't they?'

She nodded. 'They won't come back unless they have to and if they did… It would break them. And that is what scares me.'

She lifted her head and rested it on Sean's chest. 'I know that I am in a different place in my life, and there are lots more opportunities out there for me, but do you know what? I am not so very different from my folks. I want my own business so badly and I don't know how I could cope if my dream fell apart. Six months ago I was working for a big tea importer and going to night school to study business most evenings and weekends. But Lottie changed that when she asked me to join her in the tea rooms. The time seemed so right. I have volunteered to run the festival and I felt ready to do anything.'

'You are ready. I know it.'

She looked up into his smiling face but stayed inside the warm circle of his arms.

'How do you know what your limits are?'

'You don't. The only way to find out is by testing yourself. You would be astounded at what you are capable of. And if you don't succeed you learn from your mistakes and do what you have to do to get back up and try again until you can prove to yourself that you can do it. And then you keep on doing that over and over again.'

'No matter how many times you fall down and hurt yourself?'

'That's right. You've got it.'

Dee turned slightly away from Sean and looked out towards the horizon, suddenly needing to get some distance, some air between them. What he was describing was so hard, so difficult and so familiar. He could never know how many times she had forced herself to smile after someone had let her down, or when she had been ridiculed or humiliated.

Dee blinked back tears and pulled the collar of his jacket up around her ears while she fought to gain control of her voice. 'Some of us lesser mortals have been knocked down so many times that it is hard to bounce back up again, Sean. Very hard. Can you understand that?'

Sean replied by wrapping his long arms around her body in a warm embrace so tender that Dee surrendered to a moment of joy and pressed her head against his chest, inhaling his delicious scent as her body shared his warmth.

His hands made lazy circles on her back in silence for a few minutes until he spoke, the words reverberating inside his chest into her head. 'Better than you think. Working in the family business is not all fun. I have been in these hotels all my life one way or another. And I still have a lot to learn.'

Dee shuffled back from him, laughed in a choked voice and then pressed both hands against his chest as she replied with a broken smile.

'So that makes two of us who are stuck in the family trade. Am I right?'

'Absolutely. How about a suggestion instead? I know a couple of venture-capital guys who have money to invest in new business ideas. All I have to do is make a few phone calls and… What? What now?'

'I don't want to carry any debt. No maxed-out credit cards; no business loans; no venture capital investment. That's how my dad got into so much trouble and there is no way that I am going there. So thank you, but no. I might be hard up, but I have made some rules for myself. I have already maxed out my credit on my share of the tea shop. I can't handle any more debt.'

Sean inhaled very slowly and watched Dee struggle with her thoughts, her dilemma played out in the tension on her face.

She was as proud as anyone he had ever met. Including himself. Which was quite something.

And just like that the connection he had sensed between

them from the moment he had laid eyes on her in the tea rooms kicked up a couple of notches.

And every warning bell in his body started screaming 'danger!' so loudly that in the end he could not ignore it any longer. And he pulled away from her.

She shivered in the cool air, fracturing the moment, and he grabbed her hand and jogged back across the balcony. Sean slid open the patio doors and wrapped his arm around her waist, hugging her to him, the luxurious warmth from the penthouse warming their backs.

'Oh, that's better. Won't you get into trouble with the boss for wasting heat? Oh—you are the boss! Well, in that case, carry on.'

'We should be getting back to the others,' Sean whispered, only his voice sounded low and way too unconvincing. 'They might be missing us.'

She must have thought so too, because she took a last step and closed the distance between them and pressed the palms of both of her hands flat against the front of his white dinner shirt. He could feel the warmth of her fingertips through the fine fabric as she spread her fingers out in wide arcs; the light perfume enclosed them.

'This has been a magical evening. Thank you for inviting me,' she whispered.

Every muscle in his body tensed as she moved closer and pressed her body against his, one hand reaching in to the small of his back and the other still pressed gently against his shirt. He tried to shift but she shifted with him, her body fitting perfectly against his, her cheek resting on his lapel as though they were dancing to music which only she could hear.

So he did the only thing he could.

He kissed her.

She lifted her head and her hair brushed his chin as she

pressed tentative kisses onto his collarbone and neck. Her mouth was soft and moist and totally, totally captivating.

With each kiss she stepped closer until her hips beneath the sari were pressed against his and the pressure made him groan.

'Dee,' he hissed, reaching for her shoulders to draw her away. But somehow he was sliding his hands up into her hair instead, holding her head and tilting her face towards him. Then he was kissing her, his tongue in her mouth, her taste surrounding him.

He stroked her tongue with his and traced her lower lip before sucking on it gently. She made a small sound and angled her head to give him more access.

She tasted so sweet, so amazing. So giving.

She gazed at him with eyes filled with such delight, as if she was expecting some suggestive comment about the fact that this penthouse came with a king-sized bed...

And that look hit him hard.

He did not just want Dee to be his stand-in date for tonight. He wanted to see her again, be with her again. He wanted to know what she looked like when she had just made love. He wanted to find out what gave her pleasure in bed, and then make sure that he delivered precisely what the lady ordered.

She was as proud and independent as he was. And just as unforgiving with anyone who dared to offer her charity or their pity.

By some fluke, some strange quirk of fate, he had met a woman who truly did understand him more than Sasha had ever done. And that was beyond a miracle.

Could he take a chance and show her how special she was? And put his heart on the line at the same time?

He slid a hand down her back to cup her backside, holding her against him as he flexed his hips forward, and one hand still in her hair. She shuddered as he slid his hand in slow circles up from her back to her waist, running his hands up and down her skin which was like warm silk, so smooth and perfect. He ducked his head and kissed her again, his hands teasing all the while until he was almost holding her upright.

When their lips parted, Dee was panting just as hard as he was. She looked so beautiful, standing there with her gold sari brilliant against the night sky, her cheeks flushed pink and the most stunning smile on her face.

His response was to wrap his arms around her back and, holding her tight against him, rested his chin on her top of her hair.

Eyes closed, they stood locked together until he could feel her heart settle down to a steady beat.

All doubt was cast aside. Her heart beat for him, as his heart beat for her.

Dee moved in his arms and he looked down into her face as she smiled up at him, not just with her sweet mouth but with eyes so bright, fun and joyous that his heart sang just to look at them. And it was as though every good thing that he had ever done had come together into one moment in time.

And his heart melted. Just like that.

For a girl who was just about as different from him and his life as it was possible to be.

And for a girl who had made her tiny flat the size of the hotel's luggage store into a home and was willing to share her joy with him. And who wanted nothing in return but a chance to see a meteor shower from a penthouse balcony.

God, he admired her for that.... Admired her?

Sean stopped, his body frozen and his mind spinning. He didn't just admire Dee, he was falling for her.

Just when he thought that he had finally worked out

that he had nothing to give to any woman in the way of a relationship.

Think! He had to think. He could not allow his emotions to get the better of him.

If he cared for her at all then he should stop right now, because the last thing Dee needed was a one-night stand which would leave her with nothing but more reasons to doubt her judgement.

He wouldn't do that to her. Hell, he wouldn't do that to himself. It would only be setting them up for heartbreak down the road.

'I think we might want to rethink the whole getting back in time for dessert…' She grinned as though she had read his mind.

'Right as always,' he replied, and stroked her cheek with one finger. 'God, you are beautiful. Do you know that?'

Dee blushed from cheek to neck. It was so endearing that he laughed out loud, slid his arms down to her waist and stepped back, even though his body was screaming for him to do something crazy. Like wipe everything off the dining-room table and find out what came next.

He sucked in a breath.

'You are not so bad yourself. I had no idea that hotel managers were so interested in astronomy.' And then she bit down on her lower lip and flashed him a coquettish grin. 'Or did I just get lucky? You are one of a kind, Sean.'

Lucky? He thought of the long days and nights he had spent working for the company to the exclusion of everything else in his life, including the girls who had cared about him. Sasha had lasted the longest.

He had sacrificed everything for the family hotel chain. Everything.

Now as he looked at Dee he thought about what lay

ahead, and the hard, cold truth of his situation emptied a bucket of ice water over his head.

His hands slid onto her upper arms and locked there, holding her away from him and the delicious pleasure of her body against his.

'I am not so sure about the "lucky" bit, Dee. Right now I am in London for a few days to sort things out and run a few classes, then Paris for a month at most. Then I'm off to Canberra...and my diary is full for the next eighteen months. Constant pressure. And all the while I feel as though I am running and running and not getting anywhere.'

'Then maybe you should stand still long enough to look around and see what you have achieved,' she said. Dee tilted her head to one side. 'Somewhere along the way to being the best, I think you forgot the fun part. But I think that funny and creative side of Sean is still inside you, all ready to get excited about new things and have the best time of his life.'

Stretching up onto tiptoes, she kissed him on the lips. 'You deserve it.'

She stepped back and patted him twice on the chest. Then she laughed. 'And now it is time to head back downstairs before I embarrass myself even more.' And she moved a step backwards with a smile.

He frowned, nodded just once and muttered something under his breath along the lines of what he did for the firm. Then he lifted his head, turned towards the door and presented the crook of his arm for her to latch onto. 'Shall we go to the ball, princess? Your audience awaits.'

CHAPTER ELEVEN

Tea, glorious tea. A celebration of teas from around the world.
Astrologers have long used tea leaves to predict the future. Try it for yourself by leaving a little tea in the bottom of your tea pot with the tea leaves. Stir the brew three times, empty the tea pot into your saucer, then inspect the pattern the leaves make in the cup. Each specific pattern has a special meaning.

From *Flynn's Phantasmagoria of Tea*

Friday
A week later

SEAN STROLLED INTO the bar at the Beresford Riverside and nodded to the head barman who was serving after-dinner drinks to guests wandered in from the dining room.

The light strains of a cocktail piano could just be heard in the background against the chatter and laughter from the guests.

He quickly scanned the bar and lounge area to see if Dee was still there. She had called him a couple of times during the afternoon to let him know that Prakash and his team had done an amazing job and all of the last minute worries that had kept her awake were sorted.

The tea festival was all set to go tomorrow.

Then he heard her laughter ring out from a table of Japanese guests who had clustered around the tables next to the long patio doors which led onto the landscaped gardens.

Ribbons of white outdoor lights trailed over the budding branches of the cherry trees which Dee had enjoyed over the past few days.

The first smile of the day slid over his mouth. Hell. His first smile all week. Last minute presentations, flying visits to France with his dad and two days scouting for locations in Scotland meant that he had hardly seen Dee since the night of the dinner.

He missed her like crazy.

Dee was sitting at the table, and spread out in front of her was what looked like a makeshift kitchen. White saucers from the kitchen were scattered all around her, and on each was a tiny sample of what looked to Sean like clippings from the evergreen plants outside in the garden but were no doubt some example of specialist tea leaves.

Whatever they were, the hotel guests seemed enthralled. They were picking up the saucers, sniffing, tasting and chatting away with enormous enthusiasm and clear delight. Nodding, delighted, bewitched.

Because at the centre of it all was Dee.

Sean paused at the bar and leant on the rail, happy just to watch the woman he had come to find.

Her long, sensitive fingers flitted above the table gesturing here and there, no doubt on some terribly important point about growing conditions and water temperature, and he could see the glint of gold in the bangles around her wrists.

She was wearing what for Dee probably passed for quite a conservative outfit of a fitted jacket in a knitted navy fabric which clung to her curves as she moved. But of course that was offset by a stunning scarf which shimmered in shades of blues and greens, highlighting her fair complexion, and even though her head was down he knew that those pale-green eyes were going to be totally enchanting.

This was the real Dee. Sharing her passion and enjoying every second of it.

The Dee he had fallen for the minute he had looked up from a tea room floor and was sucked into oblivion by those eyes. Why wouldn't he? She was stunning.

Recognition came flooding in, and instead of pushing it away Sean held it in his mind and treasured it like a precious gift that he had never expected to receive but adored.

He was falling for Dee Flynn. In a big way. This was way beyond attraction. He cared about her and wanted to be with her, in every way possible.

And the very idea shocked him and terrified him so badly that he could only stand there and take it like a sock in the jaw.

His life had been a roller coaster for so many years, he had forgotten what it felt like to make connections with people and form bonds that went beyond business transactions, contracts and meetings in windowless white rooms.

But why now?

He slid silently onto a high-boy leather bar stool.

This was the way he was going to remember her.

He had only been standing there for a few minutes in silent ogling when he saw her head lift and her back straighten.

Almost as if she knew that he was watching her. So that, when she stood up and looked over her shoulder at him, he should have been ready for the impact that seeing her smile transform into a grin that was laser-focused on him would cause.

Impossible. Nothing could have prepared him for the blast of that smile.

She had never looked lovelier. And she literally took his breath away.

Mesmerized, Sean could only watch as she excused herself with several deep bows to the guests, who returned her bows with gentle warm waves and smiles.

Oh yes, she was good.

She skipped between the tables and was at the bar in seconds.

Instantly she flung her arms around his neck as he bent down to kiss her on the cheek, much to the amusement of the hotel guests.

'You have been away far too long, Sean Beresford.'

'Agreed. Only, I think your fan club are taking our photograph on their smart phones.'

Dee peeked around Sean's back and waved back. 'Oh no, those are proper cameras. We are probably already online. But I'm not in the least ashamed. This has been a brilliant afternoon.' And, just to prove it, she went up on tiptoes and pecked him on the lips so lightly that he barely had time to register the sensation of her warm, full lips on his before she stepped back into her shoes.

'I hardly dare to ask,' he replied, but kept his arms tight around her waist. 'But could it be anything to do with the party of visiting Japanese academics?'

Dee pressed one finger to her bottom lip and tried to look innocent, but failed.

'You do know that they brought their own tea with them, don't you? The word is out Mr B—there is not one hotel in the whole of London who serves speciality Japanese green tea of the quality your guests demand and in the way they like. I think this is quite shocking news. Just imagine the impact on the hotel trade. If only you knew someone who could import some of that fine tea for you. Just imagine what a difference it could make. Now... I wonder what we can do about that?'

Then she fluttered her eyelashes at him in the most outrageous, over-the-top way and a bubble of laughter burst up from deep inside his gut and exploded into a real bellylaugh. The kind of laugh which turned heads and made the barman look at Sean over the top of his spectacles.

And why not? It had been far too long since he had laughed out loud—really laughed.

He had almost forgotten what it felt like, which was more than sad. It was a judgement of the life that he had chosen for himself and had never stopped to question— a roller coaster of work and travel, then more work and more travel, which never stopped long enough for him to get off and see the view now and then. It was too fast, and the highs and lows were so exhilarating, that it was impossible to look anywhere else but straight ahead because he never knew what was going to happen next.

It was a life that was as addictive as it was exhausting. A rush of daily adventure and excitement that called for his total focus and attention.

That was why he had been so attracted to Sasha.

They loved the hotel trade, and the rush of pulling off seemingly impossible projects and delighting his father and their hotel guests along the way. Sasha had been on her own roller coaster and at first they had been side by side, project to project. But slowly their tracks had simply drifted apart, further and further away, until they hadn't been able to see one another. Both of them had been strapped in and going for the adventure of their lives.

It was true. His life was one long roller-coaster ride. He had jumped on when he was sixteen and was still strapped in at thirty-one.

Almost half of his life.

Strange. He had never thought of it that way until now.

And he knew exactly who he had to thank for that.

The girl with the twinkling green eyes who was grinning up at him.

The girl who had swept into his life like a warm breeze on a cold day.

The girl who he was going to leave behind, and sooner than he had planned.

Sean slid one of his hands from her waist and onto the bar so that he could lean forward slightly. He inhaled the light floral fragrance that she was wearing like the aroma of a fine wine. Intoxicating and provocative. Heady and enticing. Daring him to find out if her skin tasted as delicious as the aroma promised.

'I still haven't forgiven you for texting me when you knew that Tuesday was our Bake and Bitch Club night. The girls were scandalized by that sort of suggestive language.'

'How could I forget our first anniversary? And you did call me brazen last week. I have a reputation to maintain, young lady,' he whispered into her ear in a voice that was not meant to be overheard, especially by the hotel staff.

Her eyes met his without hesitation or excuse. Beguiling. Honest. True. And, oh, so magical.

'I know. And I am certainly not complaining,' she said.

Sean swallowed down a lump in his throat.

Dee was so close. So very close. Her gaze was locked onto his face, as though it was the most fascinating thing that she had ever seen, and he almost flinched with the loss when a guest sidled up behind them at the bar.

'That colour looks great on you.' He smiled. 'Stylish and...' He paused and, when he was sure that she was looking at him, silently mouthed the word 'hot' before slipping off the bar stool and grabbing her hand.

Her eyebrows lifted and she replied with a girly giggle and a small shoulder-wiggle, which was so endearing that he had to distract himself by focusing on the way her fingers felt clasped inside his.

Time to move to something less likely to scandalize his staff.

'I think it's about time you showed me what you have been up to in my conference suite. Don't you?'

Dee paused outside the main doors to the conference room where she had spent most of the day with Prakash, and a stream of porters, delivery drivers and other people who she had never met before but who somehow seemed to be able to transform her sketches and lists into reality.

She raised one hand, palm upwards. 'Now, it might come as a bit of a shock. So prepare yourself.'

Sean nodded just once. 'I have been through everything, from Mardi Gras to beer festivals. I can handle it.'

Dee stretched out her hand towards the brass door plate, then lifted it back and whirled around on her heel. 'First of all, I should say that Prakash and the team were amazing. Just amazing. And they did it all in one day! Totally brilliant, in fact. I couldn't have done any of this without them… And now I am babbling, because I'm so excited and it's wonderful, and did I say that it is amazing and the festival is tomorrow and…?'

'Dee.' Sean smiled and gently rested a hand on each of her shoulders. 'I spoke to Prakash. He helped, but this is your idea. Your design, your colour scheme, your concept. So I know that it is going to be wonderful.'

'Perhaps you should come back tomorrow when the exhibitors are setting up. There will be such a buzz.'

Sean looked over her shoulder into the middle distance and seemed about to say something, but changed his mind, turned back and lowered his head so that his nose was almost pressed against hers. He spoke in a jokey, firm voice.

'Dee. I want the full tour and I want it now.'

'You are so bossy!'

'I know. But that's why you like me.'

'Really? Is that the reason? I thought it was your snazzy ties and shiny shoes.'

'They only add to the allure. And you're putting off the inevitable. What is it? Why don't you want me to see your design? You know that I am going to, one way or another. '

'Yes. I know. It is your hotel. It's just that…' She sucked in a breath then exhaled on one long string of words. 'I am seriously nervous because this is the biggest thing that I have ever done on my own and I know that it's mad but my whole future depends on this being a big success.'

Then she stopped, but Sean kept looking at her with that smile on his face, as though he was waiting for her to carry on.

Then without waiting another second he stepped forward, pushed open the doors to the conference suite with both hands and stood to one side.

Then he nodded towards the space behind him, reached out and grabbed her hand. 'Come on.' He smiled. 'Show me what you have done. Show me what your imagination has created. Share it with me. Please.'

For the next ten minutes Sean walked slowly around the room as Dee explained each of the display panels in turn, starting with the history of tea production, then slowly walking from stand to stand.

She didn't need to. But he liked hearing her voice, so he let her carry on.

The whole room was decorated in co-ordinating shades of green with stencils of green tea leaves against cream, pale gold and emerald green. There were plenty of stands for the exhibitors, power points, fresh water dispensers. And a portable professional kitchen. All ready for the morning. He couldn't have been prouder.

'So this is where the magic is going to happen. I love it. Professional, elegant and attractive. It's a hit!'

'Do you really think so?' Dee screwed up her mouth.

'It looks fresh and inviting. And the colour scheme is great.'

His hands moved in gentle circles on her shoulders, up and down her arms, and slowly, slowly, the stiffness in Dee's neck relaxed and she felt her shoulders drop down from around her ears.

'You must think that I am a total idiot,' she chuckled. 'All of this work for a one-day festival of tea. The world will not end if nobody turns up to drink the tea and buy the china. And on Sunday I can go back to the tea rooms and carry on as normal. I know that; I've known that from the start. But being with you and working in the hotel here has given me so many ideas for new projects, and new ways I can sell my blended tea, I can hardly sleep at night. It is so exciting. So, whatever happens tomorrow, thank you, Sean. Thank you for helping me.'

His response was to step forward and gather her into his arms, holding her tight against his pristine shirt, not caring that he was crushing his superb suit jacket in the process. Holding her with such tenderness and warmth that she melted against him with a gentle sigh. Instantly his chin slid down and rested on the top of her hair, and his arms relaxed their grip and rested gently on her back.

It had been so long since she had felt so close to another human being. Lottie and the girls were her best friends, and she loved every one of them, but this was different, felt different; this was special.

It had been ages since her last boyfriend in the tea

house. Years of watching other girls go on the dating scene, and comforting them with tea and cake as each broken heart had healed and they'd gone out again so full of hope.

Not for her. She did not want that emotional destruction. She knew that she was too different for most men. Too quirky. Too obsessed. Too unusual.

She was not the girl that the boys in catering school introduced to their parents. She was the girl they dated until someone better came along. And it had taken her a while to realize that she was not putting up with being second best. And she never would.

Until Sean had shown her that she was a woman a man could admire and want to be with.

Sean had chosen her. Picked her out. Made her feel special. Made her feel that she was capable of running her own business and making her dream come true.

Sean. The man who was holding her in his arms at that moment.

The man who meant the world to her. But she was too afraid to tell him.

She revelled in every sensation, her eyes closed, locking each tiny moment into her memory. The heady aroma of Sean's body wash or aftershave blended with the subtle scent of laundry lavender, and a lot of Sean that only a long day in a hot office could produce. If only she could bottle that aroma, she would never be lonely again.

This was one man who had listened to what she wanted and helped her make it happen in a way which was even better than she had imagined.

She wanted this moment to last as long as possible. She wanted to remember what these little bubbles of happiness felt like.

'You are most welcome,' he replied, the sound muffled as he spoke into her hair, but the sound reverberated through her skull and came to rest in the centre of her heart. Where they exploded into a firework display of light and colour.

Exploded with such force that they made her shuffle back a little so that she could look up into Sean's face and trace the line of his jaw with her fingers. Her reward was to see his eyes flutter just a little as her fingers slid down onto his neck and throat.

This man had pressed buttons that she did not even know that she had.

'If you ever see that Frank Evans, be sure to thank him for me.' She grinned. 'Because it seems to me that I came out with a pretty good deal.'

Sean rested his hands on her hips and nodded. 'True. The Beresford Riverside is a rather more impressive venue than the Beresford Richmond Square, and you did get it for the same price. That was what you were referring to… wasn't it?'

Dee dropped her head forward onto his chest with a short laugh, only too aware that she was blushing and her neck was probably a lovely shade of scarlet.

When she did dare to lift her head, Sean was looking at her, his eyes more blue than grey in the artificial lighting above their heads, and as her eyes locked onto his the intensity of that gaze seemed to penetrate her skin.

For one fraction of a second all the need and passion of this remarkable man was revealed for her to see.

In one single look.

It took her breath away and she lifted her head higher. So high that, when his head tilted and he pressed his lips against her forehead, and then her temple, she was ready.

More than ready.

She was waiting for his kiss.

She had been waiting all day for his kiss, to see him again and to hear his voice.

And it had been totally, totally, worth the wait.

Sean took one step forward, and before Dee realized what was happening he wrapped his hand around the back of her neck, his fingers working into her hair as he pressed his mouth against hers, pushing open her full lips, moving back and forth, his breath fast and heavy on her face.

His mouth was tender, gentle but firm, as though he was holding back the floodgates of a passion which was on the verge of breaking through and overwhelming them both.

She felt that potential, she trembled at the thought of it, and at that moment she knew that she wanted it as much as he did.

Her eyes closed as she wrapped her arms around his back and leaned into the kiss, kissing him back, revelling in the sensual heat of Sean's body as it pressed against hers. Closer, closer, until his arms were taking the weight of her body, enclosing her in his loving, sweet embrace. The pure physicality of the man was almost overpowering. The scent of his muscular body pressed ever so gently against her combined with the heavenly scent that she knew now was unique to him.

It filled her senses with an intensity that she had never felt in the embrace of any other man in her life. He was totally overwhelming. Intoxicating. And totally, totally delicious.

And, just when Dee thought that there could be nothing more pleasurable in this world, his kiss deepened. It was as though he wanted to take everything that she was able to give him, and without a second of doubt she surrendered to the hot spice of the taste of his mouth and tongue.

This was the kind of kiss she had never known. The connection between them was part of it, but this went beyond friendship and common interests. This was a kiss to signal the start of something new. The kind of kiss where each of them was opening up their most intimate secrets and deepest feelings for the other person to see.

The heat, the intensity, the desire of this man, was all there, exposed for her to see ,when she eventually opened her eyes and broke the connection. Shuddering. Trembling. Grateful that he was holding her up on her wobbly legs.

Then he pulled away, the faint stubble on his chin grazing across her mouth as he lifted his face to kiss her eyes, brow and temple.

It took a second for her to catch her breath before she felt able to open her eyes, only to find Sean was still looking at her, his forehead still pressed against hers. A smile warmed his face as he moved his hand down to stroke her cheek.

He knew. He knew the effect that his kiss was having on her body. He had to. Her face burned with the heat coming from the point of contact between them. His heart was racing, just as hers was.

Dee slowly, slowly slid out of his embrace and almost slithered onto the floor. And by the time she was on her unsteady legs she was already missing the warmth of those arms and the heat of the fire on her face.

She had to do something to fight the intensity of the magnetic attraction that she felt for Sean at that moment. Logic screamed at her from the back of her mind: they were both single, unattached and they wanted one another.

She had never had a one-night stand in her life. And, if she was going to do it, this was as good a place as any, except of course it would never be casual sex. Not for her. And, she suspected, not for Sean either.

Would it be so ridiculous if they spent the night together?

Sean gently drew her back towards him so that their faces were only inches apart at the same height.

His hand moved to her cheek, pushing her hair back over her left ear, his thumb on her jaw as his eyes scanned her face, back and forth.

Her eyes opened wide and she drunk him in—all of him. The way his hair curled dark and heavy around his ears and neck; the suntanned crease lines on the sides of his mouth and eyes. And those eyes—those amazing blue eyes which burned bright as they smiled at her.

She could look at that face all day and not get tired of it. In fact, it was turning out to be her favourite occupation.

Sean was temptation personified. And all she had to do was reach out and taste just how delicious that temptation truly was.

Did he know what effect he was having on her? How much he was driving her wild?

Probably.

Panting for breath, she rested her head on his chest, listening to the sound of Sean's heart under the fine cloth, feeling the hot flood of blood in his veins and the pressure of his fists against her back. She could have stayed there all night but suddenly the silence of their private space was broken by the loud ringtone from the mobile phone inside Sean's jacket pocket.

'That can wait,' he whispered and carried on stroking her hair. 'Now, tell me about the tea. What delicious aromas can the hotel expect…?' But he never got to continue because his phone rang again, and this time is was a different ringtone.

'Oh, I don't believe it.' He sighed, stood back, tugged out the phone and checked the caller ID. 'It's my dad's personal line.' He shook his head. 'I am so sorry about this. Stay right where you are. Two minutes.'

* * *

Dee sat down at the reception table just inside the door and watched Sean stride out into the main hotel space, the phone pressed to his ear. He was pacing up and down, one hand pressed against the back of his neck in a nervous gesture that she had seen him use a couple of times.

She pressed her fingers to her mouth, which was feeling slightly numb, and covered a chuckle. He didn't even realize that he was doing it.

Dee stood up and strolled into the kitchens between the display areas. She was just about to pour some water when one of the flyers dropped to the floor in the cool breeze from one of the floor-to-ceiling sliding glass doors that was still half-open.

But, instead of closing it, Dee stepped onto the stone courtyard area outside the conference room and slowly inhaled the cool evening air.

After the heat of the past hour it felt deliciously cool on her hot skin.

In the cool February air she could see the lights of the high-tech businesses, city offices and homes which lined the opposite bank of the river Thames. The hotel was partly shaded from the riverside public footpath by landscaped grounds and trees creating a calm and open feel.

It was exactly what she wanted: no white plastic underground basements, just a well-lit and modern space which opened up to the air whenever she wanted.

There was a faint rustling from the room behind her, and Dee looked over one shoulder as Sean came to join her on the terrace. His face was in shadow but she would recognize his shape anywhere.

A soft and silky Sean-warmed suit jacket was draped over her shoulders and she snuggled into it as a cold shiver ran down her spine.

She could feel the warmth of his chest through the many layers of clothing as he pressed his body against her back and wrapped his arms around her waist so that they were both facing the river and the superb view of the city spread out in front of them.

It was as if they were the only people alive at that moment and in that space.

Instinctively she leant backwards so that the back of her head was resting on his chest. The beat of his heart was steady in her ears, then faster.

She did not need to hear it to know that it grew faster for her.

Sean was breathing faster, his pace matching her own.

'No stars tonight,' she whispered and pointed up at the clouds which had already covered the crescent moon. 'But you can still make a wish if you like. You don't need a shooting star to have your dream come true. I know that now. So tonight is your turn.'

His reply was a hoarse whisper and she felt his hands slip away from around her waist as he spoke. 'I wish I could. But I can't. In fact, I have to go and get packed straight away.'

Dee slowly turned around in the circle of his arms so that they were facing one another, and suddenly a shiver ran across her shoulders. In the light from the room she could see the new harsh lines on Sean's face. All easy chatter and smiles had been wiped away as if they had never been there.

'Packed? I don't understand. You are not due in Paris for another few days and you've only just got back. You told me that yourself. You don't need to get packed tonight.'

He licked his lips and looked at her, his gaze darting across her face. 'I thought that I had at least a week. But that telephone call changed everything.'

Sean lifted his chin as though he was preparing himself.

'I am sorry, Dee, but I am booked on a flight to Chicago. We have an emergency at the new Beresford hotel we opened at Christmas and they need me to help sort things out. I have to go. And I have to go tonight. So you see, I'll be gone by the morning.'

Dee stepped backwards and out of his arms, her fingers running down his shirt sleeves so that she was clinging on to him with only a thin layer of fine cotton.

'Tonight? Do you really have to? We have worked so hard on this together. I…I was hoping that you would be here for the festival tomorrow.'

Dee turned and stared out into the dark night. Her eyes fixed on the movement of the wind in the trees that she could just see in the light from the hotel. There was a cold, damp wind blowing up from the river and she could feel the moisture cooling her face. But it didn't help to cool the fire burning inside her head.

She felt as though she had been caught in some kind of tornado that had been spinning her round and round from the moment she'd met Sean. Spinning so fast that she had never truly had the chance to get her feet back on the ground.

She had always known that his work in London was temporary, but Paris was only a few hours away by train. They might have had a chance to stay in touch and to stay close. If they worked at it.

If they both wanted it enough.

If he wanted it as much as she did.

He was leaving.

Just as her parents had decided to leave behind the cold, grey British winters and go back to the sunshine and the life that they loved. Just as her friends from catering college had left for jobs all over the world. Just as Josh had gone back to his real girlfriend and left his stand-in, second-best girl standing on the pavement outside his apartment reeling from what the hell had just happened.

She had coped with saying goodbye and managing the shock. And she still had Lottie and Gloria and the girls in the baking club. She could cope with saying goodbye to Sean. She was going to have to; he wasn't giving her any other choice.

It wasn't meant to be this hard.

She just wanted him to stay with her so badly.

Sean snuggled up next to her in the silence, the whole left side of his body pressed against her right side. Thigh to thigh, hip to hip and arm to arm.

She wanted to rest her head on his shoulder, and her whole body yearned to lean sideways against him for support, but she fought off the temptation.

She had to.

It was almost too much to bear when his fingers meshed with hers, locking them together in the dark.

Slowly, slowly, she found the strength to look up into the most amazing blue-grey eyes. In the bar they had been like clear, blue, fresh tropical seas, alluring, tempting and begging her to dive in. But now they were dark and stormy. Dangerous.

The warmth had been replaced with an intensity and concern that she had never seen before.

It was all there in the hard lines of his handsome face. The face that she had come to love so much over the past week or so, though she did not dare admit that to herself.

The planes of his face were brought into sharp contrast by the light from the room.

She had been so wrong to imagine that the son of Tom Beresford would have an easy office job handed down by his father.

Sean worked so very hard. And she admired him for that. But why now? Why did he have to go tonight?

'What kind of emergency is it?' she asked in a voice which was quaking a lot more than she wanted. 'Not another flood, I hope.'

His lips parted and he took in a long, shuddering breath before replying in a low, hoarse voice which to her ears seemed heavy with regret and concern.

'No; worse. Food poisoning. Rob thinks that it's a norovirus, and he is already on site working with the authorities, but the hotel is closed and guests are on lockdown. And I really do not want to talk about kitchen detox at this precise moment.'

His fingers clenched around hers and Dee tried focusing on the flickering lights on the riverbank but she could sense every tiny movement of his body which made vision a little difficult.

Her eyes fluttered closed as he took a tighter hold of her fingers and stepped away and she instantly yearned to have his body next to her again. Instead he gently lifted her hand to his mouth and kissed the back of her knuckles, forcing her to look up into his face.

'I wanted to be there tomorrow. To share your triumph. Because that is what it is going to be—a triumph.'

His head tilted slightly and one side of his mouth lifted up into a half-smile. 'You are going to be amazing. I know it. And Prakash has promised me a full report with video and photos.'

'Video?' She spluttered. 'That wasn't on the list.'

His gaze was focused on her hair and he casually lifted a stray strand of her lop-sided fringe and popped it behind her ear in a gesture so tender and caring that she almost cried at the pleasure of it.

'I ticked all of the optional extras on the checklist for you. Courtesy of the hotel management.'

'Wow,' she whispered and was rewarded with a quick nod of reply and a flash of a smile.

'Sean?' she asked in a quiet voice, and she closed the tiny gap between them. 'How long are you going to be away in Chicago? A week? Two? Then you are going to be in Paris, right?'

'I don't know. Weeks, most likely. As for Paris? There is no way I can handle that now. My dad is going to take over the project and find another manager.'

Dee exhaled a long sigh of relief. 'That's great. So when are you coming back to London? I will have so much to tell you.'

His head dropped down so that his forehead was almost touching hers and she could feel the heat of his breath on her face.

So that there was nowhere for her to escape to when he formed the words that she had been dreading.

'You don't understand, Dee. Paris is cancelled. My next assignment is in Brazil for a couple of months and then back to Australia in the autumn. I'm not coming back to London.'

CHAPTER TWELVE

Tea, glorious tea. A celebration of teas from around the world.
A simple infusion of chamomile flowers can help to relax the nerves and aid in sleep by creating a general feeling of relaxation.

From *Flynn's Phantasmagoria of Tea*

'NOT COMING BACK? Then I only want to know the answer to one question—and I don't want to hear it over the phone or in an email. Don't treat me like one of your managers. Talk to me. I want to hear your answer here and now. In person. To my face.'

She pressed both hands flat against his shirt so that the racing beat of his heart flittered up through her fingertips.

He was hurting just as much as she was.

'Do you want to see me again, Sean? Because if you don't it would be better if you told me now and be done with it, so that…' She lifted her chin. 'So that we can both get on with our lives.'

'Do I want to be with you? Oh, Dee.'

His right hand came up and flicked his suit jacket onto a patio table, exposing her skin to the cold night air, and instantly she could feel her nipples pebble with alertness. His long fingers slid down the whole length of her body from her neck, down the treacherous front of her jacket to her hips and back again.

Without asking for permission or forgiveness he slipped his warm hand up inside her jacket and cupped her breast. His thumb moved over her nipple with the perfect amount of pressure to fire up every nerve in her body.

But Sean had found the perfect distraction, kissing her forehead, temple and throat with such exquisitely gentle kisses that any idea of a question was driven out her mind as her desire for him built with each touch of his lips on hers.

And, just when she thought that her legs were going to buckle, his fingers slid away until her entire breast was being cupped by his hand and her bra was redundant and getting in the way of the exquisite pleasure.

Then slowly, slowly, his hand slid lower onto the bare skin at her waist and rested there for a second before moving away.

Arms wrapped around his head, Dee hung onto Sean as he wrapped both arms around her and held her to him.

She could feel the supressed power of his answer pressing against her hip and his short, fast breaths on her neck, fighting, fighting for control.

'Oh, Sean,' she whispered through a closed throat, and she dropped her head down to the safety and warmth of his broad chest.

They must have stayed there for several minutes, but time seemed to stand still, and it was Sean who broke the silence.

'I have been down this road before, Dee. My last girlfriend was so patient and we tried so hard to make it work. But in the end we were both worn down with the constant struggle to make time for one another between going back and forwards to the airport. It was exhausting. And it killed a great friendship. I don't want that to happen to us, Dee. Not to us.'

He was stroking her hair now, running his fingers back from her forehead. 'It could be six months before I get back here, and even then it would only be for a flying visit. There will always be some crisis somewhere, like tonight, which needs me to fly out at a moment's notice. I can't plan holidays or down time. You deserve better than that. A lot better.'

Dee looked up into his face and blinked, her mouth part open. 'No. I deserve you. All of you.'

Her words stung like ice on hot skin, burning into his brain and leaving a scar.

'The last thing I want to do is hurt you, Dee. That's why it's better that we part now and remember the good times.'

She laid her cheek on his shirt and dared to finally find the words. 'Does it have to be that way, Sean? Is there truly nobody else in the company that can cover your job? What happens when you are ill or burnt out? You can't keep going like this for ever. You have to take a break some time.'

'Don't feel sorry for me, Dee,' he replied, his hand cupping the back of her head. 'My family are very close, we always have been, and I owe my father everything. This hotel chain is my life and I want to make it special.'

'It seems to me that you have paid your family dues, Sean. Paid in full.'

'What do you mean?

Dee forced herself to raise her head and slip backwards so that she could look up into his face. 'This is your decision to leave tonight. Not your father's. Or your brother's. Yours. You have recruited an amazing team of talented professionals who would be only too happy to take on some of those troubleshooting challenges if you gave them the chance. You have made these hotels your life—and I understand that. Look at me—the tea grower's daughter who wants to set up her own tea company. We are both following in the family trade. But maybe it's time to think hard about what you want to do with your life. And who you want to spend it with.'

Then she stood back and slowly slid her fingers from his, one finger at a time, breaking their connection with each movement as she spoke.

She stood on tiptoe, pressed her lips against his in one last, lingering kiss, then ran her finger along his jaw and smiled.

'Good luck, Sean. Goodbye and thank you for everything.'

Then she turned and walked away, back into the conference room and out of his life. Without looking back.

And this time he didn't follow her.

CHAPTER THIRTEEN

Tea, glorious tea. A celebration of teas from around the world.

The traditional treatment for shock in Britain is a steaming beaker of piping hot Indian tea with milk and plenty of sugar. This remedy should be repeated until the symptoms subside.

From *Flynn's Phantasmagoria of Tea*

Saturday

HER BEST FRIEND slid a plate in front of her in the early-morning light streaming in through her bedroom window.

Dee squinted over the top of her extra-strong English Breakfast at the slice of a tall extravaganza of green-and-vanilla-coloured sponge layers.

It was very green. And smelt of a florist shop. And no amount of strong tea was going to be able to wash down that amount of sugar and fat.

'I am calling this my tea festival special. It's a Lady Grey flavoured opera cake with a rosewater cream filling. What do you think?'

'Think? I am too tired to think, and my taste buds are fried. Thanks, Lottie. I am sure it will be a brilliant hit.

It looks wonderful, but I just can't face it at the moment. Way too nervous.'

Lottie rubbed the back of Dee's shoulder and kissed the top of her head.

'I had a feeling that it might be a bit over the top for six a.m. Did you get any sleep at all?'

Dee shook her head. 'Maybe a couple of hours at most. Kept waking up and couldn't get back to sleep again.'

'Never fear. I have donuts, and cheese and ham croissants. The breakfast of champions. I'll be right back.'

'You're my hero,' Dee replied and smiled after Lottie as she took the stairs down to the bakery from her apartment.

Her hero.

Dee stretched out her arms on the small table, dropped her head onto her hands and closed her eyes.

She was exhausted and her day had not started yet.

This was the most important event of her career. Months of planning. Weeks of phone calls, emails, checklists and constant to-ing and fro-ing from the hotel. And it all came down to this.

One girl sitting alone in her bedroom, drinking tea in her dressing gown. Feeling as though she had just gone through twelve rounds of a professional boxing match and lost.

Every part of her body ached, her head was thumping and she could easily fall asleep sitting upright in this hard chair.

Little wonder.

Lottie thought that she had stayed awake because of nerves about what today would bring. And that was true. But it was not the real reason she had tossed and turned until her duvet was on the floor and her sheet a tangled mess, wrapped around her like a restricting cocoon.

Sean. All she could think about, every time she closed her eyes, was Sean.

How he looked, tasted, smelt and felt. Sean.

And the worst thing?

The more she thought about what he had said to her, and repeated their conversation over and over in her head, the more she knew in her heart that he had been right to walk away and end what they had.

Sean had let her go rather than prolong the agony of always expecting her to take a place in the long line of other priorities that came with his position in the company.

He had done a noble thing.

He had given her up so that she could find someone who was able to put her first.

She *did* deserve better than to feel that she was always going to take second place in his list of priorities.

She *was* worthy of having someone to be there when she needed them. Like today.

Her parents had always put work first before her. Not because they intended to hurt her; far from it. They loved what they did and had explained many times that they wanted to be happy so that she could share that happiness.

Shame that it had never made it any easier to accept.

Shame that she would have loved to have Sean with her today of all days. To share her excitement and sense of achievement. To share her joy with the man she had come to love. The man she still wanted to be with.

The first man that she wanted to be with.

This was all so new and bewildering. Oh, there had been plenty of teenage crushes before. And broken hearts galore. But the way she felt this morning was something very different.

It was if she had tasted something so wonderful that it was terrifying to think that she might never taste it again.

Dee raised her body back to a sitting position and peered glassy-eyed at the photograph of her smiling parents, and

Lottie's bizarre but no doubt totally delicious cake, and a small chuckle made her shoulders rise and fall.

Even in the daily mayhem that constituted her mad world, falling for one of heirs to the Beresford hotel dynasty was surely the craziest.

She picked up the fork, speared a small chunk of cake and closed her lips around it, savouring the different flavours. Letting her tongue and the sensitive taste buds that made her job possible do the work before chewing for a moment and swallowing it down.

'Oh, you tried the cake. Brave woman. Go on. Hit me with it.'

Lottie marched into her bedroom with a tray, sat down on the bed and bared her teeth in fear of the honest review.

Dee raised her eyebrows and licked her lips. 'You put ground black pepper in the cream to offset the rosewater. And I am tasting orange zest and a hint of cloves and cardamom in the tea-scented sponge.'

'Absolutely. I knew that you would get it. So? Lady Grey or a green tea?'

Dee took the tray out of Lottie's hands. 'Green. But a special one. This is good. This is very good. Congratulations, Miss Rosemount. You have just succeeded in creating one of the toughest tea-matching challenges I have ever come across. Please accept this hand-crafted medal.'

'This is not a medal. It's an exhibitors badge for the tea festival.'

'Well, you don't think I would face the ravenous cake-eating hordes without you there to serve it and bask in the glory, did you? And, after all, we can't have tea without the cake to go with it! Foolish girl.'

Then Dee's smile faded and she reached out and took Lottie's hand. 'Can you come with me? Just for a couple of hours. Please? Gloria and the gang will look after the tea rooms. I just… I just need a pal by my side today. It turns out that being a tea magnate is not half as much fun when you don't have someone to share the excitement with. And I didn't expect that. I didn't expect that at all.'

Sean dug into his pocket, pulled out his mobile phone and dialled the number with shaking fingers.

He had been up most of the night, talking to Rob, who was fighting health inspectors in Chicago, and his father, who was fighting to stay awake after two hours of pacing back and forth going over the business plans for the hotel chain and where Sean was going in his career. And his life.

Please still be there.

Please answer.

Please don't throw the phone out of the window when you see who is calling you. Please take this call.

The only voice in the world he wanted to hear whispered, 'Hello?'

'Dee. It's Sean. I'm standing outside the tea rooms but I won't come in unless you want me to. Please say yes.'

The fraction of a second before she replied seemed like an eternity. 'Sean? What do you mean you are outside the tea rooms? I thought that you would be in Chicago by now.'

'Long story, but I'd like to tell you about it in person instead of on the pavement in the dark at the crack of dawn.'

'Okay. Yes, Lottie will let you in.'

It took Sean three seconds to give a very startled Lottie a quick wave, then bound up the stairs two at a time and stand puffing and panting outside Dee's bedroom.

His hand stretched out towards the door handle. And then he snatched it back.

Eyes closed, he blew out a long, deep breath, his head suddenly dizzy with doubt as the blood surged in his veins.

What was he doing here? What if she said, thanks, but no thanks? This was crazy.

He loved this woman and he had been willing to let her go because he was afraid of changing his life? Mad.

For once he was going to risk their future happiness on a crazy decision to trust his heart instead of his head.

And what if she said yes? She could be committing herself to a life where he could be on the road or in a different hotel most of the year. Was that fair?

Yes. Because he was just as determined to show Dee that he was able to give her a fraction of the love she felt for him.

And he had to do it now. Or never. Perhaps that was why he felt so naked. Exposed.

Sean straightened his back and just prepared to knock, but at the very second he did so there was movement on the other side of the door, and the handle turned on its own and cracked open an inch, then wider…and Dee was standing there.

Her eyes locked onto his as she looked at him with the kind of intensity that seemed to knock the oxygen from his lungs.

Then those eyes smiled and he took in the full effect of that beautiful face. No camera in the world could have captured the look on Dee's face at this moment.

He felt as though the air would explode with the electricity in the air between them.

'Hi,' she whispered. 'Has something happened to bring you back? Are you okay?' There was so much love and concern in her voice that any doubts Sean had about what he had to do next were wiped away.

Sean stretched out his hand and stroked her cheek, his eyes never leaving hers.

'I haven't stopped thinking about what you said. And

you were right. Leaving last night was my decision. So I did something about it.'

Sean breathed in, his heart thudding so loudly that he suspected that she must be hearing it from where she was standing so quietly, dressed in her kimono. 'I know now that I will always love you, Dervla Flynn, and it doesn't matter where I am in the world.' He licked her lips. 'I want to be with you. Love you.'

Her mouth opened to reply but he pressed one finger on her lips and smiled, breaking the terror. 'You see, I'm not as brave as you are. As soon as I left you last night, I knew that I couldn't leave the woman I have fallen in love with without trying to come up with some options.'

He grinned at her and slid forward so that both of his hands were cupped around her face as tears pricked her eyes. 'I love you way too much to let you go. I need you, Dee. I need you so much. Nothing else comes close. What would you say if I told you that I would be working out of London for the next twelve months?'

Her reply was to fall into his arms and he swept her up, holding her body tight, tight, before tilting his open mouth onto hers in a hot, hot kiss.

He cupped her face with both of his hands, his thumbs wiping away tears and water from her cheeks, and then he poured into his kiss the passion and devotion, the fear and doubts, which came with giving your heart to another human being.

'I didn't expect to be saying this standing in a cake shop, but it doesn't change a thing. I am so in love with you.'

'Oh, Sean. I wasn't sure I could go through with today without you. Can you forgive me? I have been such an idiot. Of course your family need you. You love them and want to do the right thing. I know what that's like.'

'Better than you think. I have done something rash—

there's a limo on the way to the airport at this very minute to collect two very special first-class passengers from
a flight from Sri Lanka. I knew that you wanted your parents with you today to see all that you have done. Are you
okay with that?'

'Seriously?' she asked, stunned. 'You flew my parents
to London for the festival? You did that for me?'

He nodded. 'Seriously.' His thumb was still moving
across her cheek. 'It's time that I met your parents. Because I am thinking of taking a break for a couple of months
and Sri Lanka is on my list of destinations. If you come
with me.'

'Oh, Sean. Do you mean it? Yes? Oh, I love you so
much.'

He closed his eyes and pressed his forehead to hers, his
entire world contained within his arms.

They were still standing there, kissing passionately,
when there was the sound of loud voices breaking into
their private world. Lottie had opened up downstairs and
the first customers had arrived.

'But what about your work? Chicago? Brazil?'

'I had a long conference call with my dad and Rob last
night, and we have agreed to give some senior managers a
chance to show us what they can do. Plus, my dad offered
me a new job this week. Could be challenging.'

'Difficult?'

'Very.' He grinned. 'Apparently he needs a new manager for the Richmond Square hotel who can fit in a bit
of training now and then. Within walking distance of this
cake shop and the woman I've fallen in love with. And all
the tea I can drink. How could I say no?'

* * * * *

A sneaky peek at next month...

Cherish™

ROMANCE TO MELT THE HEART EVERY TIME

My wish list for next month's titles...

In stores from 21st February 2014:

☐ The Returning Hero – Soraya Lane

& Road Trip With the Eligible Bachelor – Michelle Douglas

☐ Lassoed by Fortune – Marie Ferrarella

& Celebration's Family – Nancy Robards Thompson

In stores from 7th March 2014:

☐ Safe in the Tycoon's Arms – Jennifer Faye

& The Secrets of Her Past – Emilie Rose

☐ Awakened By His Touch – Nikki Logan

& Finding Family...and Forever? – Teresa Southwick

Available at WHSmith, Tesco, Asda, Eason, Amazon and Apple

Just can't wait?

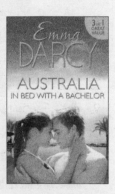

Join the Mills & Boon Book Club

Want to read more **Cherish**™ books?
We're offering you **2 more** absolutely **FREE!**

We'll also treat you to these fabulous extras:

- **Exclusive offers and much more!**
- **FREE home delivery**
- **FREE books and gifts with our special rewards scheme**

Get your free books now!

visit www.millsandboon.co.uk/bookclub
or call Customer Relations on 020 8288 2888

Discover more romance at

www.millsandboon.co.uk

- ❤ WIN great prizes in our exclusive competitions
- ❤ BUY new titles before they hit the shops
- ❤ BROWSE new books and REVIEW your favourites
- ❤ SAVE on new books with the Mills & Boon® Bookclub™
- ❤ DISCOVER new authors

PLUS, to chat about your favourite reads, get the latest news and find special offers:

- Find us on facebook.com/millsandboon
- Follow us on twitter.com/millsandboonuk
- ❤ Sign up to our newsletter at millsandboon.co.uk